# Kiss Me When I'm Dead

Dominic Piper

© Dominic Piper 2017

Published by Opium Den Publishing

Dominic Piper has asserted his rights under the Copyright, Design and Patents Act, 1988, to be identified as the author of this work.

All rights reserved. No part of this publication may be reproduced, distributed, or transmitted in any form or by any means, including photocopying, recording, or other electronic or mechanical methods, without the prior written permission of the publisher, except in the case of brief quotations embodied in critical reviews and certain other noncommercial uses permitted by copyright law.

All characters in this publication are fictitious and any resemblance to real persons, living or dead, is purely coincidental.

# Books by Dominic Piper

Kiss Me When I'm Dead

Death is the New Black

Femme Fatale

Bitter Almonds & Jasmine

# 1

## THE PRIVATE INVESTIGATOR

The moment I saw her, I knew we were going to sleep together.

She's mid-twenties; about five foot eight in four-inch heels with a knockout, pneumatic figure trapped in an expensive black suit that seems designed to show off those inescapable curves. The skirt is maybe six inches below her knees with a twelve-inch split up the left-hand side. She's wearing a white cotton blouse under the jacket with a blue bead necklace around a perfect, porcelain white neck. I inhale from her cloud of L'Air du Temps and momentarily forget where I am or what I'm doing.

If I had a secretary or a PA or whatever the hell she is, this is how I'd want her to dress. I'd actually be looking forward for the alarm to go off each morning so I could get in to see her. It's that bad.

'Mr Beckett? How lovely to meet you. Come in. Mr Raleigh is expecting you.'

We shake hands. I make sure my grip is gentle and light. Hers is soft but firm. It's more like a caress than a handshake. I smile at her and she smiles back. Her pupils are so dilated I can't quite work out what her eye colour is. The front door closes behind us and I follow her down a long corridor lined with fake Regency chairs that no one ever sits on.

She has a sexy, swaying walk that drags the eyes to those wide hips and keeps them there. I'm aware that my mouth is open. If things weren't bad enough already, she tosses her mane of black hair back and runs her fingers through it, like she knows I'm watching.

The effect of all this self-conscious body language is overwhelming and I try to think of something else, like changing the tyre on a car. Beautiful women easily distract me and I'm still not sure whether it's a good or a bad thing. It's probably both.

After what seems like three long, frustrating months, we arrive in what I assume to be her office. It's white and modern with black furniture. I wonder if she dresses to match her working environment or whether the place was decorated to match her clothes. Either is possible. Her desk is made from glass with a three-drawer pedestal on the right-hand side and I wonder if someone chose it so that they could see her legs while she was sitting down.

'Mr Raleigh is just taking a call from Oman,' she says. 'He shouldn't be too long. Take a seat. Would you like something to drink while you're waiting?'

I sit down and ask for a coffee. I continue to watch her as she slides a plastic thing into a coffee-making machine. She turns around to face me. I avert my gaze, but not quickly enough. She smiles, pleased that she's caught me out. I'm beginning to think that I'm not quick-witted enough for this subtle courtship dance that we're having.

'I'm Anjukka, by the way. I'm Mr Raleigh's personal assistant.'

She waits for a reaction to this unusual name. 'That's Finnish, isn't it?' I say, as if I didn't know. She looks pleasantly surprised.

'Yes it is. My mother was Finnish. From Jakobstad.'
'Right on the coast.'
This time, her eyes widen.
'You've been there?'

She walks over and hands me a coffee in a white china cup and saucer. I can feel a change in the air. She's more relaxed. The effect of her perfume persists.

'Not to Jakobstad. I went to Finland on holiday when I was a student. Visited Helsinki for a few days.'

'Helsinki's amazing, isn't it? I haven't been there since I was a little girl. I'd love to go again.'

I haven't been there at all, of course. I can lie my way around the globe and make it sound like the biggest truth you've ever heard in your life. I know I'm digging myself a hole, but I can't help it.

'Yes. It's a fantastic city.'

She's wearing an engagement ring. It's diamond and sapphire, but it looks old and the silver band is slightly tarnished, so either it's an antique or a family heirloom. Maybe she's not really engaged and she's borrowed it from someone to get guys off her back. It has been known.

She walks over to her desk and sits down. Good posture, straight-backed and a self-conscious hand through the hair again. She crosses her legs beneath the see-through desk. I pick up a copy of *Jane's Defence Weekly* and flick through it, turning slightly away from her. My peripheral vision is good, though, and I can see she's staring at me while doing something close to nothing on her computer. I stare blankly at an article about Hungary supplying jets to Bulgaria and wait for her to break the silence. As she speaks, I watch her mouth. She's wearing dark red lipstick, made all the more striking by the contrast with her pale skin.

'Mr Raleigh said you were a private investigator of some sort.'

'Yes, that's right. Missing pets, lost house keys, that sort of thing.'

She gets the joke, thankfully. 'Must be exciting!'

'It has its moments.'

'Have you recovered any missing pets recently?'

'Not a single one.'

'You don't look like, um…'

'Some middle-aged, heavy-set, bitter ex-CID man with a drink problem and a bedridden wife?'

She laughs. It's a genuine laugh. This is good, but unfortunately it can't continue. A buzzer starts buzzing somewhere on her desk. I can see a flashing orange light illuminating the lower part of her face.

'Mr Raleigh will see you now, Mr Beckett. Through the blue door.'

'OK. Thank you for the coffee, Anjukka.' I get up and place one of my business cards on her desk. 'If you ever need a missing library book tracked down, give me a call.'

She picks up the card and looks at it, then looks up at me. 'I'll be sure to.'

We make brief eye contact and I head through the blue door. I think that went quite well.

I'd been expecting to walk straight into Raleigh's office and find him sitting behind some gigantic fuckoff desk with a cigar stuffed in his mouth, but this is not the case. I'm in a room about half the size of Anjukka's and there are two men standing there. They are not smiling.

Both of them look like they've been pumping iron since they were six years old and wear matching grey suits with white shirts. Thankfully, they have different coloured ties on so that I can tell them apart.

Blue Tie stands with his hands clasped just below his waist. I can just see a massive gold watch peeking out of his cuff. He is, for want of a better word, 'guarding' a solid-looking wooden door to his right. This, I assume, must be the entrance to Raleigh's office. Blue Tie has a big-boned face, short black hair and a swarthy complexion, topped off with a fashionable hint of five o' clock shadow. He's ex-armed forces for sure.

It's hard to guess his nationality, but I'm guessing Mediterranean, possibly Israeli, but I can't be a hundred per cent sure until he speaks. He doesn't seem like the speaking type. He has a forced, sloth's smile on his mouth, but his eyes are dead and stupid. He's in his late thirties and I can tell he's willing me to do something mad and unpredictable so he can kill me. As far as I can make out, he isn't carrying a weapon, though I'm sure he'd like to be. Men like this aren't happy or complete without a gun or a samurai sword in their hand.

Purple Tie is standing an intimidating three feet away from me and is almost invading my space but not quite. His hands are at his side. He has a shaved head and rugby player shoulders that are about a foot wider than Blue Tie's. He has a florid, veined complexion that hints at a past or present drink problem. He may never have laughed in his life.

Purple Tie is also ex-armed forces, judging from his bearing. He's older than Blue Tie but not by much. He smells of aftershave and menthol mouthwash. To be intuitive and sensitive for a moment, he gives off such bad vibes you could cut them with a knife. There's no doubt that Purple Tie is in charge of Blue Tie. Purple Tie also carries no weapon.

This room is a stop and search zone and I can understand why it exists. Nathan Raleigh is an arms dealer. He's low-key and not in the public eye. He's one of those mysterious movers and shakers who flit through the international armaments business making a stupendous deal here and a colossal deal there, and not many people are truly aware of who he is and what a force he is.

Despite his anonymity, there was a kidnap attempt on him just over three years ago and he was lucky that it was foiled, mainly due to the incompetence of the would-be kidnappers, who were a strange mix of French, Australian and Polish. Needless to say, this kidnap attempt didn't make the papers. People like Raleigh have the power to keep things like that quiet. They also like to exercise that sort of power from time to time, just because they can.

That whole affair obviously made him jumpy, though, hence the designer monkeys giving me the tough-guy stares in this cute little antechamber, presumably standing around all day like they're waiting for a member of the royal family to arrive.

There are two obvious security cameras in here. One is high up on the wall to the left of the solid-looking wooden door and the other is almost directly behind me, above the blue door I came in through. I can't see it, but I can hear the high-pitched whine it's giving off. They should get it serviced.

There are two other cameras, however, that you're not meant to notice. One of these is in the arm of a padded ballroom chair to my immediate left and the other is on the floor about an inch away from the wooden doorframe. Both have miniscule red lights like the others and are crying out to be as inconspicuous as possible.

Somewhere, someone is watching this room on a couple of monitors and I wonder who it is.

As I'm taking in all these more-money-than-brains security measures, Purple Tie flashes me a huge insincere grin and takes a step forward.

'Excuse me, sir. Could you raise both of your arms to shoulder height?'

'No.'

He's still smiling but his eyes have gone dead.

'This will only take a minute, sir.'

He has a rough-sounding north London accent which he's had no success in making sound even remotely refined.

'I'm sure it will,' I say. 'But the answer's still no.'

'In that case – sir – we can't allow you to see Mr Raleigh.'

'That's fine by me. It was Mr Raleigh that wanted to see *me* – not the other way around. Give him my regards while he's firing you. See you, lovebirds.'

I turn around and head back to the blue door and the scented heaven of Anjukka. I wonder if she dresses like that to piss off these two cavemen. I certainly hope so. I wonder what her underwear is like. Expensive, I shouldn't wonder. Would it be too much to hope that it was also black?

'Would you hold on for just one minute, please, sir?' says Purple Tie through gritted teeth.

I stop and turn to face my astonished pals. I just know that this has never happened to them before, but it's tough. There's no way I'm going through a demeaning physical search just so some sonofabitch billionaire can feel like Mr Big. Besides, if I wanted to kill someone like Raleigh, I wouldn't need a gun or a knife.

Purple Tie turns the handle on the wooden door and goes inside. Blue Tie's face wrestles with aggression, irritation and bafflement. This is probably the worst day of his life so far and it's all my fault. He looks me up and down with a sneer on his face, as if to say 'who the fuck do you think you are?'

I give him a cheery smile. 'I bet this makes a change from turning away kids with fake ID, eh?'

His face actually darkens. It really does. I know I shouldn't be this cruel to the poor bastard, but there are some things that really rub me up the wrong way and that disdainful sneer was one of them. I'm wondering where Purple Tie has gone and whom he's talking to. I continue my one-sided chat with Blue Tie.

'Smart casual. No trainers. Sound familiar?'

Before he cracks and launches himself at me, Purple Tie reappears and he looks almost bereaved. 'Mr Raleigh will see you now. This way, please.'

He indicates the door with an outstretched hand, in case I hadn't noticed it. As I walk past him into Raleigh's office, he gives me a little deniable jostle against my right shoulder. I turn and look him straight in the eye.

'Sorry to spoil your fun, girlfriend. Maybe next time, eh?'

'Enjoy your meeting, sir,' he growls. I don't think he means it.

'Thank you. I will.'

Just before the door closes behind me, I hear one of them give a contemptuous little snort of disgust. I'm sure they're already making their way to the cupboard where the baseball bats are kept. I've always been fascinated by security guys like this; employed for their brawn, but having to dress up like waiters, spitting their resentful fake politeness out through gritted teeth and being so dim they think nobody notices.

It must be murder if you were once in the armed forces and you still have to call everyone 'sir'. In the armed forces, you knew your place, you knew what you were doing with your life and you had people who looked up to you. You had respect. Now all those skills you acquired are mostly useless in the civilian world and you have to take shit from people like me, while sucking up to and working for the sort of people who you once wouldn't have given the time of day to.

Still, I should care. Fuck 'em.

# 2

## PORTRAIT OF A LADY

After all that, there's no one in the office. Maybe Raleigh's putting on a bulletproof vest or wants to make some sort of dramatic entrance in a tank or something. That's fine, though. It gives me a chance to look around.

I'd assumed that this was purely a workplace, but now I'm not so sure. This is a large room and it's decorated like the study of a university professor from the 1940s. There's a barely discernible smell in here that reminds me of carbolic soap, but otherwise the predominant scent is of leather, emanating from the two enormous Natuzzi sofas and probably from the bookshelves.

Between the sofas, there's a wooden coffee table with big frosted glass panels on top that are somehow lit up from beneath. Three large books rest on the surface, all to do with big game hunting. One of them is so heavy I have difficulty lifting it with one hand.

Checking out Raleigh on the net was virtually impossible, but I did come across a small company called BRT Systems which manufactured bespoke hunting guns and which was owned by Praesidium International. Raleigh's name was down as one of the non-executive directors. Apart from that he was the invisible man.

But I know about his main business, which is the

supply of light arms and heavy artillery to anyone who can afford them. He's a major vendor of what I would call accessories, like CS gas cartridges and stun grenades. He's also recently moved into surveillance equipment and micro technology. I seem to recall an attempted upgrade into jet aircraft a few years back, but nothing came of it. He has a degree in chemistry from Heriot-Watt University and I would guess he's worth billions.

There's quite a bit of art in the room. Behind his desk, there's a large red and blue painting that looks like a Monet, and as I imagine he's not the sort of person to buy prints from AllPosters, I'm guessing that it's an original.

Behind me, there's a large, striking painting of a table groaning with fruit and oysters. At the centre of the painting are a peeled lemon and a brown wine glass. It isn't familiar to me, but looks as though it's from the mid-1600s and probably Flemish.

On the wall to my right, there's what looks like an Egyptian tomb painting, with the god Anubis leaning over the prostrate form of a pharaoh. Anubis was the keeper of poisons and medicines and the patron of embalming; a benevolent god, but still creepy-looking with that black jackal head. A strange thing to have in your office, but there's no accounting for taste.

But the painting that really catches my eye is a large, arresting portrait of an extremely beautiful woman. She's sitting in a pale brown armchair, with a black cushion behind her back. She's naked from the waist up, with high, medium-sized breasts and large, dark nipples. The style is vaguely impressionistic, so it's hard to tell whether she's just wearing a skirt or whether it's a dress that has been pulled down. She appears to be holding a white fur coat, which partially covers her thighs and all of her right forearm and hand.

She's staring to her right, her long blonde hair falling down to her neck and almost obscuring one of her deep blue eyes. Her mouth is full and sensual, but the artist, whoever it was, has captured a moue of boredom or contempt, which makes the whole thing rather unsettling.

It's quite unlike anything I've ever seen before and I can't tear my eyes away from it. It's sexy, sure, but there's also something sinister about it, something *wrong* with it. Who knows, maybe that's part of the sexiness? It's also completely impossible to tell how old she is. But I don't know that much about portrait painting. Maybe all of this was intentional.

'You like it, Mr Beckett?'

I snap out of it and turn to face Nathan Raleigh. He's grinning at me. I assume he's pleased that someone is admiring one of his works of art. I feel annoyed that I didn't hear him come in.

'It's fascinating. Who's it by?'

He's in his seventies, and in the past would have been described as 'dapper'. Green tweed jacket, white shirt, red bow tie, brown cords, brown Hush Puppies, red socks that match the bow tie. Only a few flecks of grey in his hair, unless it's been expertly dyed.

He has a strangely shaped and fairly recent scar an inch above his left eyebrow. It's about the size of a peanut and is mostly circular, apart from the bottom, which is a dead straight line. I can't imagine how he'd have acquired it.

'Oh, no one you'd have heard of, I fear. I had it commissioned by an artist who was recommended to me by a friend. It's my wife. Her name's Rosabel.'

'Your wife? Well now I feel embarrassed for looking at it. Please convey my apologies to her.'

This makes him laugh. 'It's there to be looked at, Mr Beckett! You don't have to be embarrassed. I'm sure *she* wouldn't mind. My wife is a very liberated woman.'

She wouldn't mind me looking at her *portrait* or she wouldn't mind me looking at her while she was half undressed? I don't pursue this line of thought with him. It's probably not a good idea.

'She's very beautiful.'

'Don't think I don't know that. A lot of men would kill to have snagged a beauty like that. Don't think I'm not aware of my good fortune. I'm a very lucky man.'

He sure is. She's quite a bit younger than him, by the look of things. It's hard to guess from a painting, but I would say she'd have been between thirty-five and forty when this was painted. If it's recent, she'd be around thirty years younger than Raleigh.

'Do you want something to drink? Or did my girl get you something? I'm sorry I was a little late for our meeting. Tedious business call, but they have to be dealt with. Am I sounding fractious? If so, I apologise. I'm a little stressed.'

'Don't worry about it. And no – I had a coffee a few minutes ago.'

'Take a seat, Mr Beckett.'

I sit on one of the sofas and Raleigh sits across from me. He's scrutinising me, almost as if I'm not really meant to be here. When you become obscenely rich and successful, your social skills are usually the first thing to go to the wall. His face breaks into a smile again.

'You know Athos Baresi.'

'Yes. I worked for him in Milan.'

'That's right,' he says, as if I'd managed a correct answer in some quiz about myself. 'He recommended you to me. He said you were one of the most efficient insurance investigators he'd ever come across and he's a hard man to please, I can tell you *that* for nothing! Said you worked fast. Said you were discreet.'

Baresi was a big man (and I mean that quite literally) in the world of fine art insurance. Some robbers stole a painting by Giuseppe Veneziano from a swish private gallery and he suspected it was an inside job but couldn't prove it. He was right. It was the owner's asshole son. I didn't quite beat the truth out of him, but it was a close thing.

Well, it's nice to know that Athos remembered me. That must have been almost three years ago. I wonder how Raleigh knows him. Perhaps all of the very rich are mates and send each other Christmas cards, which are full of miscellaneous recommendations.

'Well, speed can be of the essence, sometimes,' I say, pointlessly, wondering when he's going to get to the point, whatever the point may be.

'Why were you working in Italy in the first place? I hope you don't mind my asking.'

You can ask all you like, but you won't get a straight answer. 'I just fancied a change.'

'And some decent, warm weather, I'll bet!'

'Of course.'

'I would like to hire you, Mr Beckett. If you're free, that is. Have you ever dealt with missing persons?'

'No. That's usually a job for the police.'

'The police. Yes.'

He leans back and looks at the ceiling. The meeting seems to have gone into suspended animation for a few seconds. For the first time, I notice there's a stuffed dog sitting by a door to my left. It's a big breed, possibly a Doberman mixed with something else. Oh well, each to his own. After a minute has passed, he leans forwards, gripping his hands together tightly until the knuckles are white.

'This is not going to be very easy for me, Mr Beckett.' He gives me a smile, expecting a sympathetic response. 'I have a daughter. You wouldn't know that, of course. How could you? Her name is Viola. Viola Imogen. She will be twenty-four in a few months, but I haven't seen her for two years. Just over two years, to be exact. Two years, two months and eleven days.'

'I see.'

He looks down at the floor. When he looks up, his eyes keep darting to the left. 'We used to have an ordinary relationship, just like any father and daughter might have. But as she got older, she started going off the rails. It's that old cliché – she got in with the wrong crowd.'

I nod sympathetically. He stands up and wanders over to take a look at his wife's portrait. This seems to be pretty painful for him. He's fidgety and there's a tremor in his voice, which he can't seem to control. I'm not really sure whether it's genuine or not.

'I don't know whether this was some act of rebellion against me personally or just a fault in her psychological makeup, but she developed a heroin habit and in due course drifted into prostitution to pay for it.

'Even now as I'm telling you this I can't quite believe it's true. It is as if I'm talking about someone else. The last time I saw her, we had a flaming row. She told me all about it. Her job, I mean. What she did, the sort of people she saw – everything. It was the sort of thing that no father ever wants to hear. Are you married, Mr Beckett?'

'No.'

'Of course not. You're probably too young. Or are you? I don't know. You look early thirties to me.'

'That's about right.'

'People marry when it suits them, I suppose. I married late. There just wasn't time for it when I was younger. I had a lifestyle – is that the right word? – that didn't allow me much time for social affairs. Then I met Rosabel and everything changed. I hope that doesn't sound too clichéd.'

'Not at all. How frequently were you in contact with Viola before the row?'

He turns away from the painting and sits down opposite me again. These sofas are incredibly comfortable. I must get one when I win the lottery. I don't do the lottery.

'She visited me every three or four months, and it was usually to get money. But after our altercation the visits stopped. After a while, maybe three months, I went to the police and reported her as a missing person. I don't know if I was being stupid, but it seemed the thing to do. That was, as I say, over two years ago. I had no idea what had happened to her. I didn't know whether she was dead or alive. You can't imagine what it was like.'

'And the police haven't been in touch about it since?'

'Well, that's the funny thing. They have. I got a call from a detective. Some bloody woman. Bream, her name was. Like the fish. And she said that as I was next of kin, they had to tell me that somebody *else* had reported Viola as a missing person *three weeks ago*.'

'Did they say who it was?'

'They couldn't. Or they wouldn't. But the whole point is that Viola is still alive. Or at least she was three weeks ago. I didn't know what to think. I suppose I was relieved, or I should have been relieved, but I really don't know what I thought.'

His speech is hesitant, as though he's not used to talking to people about his feelings. 'I think I was afraid for her all over again. It was as if she'd come back into my life and then gone again. Does that sound strange?'

'Did they tell you anything at all?'

'They said she'd been a guest in a hotel somewhere near Green Park tube station. I think they were rather amused by it all. That was my impression, anyway. They said that other than letting me know, there was nothing they could do about it. As Viola is over eighteen, if she wants to go missing that's her affair, and if she doesn't want anyone to know where she is, that's her affair, too. I think they thought they were doing me a kindness. Bloody condescending, I call it. She might have been abducted or she might have been murdered, but they're still keeping her on the missing persons file as if the whole thing was of no importance whatsoever. Do you know how many people are reported missing in London each year?'

'No idea.'

'Roughly fifty thousand. Fifty thousand! I mean, there's no way on earth that they have the manpower to investigate all of those. This bloody woman said they would do their best, but I don't consider their best is good enough. I'm afraid I lost my temper with her on the telephone. I'm sure that didn't help things, either. I know the police have a lot on their plate, but I suppose I expected more because it was me. I thought I might have received special treatment. I'm stupid, I know.'

'But it must have relieved some anxiety. At least you know she's not dead. Or at least you knew that she wasn't dead three weeks ago.'

I guess there must be a limit to how many times a person can be reported missing before the police decide that they actually *want* to be missing.

'Knowing that she's not dead is not quite enough, Mr Beckett. God knows what sort of life she's been leading. God knows what sort of people she's been hanging around with. God knows what sort of physical shape she's in or what diseases she's picked up. She's probably a junkie, I can accept that, but I can *help* her.'

His eyes now fill with tears. This is killing me. He licks his lips.

'She's my daughter. When I reported her missing she may well have been safe in some sense of the word. Not dead, anyway. Do you know what the police call that? When they're found dead? A fatal outcome. God Almighty. But now someone else is obviously concerned for her safety and this time she may not be so lucky. Do you understand? I'm not articulating this properly. You must forgive me, Mr Beckett.'

I give him my understanding and sympathetic half-smile. I practise it in the mirror and it's pretty good.

'I just want to know what has happened to her and I want her back. I want her safe. If she's got problems I can help her. If she's still got addiction problems I can pay for her to go somewhere. I just can't stand the idea of her being out there somewhere. I just want peace of mind, can you understand that? I'm seventy-four now. I don't want to die without ever seeing her again.'

Seventy-four. Viola is almost twenty-four. Sexy blonde

wife. Good work.

'Well, as I said, I haven't done missing persons before, but…'

'How much do you charge, Mr Beckett?'

'A thousand a day plus expenses and what I consider expenses are non-negotiable.'

'Fine. I'll double that and give you a twenty thousand bonus if you find her. I'll give you three days' money in cash right now.'

Well, now he's piqued my interest. He gets up, walks over to a big Richmond Hall wall safe and takes out six slim packs of fifty-pound notes. Out of the corner of my eye, I can see that the safe is absolutely stuffed full of cash. Why do that? If I was as rich as this guy I'd make sure all my money was in a bank. Maybe he needs cash for bribes.

I do some quick mental arithmetic, based on the stacks of notes and the size of the shelves; depending on the denominations and currencies, there could be half a million in there. He picks up a white Jiffy Bag, slides the banknotes inside and places it in front of me on the coffee table. All sorts of deranged methods of spending this money flash through my head. I also think of coming back here and robbing his safe.

'And when I find her?' I say, as casually as possible.

'You just tell me where she is.'

'And that will be the end of the job.'

'Yes.'

'And what happens if I find her and she's dead?'

He looks rattled. 'What? What do you mean?'

'Well, from my point of view, the same amount of labour will go into this investigation whatever the endpoint will be. Therefore, it should make no difference whether I present you with a living, breathing girl or a cadaver. You just said she was still alive, but we only know that she was still alive three weeks ago. She may have been dead five minutes after the person who reported her as a missing person did so. She could even have been dead before that call was made. Understand?'

I get a bit of the silent treatment for this, but it had to be said. I can tell he's chewing the inside of his cheek. I hate people who do that. He's staring very hard at me, as if he expects me to back down, but that's not going to happen.

'Very well, Mr Beckett. The bonus stands whatever the result.'

'OK. I'll do it. But I'm going to need some help from you. I'm going to need a recent photograph, for a start.'

'I have already anticipated that. My head of security, James Fisher, has some photographs and has prepared a meagre but helpful document for you. I think perhaps he should join us.'

He presses a button on his desk. Where there had been angst and distress, there's now a wolfish grin. This is a man who likes getting what he wants.

# 3

## A MISSING PERSON

'You offended my boys, Mr Beckett.'

'Oh no.'

James Fisher is about six foot five and looks like he's the father of the two security goons, who, for all I know, are still standing in that anteroom and trying to look tough for the security cameras. Maybe he *is* their father. Maybe there's a place where insecure macho security thugs are specially bred.

His comment is an attempt to make light of the supposed offence, but I know I've pissed him off. He's holding a bright green plastic folder. He's suited up, but in a much more expensive way than his two halfwit sons. Ex-army like Purple Tie, I would say. I wonder where Raleigh gets them all from. Perhaps there's a high street agency.

I stand up and shake his hand. He attempts a punishing bone-crusher, but I'm ready for it and press a nerve on the side of his wrist with my ring finger. His hand jerks open and he glances at it with confusion, as if he's unexpectedly developed some painful carpal problem. I know that would have hurt like fuck, but he took it pretty well and isn't breaking down in tears or anything.

'Cramp?' I say to him, innocently.

He looks at me uncertainly, flashes a matey grin at Raleigh and sits down next to him on the sofa. I'm not really sure why Raleigh should have a head of security, but I'm sure I'll find out in due course. I recognise Fisher's type from long experience and from the in-control tough guy stare he's attempting to intimidate me with.

You're quite welcome to join one of the armed forces and serve your country and get shot at if you wish, but no one's forced you to join up, and it doesn't mean you have to be a grim, humourless wanker who doesn't suffer fools gladly for the rest of your life, but people like Fisher just can't help themselves.

'Wouldn't let the boys search him when he came in, sir,' he says, rubbing his wrist. 'Sherwood had to ask me if it was OK. I decided he wouldn't be a threat. You're no threat, are you, Mr Beckett?' he jokes, flashing his teeth at me.

I must assume that Fisher must have been watching the aborted search on CCTV somewhere and decided I was safe. I don't answer him and look at Raleigh, giving him the chance to appear like a nice guy.

'You must think I'm rather eccentric having all these security precautions,' says Raleigh, with a self-depreciating smirk. 'The fact is – and this doesn't leave this room – some people tried to kidnap me a few years ago.'

'Really? That's awful.'

*This doesn't leave this room?* Damn.

'Luckily, my chauffeur of the time, man named Peters, managed to see them off. I don't think they were proper professionals and I don't think they were expecting any resistance.'

I notice that Fisher is wringing his hands and looking

at the floor with more interest than it can possibly warrant.

'What made them pick on you?' I say, placing an edge of sincere concern in my voice.

'I don't really know. I imagine money was the main motive.' He smiles in an appealing, modest way. 'I suppose I'm one of the super-rich. I try to keep a low profile, but these things get out and it's inevitable that the wrong sort might get hold of the information and decided to act upon it.'

This doesn't sound like the truth to me. That little gang was too international, but basically I don't give a shit. Fisher opens up his little folder and places the contents on the coffee table. He pushes an A4 size photograph over to me and I pick it up and look at it.

So this is Viola Imogen Raleigh; junkie, prostitute and AWOL billionaire's daughter. It's a head and shoulders shot. She's breathtakingly beautiful and is clearly the daughter of the woman in the unsettling portrait on the wall.

She has thick, shoulder-length, blonde hair, exquisite cheekbones and a sensual mouth, with eyes that are intelligent, flirtatious, humorous and tragic. She's wearing a turquoise, off-the-shoulder top or perhaps it's a dress. This looks like a professional photographer did it. If she still looks anything like this and is working as a call girl, I can't imagine how much she must go out for. If you were a tired businessman and she turned up at your hotel room, you'd think you'd hit the jackpot or were dreaming. I can see that Raleigh has gone all misty-eyed.

'How long ago was this taken?' I ask him.

'That was when she was twenty-two, I think. Maybe earlier. She had a series of photographs taken of herself by some photographer. I don't know why. They weren't for me, that's for sure. I just came across this when I was going through her things. There were more, but I don't know what happened to them.'

'So two years old. Have you got anything more recent?'

'No, but there's this one.' He nods at Fisher who pushes over a smaller, slightly blurred, full body photograph of a much younger looking Viola. Some sort of holiday snap taken on a white sand beach. Not the UK, judging by the sky and sea colour. Her hair is shorter and is being blown over her face by the wind, but it's definitely the same girl. She's in a swimsuit. Nice figure. Slim and busty. Great legs. Drug problem or not, a girl who looked like this would probably exist at the upper end of prostitution; high-end escort stuff, definitely not street corner.

'That was taken when she was seventeen. Just to give you an idea of her body shape.'

It certainly does.

'She was a very attractive young girl, Mr Raleigh,' says Fisher.

'Yes,' agrees Raleigh. 'She was.'

I suddenly feel like I'm part of a cabal of perverts, ogling private photographs of teenage girls. Fisher hands me an A4 sheet with all of her vital statistics on it. Height, weight, eye colour, hair colour, clothing sizes (including bra size) distinguishing features; everything I could want is there. This is all very well if I'm going to accidentally walk past her on the street, but I'm going to need a little more. I need somewhere to start. Luckily, Fisher is able to oblige.

'We don't have a great deal of information about her

friends from the last few years, if indeed she had any,' he says, smiling apologetically. 'But I've typed out a list of names on this sheet that may help you get started.'

At the top of the sheet is the name and telephone number of the police officer that contacted Raleigh. Detective Sergeant Olivia Bream, Metropolitan Police, Seymour Street W1. I know it. Nearest tube station is Marble Arch.

'Would it be OK with you if I contacted this officer?'

Raleigh shifts in his seat. He looks a tad uncomfortable with this suggestion. 'I'm not sure. As I said, I wasn't very polite to this woman on the telephone and I'm not sure if – it's just that I don't think this is a very high priority for the police and I'm not sure if them knowing that I'd hired someone from the private sector would make things worse.'

'You feel that my presence would be insulting to them and they might make your daughter a lower priority than she is already?'

'Well, if you put it that way – yes.'

'And you're afraid that they might do nothing, as opposed to not very much.'

Police attitudes may have changed for all I know, but I can't imagine that searching for absentee call girls is a big deal for them. These are not the sorts of missing persons that make the newspapers or require elaborate press conferences, no matter how rich and powerful their father may be. Fisher glances at his boss as if he's asking for permission to speak. Raleigh nods at him.

'The way I see it, Mr Beckett, is I don't think the police are going to share any information from their file on Viola with a civilian, which, with all due respect, is what you would be to them.'

'And they might view it,' adds Raleigh, 'as some rich old man interfering with an ongoing police investigation, if that's how whatever they're doing can be described.'

'Well, I'll have a word with them anyway. I can be very persuasive.'

'As you wish,' says Raleigh, without enthusiasm.

Underneath the police details is the name of a hotel, The Bolton Mayfair, Bolton Street, London W1. A fairly new luxury hotel that's just off Piccadilly and a short walk from the Hard Rock Café. This is real call-girl territory; top clubs, top bars, top restaurants, top hotels, top businesses, top shops and top prostitutes.

'So what's this hotel?'

'That is the name of the hotel where Viola was staying before she was reported missing,' says Raleigh, with a bit of a choke in his voice.

'I see. And that information was given to the police by whoever it was that reported her missing three weeks ago.'

'Yes.'

'Did they give you the room number?'

'No. No room number. But the person who telephoned the police did say that she was staying there, apparently.'

And we don't know who made that call; though I'll bet any money it was Viola's pimp. Viola goes to the hotel to meet a client and disappears. This isn't looking good.

On the other hand, why would Viola have booked a room there if she was entertaining a client? Is that how it works now? I thought it was the client who booked the room and the call girl just turned up. I could be wrong, of course.

Without looking up from the sheet of paper, I can see

that Fisher is eyeballing me intently. Perhaps he's wondering why his boss won't let him deal with this. Perhaps there's little bit of manly jealousy going on here; hurt pride, that sort of thing.

There's another name and telephone number underneath the hotel details.

'Who's Taylor Conway?'

Raleigh purses his lips and looks pissed. Fisher looks away, his eyes resting on Mrs Raleigh's portrait.

'I don't know if that name will be of any use to you, Mr Beckett,' says Raleigh, his eyes looking pained. 'That's one of Viola's friends from quite a while back. One can never know these things for sure, but I suspect he's the one who got her started on drugs. He was the kingpin of the crowd that she hung around with about three or four years ago. It could actually be longer ago than that. I don't know if he could be called a boyfriend, but she did mention his name from time to time, usually when she was trying to make me angry. I never met him, so I don't really know what he's like, but I can imagine. That telephone number was in her address book, but I don't know whether it's still in use.'

It's a landline number, not a mobile, so I might get lucky if I have to speak to him.

'You don't have his address, by any chance?'

'No. Her address book was a rather Spartan affair. Just names and telephone numbers. Most of them were friends of hers from long ago. School, that sort of thing. She'd had that address book since she was about fifteen, I think. She mainly used it as a kind of notebook. It was covered in scribbles and sketches. She was very good at art. I thought she might actually study art in university, but it was not to be.'

'Can I see it?'

He suddenly looks a little shifty. 'I don't have it anymore. I don't know what happened to it. I remember writing down that boy's number in my own address book in case I ever had cause to call him, but that was well over a year ago. I must have mislaid it.'

What a shame. I'd have like to have seen those scribbles and sketches. And those other numbers. Never mind. So all I have to go on is the name of a police sergeant, a hotel and some old boyfriend/dealer.

Raleigh and Fisher are both breathing heavily and staring at me. I think I should say something.

'OK. I'll do the best that I can to find her — or at least find out what's happened to her — and I'll do it as fast as I can. But you have to prepare yourself for the worst. I can't promise you good news, as I'm sure you understand.'

Raleigh leans forwards and looks straight into my eyes. 'How long do you think it will take?'

I wave my hand at the photographs and the sheet of paper in front of me. 'This is not much to go on, to be honest, but I should have something for you in less than a week.'

He visibly brightens at this news. 'Less than a week! But that's marvellous! I thought you were going to say a couple of months. I knew I'd made the right decision with you. The police will take forever with this, I just know it.' He nods his head, mentally congratulating himself. 'There is another thing that I have to tell you, and I don't want you to think I'm callous. I mean, life goes on and all of that.'

'Go ahead.'

'I can't go into details, as I'm sure you understand, but

I'm in the middle of brokering an extremely lucrative deal with the Sultanate of Oman. I presume you know that I deal in weaponry.'

'I had heard. Well done.'

'In ten days, I have a meeting with two of their security ministers. I'm sure it will go well, but this Viola business has been really getting to me and…'

'I think Mr Raleigh just wants to make sure he has a clear head during the negotiations,' interjects Fisher. 'And it would be nice if this matter was cleared up one way or the other.'

'I understand.'

'And as you have said less than a week, that's – that's a huge weight off my shoulders,' says Raleigh.

Hence the doubling of my rate and the twenty thousand bonus if I find her. Well, it sounds like a lot of money to me, but it's probably chicken feed to him. Knowing what Oman usually spends on defence he's probably looking at a billion or so, if all goes well. Maybe more. I wonder idly how you actually get to *be* an arms dealer. I don't recall it being mentioned in my school's career evenings.

'OK. I'll be in touch with you as soon as there are any significant breakthroughs.'

I catch Fisher giving Raleigh a small portion of eye contact.

'Ah. I take it, then, that you won't be letting us know how you are doing on a daily basis,' Raleigh says.

'No point. Information you glean one day may not have any relevance until the day after. It may turn out to have no relevance at all. I'd just be wasting your time, or worse still, giving you hope when there was none.'

There's another tiny little visual exchange between the

two men. What is all this about? I wonder.

'I didn't think of that,' says Raleigh. 'And I quite understand what you mean. I have complete faith in you, Mr Beckett. Athos Baresi is always a good judge of men.'

'He was a real character,' I say, smiling. Actually, he was totally bent and corrupt, but knew how to have a good time, which is why I liked him.

'I understand he was also a good judge of women!' says Raleigh, now cheered up slightly. 'From what I've heard, anyway.'

We all laugh, stand up and shake hands like men. Fisher doesn't attempt another bone-crusher. Before I go, I've got to know about the stuffed dog. I think the atmosphere is light enough now for me to mention it. I look in its direction and point. 'Is that, um…'

'That's Lincoln. You probably surmised that he's mainly Doberman, but he has a touch of Beauceron in there, too. They're fantastic dogs, but prone to various diseases. Lincoln died of congestive heart failure, but he wasn't going to get away from me *that* easily.'

'Attractive markings,' is all I can say to that.

'Indeed.'

Fisher hands me the folder and Raleigh accompanies me to the front door. As we pass through Anjukka's office, I stop and turn to face her.

'Thanks once again for the coffee.'

'My pleasure, Mr Beckett.' She gives me a quick, innocent smile that tells me things aren't quite over between us yet.

Raleigh and I stand on the steps and look out into leafy Holland Park. It's starting to get cold and the leaves are beginning to turn yellow. This is the sort of street that would have once been entirely residential, but is now home to anonymous operations like Raleigh's, with discreet brass plaques being the only clues to what may or may not go on inside.

'Did you bring a car?'

'No. I took the tube.'

'Wise man. You – you don't think I'm being too cynical about the police, do you? I want to do everything I can to find Viola. I don't want to annoy them in any way.'

'I think you're right to assume that this will be low priority for them. Look at it from their point of view. A young woman is reported missing two years ago and three weeks ago she's reported missing again. That means that she was back on the radar, albeit for a short time. I think that's the sort of thing they'll put on the back burner.'

'Yes. Yes, I'm sure you're right.'

'I'll be in touch. Nice to meet you.'

We shake hands once again and I go down the steps, out of the gate and onto the pavement. Several cabs go by, but I decide to walk down to Holland Park Avenue and pick one up when I start to get tired. I'm aware that Raleigh is still standing there, watching me.

I probably won't start work on this today as it's far too late, but I want to let the facts float around in my mind and see if anything clever pops up, like a smart solution to the whole thing so I can pick up the rest of my payment tomorrow afternoon. I stuff the Jiffy Bag with the cash inside the green folder.

In an ideal world, the first person I would want to speak to would be whoever called her in as a missing person. Probably her pimp, assuming she was still working as a call girl of some sort, which I think she was.

Of course, there's a slim chance that she may no

longer be in that line of work. It might have been a real friend. But would a real friend report you missing while you were staying in a hotel? Unlikely. It all sounds a bit strange, particularly as it's usually the client who's the one with the room.

I let my mind wander and start thinking about what was probably an original Monet in Raleigh's office. Does Raleigh live in that house or is it purely for work? My suspicion is he lives there some of the time and also has premises elsewhere. Is Fisher a live-in head of security? Anjukka probably knocks off at five and goes home. The two goons who failed to frisk me probably don't live there and are bussed over when a stranger comes to call or when Raleigh needs to impress. Does Rosabel Raleigh live there? How many rooms in that place are devoted to business? Is there a garden out the back? If I had a real Monet, I'd probably get someone to paint a convincing forgery of it and put the real one in a bank vault. Maybe it wasn't a Monet at all.

I noticed that both of the ground floor front windows had a species of Berberis growing under them; thick bushes with big, vicious-looking thorns. That would not have been an accidental choice. It's an old-fashioned form of security but would still do the job as a deterrent for some opportunistic and stupid burglar who didn't realise he was about to get his hands cut to ribbons. I ball both of my hands into fists imagining what that would feel like.

Then there was the portrait of Rosabel. How much would that be worth? Sentimental value only, I suspect. I can still see that mouth, those eyes. I took the fact that her breasts were exposed on face value, if that's the right term, just like I would when looking at any nude or seminude portrait before a business meeting. But if I was commissioning an artist to paint my wife, would I have had her pose in quite that way? No reason not to, of course. It's his choice. But then to display it in your office where all your staff and visitors can see it is another thing altogether.

Can you imagine, if you were Rosabel Raleigh, walking past some slime-ball like Fisher, knowing that he knew what your breasts looked like? Perhaps she couldn't give a damn. Perhaps she likes it. Perhaps the pose was her choice and I'm just being prudish or conservative. But prudery or not, if I was deciding where to put a portrait like that, my first choice would not be in my office. Raleigh, of course, might be so insecure that he wants everyone to know what a beautiful, sexy wife he's got. Again, nothing wrong with that, but it still seems a little peculiar to me. She did have great breasts, though. Perhaps I'll tell her that if I ever meet her. I'd like to meet her. I'd like to know what she's like, with her contemptuous mouth and hot cleavage.

I start thinking about Anjukka, for some reason. I'll bet you anything that being in close proximity to a woman who looks like that must drive Fisher and his goons mad and I'll bet they've all tried hitting on her to no avail. She's probably very good at her job, but it's probably another bit of ego wank for Raleigh, just like Rosabel's portrait. All that power, all that money. It's never enough, is it? They have to keep proving and proving, showing off and showing off until they die and no one gives a shit about them anymore.

Which brings me to Viola. God Almighty – what happened to *her*? Did she become a junkie and a prostitute to piss off her father in some way? To piss off her mother? To piss off both of them? It's like an archetypical poor little rich girl scenario and I can't really feel much sympathy.

OK – I could see how the prostitution could be a direct result of the junkie thing, but even so. If I was teetering on the edge of prostitution and had rich parents, I think I'd swallow my pride and ask for money, unless, of course, I had no pride. Perhaps that was the problem. Perhaps she was messed up in ways that would be hard for me to fathom.

Perhaps she wasn't able to think straight because of the junk. It's easy to see a photograph like the one Fisher gave me and think, '*What a beautiful girl. Why didn't she find some nice guy to cherish her and love her? What happened?*' But you can't know the ins and outs of someone else's mind or of their circumstances. It's all relative. You can only make guesses and they're rarely the right ones.

Maybe her circle didn't contain many 'nice guys'. Maybe her circle was full of people like Taylor Conway, not that I have any reason to judge him. Not yet, anyway. Maybe being a rich man's daughter put her in the path of the biggest tossers and users in the country and they used her and sucked her dry like a bunch of over-privileged vampires. Maybe she was possessed of a degree of self-hatred that I couldn't begin to imagine and each day that went by twisted her a little more. I didn't ask if she had any siblings, but I get the feeling she didn't.

It's difficult for me to look through her eyes because it's difficult to imagine being a young person in a world where you can have virtually anything you want. I can't imagine Viola sifting through the change in her pocket, seeing if she's got enough money to buy another round of lager for her friends in the local pub.

And one more thing comes to mind. It sounds silly and it might be me, but I didn't like the way that Raleigh and Fisher – whichever one of them it was – had gone to the trouble of getting Viola's bra size on that sheet of paper. The beach photograph would have been more than enough. I'm trying to track her down, not buy lingerie for her. I get an unpleasant picture in my head of Raleigh rifling through her belongings until he finds an old bra to get the size off the label. What was he thinking of? How does he think I work? 'Hey, punk. I'm looking for a stacked blonde dame. Sports a 38EE. Partial to tight sweaters. You can't miss her.'

The hotel might be worth a visit. Maybe someone remembered her. Someone must have registered her when she arrived, unless she was using a different name, which is extremely likely. The 'friend' who reported her missing would have to have told the police what her real name was, otherwise they would never have contacted Raleigh in the first place.

The hotel staff, however, may never have known her real name and would only know her by the fake, assuming she was using one. If I'm going to have a useful conversation with anyone at The Bolton Mayfair, I have to know what the fake name was.

Maybe someone saw her leave. They probably have CCTV, at least in the lobby. Do they keep everything on their computer system? How long for? It's probably wiped every couple of weeks to save space and stop the system slowing down too much. I wonder if the police thought to take a look at it. Somehow I don't think they'd have bothered. I have to keep reminding myself that this is only a missing persons case for them, and they probably wouldn't bother exhuming deleted security camera footage. The police probably think Raleigh is a bit of a joke and is wasting their time.

He's an interesting personality type, though. Lots of inconsistencies in the way he was behaving; narcissistic and crowing one moment, then insecure and sentimental the next. I have no idea how you'd run a business like his, but I can't quite square employing someone like Fisher with brokering arms deals. Perhaps it's a more dangerous occupation than I'd imagined. Also, the charade with the two goons seemed totally unnecessary and collapsed as soon as I wouldn't go along with it.

A red minicab slows down right next to me and the driver leans over and asks if I need a car. When I say no, he says, '*Fuck* you, man!' and drives away.

The more I think about Raleigh, the more confused I feel, but I can't quite put a finger on the reason. OK, so he finds out his missing daughter isn't dead after two years. It must have been an incredible relief for him. But this time, he's not going to trust the police. He's going to go private. He asks around his buddies and comes up with me; someone with no experience in missing persons cases at all, but who, with the promise of all that money will certainly have a go and will maybe even succeed where the police have failed.

But if I was in his place and money was no object, I'd hire one of those big security firms full of ex-CID and have maybe half a dozen people working on this at the same time. On the other hand, some of the people I'm going to try and talk to may be able to smell former policemen a mile off and will clam up just because they can. Raleigh may be smarter than I'm giving him credit for.

I'm just on the outskirts of Notting Hill Gate when I

decided I'm fed up with walking and hail a passing black cab. The driver sniffs when I tell him Covent Garden. At least he doesn't say, 'Fuck you, man.'

# 4

## SELECT METROPOLITAN ESCORTS

I'm dropped off in the middle of Long Acre and take my usual, totally random, convoluted route home. For me, at least, Covent Garden is a great place to live; always busy, day and night, and full of tourists, workers, shoppers, drunks, clubbers and people in transit. There are also a lot of shop windows, which come in useful when you need reflective surfaces to check if anyone unwelcome is behind you.

Despite the variety, it's got a definite atmosphere and population and you can feel if something or someone is wrong. I walk eastwards along Long Acre, cross the road suddenly as if I'm heading for the tube station, but pass it by and turn down James Street, walking straight towards the market, stopping to look at a silver-painted mime, then stopping again to look through the window of The Nag's Head, as if I'm looking for friends.

I cross over to look in Fossil's window for a few seconds, then walk slowly over to the market, losing myself in the crowds and taking a hard left past the cafés, shops, classical buskers and street performers until I'm outside again. I slip around the back of the market into Tavistock Street, then down Burleigh Street and take a swift left past the No Entry sign into Exeter Street, where

I live. There's no real need for any of this, of course, or at least I hope there isn't. I just like to keep my hand in. At least that's what I tell myself. Actually, I think I'm just suffering from a healthy paranoia.

Exeter Street is one of those strange roads which is dead in the centre of London but looks like it belongs nowhere. Thirty seconds south and you're in The Strand and across the road from The Savoy Theatre, but you'd never guess it from the dingy buildings, the permanent scaffolding, the graffiti and the bins.

Many of the buildings are the back end of those in the adjacent roads and don't have obvious entrances, and it's more like a road you take to get to somewhere else. I live in a third floor flat on the north side.

I turn the keys in both enhanced Yale cylinder locks, let myself in and walk down the short hallway, carefully avoiding the nightingale floor that I had installed shortly after I moved in here, just over two years ago. In case you're not familiar with nightingale floors, they're a seventeenth-century Japanese invention, reputedly used as a defence against ninjas, though I'm not sure there are many of those in the vicinity of Exeter Street. All wooden floors creak, but these have flooring nails underneath, placed in a criss-cross pattern that makes a terrible, loud, high-pitched, squeaking, creaking noise when anyone walks on them. Sounds like birds, so they say, hence the name.

It sounds eccentric and primitive, but it works, and I have a lot of reasons for being so charmingly low-tech. Plus if anyone breaks in here while I'm asleep (if they're professional enough to get past the cylinder locks), I'll know about it in exactly one second. There's a secret, silent path through the nightingale floor, which is known only to me and Mr Oe, who built it for an extremely reasonable three thousand pounds.

Once past my archaic security zone, I'm in the large kitchen, which leads to the other rooms. I have the whole floor to myself, but it wasn't cheap, and I had to make a lot of changes, mainly to the rather flimsy windows and the hatch leading up to the roof. I didn't want any of the Exeter Street ninjas breaking in, so all of the fixed bars and window grills were a necessity, and, to my surprise, ended up looking quite cool. This floor and the one below it used to be used as a wood storage area for a local carpentry firm and there's still a faint smell of pine about the place that doesn't come from the current wooden floors, which are made from American Black Cherry.

Once in the kitchen, I take my jacket off, turn the heating on, load up my Siemens coffee maker with Bourbon Espresso beans, hit the switch and sit at the kitchen table, staring through the barred kitchen windows at the building across the road. Despite the triple glazing on the windows, I can hear people laughing on the street below. Theatregoers, maybe, but it's more likely that they're tourists or shoppers who have got lost.

I make myself a coffee and empty the contents of Fisher's folder onto the kitchen table. I take a look at Viola's portrait first. I stare hard at it, willing the solution to everything to somehow jump out of the photograph and reveal itself to me. No such luck.

Raleigh said that she had this photograph and some others done by some photographer. I flip it over and look at the back, in case there's a stamp from a photographic studio, but there's nothing. What happened to the other photographs and why did she keep this one? Perhaps this was the only decent one, and by that I mean that the others were possibly indecent.

Would she need photographs to sell herself? Would her pimp need photographs to show potential clients? What sort of photographs would they have to be? How do you go about getting a call girl nowadays? I still see cards in telephone kiosks in the West End, but these are quickly removed. But then if Viola was a high-class call girl, she wouldn't use that method.

I fire up the computer and while I'm waiting for it to do all its stuff, take another look at Viola. Such a beauty. I don't know her, but I rather hope that she's not dead. It would be such a shame. She was twenty-two when this was taken; an age when most young women are just beginning their lives and hers was already royally fucked.

Maybe it was vanity, getting these done. Maybe she just wanted some nice photographs of herself while she was still beautiful. Who knows? Maybe she left this one in Raleigh's place as a souvenir of herself, perhaps out of spite if they didn't get on. Maybe she left it there by accident.

I'm not really sure what to Google, so I type in 'high class escorts London' and, as I somehow suspected, there are loads of websites. I click on the third one down for the sake of randomness. It's called Select Metropolitan Escorts. Girls are classed according to colour, age and body type. I click on 'busty' and look at the first girl that comes up. Her name's Jasmin. No surname. There are seven photographs of her, all showing off her body. Two are in sexy lingerie, two are in a bikini and two are in what I would call business clothing. There's also one where she's topless, but her arms are crossed over her breasts. I assume there are rules about how much you can show on these sites if you don't want to get shut down.

To the right, there's a panel which gives information (which I think you'd have to take with a pinch of salt) about her age, measurements, eye colour, hair colour, build, sexual orientation and nationality. Jasmin is bisexual, Brazilian and charges three hundred pounds per hour. That's for incalls. Outcalls are three hundred and fifty, the extra fifty presumably covering travelling expenses. Each additional hour is two hundred and fifty and the overnight charge is two thousand. Jasmin doesn't look very Brazilian to me, but she certainly is busty.

At the bottom of the page, there's a section for reviews, but Jasmin doesn't have any, at least not yet. I can't imagine that many of her clients would be interested in recording their experiences, but I can see how it would be helpful, just like when you're buying stuff on Amazon.

I look at two more girls, Izolda and Raina. Both are very pretty, like Jasmin. They all have the kind of look that if someone told you they were glamour models, you'd have no cause to doubt them. There's a slight difference with Raina, though. In all of her photographs, her eyes are gently fuzzed out. Presumably there are women on these sites who don't want to be identified. It would hardly make much difference if you were a punter. If you were interested in Raina, you'd still know what sort of body she had (if that's really her in the photographs) and you'd get a good impression of her facial beauty. You just wouldn't recognise her if she walked by on the street, which I guess is the important thing. There's a chance you wouldn't even recognise her if you worked with her.

In fact, the fuzzing of the eyes makes it likely that these are genuine photographs of the girl calling herself Raina. Presumably, no business like this would last long if you booked one girl and another one, perhaps less good-looking, turned up at your hotel room.

I decide to see what would happen if I decided to book Raina and click on the relevant oblong. A new page appears asking for my requirements. They want a lot of details, such as your name, telephone number, email address, service required and the length of time you'd want to book her for. Obviously, they want the date and time, too. You could, if you wished, just book her for a dinner date. Maybe book her for half a dozen dinner dates, to see how things went and whether you had anything in common, before you booked her for a three hundred and fifty quid outcall.

There's a CAPTCHA as the bottom of the page, presumably to protect the girls from being hired by a bot. In fact, it's only this security measure, your name and your telephone number, which are the required fields. If it's an outcall, you have to put in details of the meeting point and give the room number if it's a hotel. So the client could book one of these girls using a pay-as-you-go mobile and a false name if they so wished. If anything happened to one of the girls, it would be very difficult to track down the perpetrator. Not impossible, just very difficult.

I click my way through some more girls, while my eyes keep flicking to Viola's photograph. Yes. This is a good, professional shot and there are photographs of this quality on each page of this site. So perhaps Viola was on one of these sites. The question is, of course, who booked her? And which site was she on? And what name was she using?

If you're a young woman and you fancy this type of work, there's a page where you can apply for your details to be placed on here. There's a section where you can upload up to a dozen photographs of yourself once you've been approved by whoever does the approving.

That's it, then. The photographs have to be genuine or whoever runs the site wouldn't bother themselves with you if they turned out to be fake. They'd certainly want to meet you before they allowed you on here to make sure you were genuine and the real you matched your pics.

So the site is the pimp, in a sense. They probably charge the girls for advertising themselves on here and take a cut of whatever money the girls earn. Once again, there's a CAPTCHA at the bottom, to stop bots applying to be call girls. I shouldn't really be surprised that it's like this. Prostitution has always taken advantage of the latest technology, just like it did when telephones started to catch on. Would the girls on sites like this be called eGirls as opposed to call girls?

I look at half a dozen more sites, but they're all different. Different types of girls, different prices and different target audiences. Some are scuzzy, others are high class and insanely priced. Some have girls who have appeared in famous porn films, others are 'students', currently in university somewhere in the country. Makes you feel glad your student loan was paid off in full.

Strangely, it gets a bit overwhelming looking at all this stuff after a while. All those bodies for sale, all those breasts, all those mouths, all that youth, all that beauty, all that fake eagerness, all those fake names, all those fake nationalities. An endless, unstoppable conveyor belt of lies and money and flesh and fucking; elite, exclusive, high class, choice, friendly, incall, outcall, busty, petite, Asian, ebony, English rose and mature. The clients don't care about the girls and the girls don't care about the clients. Fucking hell. Trying to track down a single, lost girl in this virtual sex world would be like looking for a needle in a haystack.

Well, at least I'm soaking up the atmosphere, but it still doesn't tell me where Viola has got to. I take a look at the other photograph, the one where she's a teenager on the beach. Seventeen years old. Four or five years later she'd be on the game and mainlining heroin, if what her father said is true. Her hair is being blown across her face, so I can't really look at her eyes to see if she's happy/distressed/fucked, but everything appears to be OK. The slightly shorter hair in this photograph suits her face shape and with that figure she must have been beating the boys off with a stick.

The sheet of paper, which Fisher prepared, is a bit of a joke, really. It's as if they were trying to do something really slick and impressive, but could only come up with four typed lines and a couple of names. I'll certainly want to visit The Bolton Mayfair, but not until I discover Viola's fake name. I could wave the photographs in the faces of the staff, but they see so many people it's unlikely they'll remember her, striking though she is. Doing that is still a possibility, but only if nothing else useful turns up.

DS Olivia Bream would have a lot of the information I need. She'd know who called in Viola as a missing person and she'd know the name that Viola was using in the hotel. The only problem with DS Bream is that Raleigh was afraid that hassling her might affect the quality of the police investigation into Viola's disappearance. On the other hand, I don't think that the police will be spending too much time on this anyway. On a personal basis, though, I'd prefer not to have to deal with the police and have found them to be pretty unhelpful in the past.

Taylor Conway sounds like he'll be next to useless.

This is someone who may not have had any contact with Viola for four years. As soon as she moved out of his circle, it's doubtful that they kept in touch. I'll keep him on the back burner.

So – hotel staff, old boyfriend and slightly involved police officer.

I pick up my mobile and punch in the number of Seymour Street police station. I look at my watch to see what time it is. Six-fifteen. I can hear the pre-recorded messages telling me to do things. I press three, and listen to more instructions, then I press one and listen to further instructions, then I press four and finally I hear what sounds like a real telephone actually ringing. Christ – what if this was an emergency? After about three or four minutes, someone finally answers.

'Hi. I'd like to speak to DS Bream, please.'

'I'm afraid she's not here at the moment,' says an impatient male voice. 'Perhaps you could call tomorrow.'

'When will she be in?'

'Hold on.'

While I'm holding on, I have time to make another coffee and drink it. My switchboard officer is doubtless doing the same thing. I know he's there. I can hear him breathing.

'Hello? Are you still there?' says the voice.

'Yes. I'm still here.'

'She's not here at the moment, but she'll be in at about seven. Can I ask what it's about?'

'It's a personal matter. It isn't to do with police work.'

*That's* told him.

'Oh.' He sounds pissed off. I wonder why? 'Well I'm not sure that I can…'

'Perhaps you could ask her to give me a ring when she

comes in. My name's Daniel Beckett.'

I give him my number, say thanks and click off. Well at least I've done something now. She might not ring back, of course, but I tried to make it sound vaguely intriguing.

After I've eaten something, I decide to go for a wander and get a drink. I don't make a habit of this, but often like to sit somewhere and get slowly hammered just before I start a case. It's a habit I picked up in Italy when I was living and working there a couple of years back. Of course it's a little bit hotter in Milan than it is in London, there are more outdoor bars and cafés and the boozing culture is different, but still.

I worked for a couple of years as an insurance investigator there, and would occasionally collaborate with a local freelancer that the big companies sometimes used. It was this guy – Flavio Moretti – who told me that all the facts of a case melted like butter into your brain after you'd had two Campari and sodas, though sometimes it took more than that – it all depended on the case. Sometimes it worked, sometimes it didn't. Sometimes you just got pissed, but it was all fun.

I walk down Tavistock Street until I find a bar that I haven't been to before and go inside. It's lit up like Christmas and is maybe half full, mostly a work crowd having a few drinks before going home. This is usually the pattern around here and the majority of the bars and pubs thin out after about eight o' clock. I order a double vodka and soda and sit at the bar, away from the workers and with a view of the doors. Like my ever-changing, convoluted routes home, this is another hard-to-kill habit. I like to be able to see who's coming in and going out for no other reason than it makes me feel more comfortable and better able to relax.

There's music playing, but I can only hear a dull thump over the noise of the other customers, and can't identify the song. I sip my drink and look at a bunch of girls dressed up to the nines, all standing about twenty feet away. One of them you notice straight away; short blonde hair, tall, very pretty and wearing a pink halter top and a tight white cotton skirt. There's a bag at her feet and it's stuffed with cards and wrapping paper. I have to assume that this is a birthday celebration or maybe she's leaving her job. It's impossible to tell.

There's something about noisy, busy places like this that allows me to focus on problems in a way that I can't when I'm home. I keep seeing Viola Raleigh's face from that photograph and wonder what her evening was like up to the time she was reported missing. Of course, I don't know for sure that she was working, but for the moment I'm assuming it was so.

I'm also still assuming that it was her pimp that called the police. There's no time limit on when you report someone as missing, unless it's something crazy like five minutes. The fact that she was booked into a room in the hotel is a little baffling to me, but I'm sure that will sort itself out in due course. Remembering what I saw on all those escort sites, some girls rent a flat where clients can come and visit. Maybe Viola did the same sort of thing, but in a hotel room. Would that be an incall or an outcall? I've no idea.

The blonde girl turns briefly and stares straight at me. We make eye contact for a millisecond and after giving me a brief, distracted smile, she turns back to her friends.

When a call girl first encounters a client, there must be a moment, fairly early on, when she makes a decision about whether she's going to take the job or not. This would depend on how high class and expensive she was; whether she could afford to turn down work.

What would make her decide not to take things any further? It could be that the client is extremely drunk or high on drugs. It could be that the client's level of personal hygiene is so repellent that she wants to call a halt to proceedings. It could be that the client is immediately abusive, creepy or violent. So she may have some way of letting her pimp know that she's going ahead with the job. Maybe she would send a text or make a call. The pimp would then know, roughly, when that job was going to end.

The blonde girl turns and looks at me again, but in a way that makes it seem like she's just scanning the bar, possibly looking for someone she knows. But her focus is slowly drifting away from her friends or colleagues and towards me.

So it's possible that Viola thought everything was OK. The client came into her hotel room and they had a few drinks. Everything's going fine and nothing seems to be out of the ordinary.

The blonde girl looks over here once more. She turns and says something to her pals. Three or four of the other girls laugh. Now they look over here, too. The bar guy sees my drink is finished and asks if I'd like another one. I say yes.

So Viola and the client start the evening's activities. They have sex, she beats him, he dresses up as a baby, whatever. As far as the pimp knows, this is going to be a typical evening for her and she'll report back in one way or another when it's all over, if that's what the normal MO is.

The bar guy places another vodka and soda in front of me. I nod and smile at him. Finally, the blonde girl peels herself off from her friends and walks over, but her bag remains on the floor.

She's smiling. Fabulous figure. I can smell her perfume when she's three or four feet away from me. 'You look lonely over here, so I thought I'd come over and say hello. Are you waiting for someone?'

She's a little nervous, but seems nice.

'Waiting for someone? No.'

She's a little drunk, but nothing too serious. She extends her hand and I stand and take it. We shake. Her skin is soft. Her eyes are dark brown like Viola's and with the same hint of flirtatiousness.

'I'm Jodie.' She indicates her friends with a turn of her head. 'They're from work. It's my birthday.'

'Happy birthday, Jodie. I'm Daniel.'

So the client's evening with Viola is going fine, but then something happens that changes things. For some reason, they must have left the hotel, possibly at the same time, possibly not.

'Hi, Daniel. Can I buy you a drink? As it's my birthday?'

'Thank you, Jodie. I'll have a vodka and soda.' This, despite the fact I've hardly started on my last one. She orders the vodka for me and a Whisky Sour for herself. Good choice. She's obviously a booze connoisseur.

We sip our drinks and stare at each other. Despite the length of her hair, she bears more than a passing resemblance to Viola; the eyes, the figure, the legs. We're standing less than a foot apart. Her perfume is getting a little intoxicating now.

'So,' she says, smiling.

'So,' I say, smiling back.

She takes a sip from her drink and places it carefully on the bar. 'Are you going to give me a birthday kiss, Daniel?'

Or maybe Viola left the hotel alone. Or maybe she and the client agreed to meet up later, somewhere else, some agreement being made that cut the pimp out of the equation. Or something bad happened there and Viola was spirited away without anyone noticing. I'm going to have to have a look at this hotel. I'm somehow going to have to get a look at Viola's room, if I can find out which one it was.

'Well,' I say. 'If you insist.'

There's another possibility. Something – maybe an actual event, maybe not – made Viola decide that she wanted to quit. She walked out of that hotel and out of that life. She didn't tell her pimp. The pimp was concerned about her because she was a good source of income for him. That's why he reported her missing. He wanted her back.

Jodie's arms are around my neck and we're kissing as passionately as teenagers at a disco. I can taste lime juice in her saliva. My hands are on her hips and I let them slide up to her waist, just below her ribs. Her body is warm against mine and her breasts press against my chest. I can hear a loud roar of approval coming from her friends. I can feel my mobile vibrating in my inside jacket pocket. For a millisecond, I start imagining I'm kissing Viola, that this is what it would have been like. But Viola didn't have innocent, slightly tipsy, fun encounters like this with a pack of laughing colleagues nearby. Viola was disturbed. Viola was damaged. And in that millisecond, I decide I'm going to find out what happened to her, and if it's bad, I'm going to find the scumbags responsible, and I'm going to punish them.

# 5

## BEAUTIFUL WHEN SHE LAUGHS

'Daniel Beckett?'

'Yes. Hi. How can I help you?'

Jodie has taken my jacket off and very carefully placed it on the back of one of the bar stools. It falls on the floor; so she squats down to pick it up. This action reveals about seven inches of bare flesh between her halter-top and the back of her skirt. It's hard to tear my eyes away from this sight, but I have to concentrate; I'm on the phone.

'This is Detective Sergeant Bream at Seymour Street police station. I got a message asking to call you.'

'Oh yes. Hi. Good. Thank you for calling back.'

Attractive, husky voice. Very slight North of England accent. Yorkshire.

Jodie runs her hands over my shoulder muscles and biceps. She keeps giving me meaningful looks and tries to start kissing again. I run a hand through her hair and slowly place a finger against my lips. Her hands snake under the back of my shirt and, for a second, I think she's going to try and take it off.

'What can I do for you, Mr Beckett?'

'I was wondering if I could have a few minutes of your time. It's regarding a missing persons case that you're involved with. I'm an investigator and I'm working for Nathan Raleigh.'

'I'm sorry – who?'

One of Jodie's friends, an extremely curvy woman of about forty, brings over Jodie's bag and drops it at her feet, raising an eyebrow at me as she does so. Jodie is standing right behind me, pressing close and massaging my shoulders through my shirt.

'Nathan Raleigh? His daughter is Viola Raleigh. He reported her missing about two years ago and she was reported missing again three weeks ago. I'm, um, trying to assist him in locating her.'

'Yes. Yes. I remember the name now. She was a guest in a hotel. I can't quiet remember…'

'It was The Bolton Mayfair.'

'Of course it was. So what are you, some sort of private detective that her father has hired?'

'That's about it, yes. So as I say, if I could just have a few minutes with you whenever you're free, it would be a great help. Nothing long and exacting, I promise.'

I try to put a laugh into my voice. Jodie is biting the back of my neck. I can feel her warmth and dampness and I can smell her sweat. I reach back and rub the front of her right thigh, while grabbing a handful of her skirt and tugging it sharply to the side.

'Well, you do understand that I can't really discuss…'

'I know there'll be a limit to what you can tell me, but really – anything will be fine at this point.'

Jodie is purring.

'Do you want to come over now? I'm just catching up with some paperwork. Where are you calling from?'

'Now?'

Jodie is panting.

'If it's not too late for you. Or inconvenient.'

'Now will be fine. I can be there in thirty minutes. I'm in Covent Garden.'

'OK. Just ask for me at the desk.'

'Will do.'

Jodie looks upset, as well she might. 'You're going?'

'It's one of my patients. Really urgent. Diabetic.'

Hopefully, she won't remember that I said that.

I disengage Jodie from my back, take her phone, punch my name and number into it and get my jacket back on. Straight away she's around my neck again. God knows what DS Bream is going to think when I turn up reeking of vodka and perfume. Or maybe she thinks that's what all private investigators are like. Jodie kisses me hard on the mouth once more. 'You owe me for this,' she says, picking her bag up and heading back to the party. As she's leaving, she turns around and smiles and I know she'll call.

I walk down to Aldwych to hail a cab and manage to get one almost straightaway. It takes us ten minutes to get to Seymour Street, so I ask the driver to drop me at a nearby Prêt à Manger so I can coffee up and hopefully clear the alcohol from my breath. There's not much I'll be able to do about the perfume, though.

Seymour Street is not a full-on police station and I manage to walk past it twice, thinking it was just offices. When I ask for DS Bream at the desk, the officer looks at me with narrowed eyes and I know immediately that he's the guy I spoke to earlier on.

I sit down on a rickety chair and wait. It's very quiet here and I'm guessing this is some sort of administrative police centre and it's no surprise that someone involved with missing persons might be based here. I'm looking down at my shoes, but I can see that Reception Boy keeps glancing at me from time to time.

After a few minutes, I can hear female steps approaching from the corridor to my right and I know it's her. I look up in time to see my deskbound pal indicating me with a pen.

'Mr Beckett?'

I stand up and we shake hands. She's slim and attractive, medium-length brown hair, freckles on her face, wide mouth and striking blue eyes. No makeup but doesn't need it, no perfume as it's not allowed. A lovely face. Probably a couple of years either side of thirty. Dark blue jeans, yellow ochre t-shirt and a faux-biker's black leather jacket with a diagonal zip down the front. Very cool.

I can see her taking me in with a single glance the same way I'm doing it to her. She realises what we're both doing and she smiles.

'Shall we go round the corner?' she says. 'There's a sort of wine bar place that serves coffee. It's usually empty at this time. Any excuse to get out of the office.'

'Sure. Fine by me.'

She turns briefly to the other officer. 'I won't be long, Roy. I've got my mobile if anyone needs me.'

'OK, Olivia,' says Roy, who gives me a look like I'm taking his fiancée out on a perilous hot date or something.

I give him a big smile. 'I'll promise she'll be back by ten.' Cruel, yes, but some people are just asking for it. DS Olivia Bream laughs at this, which only makes things worse for him.

She was right about the wine bar. Very new, very big and totally empty. It's situated in one of those areas in the

West End where you'd never think of going for a drink and I'll bet anything it won't be here in six months.

There are two grinning girls standing behind the bar in black tops, trousers and smart white aprons who look a tad disappointed when we only order coffee. I feel so bad that I consider ordering a dozen bottles of champagne just to put the smile back on their faces.

We sit down, opposite each other, at a long, black table by one of the windows. I keep thinking how this is like a first date and we'll soon be reaching over to hold hands. Very unprofessional and mildly ridiculous, but I can't help it. There's a little silver vase with a single red carnation in it. I touch the petals to see if it's real and it is. I look around.

'I bet this place can get pretty wild if the right crowd comes in,' I say, taking my jacket off and putting it over the back of the seat next to me. DS Bream eases herself out of her leather jacket and drapes it over her own seat. These tables are for six people; there are nine of them in here and several assorted smaller tables. Eleven seats at the bar, too. Someone was being very optimistic. I feel sorry for the girls and wonder what they'll do when this place closes.

'So do all private investigators wear Calvin Klein's Secret Obsession *eau de parfum* nowadays?'

I laugh to let her know she's caught me out. 'Only weekdays. At the weekend it's usually Rihanna's Reb'l Fleur. We all meet here on Saturday nights reeking of it. It's crazy and wild. You should pop in as you only work around the corner.'

'You private sector people get all the luck.' She sips her coffee and makes a face. 'Too hot.'

'That's what they say about me here on Saturday

nights. It's nice of you to see me at such short notice, by the way. I'm sure you're very busy.'

'What would you like to ask me?'

'Well, I'll just fire some stuff at you and you can just say 'no' if it can't be answered. OK?'

'OK. Off you go.'

'Can I see the missing persons file for Viola Raleigh?'

'No.'

'Good. Good start. I think I'm on a roll now.'

This makes her laugh. Her whole face changes. She's beautiful. I can't imagine being arrested by her.

'Next question. Can you tell me the name of the individual who called in Viola Raleigh as a missing person three weeks ago?'

'No.'

'Right. Do you know the number of the room that Viola Raleigh was staying in The Bolton Mayfair and the name under which she was staying?'

'Yes. Both those pieces of information are in the file.'

'Which I can't see.'

'Correct.'

'Would you consider giving me that information as a friendly, informal gesture towards the private sector on the off chance that I may be able to help you one day?'

'No.'

'Was it you who took the call from the person who reported Viola Raleigh as missing three weeks ago?'

'Yes.'

'Can you tell me anything about this telephone conversation and the person who called? Accent? Emotional content? Concern, genuine or otherwise?'

She looks upward and to the left, mulling this over. For a second, there's a glimmer of hope, which is soon dashed mercilessly to the ground.

'No. Sorry. You have to remember that when someone reports a person as missing, it's a confidential matter. The person who's missing could be found dead. We can't share this information with members of the public, which is what you are. Also, you could be a reporter or something. If we started giving out details of cases like this, it would open a whole can of worms. If I passed on information like that I may as well show you the file, which I'm not going to do.'

I'm smiling. I realise that I like listening to her talk. It's that husky voice.

'OK. Viola Raleigh has been working, I think, as a prostitute for two or three years. It's possible – probable – that she's still working as one. Is The Bolton Mayfair known to you as a place where call girls would do business?'

She tilts her head to the side. She has a long, elegant neck.

'Most big London hotels have their fair share of visiting call girls,' she says. She's trying to be helpful, I can tell, but I have to read between the lines.

'If Viola Raleigh was working as a call girl at The Bolton Mayfair, would she book her own room there? Wouldn't it be more normal for the client, if there was one, to book the room and Viola would visit them?'

'It's possible she'd book her own room, but unlikely. Visiting one of these girls in their own flat, or in a hotel room they'd booked, would probably be classed as an incall. They get more money if it's an outcall. Therefore it would be more financially viable for the girl to visit the client in their hotel room. Some of that extra money from an outcall would be used for travelling expenses, but not all of it. Having said that, there are all sorts of variations in this line of work, so nothing's a hundred per cent, but the Bolton's not a cheap hotel.'

'Would it be true to say that you strongly suspect that Viola Raleigh was working as a call girl and because of that you're not taking this seriously? This is not my opinion, but the opinion of my client.'

'We take all missing persons cases seriously, Mr Beckett.' She takes a deep breath, exhales slowly, then sips at her coffee. 'It would seem to me that Miss Raleigh does not want to be in contact with her father. There are a lot of reasons people go missing and one of the most common is family conflict. She's over eighteen. She doesn't have to see him ever again if she doesn't want to. It's not relevant in this case, but if we come across a missing person who's over eighteen, we won't pass on their whereabouts to anyone without their permission.'

'But what about the person who called in the missing persons report on her three weeks ago? Would that not make any alarm bells ring for you?'

'Not really. In fact, it could be seen as a good thing. At least we were able to tell her father that she was still alive. Also, if someone was staying in a hotel for, shall we say, normal reasons, it's unlikely that someone would report them missing.'

'So, as far as you can gather, Viola Raleigh was meeting a client in that hotel. That would be the most likely scenario.'

'I would say so, yes. I don't think she was on holiday.'

'So the person who called and spoke to you would probably be someone who was professionally connected with her, for whom alarm bells were ringing when she didn't clock off at the expected time or make contact at the expected time.'

'It's possible.'

She's so bloody cagey. I'll needle her slightly and see if I can get her to slip up in some way.

'What did you tell the person who called? Did you say it was nothing and that Viola will probably pop up again in two years?'

'When I spoke to her…'

'It was a woman.'

'Oh God, you're quick, aren't you. Yes, it was a woman. I told her that this was a borderline lost contact case, for want of a better phrase. That Viola Raleigh had a history of cutting herself off from friends and family and that it might be better to use a tracing service that may be able to expend more effort on this than we could. It was just a suggestion, though. We're still investigating and Viola Raleigh is still officially a missing person.' She looks impatient. 'Once again.'

I finish my coffee and slowly stroke my chin with my thumb. 'So you're only a missing person if someone reports you as such.'

'Technically, yes.'

'What did this woman you spoke to say when you suggested using a tracing service?'

'She didn't comment on it. Of course, it could be said it's her father who's pursuing that option by employing you.'

'Do you know anything about her father?'

'No. He's just a name and a telephone number to me. It was just a courtesy call, really. We have to contact next of kin if something like this happens, if the missing person reappears, even if it's only for a short time.'

'He's a billionaire arms dealer.'

She raises an eyebrow. 'Really? Well there you are. I wonder why he didn't hire someone like you two years ago. Or maybe a whole army of people like you. It's what I would have done. Could have saved us time and money.'

'Maybe he did, I don't know. But there's a reason he wants some sort of closure this time.'

'What is it?'

It's hard to stop a laugh appearing in my voice. 'Well this is going to sound terrible because it is. He's got a big deal coming up next week and he wants a clear head during negotiations – at least that's what he told *me*.'

This makes her laugh. 'What a wanker!'

'Yeah – um – *yeah*. That's what I thought. He wants to know one way or the other what's happened to her. If she's dead he wants to know about it and if she's alive he wants her to come home. As I said, he thinks you're doing nothing about it, or if you are it might take months, and he wants it sorted out fast while the trail is still hot, so to speak.'

'I suppose I can understand that in a way. Sorry I can't be of more assistance.'

'He wasn't too keen on my talking to you, either. He thought you'd be offended and would do even less than he thinks you're doing already.'

'He sounds like my kind of guy.'

I signal to one of the waiters who looks only too glad to have something to do. She walks over and holds a pen and a black pad, as if she's expecting us to order a complex meal. 'Could we have two more coffees, please?'

'Is this your equivalent of bribing me?' says Olivia.

'Yes. I'm hoping two coffees will loosen your tongue and you'll spill the beans.'

'Leave my tongue out of this.'

'And if that doesn't work I've got a ten-pound note in my wallet with your name on.'

'Well now you're talking.' She looks at my face and then my clothes. 'How did you get into this? Did you used to be in the job?'

She means did I used to be a police officer.

'No, no. Nothing like that. I just read a load of detective novels and thought it looked easy.'

She looks sceptical, as well she might. 'Raymond Chandler, that sort of thing, I suppose. Yes. I thought you weren't ex-police. You don't have the vibe. So what's your actual background? I can't believe you got it all from detective paperbacks.'

The coffees arrive. I have to change the subject.

'What made you join the police force?'

'Doing the right thing. And stopping people doing the wrong thing.'

Three more people come in, two young guys and a girl. Things are hotting up here. DS Bream looks thoughtful for a second.

'You don't think — I mean, this may be nothing — but you don't think there's a connection there somewhere?'

'Where?'

'Between this girl's dad being an arms dealer and her being a call girl?'

'Didn't occur to me. I did think there might be a connection between him being very *rich* and her being a call girl, you know — always busy when she was a child. No time for her, all that sort of cod psychology thing. He may have sent her away to school, I don't know. She's had a drug problem for some time, I was given to understand. Don't know about the mother. He had a big topless portrait of her in his office.'

I can see Rosabel's portrait again in my mind. I don't know if the artist was intending it to be memorable, eerie and haunting, but he or she certainly succeeded.

'*Topless?*'

I laugh at how ridiculous that must have sounded. 'Well, yes. Very classy. Very well done. Sitting down and holding a fur coat. Maybe it's just a thing that rich guys do. I wouldn't know. So what made you think…'

'Well, it would depend on who her father deals with. Arms dealers have been known to, er, entertain foreign clients.'

'With prostitutes.'

'It has been known. The Arab countries are quite big on it. If you have a client who's going to be spending a few billion, you're not just going to give them a cup of tea and a biscuit when they come over.'

'You're going to give them one or more beautiful women who'll do anything they're asked to do and make them feel like gods.'

She laughs. 'It's just a link. It may mean nothing. I don't want to colour your investigation.'

She clasps both hands behind her neck and stretches backwards in her seat. The action stretches her t-shirt against her body. Her breasts are small and ravishingly shaped. Unintentional or not, it's electrifyingly erotic. Poor old Reception Roy. I'll bet he has a terrible crush on her.

'I'll keep it in mind. Thanks.'

'I really have to get back, Mr Beckett. I'm sorry you didn't manage to prise much out of me.'

We stand and get our jackets on. I pay one of the bar girls and glance out the window as I wait for her to give me my change. Out of the corner of my eye I can see her turn towards me, then with an involuntary jerk, I fling my left arm out and catch something. A second later, I realise it's a bottle of champagne that she's accidentally knocked off the bar with her elbow and my hand is tightly gripping the neck. Both the girl and DS Bream share a couple of seconds of stunned silence before the girl laughs with shock and there's a round of astonished applause and cheering from the three people who came in a few minutes ago. I guess it was their bottle of champagne.

'Jesus Christ,' says DS Bream as we leave, staring at me with a quizzical expression on her face.

I walk her back to the police station, thanking her again for her help. Her mouth is twisted into a wry smile. I should have let that champagne smash on the floor; *Crouching Tiger* moments like that can be a bit of a giveaway.

'It was, er, interesting meeting you, Mr Beckett. If anything odd floats up to the surface from this, can you let me know? I'm a bit overdue for promotion and I need something big and spectacular.'

I smile at her. 'Sure. Can you give me your mobile number?'

'Why?'

'So I can give you a call if anything big and spectacular comes up.'

She reaches in the inside pocket of her jacket and fishes out her card. I take it and slip it into my wallet.

'I see. I thought you were going to ask me out to dinner,' she says, raising an eyebrow.

'I might at that. Have a nice evening and thanks again.'

She walks up the steps of the station, pushes the doors open and is gone.

I walk down towards Oxford Street to get a cab. It's starting to get dark now and I can feel a few spots of rain on my face. So what did I get out of that? Not much, really, but at least I know that it was a woman who reported Viola missing the second time. So far, I'd assumed that it was a man, and had a picture of some nebulous pimp from Central Casting in my mind. This changes things. Perhaps it wasn't a pimp, though there's no reason why, if it was, it couldn't be a woman. Perhaps Viola didn't have a pimp or had no need for one. Perhaps it was a genuine friend; someone who Viola liked to keep in touch with when she was out on a job for safety reasons. It could have been another call girl. I'd still like to find out who it was, though. It's a little annoying that DS Bream would have had a name and a contact number but wasn't telling, but there it is. At least I tried.

It's hard to know, but the way some of those escort agency sites were structured suggested that many of these girls worked for themselves and didn't use a pimp in the old sense of the word. The people who run the sites just take a cut of the girl's money in one way or another. It could be that the client hires the girl, pays the site and the site pays the girl afterwards, minus its commission. That sounds quite a risky method for the girls, but if one of these sites ripped them off, it would only happen once and I'd imagine word would get around pretty fast.

How many of these girls are casualties each year, in London alone? How many of them disappear into thin air without it being reported by anyone? It is a common occurrence? How much effort do the police put into these cases? It must be an added difficulty when the person who vanishes is operating using a fake identity.

Perhaps hiring me was the smart choice, only time will tell.

Just on a whim, I get my mobile out and call the number that Raleigh gave me for Taylor Conway. I think it's a long shot, but he might have some magical piece of information that will give me a breakthrough.

Well, it just rings and rings. Just at the point I'm about to click off, though, someone picks up and for two seconds I hear a distorted girl's voice saying 'Yeah? I've got…' then it goes dead. London accent, early twenties or younger, stoned rather than pissed. There was music in the background. Difficult to identify, but I think it was The Architects.

I ring the number again, but this time it's engaged. I try a third time and it's silent. Fuck it. I'll try again tomorrow. At least there was *something* on the other end, if only for a couple of seconds.

I get a black cab and get out near Leicester Square. I take out five hundred pounds from a cashpoint; walk down to Charing Cross and then up The Strand. It's crowded here tonight and I look for a bar. For a brief second, I consider going back to the one where Jodie and her friends were having fun, in case Jodie is still there, but I decide against it, cross the road into Villiers Street and find a virtually empty pub.

I sit down at a corner table and try to focus on what I'll do tomorrow. Today hasn't been that bad, all things considered. Got an almost certain date with Raleigh's PA, got mauled by a tipsy birthday girl, had a coffee with a dishy police officer and managed an abortive telephone contact with Taylor Conway. I'll try and contact him again tomorrow. I somehow feel he won't be an early riser. I'd like to have a look at the hotel, but I'd like to know Viola's *nom d'amour* before I do that.

The barman is reading *Sentimental Education* by Flaubert. He's probably a student. Three women come in; smartly dressed, possibly in their late thirties. They have spots of rain all over their clothes. It must be getting worse out there. I listen to them talk without looking in their direction. I think they're lawyers.

I have to go to the bar again and stand a few feet away from the new arrivals. The woman nearest me is more like mid-forties on closer inspection. Red hair with a few flecks of grey. Roughly five foot five in her heels, which are dark green to match her business suit. Great legs. She smiles at me as we both try to attract the attention of the still-reading barman. I'm trying by telepathy, which doesn't really work, despite all the claims made for it over the years.

'Obviously rushed off his feet, poor dear,' she says to me. Her smile is warm. Her two friends continue with their work talk. She rolls her eyes as if she's letting me know how boring they are. It's a little secret that gives us something else in common, exasperation with the barman being the first thing.

Then she snaps her fingers so hard that I can feel my ears ringing from it. I wish I could do that.

'Hey! Are you asleep over there or something?'

There's an accent that escapes when she yells like that. Australian?

The guy puts *Sentimental Education* face down on the bar to save his place and strolls over. I hope his pages get stained with lager.

'I may as well order for you now we've got his attention,' she says, looking pleased with herself. 'What are you drinking?'

'Oh, you really don't have to.'

'I'm feeling generous.'

'I'll have a vodka and soda. Thanks. Working late tonight?'

'We're really short-staffed at the moment. It's actually getting quite serious now. Lots of overtime available, so it isn't that bad, but it's so hard to get good people. I'm sure all of this sounds intriguing to you.'

'It's fascinating and subtly erotic.'

'You should hear me talk about our Internet connection. You'd salivate, I swear it.'

'I'm salivating already.'

'I wondered what that was all down your shirt.'

She laughs and orders a couple of Pinot Noirs for her friends who are still chatting away, a Yellow Tail Shiraz for herself and my vodka. I feel like I'm an alcoholic, but at least it's women who are buying the drinks tonight.

'It's starting to rain out there,' she says, smiling at me.

'I noticed,' I say, smiling back.

We smile at each other for a while, both trying to stop our smiles from turning into knowing laughs.

The barman brings our drinks over and she hands him a fifty-pound note. He looks pissed and raises his eyebrows at being handed such a large denomination. What a jerk.

She pushes the Pinot Noirs towards her colleagues who barely notice and turns her attention back to me, raising her glass.

'Cheers,' she says.

And then we're both laughing at the inevitability of it all.

# 6

## KINGPIN OF A BAD CROWD

I wake up when the sun starts streaming through the window. Another advantage of living in a Theatreland back street like this is that there's nobody about early in the morning and rarely any traffic noise, not that I'd hear it this high up. On top of that, there's the triple glazing, of course.

Eventually, I get up, go to the kitchen and start the Siemens and when I return to the bedroom she's awake. When she sees me come in, she whips the sheet off her body. It's an arresting sight and I feel slightly dizzy with sensory overload.

'Come here,' she says.

I lean over and kiss her, grabbing her red hair tightly, yanking her head back, biting her neck, giving her goose pimples. She digs her fingernails into my shoulders and presses herself against me.

'Oh, Jesus,' she says, her voice cracking.

'Fancy a coffee?' I say, with an inappropriate smile.

'White, no sugar, you bastard.'

'Back in a moment.'

'Don't be too long.'

She flops back onto the bed. I can see her red blouse and her green jacket on the bedroom floor. Her bra is in the kitchen, though, and I wonder how that could have happened, then I remember and smile to myself.

I put half a dozen croissants in the oven to warm up and check on how the coffee is doing. I'll have to buy more croissants.

'How long does that thing take?'

'Won't be long. It's a bean-to-cup affair. You won't believe the taste.'

It turns out that she wasn't a lawyer or a solicitor but a paralegal. Still, it was a pretty good guess. I look at the oven clock. 6:43. I've got a lot to do today. I want to start making some real progress on this Viola thing. I want it finished yesterday. I start thinking what I might do with the twenty thousand bonus that Raleigh promised if I cracked this.

I'm wondering what time my paralegal has to be in work and whether she works nearby. It was about nine pm when she and her colleagues appeared in that pub, so either they worked locally and had been working late (I think she mentioned something about overtime) or had come from some other area.

I take the coffees and croissants into the bedroom on a tray with some butter. She sits up and then changes position so she's on her haunches, running a hand through her hair. I'm trying not to get distracted.

'Where do you work?'

'Trying to get rid of me?'

'Obviously.'

'Inner Temple Gardens.'

Of course. I keep forgetting I'm so close to London's legal zone.

'I'm Daniel, by the way.'

'Natalie,' she says, through a mouthful of croissant. She's ravenous.

'Pleased to meet you, Natalie.'

We shake hands.

'So what's with the squeaky hallway? You really ought to get that seen to. Sounded like a million mice being tortured. I've never heard such a bloody awful sound.'

'I know. It's one of those things I'm always meaning to get done, but you know how it is.'

'This is a hell of a place; so *roomy*, so *cool*, so *minimalistic*. Was it like this when you moved in?'

'Not quite. I've added a few things. All the buildings on this side used to be storage places; that's why they're all so big.'

'You're right about this coffee. It's like fireworks in my mouth.'

I'm going to have to make appointments with Taylor Conway, if possible, and someone at the hotel. I'm trying to think who would be the best person there. The manager? Maybe I'll have to see him or her first. I really want to talk to someone who was on duty the night that Viola was there, whoever that may have been. I wonder what their security camera situation is like.

I know that the mysterious female friend of Viola made her call to the police about three weeks ago, but I still don't know the exact date that call was made or the exact date that Viola stayed there. If I can find the professional name she was using then they should be able to look it up in their files and then I can have a chat with the night manager or whatever. I'd also like to take a look at the room she stayed in. I sit down on the bed and run a hand down the side of one of Natalie's thighs.

'I've never actually met anyone who actually *lived* in

Covent Garden before,' she says. Her face is pleasantly dishevelled; hair a mess, lipstick smeared, eye shadow smudged. The overall effect is sexy and smouldering. She gasps as I dig my fingernails into her flesh.

'Well, there's a first time for everything, Natalie.'

'I discovered that last night.'

'Really?'

'Yes.'

'And I thought you were so worldly.'

'Not that worldly, honey.'

She places her plate and coffee cup on the shelf by the side of the bed, gets up and stands by the window, facing outwards, each hand gripping one of the fixed metal bars. She turns her head slightly to the side and glances over her shoulder so she can see me.

'Please.'

\*

It's when I try Taylor Conway's number as I'm walking up Charing Cross Road just after nine that someone finally answers. I didn't actually expect this and I can hardly hear anything because of the traffic noise, so I walk into Foyle's and pretend to look at some books.

'Hi. Is this Taylor?'

'Yes. Who's this?'

'My name's Daniel. Daniel Beckett. I tried to call you last night.'

'Why?'

I can tell this is going to be hard work. A woman in a blue hat stares at me. I pick up two contrasting travel guides to Barcelona so it looks like I'm in here for some reason. Perhaps it's my wife on the phone and she's helping me decide.

'Because I wanted to speak to you. A girl answered, but then I got cut off.'

'Were you the unknown number?'

'That's pretty likely.'

'Why did you want to speak to Samantha?'

'I didn't. I wanted to speak to you. She answered your phone. I wanted to speak to you.'

'What about?'

The tallest peak of the Collserola mountain range is one thousand six hundred and eight feet high. Barcelona hosted the 1992 Summer Olympics.

'Was that The Architects that was playing in the background? Last night?'

Architecture enthusiasts will be entranced by the modernist style of Anton Gaudi, as famously featured in *La Sagrada Familia*. *Tapas* is a Spanish delicacy where food is served in small portions.

'Yeah. Yeah! You like them?'

'Still listen to *Nightmares* once a day.'

'Fucking yeah. *Nightmares*. They'll never beat it.'

Barcelona enjoys an almost perfect climate. No visit would be complete without a visit to the Picasso Museum.

'Listen, Taylor. I'm a private detective. I'd like to ask you some questions about Viola Raleigh. Can I come and see you, please?'

'What – *now*? Did you say you were a detective? Viola, did you say?'

And so on and so forth for another four and a half minutes. I'm now an expert on Barcelona. Eventually I prise an address out of him. He lives in Ealing, so I walk up to Tottenham Court Road tube and twenty-five minutes later I'm in Ealing Broadway. Taylor, rather unexpectedly, lives in a small detached house in a leafy road sandwiched between a church and a small private primary school.

When he opens the door to me I'm almost knocked on my back by the smell of dope and I'm irrationally worried about what the neighbours might think if they can smell it. He's about twenty-five or twenty-six, but despite being seven or eight years younger than me he looks about five years older. I'm not saying it's anything to do with his drug intake; he just has one of those old looking faces. I'm sure he was able to get served in pubs when he was eleven and probably did. His hair is long, and has that ragged, tousled, casual look that I remember trying to achieve (without success) when I was about fifteen and which probably cost him a small fortune in some overpriced salon.

I find myself looking at his clothes (eclectic, rumpled but clean), his hair and the place he lives in, to try and give myself an assessment of how much money he must have and how much it must take to maintain his lifestyle. I don't do this for any malicious reason; I just need to compare him to Viola's financial background and social status to give myself an idea of how much she was slumming it by hanging around with him.

I don't think they were boyfriend and girlfriend, though they may have been occasional lovers. Of course, I may be disabused of that idea after talking to him. I just wish he'd let me in and close the front door before that smell starts wafting down towards the nearby police station and my interview with him is prematurely curtailed.

Before he lets me in, though, he has to assure himself

of my credentials or lack of them. It's obvious that the smell isn't as powerful to him as it is to me or he'd drag me in and shut the door immediately.

'You're not, like, the police, then, are you? You're more, like, sort of Sherlock Holmes, yeah?'

'That's right, but without the intravenous cocaine solution.'

He laughs. 'What?'

I hand him my card. All it has on it is my name and mobile number, but it's made from a thin, silvery metal with miniature micro-grills on the top and bottom. People don't tend to throw a card like this one away. He looks at it as if he expects it to do something amazing.

'Fuck. This is the coolest fuckin' business card I've ever seen in my life. Can I keep it?'

'Sure. Can I come in?'

I follow Taylor into what must be called the living room, which merges into a spacious kitchen, then a plant-filled conservatory. I can just about see a large garden, which seems to be overgrown with roses and raspberry bushes. The whole place is untidy, but it's not that bad and the furniture is comfortable.

I sit down on a sofa. There's a huge TV screen where a fireplace must once have been. It's tuned to some mad-looking American evangelist channel, but the sound is turned off. I can hear something that sounds like traditional Chinese music emanating from somewhere, but can't spot a stereo or any speakers. There's someone in the kitchen, but I can't see them.

Taylor sits down right next to me and examines my clothing. He catches my eye and looks embarrassed.

'Sorry, but I've never met like a private dick before. That's what you are, isn't it. A private dick. It sounds so fuckin' cool, doesn't it? A private dick. Hi – I'm a private dick. Fuck you. Would you like a tea or coffee or something?'

'Coffee, if it's not too much trouble.'

'Course not.' He turns away from me with a surprisingly quick movement that makes my hand twitch. 'Molly! Can we get a couple of coffees?'

Molly pokes her head around the door, looks at me, and then looks at Taylor. For a second, I think she's about fourteen but then I realise that she's just very petite and thin. She wears a green and purple crew neck jumper with hash burns all over it. It's about three sizes too big for her. When she speaks, I put her at about the same age as Taylor, perhaps a year or so younger.

'What the fuck d'you think I am? Make it yourself.'

Taylor gives me a sheepish grin, pushes himself up off the sofa and lopes off into the kitchen. I follow him. It'll save time. He prepares the coffee things and rolls a spliff at the same time. His drug paraphernalia is in a bright red Betty Boop tin. I remember seeing those in the shops in Milan and I wonder if that's where he bought it. He's got a blue Francis Francis X1 coffee maker. Classy guy.

There's a bookshelf next to the oven with two books on Moroccan cooking, *Down and Out in Paris and London* by George Orwell and *Complete Tales and Poems* by Edgar Allan Poe.

Molly has disappeared into the garden and I worry that she'll get cut to shreds amongst the roses and raspberries. I wonder what happened to Samantha. Taylor looks up and grins.

'You can't see it, can you. There's a greenhouse in that jungle out there. We're growing White Widow and Train Wreck. I've kept the garden like that so the neighbours can't see. Also, the smell of the roses and the raspberries masks the skunk smell and the thorns discourage visitors and animals. I've also encouraged stinging nettles to grow at the sides and down the bottom. They have a bad, strong smell. I planted little trees, yeah? The birds sit in the trees, they have a shit and the shit encourages stinging nettle growth. Magic, eh? D'you like raspberries?'

'They're OK, yeah.'

'I've frozen some of the ones from the garden. I'll give you some when you go. Remind me.'

'Thanks. I will.'

He hands me my coffee and we go back to the living room or whatever it is. The coffee smells good. Just before we both sit down, he lights his spliff and immediately offers it to me.

'No thanks. I'm working.'

'Of course you are. Christ, I'm stupid. You won't be able to deduce stuff after a drag off this fucker; I can tell you that for nothing.'

He sits on a chair to my left and stares at me, smiling. 'I've never met a fuckin', er, private detective before.' He tips ash into a large ashtray decorated with a Picasso portrait of Dora Maar. 'Is it dangerous?'

'Depends.'

'D'you get bad shit pinned on you so you'll go to jail instead of the real culprit?'

'Not so far.'

'Have you ever gone into a room looking for something and then someone comes up behind you and smashes you on the head with something?'

'Not recently.'

'What about really stacked women in fur coats turning up at your office and crossing their legs so you can see they're wearing suspenders.'

'Once or twice a week.'

'Shit. So how's Viola nowadays, anyway? She in trouble?'

'Why would she be in trouble?'

'Dunno. It's what she's like. If there was a rollercoaster with a sign on it saying *next stop, trouble*, she'd be the first to jump on board, know what I mean?'

'OK. Well, I just need to ask you some questions. You may not be able to answer all of them, but I'll be grateful for anything, really.'

Another girl appears, and sits on Taylor's lap. She's maybe twenty or twenty-one, bright yellow skirt, very tight t-shirt, no bra, beige espadrilles. He gives her the spliff and she takes a deep, deep drag from it. Taylor produces my business card from somewhere and hands it to her. 'Look at this fucker! Is that class or what?'

The girl looks at the card and looks at me. She's much better looking than Molly. She has violet eyes, which may be tinted lenses and black hair which looks natural. There's an upturn to her eyes which makes her face beautiful and she has good cheekbones. Perhaps this is Samantha. 'So what – are you selling business cards?' she says, a little contemptuously, crossing her long legs and leaning back on Taylor like he's not there. I recognise her voice from our brief telephone encounter. It's Samantha.

'Yeah,' I say. 'I can do you a thousand cards with your choice of design for only a hundred and sixty quid.'

'He's a private detective,' says Taylor from behind her back.

'Fuck,' says the girl, getting up and leaving. 'Are you going to have me followed, you shit?' She leans over to me on her way out of the room and whispers loudly in my ear so that Taylor can hear. 'He thinks I'm fucking other people.' I see she's still holding my card.

Taylor watches Samantha leave the room and goes into a sort of trance for a minute. Then he starts running his hand under the sofa as if he's looking for something he's lost. Then he loses interest in whatever it was.

'So,' says Taylor, 'are you not meant to give me some sort of money? For info? Isn't that what you do? You slip me a ton and I spill the beans over my best mate.' He's smiling. It's hard to tell whether he's serious or just smashed.

'Sure. When we've finished I'll give you two hundred. Think that'll cover it?' What the hell. Ultimately this is Raleigh's money. Taylor's eyes light up and I've now got his full attention.

'Sure. Sure! Fuckin' hell. This is really exciting. This is just like a film. And if it turns out to be bullshit information, you'll come back here an' fuckin' really work me over, yeah? And there'll be a car chase.'

'That's about right. And I'll tell the police to come and have a look at your hidden greenhouse.'

He laughs. He knows I'm not being serious.

'OK. Fire away.'

'This is the situation. Viola's father...'

'Oh *fuck*.'

'What?'

'Her fuckin' father. He always sounded like a real asshole.'

'OK. Well anyway, her father reported her as a missing person two years ago. Have you seen her in the last two years?'

'What did he say about me?'

'He said you were the kingpin of a bad crowd she used

to hang around with.'

This makes him laugh. '*Kingpin*? Is that the actual word he used?'

'Yes. Have you seen her in the last two years?'

'Definitely not. Last time I saw her would have been…it was actually just after my birthday, like a belated birthday party thing, so it would have been close on three years ago. Three years two months, maybe, or just a little bit more than that, three years and three months. And there wasn't any *bad crowd*, y'know? That sounds like a bunch of rich twats who all go to the same nightclubs and snort coke when they're fuckin' skiing in Phuket or somewhere. She was just like a friend of a friend, who introduced her to me because she wanted a reliable and steady source of dope. It turned out that the dope wasn't enough for her, though, y'know? People like that, they're always going to find some way of achieving the oblivion they seek, yeah?'

'Was she your girlfriend?'

'Well I shagged her a few times, but I think *girlfriend* is too strong a word. I shag Samantha who you just saw, but I wouldn't refer to her as my *girlfriend* or anything like that. You know – if you were hanging out with Viola, she was usually ripped and you could just fuck her if you wanted to. I'll be honest with you, though, man to man…'

This is too much for me and I start laughing. 'I'm sorry. It's just the way you're describing her.'

'You're not baked, are you? I'm not giving you secondary euphoria or anything?'

'I'm fine. Keep going.'

'Yeah. OK. Where was I? So man to man, Viola wasn't fuckin' much good at it. She never really got into it. You might think it was because she was off her head on skunk, but it wasn't anything to do with that. Molly out there is high most of the time and she's fuckin' great at it. Same goes for Samantha.

'Dope is like a great aphrodisiac with great orgasms at the end and most girls get off on it. Viola was, I suppose, indifferent. Yeah. That's the word. Indifferent. She was indifferent. Always made you feel like you weren't turning her on. She fucked like she'd read how to do it from a book and the book had a few important pages missing. And no fuckin' index. I used to think it was me, but I don't think it was, I think it was her. I think it might have been the school she went to.'

'The school?'

'Yeah. Some private school or other. Girls from those sort of schools always fuck bad.'

'Her father said she was probably a junkie.'

'Well, she definitely got onto smack, but that wasn't until later. She was on it when she was still coming round here, but I wouldn't describe her as a junkie. You have to work pretty hard at it to become what I would call a junkie. She used to take a lot of downers and stuff. She didn't want to be up.'

'Did you get it for her? The smack?'

'At first I did, yeah, but, er, the stuff I was getting wasn't that good. It wasn't really my speciality, know what I mean? Also, I could only get it from time to time. It was complicated for various reasons and a bit of a pain if I'm being honest. But it was a bit of a pain for her, too, as she was getting more into it and wanted a reliable supply and she wanted better stuff than I could get her. Did I say that already?'

'Was she working as a prostitute when you knew her?'

'Was she – *what*?! A prostitute? Are you kidding me? Jesus Christ. Fuck.'

He looks genuinely upset.

'That's what she told her father two years ago. Something I haven't told you yet is that she was reported missing a *second* time, three weeks ago. I don't know who it was who reported her missing, but it may have been a pimp. Whoever it was, the last place she was known to be was in a hotel room. Someone was expecting her back and she didn't make it. I think she was seeing a client there and so do the police.'

'Fucking hell.' He picks up a pair of novelty sunglasses shaped like pineapples and fiddles with them. 'Yeah. Yeah. I can see it. Her dad used to give her money from time to time but I think it all went on her general expenses and partying. I'm just guessing that, though. I really haven't got a fucking clue!' He has a break and laughs to himself for about a minute.

'She always had great clothes and she had a car. It was a VW Jetta Sport. It was red. Have you read that book with the guy with the terrapin called Jetta? The Clingfilm guy? She lived somewhere, but I don't know where it was. Possibly like London Wall. Somewhere like that. Somewhere in the City. She got cabs a lot. So she's like back from the dead and her dad wants you to find out…'

'Yes. Something like that.'

'Do you think she's dead?'

'No. Not at the moment. I may be proved wrong.'

He sighs and rolls another joint. The last one disappeared with Samantha. He lights it and takes a big drag. Magically, Samantha reappears and sits on the floor next to him. She's got changed and the tight t-shirt has gone, replaced by an unbuttoned breast-revealing white cotton shirt. Her stomach is flat and I can see tan lines where she's been wearing a bikini. She still wears a skirt, but now it's red needle cord. The last time I saw her she was wearing espadrilles, but now she's bare-footed. She takes the spliff from Taylor, takes a drag and hands it to me. Taylor frowns and takes it off her.

'He's fuckin' working, Sam.'

Sam aims a pouty little frown my way. Taylor stares at the TV screen for a while.

'She was always a bit fucked up after her mum, you know?'

'What d'you mean?'

'Well, this friend of hers – I can't remember her name – was it Alicia? Alisha? Amelia? I can't remember. Alesha Dixon. She's a fucking good-looking woman, isn't she?'

'What happened with Viola's mum?'

'It was Antonia. Yeah. So anyway, yeah, Antonia was one of the *wrong crowd*, too, ha ha. She had really weird frizzy hair. And she had a stammer. She told me that Viola's mum dying hit her really hard. Particularly the way it happened.'

'Hold on. Viola's mother is *dead*?'

This can't be right. He's got this wrong. He's mixing her up with someone else. I cast my mind back to my chat with Raleigh after he'd seen me admiring Rosabel Raleigh's portrait. He was talking about her in the present tense, definitely. There was no indication whatsoever that she might have died. Before my mind starts going down time-wasting routes I turn my attention back to Taylor.

'Particularly the way it happened? What does that mean?'

'Well, she committed suicide.'

'When?'

'When? Fuck. I think it was when Viola was fourteen. Something like that, anyway.'

That makes it about ten years ago. Is that portrait of someone else? Did Raleigh remarry and, moreover, remarry someone who looked like Viola? No. That's ridiculous. Would an event like this have been in the news? Unlikely, as Raleigh wasn't a public figure and didn't court publicity.

'How did she do it?'

'I think she shot herself.'

God Almighty. 'You think or you know?'

'Well that's what Alisha told me. She said that Viola's mother didn't leave a suicide note, but that she didn't have to.'

'What the hell does that mean?'

'Dunno, but there it is. Sorry – did I say Alisha? I meant Antonia.'

OK. Perhaps I'm giving this too much significance. It could have been one of the things that still upset Raleigh and he didn't like talking about it. Maybe it comforted him in some way to refer to her as if she was still alive. Everyone deals with this type of thing in a different way.

'There was a point when she drifted out of your circle. What happened?'

'To who?'

This interrogation is going in the sort of elliptical way that I can't stand, but I have to persevere. Taylor is in no state to be logical and I just have to work with that.

'To Viola. I understand that this might be hard for you to talk about, but I'd like to know what happened when she slipped out of your orbit.'

He purses his lips and looks momentarily angry.

'It's my fault. How long did you say she'd been on the game?'

'She told her father about it a little over two years ago. That's not to say that's when she started, though. I think it came out during an argument. It may have been going on longer than that.'

'Dates, you know? I can't really be accurate, but I think it started before two years ago. It was to do with the smack, all to do with the smack. Like I said, I had problems supplying her with the hard stuff and suggested she contact this other guy. I knew about him and I knew it was a bad idea, but she was so fucking persistent and charming, y'know?'

'Tell me about him.'

'I bet her dad thinks it was me that got her into drugs and me who got her into prostitution. It wasn't.'

'I know it wasn't, Taylor. Tell me about this guy.'

'It's this guy called Emile. He's quite old, you know? Sixty, maybe late sixties or seventy. Could be older. I don't know. I just knew through the grapevine that he was a big dealer in smack and coke. He didn't bother with dope or anything else. Everyone knew about him, but not everyone had cause to deal with him. This is the thing, though. He dealt in girls, too.'

'Go on.'

He takes a final drag from his spliff and stubs it out on Dora Maar's face.

'Well I don't know this for sure, so you mustn't take this as being, like, what happened, but I'd heard about one girl who'd started selling her ass for him in return for smack. She – there was a guy I used to hang out with called Paul Booker. His mate Niall, he used to go out with this girl but he dumped her as she was too much trouble.

It was her. He's like a poncy kind of guy, this Emile, but quite hard, yeah? Quite a bastard, apparently. He's got some really tough fuckers who do his dirty work for him. I heard that one of them beat a guy to death once for, like, nothing. I also heard – and this is worse – that one of them beat a girl to death once.'

'So you think he may have started Viola off as a prostitute in return for giving her good quality smack?'

'Well, it's possible. As I said, she didn't seem to care enough about sex for it to bother her and she didn't know what fuckin' day it was most of the time. I mean, I shagged her this one time and I saw her the next day and she didn't seem to know who I was. She asked me if I was a friend of Keith. I don't know anyone called Keith.'

Was it someone connected with this Emile who called the police after Viola didn't come back from the hotel? Some girl he got to ring the police and report her as missing? Worried about a source of income going AWOL? Taylor is talking about stuff that happened a long time ago, though. I'm getting annoyed with all of this and want to sort it out fast.

'How can I get to this guy Emile? Have you got a phone number or an address?'

'Fuck. I don't want him to think that I'm sending people like you to him.'

'I won't mention you. He'll never know.'

'Hold on.' He gets up and makes his way to a staircase, then turns back. 'Do you want another coffee?'

'I'll make it.'

'I've just got to look for something. Won't be long. Can you work the coffee maker?'

'I'll manage. Don't worry.'

I clean the old coffee grains out, put some fresh coffee

and water in and turn it on. I can feel someone behind me. Very quiet; must be bare feet, must be Samantha. I can hear her soft breathing.

'Would you like a coffee too, Samantha?'

'Yeah. One sugar, no milk. You've got pretty wide shoulders, haven't you.'

I turn to face her. She's still wearing the open cotton shirt, but now there's more breast visible and one nipple. She's reapplied her makeup. This is the sort of situation you dream about being in when you're fourteen. I can hear thumping from the room above. There's a print on the wall where the kitchen goes into the conservatory. It's a naked girl, by Bonnard, I think. Can't remember what it's called. Taylor has got some interesting stuff here.

'Thank you, Samantha.'

'My shoulders aren't like that at all.'

'No?'

Samantha is making meaningful eye contact with me and not saying anything. She runs a hand through her hair. I'm reminded of Anjukka doing exactly the same thing. I feel like I've been in this situation for an hour and it's exhausting. I'm keeping my eyes away from her breasts as I don't want to encourage her. The coffee maker beeps. Molly comes back in from the garden, stares at me and then stares at Samantha. Taylor reappears with what looks like an A3 sketchpad. I make three coffees and take them into the living room. Samantha takes hers off the tray and disappears.

'If it's anywhere it'll be in here somewhere.'

Taylor rests the pad on his lap and flicks through it. From my point of view I can see lots of drawings, scribblings and articles cut out from newspapers. At one point, there's even a pressed flower. He must use this pad for everything. I can see letters of the alphabet and names and numbers beneath them. He turns the pad upside down and squints at it.

'Yes!'

He sits next to me and points at the pad. There's a drawing of a horse and underneath it the name 'Novak', an address and a telephone number.

'That's him. I knew I had it somewhere. Of course, none of that info might be current, yeah? That looks like a mobile number. Shall we try it?'

'No. Not yet. I want to think.' I tap the name and number into my mobile and memorise the address.

'Christ Almighty. If she's dead or something it'll be down to me, won't it.'

He actually starts crying.

'Look,' I say. 'If she hadn't ended up with this guy through you, it would have been through someone else. Don't worry about it. Forget it. She was fucked up, your paths crossed, that's it.'

'She was really beautiful, too. I mean – she looked like an actress.'

'Stop beating yourself up.' I take out my wallet and hand him two hundred pounds. 'Take this. What you've given me has been really useful.'

He sniffs and takes the money.

'Thanks, mate. Look – I know you're not working for me or anything, but when you've sorted all this shit can you tell me what happened? I feel like I'm part of it now. And be careful when you go and see Emile Novak. You might get in over your head, yeah? He's into all sorts of bad shit. I've only heard rumours, but he seems to be able to get away with anything he feels like. I don't know why. Maybe he's got friends in high places.'

'Don't worry.'

'Listen. Sit down. Don't go away.'

He gets up again and runs upstairs. Now what? I want to get away and think this over. I don't want to talk to people.

Seconds later, he reappears holding a gun, which he places gently on the table in front of me. I almost spit my coffee out of my mouth. It's a Glock 17 and it looks brand new. Taylor looks enthusiastic and very pleased with himself. He speaks in a semi-whisper.

'I can get you anything like this. Anything you want. This one came from Sweden. I think the army use it, yeah?'

'Why have you got a gun, Taylor?'

'It's just one of my side-lines. There's a market for guns amongst people I know. I keep this one in case anyone comes here and tries to cause trouble.'

I pick it up and weigh it in my hand. It feels like it's fully loaded. I take the magazine out and eject seventeen bullets onto the table.

'Put these bullets in a bag and hide the bag somewhere where your girlfriends won't find it. This gun has three safety features and they were all turned off. This could have gone off when someone was fucking around with it when you were all high.'

I show him the safety features and make him repeat them back to me and then demonstrate them until I'm satisfied.

'I'm not telling you off, but Jesus, you know? You really don't want to get involved with the sort of people who'll buy or sell guns.'

And here am I working for an arms dealer.

'OK. Cool. But if you ever need anything, you'll know

where to come and I won't rip you off. I can get other stuff, too.'

I can hear Samantha padding around somewhere. I wipe my prints off the gun with a tea towel, ram the magazine back home and hide it under a cushion, simultaneously placing Taylor's sketch pad over the bullets.

'Sort that. Promise me. And while I'm here, the whole road reeks of dope when you open that front door. You don't want the police in here and them finding that gun and whatever else you've got. Just get a little bit more paranoid. Paranoia is good.'

'OK. OK. Got it. D'you want to buy a car?'

# 7

## ALL THE FUN OF THE FAIR

I find a café in Ealing Broadway and order a large coffee and two apricot Danish pastries. I sit outside and wait for the waitress to bring everything out to me. That meeting – if that's what it can be called – with Taylor Conway was so bereft of logic at times that I'm finding it hard to pick out what was relevant to this case, if anything.

Viola obviously had an effect on him, though, and I felt quite sorry for the poor sap. Despite myself, I have an urge to be able to go back in time and stop her at that point; that point when it started to go wrong, whenever it was and whatever caused it. To be able to grab her, pull her out of that life and run away with her.

According to Taylor, too, she didn't seem to have much interest in sex, but there could have been any number of reasons for that and it wouldn't necessarily stop her from drifting into prostitution. Most prostitutes don't enjoy the sex, or so I was reading last night during one of my rare ten minutes of 'research'.

The fact that Raleigh's wife had shot herself was interesting, but I don't think it really had any bearing on anything. It fits in with the wild child antics of Viola in a way. Heartless rich bastard with a trophy wife and a child he's too busy to spend time with. The wife commits suicide and the daughter goes off the rails. Tough. Her portrait flashes into my mind again. What a terrible waste.

But knowing about Emile Novak was fairly useful. If he's still at the same address I'll have to pay him a visit and I need to do it now. At the back of my mind, I'm thinking how wonderful it would be if I could finish all of this in twenty-four hours. I could pick up my twenty thousand bonus and be sunning myself in the Caribbean by the weekend.

So what do I have on Novak? Deals in hard drugs, possibly forces girls into prostitution and is 'hard' according to Taylor. But also a poncy kind of guy, whatever that may mean. Would Viola have been with him for almost three years? Would she have survived being kept on smack all that time? Would she still be good-looking enough to send out? If it wasn't Novak or one of his minions who reported Viola as missing, then perhaps he'll know who it was.

I start chewing my second Danish and am just about to see if I can get hold of Novak when my mobile goes off. Another mobile. Unknown number.

'Hi. Daniel Beckett.'

'I wonder if you can help me. I have a problem with a missing library book.'

'Hi, Anjukka. How're things?'

'Fine, thank you. How's your work going?'

'Can't complain.'

'I was wondering if you'd like to go and get something to eat tonight. If you're not too busy, that is.'

'Well, I have to eat sometime. What sort of food do you like?'

'I don't mind. Anything.'

'Anything is good for me.'

'Can we start early-ish? I don't want to go home and

then have to come out again. I hate the tubes in rush hour.'

'No problem at all. You're on the central line. Get out at Bond Street and I'll see you outside Selfridge's at dead on six o' clock.'

'Fine. I'll look forward to it.'

'Me too.'

I think of that swaying walk and wonder if she's cleared this with her fiancé. She doesn't sound like someone with a fiancé. I take a final gulp of coffee and ring Novak's number. Not working. I better get over there if I'm going to clear all this up quickly.

Having never done missing persons before, I'm not really sure how long all this is meant to take. Maybe that's an advantage. Novak lives in Bloomsbury, of all places. Of course, he may not live there anymore, in which case I'll have to use other methods to find him. I pay for my snack and walk over to Ealing Broadway tube yet again.

Just before I walk down the steps into the tube station, I stop suddenly and look in the window of a chemist's. There was another snack bar right next to the one I just used, and I fancied that a middle-aged man sitting outside that one got up and left at exactly the same time that I did.

I walk off and glance briefly over my shoulder, but there's no one there apart from a young woman pushing a pram and an old guy holding a paint-splattered ladder. Maybe I'm just paranoid from my secondary euphoria at Taylor's house. Talking of which, I realise that I just ate two Danish pastries when I never usually order more than one.

I get off at Holborn just over half an hour later and once I've orientated myself, walk up towards The British

Museum. Coptic Street, which is the address Taylor had for this guy Novak, is dingy and full of restaurants. It isn't the sort of place where you'd expect someone to live if you know London, but then neither is Covent Garden.

I find the house I'm looking for sandwiched in between a couple of snack bars. There's one of those old-fashioned shoe scrapers next to the front door and a brass plaque which reads 'Firmheath Enterprises plc'. Well, it might be him and it might not. If I was a drug dealer-cum-white slave trader I probably wouldn't put my actual name or details of my business on the door.

I press the buzzer and wait. It looks conspicuous to be standing in a road like this and several passers-by stare at me. This is a road you walk down on your way somewhere else, unless it's lunchtime.

A minute passes and still nothing. I close my eyes and listen for any sounds coming from inside. This is difficult, as the clatter coming from the snack bars either side obliterates everything I'm trying to hear. I attempt to zone out the café noise and listen out for atypical sounds originating in the house.

All these buildings have four floors and for all I know whoever lives here occupies all of them. Maybe they're at the top and are slowly making their way down. Maybe Firmheath Enterprises is long defunct. I can hear a faint mechanical noise like some sort of slow-moving machinery. Then I hear a dull thud which definitely comes from inside.

I press the buzzer once more. There's a harder, sharper sound, then something like the thump you'd expect to hear from a self-closing door with powerful spring hinges. It's barely discernible, but I can hear and feel someone walking slowly and quietly towards the front door. The reverberations tell me it's a heavy person and almost certainly male. Well, whatever's going on in here, I should know any second now.

The guy has the look of someone who's not used to opening a front door to anybody and I start to wonder if I'm maybe the first person who's ever pressed the buzzer here, or whether it's the first time he's ever opened a door, or both.

He's got broad shoulders, muscular, hairy arms, a huge gut and is a little under six foot. Smells of lavender toilet cleaner and stale sweat, which is a combination I've always adored. His demeanour is not welcoming and he's got an aggressive, smirking expression on his face, which I don't like.

This is the sort of guy who'd come up and try to pick a fight with you in a pub car park after closing time when he was a) positive he held the advantage and b) had six mates with him. His hair is ginger and cut short and his pale eyebrows are angled at about forty-five degrees, giving a clownish look to his ignorant-looking fat face. I look into his eyes and decide that he's stupid.

'Fuck *you* want?'

London accent. He could be in his late thirties or early forties. His whole body is blocking the doorway; there's no way I could sneak past him. It isn't lavender toilet cleaner; it's some sort of deodorant. Looking over his shoulder I can see a long, dim corridor. At the end of that corridor is the door that I heard close. It's metal, strong looking, and has a modern chrome keypad above the handle; nothing that couldn't be removed with a crowbar if you were motivated enough. There are no security cameras; at least none that I can see.

'I want to talk to Emile Novak.'

He stares at me without comprehension, as if I'm speaking a foreign language. 'You can't see him without an appointment.'

'OK. Can I make an appointment?'

'No. Fuck off.'

His dim expression doesn't change, but he sneers at me as he attempts to close the door in my face. I put a hand out to stop it and he looks perplexed. 'Listen, mate. Get your hand off that fuckin' door.'

'Why?'

'Or I'll fuckin' punch you in the face, that's why.'

Oh good. I've found one of those men who are always looking for an excuse for violence. 'It won't take long. I just want to ask him something.'

'You fuckin' prick with your fuckin' queer leather jacket. Fuck off.'

This is taking too long and I'm not even sure that Novak is in. My aggressive friend is nostril-breathing now and his mouth is a thin angry line. He opens it again.

'I'm going to count to five and then I'm going to sort you out,' he says, a twitch in his left eye making the left side of his face wobble like jelly.

He's breathing more rapidly, looking at me with undisguised loathing. I can't spend all day standing in the street, but I think the next time I say something he's going to attack me and I don't want that to happen. I also want to take this off the pavement and into the house, before we start to attract too much attention. I open my jacket so he can see my inside pocket and I take out my pen. The street is clear. There are three girls walking away from me about a hundred yards away and a guy with a limp on the other side of the road, who's just turned into a tobacconist's. Someone is shouting in Romanian in the snack bar to my right.

'One,' he says, smirking his head off. 'Two.'

'I'm just going to leave a message for him. Can you make sure he gets it?'

'Three.'

He looks down dumbly at the pen. I flip it around in the air, catch it and ram the blunt end into the soft flesh under the curve of his jaw. As his head rocks back and he grimaces with pain, I knee him in the balls as hard as I can and strike him in the solar plexus with the ball of my hand. This all takes one second.

He falls back on his arse in the hallway and I step in and kick the door closed behind me.

I have to assume there are other people in here, so what I have to do next has to be done with the minimum of noise. My pen, by the way, is what's known as a tactical pen, made from aircraft grade aluminium and used in the same way as you'd use a Kubotan, a small but effective martial arts weapon. Weighs a couple of ounces. Very handy and you can write with it, too.

He's recovering, and trying to work out whether to hold his throat or his balls. While he's thinking about this, I kick him in the jaw and kneel down to introduce myself, grabbing his shirt and holding the sharp, castellated end of the pen against the white of his eye. He looks pissed, as well he might. He also looks frightened.

'We're going to get up and you're going to type the combination into that keypad on the door. If you don't get it right the first time, or if you make a noise, my magic pen's going straight through your eye and into the back of your skull. Understand?'

This would be impossible, of course, but he seems convinced enough to go along with my plan. He nods and

I drag him to his feet, pushing him over to the door, which I can see now is made from reinforced steel.

Then suddenly, with a speed which surprises me, he pulls away from me and in the dimness I can see the flash of a knife and it's a big fucker. Now where the hell did that come from? He's grinning now, pleased with himself. I must be getting sloppy in my old age. It won't happen again.

'Cunt.'

He dances about a bit, waving the knife in all directions. I can tell he's not a professional knife fighter, so that's something, but it's still a dangerous and risky thing to have to deal with. So far, everything's been relatively quiet and I want it to stay that way. I avoid three or four badly aimed slices to my torso, face and neck and manage a straight punch to his face, breaking his nose. Now he's going to get careless and angry, which is what I want.

He executes a straight thrust to my stomach, which I avoid by turning aside and grabbing his wrist, then using his forward momentum and speed to bend it back at an angle that's so painful that it instantly floors him.

He grunts in pain as I kick the knife out of the way, but then he's up again, crouching in a boxer's stance. He takes two quick jabs at my face. The first one is wide, but the second almost makes contact; I dodge it and he punches a hole in the wall behind me. I can see him quickly looking for the knife, but it's nowhere to be seen. If one of those punches makes contact, I'll almost certainly be concussed, so I have to finish him off before he finishes me.

He has a sly look in his eyes now and attempts a feint, throwing a half-way punch with his left before launching a powerful right, which I block with the side of my arm, simultaneously hitting him in the centre of the face with a knife hand strike.

While he's coping with that, I grab the fingers of his right hand in both of mine and wrench his hand hard to the left, breaking his wrist, slapping a hand across his mouth to stifle the scream of pain he produces as the ligaments rip.

I grab his hair and slam his head into the wall to calm him down, and then manipulate him over to the door once more.

'Do it.'

He punches five numbers into the keypad with his left hand, his right now being useless. I make a mental note of those numbers; I don't know when I may need them again. There's a click and a green light appears. I arrange a meeting between his head and the wall once more, then hammer-fist the side of his neck twice for good measure. He drops to the floor, out cold.

I can hear the ambient café noise from both sides, but nothing more. I find the knife and drop it into one of my side pockets. It's some sort of hunting knife, with a gut hook on the blade that would have torn my insides out had he managed to get it in me. He deserved that wrist-break just for being in possession of something as nasty as this. For a fraction of a second I wonder who he is, then decide that it doesn't really matter. I open the door as slowly and as noiselessly as I can. It's heavy, and about eight inches thick.

Right in front of me, there are about thirteen steps. Carpeted, which is good, as it'll cut down the noise. I walk up slowly and hear the door click shut behind me. When I reach the top, there's a landing, a strong smell of chlorine and an unlocked door. I push the door open and step back, in case someone is waiting on the other side.

It's as quiet as the grave and I can't sense any presence, so I step inside and take a look. The chlorine smell comes from a small swimming pool. It's about twelve feet long and five feet wide. Blue lights illuminate both sides under the water. The air in here is humid and there's a slight smell of mould. No changing room and no way out apart from the door I came in by.

Across the landing is a small, old-fashioned lift with a rusty scissor gate. There's another staircase, but it seems to be going in the wrong direction, so I have to assume for the moment that the lift is the only way to get to the upper floors of this place. That mechanical noise I heard while I was outside must have been this archaic piece of junk descending with my overweight, unworthy opponent on board.

I don't waste any time wondering why a house would be built this way. I slide the lift doors open and get inside. If there's anyone upstairs, they'll be expecting my incapacitated friend, not me. Whatever's up there, I'll just have to face it.

There are two buttons inside the lift and both have peeling stickers next them. One button says 'pool', which I guess is where I am now, and the other says 'office'. I close the doors and press the 'office' button. The lift creaks, groans in protest, shudders slightly and eventually begins a slow ascension.

Very quickly, the chlorine smell fades, and as the lift passes through dark, deserted and spooky floors two and three, it's replaced by a thick, cloying smell of oranges. Oranges mixed with something else. Perhaps it's musk or cypress; some ghastly cologne or other.

The lift reaches the fourth floor and stops. So this is 'office'. There's no one here to meet me, so I slide open the gate and step out onto the landing. I leave the gate open, so when the guy downstairs recovers, he won't be able to use it. I hope that's how it works, anyway. I presume there has to be another way up here, but I can't see one and what the hell, I can't be bothered with that at the moment.

This floor is quiet, isn't dirty like the others and has a fairly new paisley carpet on the floor. To my right, there's a garishly painted door – blue and white stripes – but it doesn't seem to have any security locks attached. It's also slightly ajar, which is either useful or scary, depending on your point of view and past experience.

Keeping in mind I have a vicious hunting knife in my jacket pocket, I walk up to the door and give it a hard shove. The orangey smell is stronger now and makes me feel slightly nauseous.

'Jeremy? Who was it?'

'It isn't Jeremy. Jeremy's currently indisposed.'

He's in his late sixties or early seventies. Extremely overweight, sweaty and the proud owner of four chins. It looks as though he's wearing makeup; not eye shadow or lipstick, just some sort of facial foundation that gives him a cadaverous demeanour which I'm sure isn't intentional. It stops at the base of his neck and his natural puffy, white, veined skin takes over.

He has black-dyed, permed curly hair that reminds me of a Roman emperor. He lies propped up in a large, circular bed covered in a dark brown silk sheet. It doesn't take a detective to notice that both his legs have been amputated about a foot down from the thigh. He waggles both stumps up and down excitedly. I'm glad he's covered by the sheet. There is a pair of old-fashioned wooden crutches by the side of the bed.

Whoever he is, he isn't startled or afraid. He's confident and amused, as if he knows I'm standing over a trap door and he could operate the lever at any time. I look down at my feet, just to be sure.

'My goodness me! A visitor! And so handsome! To what do I owe this pleasure?'

He has a thick, glutinous fat man's voice which is already irritating to listen to.

'Is there another way in here apart from this lift?'

'There are some stairs at the back of the house. The door to them is on the ground floor, but it's always locked. Jeremy has the key. I have to tell you – this is tremendously exciting, *tremendously* exciting.'

'When he recovers and makes his way in here, you've got to tell him to stop whatever it is he's going to try to do. Is that understood?'

'Recovers? Whatever can you mean?'

I look around the room. Wherever that door is, it isn't in here. The only one I can see leads to what has to be a kitchen. There's a huge Bang & Olufsen stereo on a table to my right. There's a silver turntable and three shelves of vinyl.

The place is decorated in classic style and I have to say it looks very smart. It's all yellows, dark greens and terracotta. The wallpaper is William Morris with pale green leaves and white flowers twisting around pomegranates and lemons. Two prints on the wall with expensive frames, one a dark Constable with a stag in the foreground and the other a possible Frederic Leighton. There's a large, bronze bust next to the bed which looks like it may be an Egyptian woman. I wonder who cleans and maintains it. I guess it has to be Jeremy.

He sees me looking at the bronze bust.

'Ah! I can see you're wondering who that is.' He points skywards, as if he's going to begin a lecture. I hope he isn't. 'That is purportedly one of the daughters of Akhenaten. Her name was Ankh-en-pa-Aton and they say she became his last queen. Akhenaten, as I'm sure you're aware, was married to Queen Nefertiti and was the father of Tutankhamun.

'It is said that Akhenaten took quite a few of his daughters as wives, and even attempted to father children by them. Delightful, don't you think? He also counted his own sister as one of his consorts. It was a man's world in those days, eh? His name meant 'strong bull' and he was certainly that, by the sound of things!'

I drag a pale gold leather chair over to the side of the bed and sit down. He waggles his stumps up and down again. It's such a stupid-looking action that it's hard not to laugh.

'I take it you're a regular visitor to The British Museum, Mr Novak.'

'Ah! You know who I am. So this isn't a random burglary or a deliciously brutal indoor mugging. Yes. It is my favourite place in the world. I get there when I can, when I can. Jeremy hates it, of course, as I'm sure you would guess if you were so inclined.'

He gives me a long, hard look which is meant to be sinister.

'Well, this is a quandary we find ourselves in. I feel totally helpless and at your mercy. I can't say it's unexciting. That would be dishonest of me and I am an honest man, you see.'

'I'm a private investigator. My name's Daniel Beckett.

I'd like to talk to you about Viola Raleigh.'

He raises his eyebrows in mock astonishment. 'Now *there's* a name to conjure with. Little Viola. Such cheekbones. Now what makes you think I can help you with her, Mr Beckett? I'm not sure that I really remember her that well. What did you do to Jeremy, may I ask? He's not permanently damaged, is he?'

'His manner is too immediately threatening and intimidating. I had to assault my way past him to get in here. Then he pulled a knife on me which I had to take off him, then I had to break his wrist to stop him punching me in the face. He brought it all on himself. He's not very bright. I'd think about replacing him if I were you.'

'Hm. So how does one become a private investigator nowadays? Is there a college course that one can attend? In a *polytechnic*? I must say, I can smell police, or ex-police, a mile away and you don't have the odour. There's nothing wrong with that odour, of course. It can be quite bracing under the right circumstances. Little Viola Raleigh. My memory isn't as good as it was, you know how things can slip away.'

He smiles sweetly at me, but his eyes have a steely look which tells me he won't be giving out any information without a struggle. That's fine. I've got all day.

'You don't have to prevaricate with me, Mr Novak. I don't care what you do or what you've done. I'm just trying to track her down. She was reported as a missing person two years ago. She popped up on the grid again three weeks ago after someone else reported her as missing. I need to know if it was you or one of your associates.'

He adjusts his position so that he's sitting more

upright, sliding a cushion behind his back. There's a small cupboard next to the bed with a drawer at the top. He keeps glancing at it. He thinks I don't notice.

'Three weeks ago! I have not had any business dealings with Ms Raleigh for some considerable time – certainly not as recently as three weeks ago. Nor would I want to!' he says petulantly, peering once more at the drawer.

There's a noise coming from inside the kitchen. It has to be Jeremy. I hear a key rattling inside a lock and a door opening. It's going to be difficult for him to get used to using his left hand for things from now on. The door squeaks. Not used much. Novak sees that I've noticed and he acts quickly, his hand reaching for the drawer and opening it.

Unfortunately for him, I anticipated this action thirty seconds ago. I lean forwards and slam the drawer on his hand, twice, then pull it out completely and remove the Ruger P semi-automatic that he was over-optimistically reaching for. God Almighty – why are there so many guns about? Novak checks his hand for damage and looks dismayed and disappointed, as if he'd expected more of me under the circumstances.

Jeremy appears in the doorway, furious, his face bloody from his recent nose break and his remaining good fist balled in anger. I aim the gun at the centre of his head, holding it in my left hand so that I can slap Novak's mouth with my right if need be. 'Tell him!'

'All is well, Jeremy, all is well. I think you should just sit down in the corner so that this gentleman can keep an eye on you and we'll see what he has to say.' He looks up at me with an expression of near admiration. 'You broke his nose! I absolutely love it! Should his hand be quite at that angle? You have been in the wars, Jeremy, haven't you?'

Jeremy sits down as requested, but he's still tense and angry. If he saw an opportunity to take me down I know he'd use it without any hesitation, broken wrist or no. I should have searched him. I move my chair a few feet back from Novak and sit down once more, the gun still in my hand. I take the safety off and can tell by the weight that it's loaded. I'm waiting for Jeremy to make even the slightest twitch. This guy is a proper heavy and a damaged wrist won't stop him.

'OK,' I say, keeping both of them in my vision. 'This is going to be easy for both of you if you play your cards right. I'm going to ask some questions and when I feel they've been answered to my satisfaction I'm going to leave. Is that clear enough?'

Jeremy grunts and Novak gives me an oleaginous grin.

'If either of you two do something I don't like, I'll just shoot you. Believe me, Novak, I can make it look like he did it with his good hand and then turned the gun on himself. Or vice versa. Understand?'

How the hell did this get so aggressive and complicated? It's just a few questions, for God's sake. Novak stretches and clasps his hands on his belly over the sheet.

'Of course, dear fellow. And may I say how humbled I am to be in the presence of such a professional and ruthless individual.'

'Shut up.'

'As you wish.'

'Tell me how you first came across Viola Raleigh.'

'Viola, Viola, Viola. Yes. A very disturbed girl, and believe me I've seen a lot of them in my time.' He raises a hand and cleans food debris from each corner of his mouth. 'Now how old was she when I first encountered her? Doubtless early twenties, though I never asked for her birth certificate. We didn't have heart-to-hearts, of course, but I divined some trauma or traumata had gone on in her pampered past.

'She was buying very low quality heroin from somewhere, but it wasn't delivering her to the oblivion that she craved, so she was recommended to me, which is as it should be. I take pride in my work, Mr Beckett, as I'm sure you do, and it offends my sensibilities when I hear of such a powerful and effective drug being watered down for the consumption of the foolhardy. Or should that be powdered down?'

'So the stuff she got from you was considerably stronger and of superior quality.'

'The *stuff*, yes. I see you know your drug terminology, Mr Beckett. As I said, what she had been on before we became acquainted was cut with all sorts of rubbish. She brought me a sample. I almost fainted when I saw the results of the analysis. Among other things it contained toffee and brick dust. Can you imagine what must go through the minds of these people? I didn't want her to go straight on to a more powerful variant. Not immediately, anyway. I wanted her to be a long-term and regular client. She plainly came from money and so was worth cultivating.'

I can see Jeremy starting to rise very slowly from his seat. I catch his eye and give him a look that says 'no'. It's all very well threatening someone like I had threatened Jeremy, but when they're as dim as he is, they're often *compelled* to do something stupid and dangerous, no matter what the consequences might be to themselves and others. He looks pale and clammy, and I know that wrist must be hurting like a bastard. He slowly licks the sweat that's gathering on his upper lip.

'So you got her hooked with due regard to your health and safety regulations and management policies,' I say.

'Nicely put! Yes. Yes. She was a nice little customer and things went very smoothly for several months. She would arrive here every week with her money, we would have a cup of tea and a lightweight chat and then she would go to whatever she called 'home' to jab the *stuff* into her veins. I thought it would go on like that forever, or until she OD'd in some public lavatory or squat or bus station or wherever these young people go to have fun and die nowadays.' He scratches the side of his face and looks bored, but I know his mind is racing.

'But it didn't go on forever.'

'No it didn't, my dear fellow. It certainly did not. I knew something was amiss when she failed to give me two payments, one after another. Now I'm a very generous man, and her credit was good with me. I liked her, in my way. She had a very good speaking voice and a wide vocabulary. As I say, we didn't do much apart from small talk, but I surmised she had been the recipient of an expensive education of some type, rather like myself.'

'So what did you do when the money flow was interrupted?'

'I have strict rules which I always – *always* – adhere to. The first time someone fails to make a payment, I will give them their goods in good faith and expect to be reimbursed the next time they see me. This I did with dear Viola. I can…'

He pulls himself up short suddenly and looks alarmed. 'She's not *dead* is she?'

'Not as far as I know.'

'Oh. Oh good. On an aesthetic level, she was a delightful looking creature. She got a bit ratty-looking as time went on, of course.'

'What happens the second time they don't pay you?'

'Then that is *it*. They are no longer my customer. I had – and still have – a little network of people in the same business. I will put the word out to this network if a client is unable to pay for goods they have received. They will then be *fucked*, Mr Beckett. They're only junkies, after all. It's simply good business for everyone. I would expect the people in this little network to do the same for me under similar circumstances.'

'But you've got ways of making your female clients pay off their debt and maintain their habit,' I say.

He looks shocked that I should say this and is probably wondering where I got my information from. I hope that he doesn't make the connection with Taylor Conway, but it's always a possibility. Well that's tough. On the other hand, we're talking about ancient history here and it's unlikely he knows where Taylor lives, though if it was an effortless job to go and break Taylor's legs, I've no doubt he'd do it, or get Jeremy to do it for him.

'Well, well, well, Mr Beckett. You are a well-informed young man, aren't you? I wonder how much more you know about my personal affairs and business peccadilloes.' He looks straight into my eyes for a few seconds and all the bonhomie is gone. 'I wonder what would actually *happen* if I commanded Jeremy there to come over and give you a little talking to. Would you really use that gun? Jeremy was a boxer, you know. He was a boxer, then he was a builder and now he is a bastard. Isn't that right, Jeremy? The three Bs!'

I smile at him. 'I wouldn't trouble yourself with considering anything as foolish as that, Mr Novak. Your whole life would change.'

He stares at me a little longer and the humour comes back into his eyes, accompanied by a faint, pained smile. 'Hm. Yes. I can see that it would be a bad idea. I have met a number of private investigators in my time, Mr Beckett, but none of them have been capable of giving me the scrumptious little frisson of fear that I felt just then. How curious.'

'Besides, Jeremy's right wrist is broken in a pretty serious way. He's going to pass out fairly soon and I'd advise a visit to the hospital when I've gone. They may be able to help him use his hand again. That nose may need popping back into position as well.'

He turns to Jeremy and gives him a sympathetic little moue. 'Am I going to have to give you your cards, Jeremy?'

'So let's hear it about your prostitution racket.'

He takes a deep breath and sighs. I'm sure he wouldn't have chosen the indelicate phrase 'prostitution racket', and the words may make him burst into tears with their vulgarity, but now I'm needling him for my own amusement.

He scratches his head and his eyes dart from left to right. He's trying to find somewhere to start, some way of explaining everything that won't give too much away, won't incriminate him and won't leave him open to blackmail from someone like me.

'Well, as I'm sure you'll understand, I'm not a *hands on* person as far as my companies are concerned. Like all good company directors, I delegate. But ultimately, all executive decisions are mine.'

Such pretension. Such delusion. Pathetic.

'During our little chats, Viola had mentioned that she had, in the past, *offered* herself in exchange for drugs, shall we say,' he says, sounding pleased with his own sentence.

'With people she knew.'

'Yes. Some she didn't know *that* well, but the principle was the same as the girls who worked for me at that time. It's simple barter, Mr Beckett. You want something; you have to give something in exchange. I talked her into it, I rationalised her into it, I flattered her into it, I cajoled her into it and I drugged her into it. Viola seemed to have a very casual attitude to amatory matters in the first place, I must say. I wouldn't declare she was a great romantic heroine whose sensibilities would be offended by such occurrences. I would, in fact, suggest that the sexual life was not of much interest to her in the way it seemed to be to some young ladies of my acquaintance. So it was but a tiny step she had to take to become one of my, one of my…'

He pauses, trying to find the right word or phrase.

'One of my *bitches*!'

He spits the word out, with joy and malevolence, laughing with his mouth open and giving me a view of his black fillings. He waggles his stumps up and down under the sheet once more. This time, the drumming is faster than on the previous occasions. It's quite disturbing. I fear that he may be very slightly unhinged.

'Yes, Mr Beckett. My *bitches*, for that is what they are. My *whores*. My *sluts*! Pretty Viola was a little reluctant at first, it had to be said, but the strength of her addiction had got the better of her. But I couldn't just put her *out there*, you understand. She had to be put through a vigorous training regime. The most vigorous there was.

She had to be trained to show enthusiasm. She had to be trained in many different arts and skills. She was an amateur and it was my task to turn her into a professional!'

'And how…'

'How did I do that? Is that what you're about to ask? Well obviously I wasn't going to charge people to fuck the silly little bitch straight away. That would not be good business. My clients are not top drawer, as it were, but they still like to see a little enthusiasm in their whores. They like variety, they like *perversion*, they like the girls to take them to places they have never been to before, or at least take them to places that they have *thought* about visiting but have never dared to go to. This requires training, sir. This requires training and discipline.

'First of all, they have to understand that they can never turn down a client. They have to deal with men who they may personally find utterly repugnant. So with that in mind, my first act was to give her to Jeremy here for a week. Jeremy, as you can see, is a revolting, fat, brutish specimen with appalling personal hygiene and a stupid, boorish personality. He's a malodorous thug with the IQ of a lizard and that is an insult to lizards. He hates all women and is prone to inflicting callous, ferocious and savage violence against them. He is a degenerate slime bucket of the first order.'

'I think you're being too sympathetic. Are you trying not to hurt his feelings or something?'

'Very good, Mr Beckett. You have a dry wit that I wholly appreciate. You know what Viola looks like, I assume. Jeremy, as you'll probably surmise, would never get a woman as good-looking as that in a million years. She would be, as they say, totally out of his league. So you can imagine the fireworks when he fell on her for the first time. You can imagine what he did to her, hour after hour, day after day, night after night. He was like an animal, a beast, a monstrosity. He was remorseless, vulgar and pitiless.

'His tastes in outlandish hard core pornography have given him an edge, shall we say, when it comes to entertaining the ladies. After that week, Mr Beckett, there was *nothing* that the lovely Viola had not experienced. She had been totally and utterly debauched. Why, he even introduced her to several of his *chums* from the snooker club he belongs to. They *fully* enjoyed themselves with her, believe you me! No doors were closed, if you get my drift.

'My reasoning, you see, Mr Beckett, was if that if Viola could show enthusiasm and be pliant with a noxious specimen such as Jeremy, then she could do the same with *anyone*. If she could entertain Jeremy and his uncouth *mates* without a break for three or four hours, then the world would be her oyster. A Park Lane hotel room filled with Arabs would be a walk in the park for her, do you see? It would be a lovely day out at the seaside eating an ice cream!'

Park Lane? Really? I can't imagine that Novak would be the first person you'd contact if you were procuring for oil-rich sheiks, but I'll allow him his little delusion.

I want to take a deep breath and swallow, but I don't want to show that this is beginning to get to me. It isn't sympathy for Viola I'm feeling, but hatred for these two freaks. And here I am with a pistol in my hand and both of them at my mercy. Novak plainly loves holding forth like this, so I'll nod my appreciation and hope he produces something useful.

'So presumably you were present at Viola's induction.'

'I wouldn't have missed it for the world, Mr Beckett. Far more entertaining than the television is nowadays. I'm old enough to remember the golden age of television and today's rot certainly falls short in the quality department. The induction, as you exquisitely put it, wasn't done here, of course. I have some lowly premises in Willesden where the training takes place. It used to be used by a gentleman who made copper piping, so it is conveniently soundproofed. I would sit in my wheelchair and observe. I treated myself to a ringside seat, as it were. I gave her valid criticism. If she was not enthusiastic enough, I would give her a sharp slap on the bottom with my riding crop. If there were techniques that she was unfamiliar with, I would instruct her.

'Sometimes, it was easier to watch a pornographic film instead of using words. She was a bright girl, though, and she picked up most things pretty quickly. You should see some of the girls I've had to work with. You have to explain things about fifty times before it gets into their thick skulls.

'I also taught her to use some of the choicest, spiciest language. She became very good at that, eventually. It sounded marvellous coming out of her mouth with that refined accent of hers and Jeremy here was most enthused by it and so were his snooker chums. They used to call her 'Her Ladyship', which I found *most* amusing. Sadly, I am yet to pimp out a genuine member of the aristocracy, but I live in hope, Mr Beckett, I live in hope. They are about, I have heard. Some quite close to the top, if you get my drift. Some much loved by the general public, God bless them.'

'So then what happened? She went out for money to real clients.'

'Yes. Yes. I must mention that she was dependent on me for her supply of heroin. It had to be that way. I had to have her under the strictest control. I am a whoremaster first and a drug dealer second. If some top businessmen were in town and wanted her, I couldn't afford to have her nodding out like some hopeless smack hound in mid-orgy. I have my reputation to consider.'

'Of course you do, and I respect that. So you kept her heroin habit under control.'

'As I said, she sought oblivion, but I was ill disposed to let her have it, for her own good and for mine. I personally injected her, usually between the toes so the puncture marks would not be too obvious. Sometimes in the back of the neck, sometimes in the armpit, anywhere there was a vein. I thought it best that she always had to come to me for her fix, as it were. If I left it to her, she'd have had track marks over her forearms and that would never do. Oh no.' He sighs and looks wistful. 'I like to think that she thought of me as a father figure. Is that too precious of me, Mr Beckett?'

'Precious? No.'

I suddenly get Raleigh's face in my mind. I've been so wrapped up in listening to Novak's hellish narrative that I've almost forgotten what I'm doing here. So far, though, he hasn't given me much I can use.

'She was a whore,' says Jeremy, usefully.

I'm glad Jeremy spoke. I've been so focused on Novak that I let myself forget he was there for a few seconds.

'Ah, well you would know all about *that*, Jeremy,' says Novak, grinning at his slimy abettor. He turns to me and turns both palms up, in a gesture of honesty. 'Jeremy and his chums gave Viola a dose of Rohypnol one night, Mr Beckett. That and a little pinch of the finest cocaine, plus some other high-class stimulants.

'You should have seen her displays. Such wantonness! She was like a pig at a trough, Mr Beckett, a pig at a trough. I am so glad that I had the foresight to film it. A pretty penny was made *there*, I can tell you that for nought.' He flashes a sly grin at me. 'If you think it would help you in your investigations, I could sell you a DVD of the occasion at the reduced price of fifty pounds. All the fun of the fair.

'To be quite honest with you, it was difficult to categorise it. My regular DVD customers like to know what they are getting, but this had absolutely everything. We even got a couple of my sleaziest girls in to spice things up a little. Old in body, but young in enthusiasm; I'm sure you know the type, Mr Beckett.' He laughs and waggles his stumps. 'I even indulged myself with a brief cameo appearance. I had ambitions to tread the boards when I was young, but it was not to be.' He sighs at the memory. 'We even got young Viola to lick the toilet clean at one point. Hilarious. It was almost like one of those art films they show at the ICA. Do you think Blu-ray will catch on, Mr Beckett?'

'She was like a filthy fucking pig,' says Jeremy, his eyes twinkling at the memory. 'She was like a hog, a dirty fucking hog.' Jeremy looks sick now. A few more minutes and he'll be lying on the floor. I do hope he doesn't go into shock and die. 'The bitch,' he adds helpfully, laughing weakly.

'Not all of my girls are aficionados of the poppy, Mr Beckett, lest I give you that impression. Oh no. That only happens in cases like Viola's, where her addictions outweighed her finances and she was a suitable candidate for whoredom. In most cases of payment arrears, Jeremy here will use a hammer on the miscreant, sometimes a knife; it all depends on his inclination at the time of the event.

'He is a jolly fellow, don't you think? Obedient to the last. I have no doubt, Mr Beckett, that he would like to use a hammer on *you*, as would I. Does it trouble you at all, Mr Beckett, being in a room where both of the other occupants would like to hammer you?'

'Have you ever thought of getting a treadmill up here? It would save you having to go down in the lift to your little swimming pool every day.'

'Ah! And you respond with a hammer blow to my soul. Well done, sir. Bravo.'

'So Viola Raleigh worked as a prostitute for you in exchange for drugs.'

'Not that simple, I'm afraid. I think she actually *enjoyed* the prostitution. Very unusual; most of the girls don't really like it, but I think young Viola did. This is only my humble theory, but I think she thought that being at the mercy of multiple partners, being *used* so heartlessly and repeatedly, would somehow eradicate whatever it was that was eating away at her soul. Cod psychology, but it's the best I can do under the circumstances. So sorry. I shall read a book on the subject before you visit me again. I do so hate being unprepared for an intellectual chat.'

'But you have no idea what this thing was. The thing that was eating away at her soul.'

'No. But whatever it was, a regular heroin habit and her dozen or so clients a day were not enough to keep it in check. It all went well for three or four months, but then I started getting complaints. These were complaints about her enthusiasm during performance, you understand. I began to get suspicious. I am many things, Mr Beckett, but I am not stupid.

'We brought her up here, Jeremy stripped her for me and I examined every square inch of her body with a magnifying glass. I was truly the Sherlock Holmes of the demimonde. Then I found what I had been looking for. Puncture marks where there should not have been puncture marks. She had been supplementing her heroin diet, Mr Beckett. I have no idea where she was getting her supply from and I did not care. Her career with me was at an end. I had made back the money she owed me many times over and had no further use for her.'

'The bitch,' adds Jeremy, dribbling, his eyes going in and out of focus.

'When did this happen?'

'A little over eighteen months ago. I don't remember the date. Sorry. I'll mark it on a calendar the next time.'

'So you just kicked her out and left her to her own devices?'

'Oh no. That is not my modus operandi, Mr Beckett. She was still in good physical condition; she still had her looks, to a degree. She was a little skinnier than when she first came to me, but nothing that three square meals a day wouldn't clear up if someone could be bothered to get her off the Horse.

'She was from a good background, she was young, she had a good education and she was intelligent. Messed up beyond hope, perhaps, but still with many qualities to recommend her and with a lot of quality training and varied experience under her belt. There are people who are prepared to make a silk purse out of a sow's ear, but I am not one of them. I simply don't have the patience for that sort of thing.'

'But you knew someone who did have the patience.'

'Yes indeed, Mr Beckett. I did. I had, shall we say, certain *suspicions* about Viola's nature and thought very carefully about who I could sell her to. It had to be someone very clever, sympathetic and perceptive. Someone who would be able to see past Viola's troubles and use *that* body, *that* voice and *that* beauty to their best advantage. I am very capricious, you see. I had no more interest in her now.'

'So who did you sell her to?'

My voice sounds rough. I cough to clear my throat. I've been holding the gun for too long and my hand is sweating against it. I rest it on my thigh and wipe my hand on my chinos. I want to get out of here now. I'm sick of listening to this prick and keeping an eye on his drooling associate. I'm never doing missing persons again after this. It's far too sleazy and time consuming, talking to stupid people who think they're the smartest thing on the planet.

'What you are asking me for has a price, Mr Beckett.'

'I'm sure it does, Mr Novak. Here's my deal. I took five hundred pounds out of a cashpoint machine yesterday purely for bribery purposes. I've already used two hundred of that. I'll give you the three hundred if you give me the name. Obviously, I'll also need a contact telephone number and/or an address. If that's not enough money, I'll just have to get the information out of you by other means. You have thirty seconds to think this over.'

Novak slaps his hands against his thighs. 'I *knew* this was going to be an exciting day as soon as you walked in here! Threats, violence; what else could a man in my position ask for? Three hundred pounds! Did you hear that, Jeremy? We're in the money at long last.'

Novak waggles his stumps up and down again. Jeremy looks at me with a dull expression on his face. He raises a fat hand to wipe his face and looks at it to see if there's any blood. There is. Having discovered more about him in the last half hour, I really hope his nose hurts.

'What are you going to do, Mr Beckett? Torture me? I have powerful friends in the police force, some of whom I have known for many years. Or perhaps you're going to kill me. I can see that you're capable of it, but then you'd have none of the information you seek, would you. No. I think I can safely tell you to fuck off, Mr Beckett. I shall do so now. Fuck off, Mr Beckett! Fuck off!'

I have an Olympus digital voice recorder in my pocket. I think of it as new, but it's already low-tech. Still does the job, though. I take it out and show it to Novak. It wipes the smile off his face.

'I don't have powerful friends in the police force, but I do have the mobile number of a detective who is criminally underused and hungry for promotion.'

I'm thinking of DS Bream. That's an unfair and totally inaccurate description of her, but it'll give this dick something to think about. I remember her stretching back in her chair in the wine bar and that husky voice. Did I promise her dinner? I can't remember. Jeremy looks at Novak, as if awaiting instructions.

'Now I'm not sure how much this recording of our conversation would be worth in a court of law, but if I was a detective sergeant on the make and this fell into my lap, I'd certainly investigate you until your teeth rattled. I might even discover some police corruption as an added bonus, considering what you just said.' I lean forward and catch his gaze in mine. 'And who knows what else. You do have a licence for this firearm I take it?'

'Ah,' says Novak, with not a little resignation in his voice. 'It is not difficult to call my bluff nowadays. In my prime, I would have personally eviscerated you and fed you your own testicles, but those halcyon days are over. I like a quiet life nowadays, Mr Beckett, so I'll reluctantly take the three hundred. Can I see it first?'

I open my wallet, remove the notes and fan them out so he can count them. This is good enough for him. He licks his lips.

'Jeremy, would you be so kind as to fetch me my address book, a sheet of paper and a pen?'

Jeremy just about manages this before collapsing in a heap on the floor. Novak rolls his eyes, chews the top of his Biro and scribbles away.

'I shall remember you, Mr Beckett. I shall remember this little episode that we've shared today. I have friends.'

'Shut up.'

# 8

## A PIN-UP COME TO LIFE

I make sure I'm a little early for my meeting, or date, or whatever it is with Anjukka. I don't want her turning up and I'm not there. I stand next to one of the pillars beneath the Selfridge's clock and stare into space, blocking out the passers-by and their chat. Every time someone comes out of the store, there's an accompanying whiff of perfume.

On my way out of Novak's place, I encountered a sallow young girl in a short skirt who asked me if he lived there. She can't have been more than twenty and had an accent that I couldn't place. I told her that I was a doctor and had just been treating him for an infectious disease. He probably wouldn't last the night. She looked concerned, thanked me and walked off quickly along the street. I'm not sure if that was a good thing to do, but it felt right at the time. I may, of course, have sent her on a trajectory to someone or something even worse.

After that, I'd got a cab straight back to Exeter Street, had a shower and got changed. I needed the shower to get the atmosphere of Novak's place out of my system. I'd decided to put all of today's work out of my mind and think about it in an analytical way tomorrow, but it was difficult. Once someone like Novak has put images in your mind like those inspired by his description of Viola's 'training' regime, they keep sliding up to the surface and are hard to shake off.

I was surprised my little digital recorder threat worked on Novak, to be honest, but I think his type are on the way out and the services I've seen advertised on the net are the future; marginally safer, more autonomy for the girls and a little freer from the base exploitation of the type that Novak had specialised in, where the girls are basically cash cows.

I tried watching a film, but turned it off after half an hour and went back to Fisher's Viola file, pulling that A4 photograph out and staring at it for a while. It was a hypnotic image; there could be no doubt about that. The blonde hair, the intelligent eyes with that hint of flirtatiousness, the full mouth; you could stare at it for hours. This woman was definitely a cut above most of the escorts that I saw on all those websites. Many of them were strikingly attractive, but none as beautiful as Viola Raleigh.

It's no exaggeration to say that she could have been a model; not that a woman with looks like that would *have* to go into that line of business, but it would surely have been preferable to the horrors that Novak had described. Perhaps there wasn't enough oblivion in modelling. Perhaps there wasn't enough debasement in modelling. Perhaps there wasn't enough horror in modelling. I used my mobile to photograph both of these prints. You never, know, I may need to show them to someone at some point, though I'm tempted to make the one taken by the professional photographer my background.

Novak seemed to be a little surprised at Viola's enjoyment of the whole process and so am I. His theory about her reasons for this may have had more than a grain of truth in it. Was she eradicating something that was eating away at her? Was the heroin not enough? She was a functioning heroin addict, from what Novak was telling me, but after a while you just need a fix to feel normal. To get high on it again, to get the thrill of that initial buzz, you need to up your dose until the day comes when your body can take no more. This isn't always the case, but it's common enough. My brother was a good example.

So if things were that bad, why didn't she commit suicide? Well, lots of reasons. It's just against the nature of some people; their survival instinct is much too strong. Or they're frightened doing it for a variety of reasons, some of them practical. Also, suicide attempts can fail and leave you in a worse state than you were in to begin with. Maybe you have some last vestiges of religious belief. Novak told me that during Viola's training period, he could hear her crying and praying every night while she lay on her mattress, which is a little sad, I guess, but it could be the reason she felt reluctant to finish things off by her own hand. Of course, there could be some reason that I haven't thought of.

So apart from a more brutal history, what did I get from Novak? Well, anything that came out of that creep's mouth would have to be taken with a pinch of salt, but taking that into account, it doesn't seem likely that it was him that reported Viola missing three weeks ago. I've thought about it, and I can't see any reason why it would be in his interest to lie to me about that, unless it was pure cussedness on his part.

He and his monkey were not well pleased about my intrusion into their life and I'm sure he'll already be on the phone to his contacts, checking up on me. That's all I need; another reason to keep looking over my shoulder.

So now I've got the name of the next person down the line; Mrs Bianchi. Novak sold Viola to her for an undisclosed five-figure sum. He seemed to think he'd got a good deal, though it's possible that it was Mrs Bianchi who got the good deal. This would depend upon the plans she had for Viola, how smart she was and how she intended to exploit her. Just because Mrs Bianchi is female (and, presumably, Italian), it doesn't necessarily mean that she was the person who reported Viola missing, but it's better than nothing. I'll check her out tomorrow.

I start to wonder how long this is going to take. How many people am I going to have to speak to until I finally contact Viola? Will it ever happen? I have to keep thinking of that twenty thousand bonus. I'm still annoyed that I've had to go down this path when a little police cooperation would have sorted it out much earlier. But then it's only taken me a little over a day so far, so there's nothing to complain about. And I did make contact with DS Bream.

'Wow. You look totally zoned out.'

It's Anjukka and she looks fabulous. She's wearing a close fitting, short, strapless Fifties-style dress with a cinched waist that accentuates her wide hips and a boned bust that pushes her breasts up so it looks like one of the more voluptuous Gil Elvgren pinups has come to life and is walking down Oxford Street. I think they call them wiggle dresses and it's obvious why. The pattern is just as outrageous: enormous, bright green tropical leaves and dazzling red and orange flowers. You could only get away with this in London. Anywhere else and they'd think it was fancy dress. I swallow the saliva that's somehow gathered in my mouth and attempt to speak.

'I was miles away.'

We link arms and walk along the pavement towards I don't know where. Her swaying walk means her hip keeps brushing against mine and I can hear the swish of her stockings as they rub against each other. Add to this an overpowering musky perfume which I can't identify and it's one of those times where you could get run over and it really wouldn't matter; it doesn't get much better than this.

'So where do private investigators take their dates nowadays? Some low dive with sawdust on the floor where fights break out all the time?'

'Or there's an Italian Place in John Prince's Street, maybe ten minutes' walk from here,' I say. 'They've got a champagne bar. I've heard it can get pretty violent when someone orders an unfashionable type of champagne cocktail. Will that do you?'

'Sounds wonderful.'

Men keep staring at us as we walk along. That's not quite true; they stare at Anjukka and then glower at me.

'I just realised I don't know your surname.'

'It's York.'

'Anjukka York. Striking.'

'Thank you.'

'So what does your fiancé do?'

'Are you fishing, Mr Beckett?'

Then I notice that she's not wearing her diamond and sapphire engagement ring. I guess she dumped him when she met me. It happens so much that it barely surprises me anymore.

'Just curious.'

'His name is Alistair Bellamy. He's from Ascot, he's

forty-two and he runs his own business, importing gourmet foods from Europe and elsewhere. He's very successful, very handsome and drives a Mercedes E63 AMG Estate.'

'I want to have his babies.'

She laughs. 'He also doesn't exist. I made him up to stop Fisher and all the rest of them hitting on me. The engagement ring I just saw you looking for is my grandmother's on the Finnish side.'

'And does this ploy work?'

'So far. They're a pretty conservative lot and a woman who's engaged is out of bounds for them, despite their rampant sexism. In fact, I think that sexism is part of it and has worked against them in this case. I also think they're kind of afraid because my fake fiancé is rich and drives a Merc. Also, Mr Raleigh finds me invaluable and doesn't want to lose me because of any sexual harassment incidents or lawsuits. He's edgy about anything that might put him in the public eye.'

'So what sort of gourmet foods does your fiancé import?'

We turn into Ronchetti's and take a seat at the bar. She leaves the ordering to me, so I ask the bargirl for two Black Velvets while they sort us out a table. Anjukka runs a hand through her hair and drinks half of hers in one go. I like her.

'How long have you worked for Raleigh?'

'Two years. A little over two years. It's very good pay. I've made myself indispensable. Officially, I'm his PA, but I used to be a paralegal, so I'm able to deal with a fair amount of his contractual work.'

Another paralegal? How many of them are there? I think of last night with Natalie and my mouth starts to go dry. I take a sip of my Black Velvet. I must ring her when all this is over. I think there's more to explore with someone like that.

Anjukka crosses her legs. I'm looking at her face, but my peripheral vision has picked out the tops of her stockings and her suspender clips.

'And that place in Holland Park. Is that the HQ? I got the impression he lived there.'

'No. The headquarters is in the City. That's where I work most of the time and that's where most of the day-to-day business is done. That's where the fiancé ploy *really* comes in handy. It's as if someone rounded up all the creepy, ugly, loud, privately educated, insecure males in London and dumped them in one office.'

'Sounds like heaven on earth for an attractive young woman.'

'*That's* for sure. Sometimes he'll use the house in Holland Park when he's seeing people and wants to give them the impression that the business is not some big impersonal conglomerate in a skyscraper, which of course it is. He has another big house in Richmond. I know the address, but I've never seen it.'

She finishes her drink. I order two more even though I'm only half way through mine. I think she's drinking quickly because she's nervous.

'He does stay at the Holland Park place overnight sometimes, though. It depends what he's doing. He often entertains clients in the West End, so Holland Park is nice and handy. I think there are a couple of bedrooms in the house, but I've never seen them. There's a lot of security because he keeps some stuff in filing cabinets that's confidential and there're the computers and so on.'

'Not to mention his art.'

'Yes, well there's that, too.'

'What do you think of his wife's portrait in the office?'

'Oh my *God*! Isn't that the most outrageous thing? I mean – *really*? I've never met her, so I can't judge, but if that was me I'd just drop dead of embarrassment whenever anyone was in there. I mean – I'd drop dead of embarrassment just having the painting done in the first place!'

She doesn't know that Raleigh's wife is dead. But then why should she? Most people don't know anything about their employer's private lives. I'm sure there's nothing significant in this. It's interesting, all the same because he was talking to me about her as if she was alive. I'm trying to think of something to say that will flatter her and get me some more information at the same time. She takes a sip of her drink, looking at me over the rim and uncrossing her legs. I hear the seductive swish of her nylons again.

'She's very attractive, though,' I say, watching her carefully.

'Do you think so?'

'For that type of figure.'

'And how would you describe that type of figure, Daniel?'

'Slim. Willowy.'

'And is that the sort of figure you go for?'

'So you wouldn't ever have a portrait like that done yourself, then.'

'I don't know. It would depend.'

'On what?'

'On who was painting it. I don't think I'd be too bothered if it was a woman.' She giggles. 'It would be just like when you were in the ladies' changing room in the gym, but someone was painting you.'

'But if it was for someone special, you might consider it?'

'Yes. Yes, I think I would.'

'Quite expensive, I would think,' I say.

'It probably is. But I think if you wanted someone to have a portrait of you like that, it would be worth the money.'

'I think so too. Where would you hang it?'

'It would have to be in the bedroom.'

'You're probably right.'

A waiter appears. Our table is ready. Anjukka finishes her drink and gets up. She loses her footing for a second and falls forward, grabbing my forearm for support. I place a hand gently against her waist as we're led to our table.

'High bar stools,' I say. 'Always a hazard.'

'They're going to think I'm pissed.'

We sit down and the waiter hands us a menu each. As we make our choices, she looks up at me. 'You didn't answer my question.'

'Which one was that?'

'When you described Mrs Raleigh's figure as slim and willowy. I asked you if that was the sort of figure you went for.'

'Did you?'

'Yes.'

'What did I say?'

'You didn't.'

'Well, on careful consideration, I'd say it wasn't the sort of figure I went for. I prefer curvier women.'

'I thought so.'

'Did you?'

'Yes. You look the type.'

'Thanks.'

'You're welcome.'

We order our meals and I order a bottle of champagne. Neither of us fancies a starter. We both have the same thing – spaghetti alla puttanesca. I like it here because the portions aren't too big. I hate feeling bloated after a meal.

We eat in silence for a while, our eyes occasionally meeting across the table.

'So how are you doing with finding Mr Raleigh's daughter? I can't imagine how stressful that must be for him. He had to tell me about it in case I had to deal with you in some way or other. Taking messages, logging payments and so on.'

I have no idea how much she knows about what's going on.

'It's keeping me busy.'

'Oh, sorry. You can't really talk about it, can you?'

'It depends. Tell me what you know.'

'Well, she went missing a couple of years ago and I think he just got fed up with the police doing nothing and hired you.'

'That's about it. I'm just doing the usual – checking with people she knew, old friends, that sort of thing. Sometimes one thing will lead to another. It's pretty tedious. I think the trail may have gone cold, unfortunately.'

'They had a big confab after you'd gone. Mr Raleigh and Mr Fisher, that is. They were in Mr Raleigh's office talking for at least half an hour.'

'Do you know what they were talking about?'

'I got the impression that Mr Fisher was a bit annoyed

that Mr Raleigh got someone in from outside the company to help.'

'Really?'

'Yes. I think he thought that Mr Raleigh might ask him to do it, as he'd been in the army and so on. I don't think that's what they were talking about, though. I think they were talking about you. Anyway, I'm glad he's annoyed. I don't like Mr Fisher. He's a creep. Just thinking about him makes me feel ill. He's always turning the conversation around to sex.'

'I didn't know he'd been in the army. He might have been doing radar or something, though. Doesn't mean he could do this. So you pretend to be engaged in work. Are you seeing anyone at all?'

'No. Not at the moment. Not for some time, actually. This is the first date I've been on for two years.' She purses her lips. 'And it was me that had to ask *you* out! That's the price I pay for my betrothal to Alistair and his posh foodstuffs. I don't mind, particularly, but I do love going out. I go out with girlfriends from time to time, but it's not the same.'

'Two years. That's incredible. I'm not being rude, but you're one of the most gorgeous women I've ever seen. I really can't believe you're unattached. Don't take that as any sort of come-on, though. I say that to everybody. I don't think I would let Alistair and his Mercedes stop me asking you out, though.'

'Well, it didn't stop you, did it. I could see you noticed the ring, but you still gave me your card when there was no real need to. That's why I rang you. That's why we're here now.'

'You see right through me.' I take another sip of champagne. 'Why is Mr Fisher a creep?'

'Well, he – I shouldn't be telling you this, I suppose – he does things for Mr Raleigh that I find a bit distasteful. In fact, there are certain aspects of this job that I've really begun not to like. To be honest, I've been looking for something else for a couple of months.'

'I don't think you'll have any problems finding anything.'

'I hope not.'

I pour some more champagne into her glass. Her skin is attractively pale against her black hair. The combination of her beauty, her perfume and the champagne is making my mind wander. I must keep focussed.

'What sort of things does Mr Fisher do that you don't like?'

She drinks and purses her lips again. It's quite an endearing gesture.

'Well, you know that Mr Raleigh is in the arms business I take it.'

'Yes.'

'He does a lot of business with the Emirates; lots of other countries, too. I don't know the full extent of it, really. He sees people when they come over. I don't know who half of them are. Sometimes they're royalty, sometimes they're government officials, and sometimes they're armed forces personnel. It all depends.'

'Go on.'

'Well it's no secret that a lot of these people expect to be entertained well when they're over here and that means prostitutes, among other things. They want to be treated like little gods, just because they have money and want to buy guns or whatever. I find it dreadful, actually, that Mr Raleigh sucks up to them like he does. It makes you have no respect for him, I suppose. The whole thing is dreadful.'

'I know it is. Powerful men tossing off other powerful men by proxy.'

She laughs. I use this opportunity to slide my hand over the table and hold hers.

'Well Mr Fisher is very closely involved with the entertainment side, if that's the word for it. Once, when we were in the main HQ, I was walking past his office and I could see that he was looking at some site or other that had semi-naked women on it. I don't mean pornographic, just women in sexy lingerie and bikinis and so on.'

'So you think he was hiring call girls?'

'He was *definitely* hiring call girls. I was working late that night, so I waited until he'd gone home and there was no one about and I switched on his computer to see what it was he'd been looking at. It was easy to find out the password for his Internet server. There's a list of the passwords in a file in the management menu, which I have access to. Stupid, really, but those office computers aren't really used for all the confidential stuff. They're mainly used for admin matters. He hadn't bothered to clear his search history, so I took a peek.'

Jesus Christ. She was sailing close to the wind doing that. There are dozens of ways to find out if someone has been looking at things on your computer. She would have altered the way the search history looked just by clicking on one item. I've come across people who are so paranoid about this that if they don't erase it, they make a screenshot note of what their search history looked like and check it the next time they log on. She was lucky that Fisher wasn't one of those people.

'So what did you find?'

The waiter appears with a dessert menu. We take one each and try to choose something. They do a great affogato here, so I'll have that. Anjukka has strawberry macaroons with toffee-flavoured cream blobbed on top of them. I order another bottle of champagne.

'Can I try some of your dessert when it arrives?' she says.

'Sure. They use very strong espresso in it, though. You may get heart palpitations.'

'I'm getting them already.'

'Really? Then you might die.'

'Die from an Italian dessert? I'll take the risk. You only live once.'

Our hands separated while the dessert was sorted, now they slide effortlessly together again. The waiter smiles as he places the champagne bucket beside the table. If I'm not careful they'll send a violin player over here in a minute. I start to think about Viola Raleigh and how this sort of male/female intimacy would have been alien to her.

'I don't think the result would be unattractive, though,' says Anjukka, grinning wickedly.

'Sorry?'

'If I had a portrait done in the same style as Mrs Raleigh's.'

'I don't think it would be, either. Would you choose exactly the same pose?'

'I'm not sure. I think if you were going as far as exposing your breasts, then you may as well go all the way. I think I'd dispense with the fur coat across the lap.'

'Too coy?'

'Something like that. Too flash and ostentatious, also. I don't think I'd sit in an armchair, either. If I was going to be sitting down, I think an ordinary chair would be much better. My bottom's one of my best features and I'd want it to be seen. *If* I was going to have a portrait like that done, of course.'

'Of course.'

'Also the dress she's got on, if it is a dress. I don't think I'd bother with that. I mean, it's quite erotic if it *is* a dress, I suppose. There's the hint that it's been pulled down to expose her breasts for the portrait. But once again, why bother with it? You may as well go all the way.'

'I thought it was maybe a skirt. It's hard to tell.'

'Whatever it is, it would have to go. I wouldn't want someone to have something boring and dull hanging on their bedroom wall.'

'I had no idea you were so considerate.'

'It's one of my best qualities.'

The desserts arrive. Anjukka looks at mine while eating the first spoonful of hers.

'Go on. Try some.'

'What's the ice cream?'

'Vanilla.'

She takes a spoonful, making sure she has enough of the coffee. As she swallows, her eyes roll up into her head. 'Dreamy. I didn't think it would be so sweet.'

I'm interested in the fact that Fisher hires call girls as part of his job for Raleigh, if Anjukka's got her facts right. I'll have to bring that up again soon as it seems to have drifted away as part of the conversation. I can't quite work out whether this is significant in any way. I shouldn't be drinking this much; it affects my cognitive abilities.

Is Fisher somehow involved in this? Is he screwing

over his boss in some way? I can't imagine how. Let me try and think a little more clearly. Could it have been Fisher who was Viola's mysterious client that night in the hotel? Did Viola realise who he was, go a little crazy and run off into the night, never to return? Would she have known who Fisher was in the first place? I'm not sure whether their respective roles in Raleigh's life overlap or not.

Most people don't have enough involvement in their parents' jobs to know or recognise individual members of staff. On the other hand, Fisher seemed to know Viola well enough, if only through her photographs and his research. If Viola was an occasional visitor to the place in Holland Park, she may well have encountered Fisher and he her.

It could be just coincidence, however, and it's difficult to make anything of it. DS Bream, however, picked up on it straight away. What was it she said? Something about not giving arms clients just a cup of tea and a biscuit? She said that it might not mean anything and she didn't want to colour my investigation. Well, maybe she's right. Maybe it just muddies the waters, thinking like that.

But what if Fisher really is involved? Could he conceivably be entertaining Raleigh's clients with Raleigh's own daughter? Is all this help and sympathy just a front? No. That would be an insane thing to do. If that was the case, and Raleigh found out, Fisher would be finished. I wouldn't put it past Raleigh to actually have Fisher killed. I'm sure he has the contacts for something like that.

'You were telling me about Fisher's search history.'
'Oh yes.'

She finishes what's left of her dessert and drains her

glass of champagne. I refill it. Her face is a little flushed now. She's enjoying herself. I'm glad. She's nice.

'It was all websites for very, very expensive call girls. I'm no expert, but they all looked top of the range to me. All very beautiful. Like models. Some of them had their faces blanked out, some of them it was just the eyes. Others, you could see their faces clearly. They were usually dressed in lovely evening gowns, though many of them were in lingerie or swimwear.'

'Expensive? The girls, I mean?'

'God, yes. Average was something like a thousand an hour, two thousand for a dinner date and almost four thousand for overnight. I imagine they'd spend a fortune on clothes and grooming. And shoes! But now I think of it they didn't really look like models. Not British ones, anyway. British models look too quirky. These had a bit too much forced glamour. More like high end Page Three girls, if anything. Or maybe glamour models. The sort of girls you'd see in saucy lingerie catalogues, not that I've ever browsed through anything like that.'

'Of course not; me neither. How long has Fisher worked for Mr Raleigh?'

'I don't know. Certainly before I arrived on the scene. One of the girls told me that Fisher was head of security when that kidnap attempt happened and that was about three years ago. He wasn't present when it actually happened, but I think Mr Raleigh was a bit annoyed at him, and she said that Fisher had become much more of a suck-up since that time. It was as if he was always trying to prove himself, even though there was nothing he could have done about the kidnapping stuff. I suppose the search thing they tried on you was one of the side effects of that.'

'You're probably right. I should be careful looking at other people's computers like that, though. There are a million ways of telling what someone's been looking at and at what time.'

I finish my dessert and place my spoon by the side of the bowl. 'Would you like anything else? A coffee or something?'

'We could have coffee at my place, if you like.'

'Sure.'

After several attempts, I manage to attract the attention of a waitress and pay the bill. As we leave, I slip my arm around Anjukka's waist and she moves in close. I must find out what that perfume is.

The evening is still warm as we stroll down towards Oxford Street. I'm still having problems connecting Fisher's perusal of call girl sites with Viola. It's almost certainly part of his job to procure girls for Raleigh's clients and he would know what Viola had been up to, but the more I think about it the more I'm inclined to think that it's just a coincidence. It could be that he's the sort of man who hires call girls for himself.

Just as we walk past The Old Explorer pub I get a little moment of light-headedness, as if someone's attention is on me, and I know we're being followed.

# 9

## BURNED IN LIBERTY'S

I don't know who this is, who they work for or what they want, but I'm damned if I'm going to let it ruin my evening with this girl. We keep walking at the same slow pace, enjoying being in such close proximity.

We cross the road at Great Castle Street and I manage a quick glance behind us in the reflection of one of Ponti's windows. There's an unshaven man in his forties in a bright red Vans hoodie and faded black 501s on the same side as us. He's got a big spirit level slung over his shoulder and is smoking a small cigar.

On the other side of the road, a middle-aged woman in a dark red business suit carrying a pale green leather tote bag is looking in the window of a branch of BHS. The window display is all beach towels, deck chairs and picnic hampers. The woman. The bag. The display. Her interest level. Not right. It's her.

'Where do you live?' I say to Anjukka, just to keep things as normal as possible under the circumstances.

'I never give my address to strange men.'

'Is that right?'

'You never know who might turn up in the middle of the night.'

I spin her around so that she's facing me. 'How do I

make myself a little less strange to you?'

As we kiss, she presses her body close to mine. I hold her waist firmly just beneath her breasts. I look up to see Tote Bag walk slowly away from the window she was inspecting. This is a bad road to loiter in without looking conspicuous and she knows it. I suddenly get the whole plan in my head, complete in every detail. It's not perfect and it's a little risky, but it's the best I can do after drinking two Black Velvets and the best part of a bottle of champagne.

I disengage from Anjukka. Her lips are parted and she's panting slightly. 'I live in Battersea. Do you know it?'

'I've heard of it. And you've definitely got coffee? I wouldn't want to get there and find you only had tisanes or something.'

'I've definitely got coffee. And I'm sure you'll like the taste of it.'

'I'm sure I will. Let's walk down to Regent Street. Better chance of getting a cab coming up from Piccadilly.'

She gives me an arch look. 'Are you in a hurry?'

'No hurry. We could even look in Liberty's, if you like.'

'I love Liberty's.'

We continue our slow pace as we walk down to Oxford Street. We're now holding hands. Ditching a tail while accompanied by a woman wearing an ostentatious, strapless, green, red and orange dress is not something I've ever done before. I also have to keep it a secret from her that we're being followed. I don't want her to get frightened and I don't want her to turn around and look at Tote Bag, who doesn't yet know I've pinned her, but she soon will.

We cross over to the south side of Oxford Street. Once again I check out what's behind me in the big window of an optician. My new friend is staying on the other side of the road but still tracking us. Very smooth. She's looking in shop windows like I am. I think she's alone.

'You know,' I say, keeping up a normal-looking conversation for Tote Bag's benefit, 'if I manage to track down Viola, I'll get quite a big bonus.'

'What are you going to spend it on?'

We turn right into Regent Street. The crowds are thick and chaotic, which is good. If I was on my own I'd have lost her by now. We keep to the west side of the street.

'You're going to laugh. Or be appalled.'

'I'm intrigued. Tell me.'

Out of the corner of my eye, I can see the pale green tote bag and the red business suit about six yards behind me on the other side of the road. It's a bad colour combination; too conspicuous and jarring. What is she? Another investigator like me? She needs a bit of advice about her work clothing.

'It was your description about how you'd pose for a nude portrait. As soon as you started talking about it, I thought that it would be a portrait I'd like to see.'

'Oh, *would* it now?' Her eyes are sparkling at the idea.

'So are you about to laugh or are you appalled?'

She laughs. 'I'll tell you later.'

It's getting more crowded. We push through the ever-increasing surge of pedestrians and tourists and I keep getting jostled in the shoulder. I have my hand on Anjukka's waist and gently guide her in the right direction. We're opposite Great Marlborough Street now, and cross the road to get to Liberty's. The traffic is hell and we almost fall victim to a black cab, then a cyclist, but it gives me an excuse to look from left to right. Tote Bag has dropped back about six yards and pretends to look for something in her bag. She acted quickly when she saw we were about to head in her direction.

Still behaving casually, we head for Liberty's main entrance, my hand now resting on Anjukka's bottom. This is not how someone who suspected they were being followed would act. At least I hope not.

'It would have to be a female artist, of course,' I say, as we enter the main part of the store. We walk around casually, just like a normal couple.

'Goes without saying.' she replies, running her hand over a selection of expensive silk scarves. 'Although a man I don't know seeing me naked has a certain *je ne sais quoi* to it.'

I turn swiftly and face the main entrance. Tote Bag would have had time to catch up with us and could be in here by now, but she's holding back and I can understand why. When someone you're following comes into a place like this, you might find yourself face to face with them as soon as you walk through the door, with whatever consequences they decide upon.

There's another entrance at the side of the building that leads into the perfume department, which is where we seem to be heading. Tote Bag could stand at the corner of the building and observe both exits. I don't make any suggestions as to what we might look at. I let Anjukka make all the decisions for the sake of randomness.

'Although you may find that posing for a painting is a little boring,' I say. 'I think you'd have to sit still for a long time.'

She sprays a sample of a perfume called Carnal Flower onto her wrist and holds it up for me to smell. Very strong scent of tuberose and some notes I can't identify.

'I don't think sitting still for a long time would be hard work, do you?' she says, smiling.

'Perhaps they'd let you watch a movie.'

'Pornographic?'

'Action/adventure.'

She starts looking at various makeup counters and I move away from her to get a better view of the entrance area. I tell her I'm just going to have a quick look at the stationery. As I'm half way across, I see Tote Bag. She's pretty smart and she held back for a few minutes before coming in. It's a risky strategy as we could have been on the third floor by now, but in her case it still won't work.

She hasn't seen me yet, but she's scanning the store as if she's looking for a friend, while examining the scarves. If I was her, I'd be looking for Anjukka's conspicuous dress. I swiftly take my jacket off and let it drop to the floor. When she's scanning for me her brain will be locked into 'black leather blazer', not 'pale blue shirt'. This deception won't last long, but I don't need very long.

A security guy is wandering around by the handbags, trying to look inconspicuous, but his darting eyes identify him to me straight away, and the fact that he's inspecting handbags, and the fact that he's wearing a smart Hugo Boss suit to go shopping in. Someone needs to talk to him, but it's not going to be me. The store is closing fairly soon and he probably thinks another boring day is over. He's watching two French girls wiggle by and isn't focussed on ordinary customers. Good.

I approach him in a chummy, matey way, like I'm an

ordinary bloke who's just trying to help. He gives me a hard stare.

'Excuse me, mate. I'm sorry to bother you and I know it's none of my business, but that lady in the red suit holding the green bag over there has just stuffed three of your Vivienne Westwood scarves into it. Thought I'd better tell someone. Cheers.'

He frowns, looks at me, and then looks straight at Tote Bag. She sees the both of us staring at her and knows she's been rumbled. She looks flustered and as guilty as hell, which only serves to convince him I'm telling the truth. He nods to a grim-looking, trainee Sumo colleague who I didn't notice and who comes up behind her and gently takes her arm.

'Thanks, mate,' says Security Man.

'That's alright, squire.'

I collect my jacket and return to Anjukka, who's spraying something called Carthusia over her neck.

'Shall we go?' I say. 'I'm starting to get a craving for that coffee.'

We step out of the store and I hail a cab.

On the way to Battersea, Anjukka and I engage in small talk, eavesdropped upon by the cab driver who occasionally interjects with useless comments about the weather and/or traffic. I rest a hand on the top of her nearest thigh and sporadically dig my fingernails into her flesh. She slaps my hand but doesn't make any attempt to remove it. She smells like Liberty's perfume department and it's pretty intoxicating.

I'm still thinking about Tote Bag. There is no doubt that she was a professional, just not a very good one, at least not for the job she'd been given. There are a lot of people from my past who would have good cause to have me followed, but none of them would hire people who were that easy to shake off.

So who was she? My first thought is that Raleigh was having me tailed to make sure I was doing my job properly. That sounds ridiculous, but you never know. But if that's what was going on, why not hire someone a little better? And why do it in the evening, when I probably wouldn't be working? Perhaps he didn't want to spend any more money on private investigators than he absolutely had to. Perhaps whichever company he hired told him that they were very good. Perhaps they *were* very good, but one of their operators had the bad luck to be following me.

Another possibility is that they were following Anjukka. Now why would someone be doing that? My train of thought naturally returns to Raleigh, maybe Fisher. But what would their motive be? Perhaps Fisher is stalking her in some roundabout way. Maybe some PI's daily reports about what she's been doing turn him on. Anjukka said that Fisher and some others had been hitting on her. Is someone there checking on whether she's really got a fiancé?

It's a possibility to keep in mind, but my gut instinct is that it was me that was the target. This is unsettling, mainly because it demonstrates to someone that I can spot a tail and lose it less than five minutes without really trying and while I've got company. To be honest, I really can't be bothered thinking about it right now, but I'll ratchet my vigilance up a few notches just the same.

Anjukka lives on the seventh floor of a smart, modernistic block of apartments with a view of the duck pond in Battersea Park. Just after the taxi dropped us off, the driver murmured, 'Some people have all the luck.' I'm not sure whether he was referring to the fact that she lived in such a nice place or whether I was the lucky one for having my arm around the waist of such a beautiful woman.

Inside, her apartment is light and airy with white being the predominant colour. Everything looks new, and I'm reminded of one of those fabulous places you see advertised in the back of glossy magazines.

Despite the size of the place, she's kept it sparse and free of clutter. In what I assume is the main living area, there's a black leather sofa in front of an enormous television, a big wooden coffee table, four sizeable bookshelves containing either books or ornaments, and a black leather chaise longue beneath the large windows. There's also a small glass dining table with four chairs.

I can see two stereo speakers on the wall to my left, and there's a Bowers & Wilkins wireless music system lying on the coffee table. The white of the walls is only broken by two predominantly dark blue prints, Lady with Hat by Klimt and Donna in Blu by de Lempicka.

'Wow,' I say, grinning. 'This is a great place.'

'Oh, stop it.'

'I mean it! It's fabulous. I'm going to live here. Let's get married.'

'Would you like the grand tour?'

'Let's go.'

We head into the kitchen, which is white like everywhere else here. 'This place was too expensive for me really,' she says, 'so I made sure I got high quality basic stuff to fill it up with; stuff that wouldn't break down in a hurry.'

'Good idea. It looks good. Very minimalistic.'

The kitchen has a central food preparation area with

an inbuilt chopping board. There's a microwave above the oven hob and an impressive collection of juicers, food processors, electric knife sharpeners and the like. I start to wonder how much Raleigh is paying her. Of course, it may not be just from him; she's been working for a while now. Perhaps her parents helped her out with all of this.

'This is the kitchen.'

'Really?'

'We'll return here shortly for that coffee I promised you.'

'I hope so.'

I follow that sexy, swaying walk along a hall. She points towards another white room.

'Bathroom. Bedroom one. Bedroom two. Office.'

Bedroom one is like the main living area in negative; powder blue walls and white linen on the bed, a black and white print of a laughing Sophia Loren, big wardrobes and a transparent thing containing loads of pairs of shoes. Bedroom two is full of plastic boxes like the storage ones you see in Staples. The office has a small table with an eleven-inch MacBook Air, another, smaller bookshelf filled with paperbacks and a small chest of drawers which is covered in magazines.

We head back to the kitchen and she starts making the coffee. I'm surprised to find that she uses a cafetière, as opposed to some hi-tech machine that fills a whole wall. As she waits for the kettle to boil, she excuses herself and pops into the bathroom. When she emerges a minute later, she's reapplied her lipstick. She pours two cups and we sit down opposite each other at the dining table.

'So how did you become a private investigator, Daniel?'

Here we go. I really haven't got the energy to lie, but

I've got to find that energy from somewhere. I sip my coffee to give myself a few seconds to think of something convincing. Anjukka is not stupid. That's why she's so sexy.

'I worked in insurance, investigating suspicious claims. The job entailed a lot of fieldwork and you were given special training to cover all the possibilities that you might encounter. I went on courses run by people who had worked in corporate security and eventually picked up enough skills to go freelance. I got bored with the insurance stuff after a while and branched out into different areas, like the job I'm working on now.'

It's getting better with each telling.

'I guess the money's better, too,' she says, grinning. 'Particularly if you're considering blowing a huge bonus on commissioning a nude portrait of someone you've only just met.'

'I'm impulsive that way. You said that you'd tell me later whether you were about to laugh or be appalled at my impudent suggestion.'

'Oh, I'd forgotten about that.'

'I don't doubt that for a second. Well, this is later. Have you made your mind up?'

'I don't think I'd laugh and I don't think I'd be appalled, either.'

'So you'd be…?'

'Interested. That would be the word I'd use.' She laughs and bites her lower lip. 'Only if you're paying, of course. I'm not as wealthy as this place might suggest.'

'Goes without saying. After all, it'll be hanging in my bedroom.'

'Hold on.'

She smiles at me, gets up and vanishes down the

hallway into bedroom one. I can't imagine what's going to happen next. My mind drifts back to Tote Bag. What is she going to say to whoever her employer/employers was/were? 'Sorry sir/madam/whatever, I was professionally burned in Liberty's handbag section by some sort of counter surveillance expert with superb situational awareness even though he was mildly plastered and with a girl?'

Anjukka returns wearing a dark blue silk kimono loosely tied with a white sash belt. I try my best not to look too astonished. She sits down opposite me again. Out of that dress, her breasts are wider and fuller. I know she's aware of this. I want to take her; immediately, fiercely, and I know she'd respond, but I'm enjoying the tension.

'I think the difference between the portrait that Mrs Raleigh had and the one that I, in theory, would have, would be that she was basically in a state of undress.' As she says this, she tightens the sash belt around her waist, emphasising her curves a little more, in case I'd missed them.

'And you said, I recall, that if you were going as far as exposing your breasts for a portrait, you may as well go all the way.' I take a sip of coffee as my mouth is getting dry.

'That's right.'

'So, no fur coat, no pulled down dress, just you with an accent on your best features.'

'Which best features would those be?' she says, rubbing her shoulder and allowing the robe to slip down very slightly.

'I think you mentioned your bottom.'

'Did I?'

'Yes. And you mentioned posing on an ordinary chair,

as opposed to an armchair.'

'Or the chaise longue over there. Shall I try a few poses out, just in case you have to talk to anyone about this? It's always best to be prepared for things.'

'I think that would be a good idea.'

She stands and walks over to the chaise longue. I get up and follow. She turns to face me and lifts up the sash belt in her hand. 'Would you mind?'

I pull the belt down. She shakes her shoulders and the kimono falls to the floor. She turns and heads towards the chaise longue. That sexy, swaying walk is really something. She's right about her bottom being one of her best features, though it isn't the only one. She lies on the chaise longue and runs both hands through that mane of thick, jet-black hair.

# 10

## *L'OPINION D'UN ARTISTE*

In the morning, Anjukka wakes before me and is in the shower while my eyes are still shut. It's a few minutes past seven and she has to get to Holland Park earlier than usual, to catch up on some preparation work for a meeting that Raleigh has at ten o' clock. Raleigh has an important visitor; some banking guy or other who's involved with the money for Raleigh's upcoming big Oman deal.

She comes back into the bedroom wrapped in a dark blue towel and I sit up in her bed and watch her dry her hair, apply her makeup and get dressed. She spends ages on her hair. I wasn't sure that I believed her when she said that she hadn't been on a date for two years, but after last night I can see that it was true.

It's only now that the memory of Tote Bag pops into my mind. I'm still unsettled by that, and the more I think about it, the more I suspect that Raleigh was behind it, but once again, I can't really imagine why. As Anjukka continues to work on her hair, I get up and look out of the window.

The road outside is covered in various markers to stop motorists parking or even stopping, so there are no suspicious cars or vans. I can see three people walking down the road. One is a guy holding a skateboard under his arm and the other two are a pair of women in smart business suits on their way to work.

I turn back to Anjukka, who's now in her underwear and attaching the metal clips of her six strap suspender belt to her stockings. She looks great. I really must look into getting her portrait done today if I have any time. I have to get back to my flat for a change of clothing, so I'll have a quick Google before getting on with the day's work.

I'm getting ahead of myself, of course. I still have to find Viola so I can get my bonus, otherwise I won't be able to afford anything. Actually, I have no idea how much a portrait costs or how long it would take, but the concept has taken root in my head now and I just know that I have to have it.

I promise to call Anjukka as I leave and walk down the road where she lives, which is already starting to get very busy. The advantage of this is that I get a cab almost immediately. On my way to Covent Garden, I start to think about Mrs Bianchi and wonder what she's like. This is assuming, of course, that Novak's information was good. What sort of woman *buys* a girl like Viola off a scumbag like Novak? I guess she has to be some sort of major scumbag herself.

I almost call the number that Novak gave me, but decide it's too early. I take the piece of paper with Bianchi's address on and stare at it. She lives in a house in Portman Street. That's virtually around the corner from Seymour Street police station, which makes it almost certain that she was the person who reported Viola as missing. She could even have done it on foot. I'm vaguely aware of the houses in Portman Street; Edwardian listed buildings that are either business premises or expensive flat conversions. This area is dead in the centre of the West End, where your local supermarket would be Selfridge's, so you'd have to be fairly wealthy to live there.

I get the cab to drop me off by The Royal Opera House and walk down the whole length of Floral Street, checking reflections and executing sudden stops by random shop fronts. By the time I'm down the bottom of Garrick Street, I know I'm clean.

The next time I feel a tail and I'm alone, I'm going to turn the tables on whoever it is and tail *them*. It's probably still too early for someone to be following me, and I'd guess that Tote Bag is going to spend this morning convincing her bosses that she's still worth employing after yesterday's fiasco, but if whoever set her on me is persistent, she'll be replaced by someone else, so I have to keep on my toes.

When I finally get back, I dump yesterday's clothes in the washing basket, fire up the computer and take a long shower. I get a strange feeling that I haven't done enough yet, but then remember that, strictly speaking, I'm only at the beginning of day two. I must learn to relax more, but it's difficult.

I sit down with a coffee and look for female portrait artists. I must be entering the wrong combination of words as nearly everything that comes up is to do with photography, boudoir photography in particular, which seems to be an up-and-coming industry.

Eventually, after inserting the words 'oil' and 'paint', about half a dozen possibles in the central London area appear. Unfortunately, most of them seem to be out in the suburbs and many of them work from photographs, which is not what I want. One or two look quite good, but they're too reasonably priced; if the artists were that good, they'd be charging a lot more.

Then one in Bond Street catches my eye. Usually this is a place associated with massively expensive original art, but the address says 'second floor', so maybe it's not connected to a professional dealer. I don't mind spending money on this, but I don't want the bill to run into millions.

I peruse the site as I dial Mrs Bianchi's number. It's almost nine o' clock and whatever her occupation she should be thinking of getting up by now. If not, it's just tough. Predictably, though, there's no response from the number that Novak gave me. If I find out that that fucker's taken my three hundred for nothing, I'll be extremely upset. I get a feeling of nausea just thinking about him and his whole putrid attitude, particularly when he was bragging about what Jeremy and his pals got up to with Viola.

I'll have to go to the Portman Street address and hope I have more luck there. I'm a little annoyed, as I hate making cold calls; the look on people's faces when they open the door to you and the fact that you have to explain yourself to them while standing in the street. Plus the frequent displays of incredulity that you're a private investigator. It never fails to bug me.

This artist with the studio in Bond Street is Louisa Gavreau and she specialises in nude portraiture of women, but will also do men. Perhaps men don't mind being painted nude by a woman as much as women mind being painted nude by a man. Who knows? There's a gallery of portraits she's done on her site and they all look pretty good to me, though not all are nudes. There are no prices, though, which is a bit of a pain. Maybe each portrait is priced according to what the client wants. I decide to give her a call to get it out of the way. She answers instantly, which I always like.

'Yes?'

'Good morning. Is that Louisa Gavreau?'

'Yes it is. How can I help you?'

Scottish. Probably Edinburgh. With that surname I was expecting a French accent. Aged between forty and fifty, at a guess.

'My name's Daniel Beckett. A female friend of mine wants to have a nude portrait done and I want to get it for her as a gift. She'd prefer to have a female artist paint her. I'm in your area this morning and I was wondering, if it's not too inconvenient, if I could pop in and see you for a chat about what has to be done.'

'In the area this morning are you? Um, I suppose that would be alright. Do you know where I am?'

'I've got your site up in front of me as I speak. The Old Bond Street address?'

'Yes, that's the one.'

'Would nine-thirty be OK for you?'

'Nine-thirty? I can't see why not.'

'OK. I'll see you then. Thank you.'

'I'm above the Sarah Chaisty Fine Art gallery. You can't miss it. There are big purple abstracts in both windows. Appalling. Just press my buzzer.'

I decide to walk to Bond Street and stop off at a cashpoint to get out some more bribery money on my way there. If I spend half an hour talking to this woman, I can get a coffee and a snack when I'm finished and be up at Portman Street at about ten-thirty to see Mrs Bianchi, if she still lives there, or if she even exists.

If she does exist and if her proximity to the police station at Seymour Street makes her the person I need to talk to, I can then get on with visiting The Bolton Mayfair. I want to cram as much into this day as I possibly can.

As I walk along Piccadilly, I realise that Bond Street isn't that far from the hotel. I may walk past it after I've sorted this visit out, just to have a look, if nothing else. I can't have walked down Bond Street for years and there are more fashionable clothing shops than I remembered. There's still a lot of work going on here, though, and there are skips and scaffolding everywhere.

Suddenly, I get a feeling that there's someone with me. I cross over the road and look sharply to the left, as if looking for oncoming traffic. There's a middle-aged man in a cream suit walking away from me on the other side of the road, an elderly woman in a huge fur coat with a walking stick, a girl in a short yellow skirt with five- or seven-inch heels and great legs, a fat guy in an oversized powder blue suit yapping into his mobile in a language that could be Armenian. No eye contact, no unusual or sudden moves. Maybe I'm just getting progressively more paranoid.

The Sarah Chaisty Fine Art gallery is on the left of Bond Street as you walk up from Piccadilly. It's one of the older buildings here and the front is well-kept redbrick. As Ms Gavreau said, there are two large windows with purple abstracts. I look up to the second floor, perhaps hoping to see her leaning out and waving to me. Ornate cast iron balconies front each window. This must have been a very fashionable address once upon a time, but I'm not sure about now. Shops and galleries moved in as families moved out.

Just as I'm about to press Louisa Gavreau's buzzer, my mobile bleeps and there's a message from Anjukka. She's been in Raleigh's office, hopefully when no one was around, and has taken a photograph of Rosabel's portrait. Below are the words 'Don't forget!'

It makes me smile. This is all rather insane and rushed, but I want this done for her and she wants it done for me. Neither of us have analysed it; it just feels right. Actions like this take us both a little further from reality, which is fine by me; reality's overrated.

I make my way up a narrow staircase and Louisa Gavreau is waiting for me on her landing.

'Mr Beckett? Please come in.'

I follow her down a hallway and we turn left into her flat. I'm surprised. Somewhere in my head, I'd been expecting some clichéd version of an artist's studio, with paint all over the floor, canvases propped up against walls and wooden easels. This is just like someone's flat.

'So what did you think of the art in the window downstairs?' she asks. 'Don't think. Just your immediate impression.'

'It was very...purple.'

'My thoughts exactly. Some Russian artist that Miss Chaisty is sweet on at the moment. I think it's condescending, personally. Perhaps even racist or borderline fascist. If any British artist had come up with such tripe, you can bet your life it wouldn't be being sold within a hundred miles of Bond Street. Still.'

'Yeah,' I say, stupidly.

'Coffee?'

'Yes please. White, no sugar.'

I sit down on an amazing fake tiger skin sofa. The whole place is entirely decorated with such items. Everything on the wall is pop art and there's a huge Andy Warhol print of Jackie Kennedy above the fireplace.

Looking at the building from the outside, you'd never imagine this interior. Louisa Gavreau is older than my assessment from her voice. Probably in her mid-fifties or early sixties, salt and pepper hair in a pageboy, slim, attractive and dressed entirely in black. No shoes. Tattoo of a green bird on her left ankle.

'So this is your girlfriend who wants the portrait, yes?'
'Well, sort of.'
'Sort of portrait?'
'Sort of girlfriend.'
'Birthday present?'
'Ordinary present.'
'And she wants a nude; no clothing at all, no subtle draperies, no breasts peeking shyly out of loose-fitting blouses, a total absence of coyness, demureness and modesty?'
'She thinks that if you're going to show your breasts, you may as well go all the way.'
'Quite right.'
'And she'd like to sit on a chair or a chaise longue.'
'Well, I'm going to tell you two things, either one of which may or may not put you or your sort of girlfriend off. First, the time that one of my portraits will take. I'm a fast worker and can usually manage something you'll both be pleased with in two sittings. Each sitting will last a minimum of five hours. Having said that, it might take longer and I may need to get the sitter back a few times after the last sitting. It's unpredictable. The sittings can be spread out if you wish, though it's better if they're done as close together as possible. I realise that people work in real jobs, so I'm prepared to work weekends and will do evenings as well.'
'And the second thing?'

'The second thing that may or may not put you or your sort of girlfriend off is the price. For what I have just described, I will charge three thousand pounds.'

'Fine.'

'Fine? Good. In cash, if you can manage. Cheques reluctantly received. Come in here.'

I get up and follow her into a large room with no windows. She puts the light on. It's like an art gallery of her work. About half of them are female nudes. All superb, realistic and sexual; far better than I could possibly have imagined from the material on her website. I take a close look at a ravishingly erotic painting of a short-haired, full-bosomed woman who is kneeling down looking into a large wall mirror, so that her body can be seen from the back and from the front. It's hard to see any brush strokes.

'You like that one? She complained and complained about that pose, the silly mare. Kneeling down sounds like an easy thing to do, but it's murder on the calves and the front of the ankles after half an hour. Still, it's a good effect. She was very proud of her breasts and of her bottom, so I thought it was a clever way of getting them equal attention.'

'It's incredible.'

'Thank you. I don't put these ones on my site for the sake of my sitters. Many of them value their privacy, for some reason. When I've finished a portrait, if I'm pleased with it, I'll have it photographed and framed. That is what you see in here.'

'They're fantastic. I can't wait to see what you'll do with my sort of girlfriend.'

'What's her name?'

'Anjukka York.'

'Well, I'll certainly remember that. Here's my card. Get her to text me or call me and we'll set up an appointment or appointments. I just hope she doesn't mind sitting still for hours on end. Many of them do, you know. They complain about it like the one you were just looking at. I tell them to go and get some of those passport photographs done if they want speed and comfort. It's the way I work and they can stuff it if they don't like it. She can bring her own music if she likes, as long as it's something that I want to listen to as well.'

'Sure. I'll let her know,' I say. I hadn't thought of that. I suppose you have to have some sort of stimulus to alleviate the possible boredom caused by sitting still for so long. I just imagined that the artist and the sitter would have an interesting chat, but even an interesting chat can't be sustained for five hours.

'Do you live in different places? You and your sort of girlfriend?'

'Yes.'

'Whose place is this painting going to be in when it's finished? Yours or hers?'

'Does it make a difference to what you'll do?'

'If it's for you and it's something you'll be seeing every day, I can add a certain erotic undercurrent that you'll find stimulating.'

'Well, I haven't thought about who'll be having it. Add the undercurrent anyway.'

'All right. Was it your idea?'

'Her having a nude portrait done? Not really. It was just something we were talking about. There's a nude where she works and she was just saying that it wasn't the sort of thing that she would have had done. Or rather, she would do it in a different way. In fact…'

I get my mobile out and find Anjukka's message.

'…she texted me this photograph of it when she got into work this morning.'

'Well-known nude? Venus Verticoria? Something like that?'

'No. It was commissioned fairly recently. It's her boss's wife.'

'Can I see?'

'Of course.'

I hand her the mobile and she squints at the portrait of Rosabel Raleigh. She then produces a pair of half-moon reading glasses and squints again. We walk back into her living room, or whatever it is. Now I can spot a couple of banks of lights on the ceiling that I hadn't noticed. This must be the room she does her painting in.

'Well this is no bloody good. This is tiny. Can I take?'

She holds up my mobile and walks over to her computer. She draws a wire out of the CPU and attaches it to my mobile. She sits down and taps a few times on the keyboard and Rosabel's image pops up on her computer, filling the nineteen-inch screen. She stares at the image for a while without saying anything.

'Interesting.'

'Anjukka didn't really see the point of the fur coat or having just a skirt on or whatever…'

'It isn't a skirt, it's a dress. The dress has been pulled down to show the breasts. Do you know who the artist is?'

'No idea.'

'She's very beautiful, isn't she? The style is vaguely impressionistic and this type of pose is quite old fashioned now. Just my opinion, of course, you can take it or leave it. It's a bit of conceit, is what I mean. She wants to show off her body, but at the same time she wants you to know she's got a fur coat.' She leans forwards with both hands resting on the desk and looks more closely at the image on the screen. 'There's something a little odd about it, don't you think?'

'Odd? In what way?'

'Hard to put your finger on. How old is she? Do you know?'

'No. I would say she was mid-thirties.'

'You're probably right. When was this painted? Any idea?'

'At least ten years ago, I would guess.'

'Obviously the artist has taken certain liberties in the way he or she has painted this woman; it isn't entirely realistic, but then who wants a bloody photograph?'

'So what's so odd about it?'

'The way the eyes and the mouth have been painted. If this was done from life, it's a little sloppy in some ways. Was the person who commissioned this rich, by any chance?'

'I would say so, yes.'

'So this would have to be someone pretty good, or at least pretty expensive. Even so, the pose is a little strange. I think if you were having your wife painted, the idea of having her dress pulled down to reveal her breasts and then to have a fur coat on her lap – well, it's not what people would normally have done. On top of that, her posture is slightly odd, the way the arm rests on the coat and the aspect of her shoulders compared to the position of her head.

'And her facial expression is slightly unusual. That look in the eyes and the pouting lips, I think they were not taken from life. Just intuition, really. Intriguing. The more you look at it, the odder it becomes. Of course, many portrait painters strive to make the painting more attractive than the reality; it's often what the subject or the commissioner asks for. Sometimes portrait painters do it even if it *isn't* asked for.'

'I don't understand what you're trying to say.'

'Could you text me that painting? I'd like to text it to someone else. It won't take long. If it's alright with you, that is.'

'Of course.'

I have no idea what this is all about. I forward Anjukka's text message to the mobile number on Louisa's business card. A couple of seconds later I hear her mobile bleep. She takes a look at the image, fiddles with her mobile and then starts to call someone.

'My sister,' she says to me. 'I'm just going to forward this to her and then have a quick chat. She's a doctor. It may be a waste of time, of course. She might even be busy, shovelling some patient's intestines back in.'

'Fine by me. I'm in no hurry.'

She waits for a while as her sister's number rings. She looks mildly irritated as no one answers straight away, then her face brightens.

'Leonie? Me. Did you get that text? Have you got any means of blowing it up to a decent size wherever you are at the moment?'

She covers the wrong part of the mobile with her hand and looks at me. 'She's in her office at the hospital.'

'Good.'

I still don't know what's going on. She's back on her mobile again.

'Yes. Yes, I know these things are too bloody slow. Well, maybe it's your computer. I suppose they're still steam-powered in the NHS are they? I'm fine. Corin got rid of his car afterwards. Yes. They were asking too much to have it repaired so he gave it up as a bad job. Ha ha. You saw them? Bloody awful, aren't they? OK. Have you got it on a decent screen now? I'd like your immediate impression. Don't bother thinking about it. Just say the first thing that comes into your head. Yes. Yes. Ah. Well that's interesting. I had a feeling about that but common sense overrode. No, I don't know her. Some person I've got here. Are you still OK for Saturday? OK. OK. OK, darling. Later. *Ciao.*'

She places her mobile next to the computer and folds her arms. I notice that she has a long, faded scar down the whole length of her left forearm. Painting accident?

'My sister doesn't know much about art, I'm afraid. But as soon as she saw that painting she said that someone had done a very, very good job of disguising a Hippocratic countenance. Not so good, though, that she couldn't spot it. She was always the brainbox of the family, though I was actually better at science in school that she was. People never believe that, but it's true.'

I have to laugh now. I'm totally lost. 'Sorry – what's a Hippocratic countenance?'

'It's a painting of a corpse, dear. Very well executed, that goes without saying. It could even be said to be a true work of art in the technical sense. It's almost like something one of these Britart types might have thought up in the Nineties. You look at her and you think what a beautiful sexy woman she is; the come-hither eyes, the succulent mouth, the pert breasts, the hard nipples.

'You'd need the combination of an artist and a medical person to spot something like that and even then it might pass you by. It's possible that the subject was preserved in some way or other. Embalmed or something. That's just a guess. Personally, as a professional portrait painter, I can't imagine a more disturbing commission, or, while we're at it, a more disturbing scenario. In fact, I get a little shiver down my spine just thinking about such a thing. Imagine trying to sleep at night while something like that was sitting in your studio. Yuk. On the other hand, it would certainly deter burglars!'

I get a little surge of adrenaline and my mouth is dry. 'Could I have another coffee, please?'

'Certainly.'

I sit down and look hard at the image of Rosabel Raleigh on the computer screen. Despite what I've just been told, I still can't see it and I don't really believe it. It's too early in the morning for this sort of thing. My brain isn't capable of assimilating this type of information and all its repercussions.

'Coffee.'

'Thanks.'

'I'm sorry, darling. You look a bit rattled. I hit you with that pretty hard, didn't I!'

She laughs. It's a sexy, throaty laugh.

'I wouldn't say I was rattled. More like *baffled*. It's just, it's what – what, why the fuck would you get someone to paint your wife's embalmed corpse? It's crazy. Having them embalmed – if that's what's happened – having them embalmed in the first place would be bad enough, but then to have them…'

'Well, what interests me,' says Louisa, lighting an unusually long cigarette, 'is how you would find an artist who would do such a thing? I can't imagine how you'd word it when you rang them up!' She laughs again.

'Have you ever heard of anything like this before?'

'No. But we could be wrong, sweetie. You have to take that into account as well. It was a snap judgment made by two people in a matter of minutes. It's bizarre, certainly, but perhaps it's so bizarre that it couldn't possibly be true. Although, it could be said that the fact we're even talking about it makes it true. Does that make sense? I don't think it does.'

'Let's say it's true. Why would you do it? Let's start with the embalming.'

She takes a deep breath. 'Madly in love with the wife? Couldn't bear to lose her? I must say that I'm no expert on this sphere of life. I assume it's legal in this country?'

'I've no idea whether it's legal or not. I presume it is. Even if it wasn't, this is a guy who could probably pull some strings to make it happen. If you're mega-rich, things like the law don't matter that much.'

'Alright, my love. It's legal. So you've had your darling wife stuffed or whatever…'

It's no good; both of us crack up laughing at her use of the word 'stuffed'. It takes us a couple of minutes to recover.

'OK,' I say. 'She's been stuffed, embalmed, whatever, but that still isn't enough for you. You want a sexy portrait of her.'

'Once again, I'm no expert,' says Louisa, smiling broadly, 'but I don't think that an embalmed corpse would last forever. Maybe you'd want to get her immortalised in oils before she started falling apart.'

Another laughing jag ensues. We shouldn't be laughing at this. This is really weird, sad, sinister and disturbing, not funny at all. We continue laughing for a few more minutes.

'So then you'd be looking for a really good artist who

had the stomach for this and who would keep his or her mouth shut,' I say. 'You'd probably have to sling them a pretty large amount of money. Much more than three thousand pounds.'

The image of Raleigh's currency-stuffed safe pops into my mind and so does the twenty thousand bonus he promised me if I found Viola.

'That, my dear, would be the difficult part. If someone approached me with a job like that, I don't know that I'd do it for any amount. I mean, no one wants money that much, do they? It would be gruesome!'

'Yes they do. A lot of people do. I think if you were wealthy enough and knew where to look you could find someone in a couple of days.'

'Perhaps we're making it out to be too sinister. Perhaps that portrait is the conclusion to one of the great love stories of our time. Perhaps we're looking at a twenty-first century Dante and Beatrice!'

'I don't think so. She committed suicide.'

'You seem to know an awful lot about your sort of girlfriend's employer.'

'Yeah. You pick things up, you know?'

We sit and stare at Rosabel's portrait. Taylor Conway thought that the suicide happened when Viola was about fourteen. Assuming his guess was accurate, that's about ten years ago. So Raleigh's wife commits suicide, he has her embalmed and then he has someone paint her. He keeps the painting in his office and talks about Rosabel in the present tense.

Viola grew up knowing, presumably, that her mother had shot herself. If Louisa and her sister are right about this portrait, and I somehow think they are, Viola may also have grown up with that ghoulish souvenir of her mother always around the house somewhere.

There's no way of knowing whether she realised her mother was painted post mortem, but if she did, the mental and emotional damage would have been considerable, one would guess.

By the time Viola was about twenty, she had a dangerous drug habit, a bunch of weird but essentially harmless friends and was beginning to drift into prostitution. A couple of years later, she was being ruthlessly and sadistically exploited by that fucker Novak and his chief monkey.

Eventually, she pissed Novak off so he sold her to the mysterious Mrs Bianchi. Now Viola's disappeared while on a job and her dad hires me to find her, while possibly having me followed by another private investigator, albeit an inept one. Her dad's lieutenant, Fisher, cruises swanky call girl sites on the Internet, presumably looking for suitable girls for his boss's important scumbag clients.

I think I need to get an A3 pad like Taylor and make a big flowchart with all this stuff on. It's giving me a headache having to think about it. I've got a vague feeling that all these things are connected in some way, but I really can't imagine how at the moment. I suspect, though, that there is information that I don't yet have that would make sense of at least some of this.

I think it's time to break the silence and get out of here.

'OK! Well, thank you very much for your time. I'll get Anjukka to get in touch when she's ready. I'll let her know that I think you're the one. If she should ask, don't tell her how much you charge. Perhaps you could cut the amount in half or something.'

'Will do. Sorry you had such a creepy time here! If you

like, I can text you some photographs of the portraits I showed you in there. I'm sure she'd be interested.'

'Thanks. That would be really useful.' I hand her my business card, which she pings with a forefinger to see if it makes a noise. It doesn't. 'My number's on there.'

'Oh, one more thing, Mr Beckett.'

'Yes?'

'If what we've just been speculating about is all true, then it puts a whole different complexion on certain aspects of that portrait. I mean the breasts being bared in that way and the unmistakable erotic charge that the painting gives off. It did occur to me, well…'

'What? Say it.'

'The top of the dress around her waist could have been like that for two possible reasons. That's if we're right about her being dead while it was being painted. Either the dress was pulled down to expose her breasts for erogenous effect, or they were unable to pull the dress up over her arms because she was inflexible, if you get my meaning.'

'That's certainly something to think about. Thanks again.'

'One more thing. If I was your sort of girlfriend and I was working for the man who had that portrait commissioned, I would seriously think about getting myself another job. Just a thought.'

We shake hands and I walk down the staircase and out into Bond Street, wondering if the man I'm working for is entirely sane.

# 11

## AN UNEXPECTED BEATING

It may be nothing of course. If I can keep the discovery about the Rosabel Raleigh portrait separate from the investigation into Viola's disappearance, then I'll be able to keep on working with a clear head.

I can do this by viewing Nathan Raleigh as nothing more than an eccentric millionaire who had his heart broken. He married a beautiful woman who was perhaps mentally disturbed in some way. She committed suicide, leaving him to bring up a teenage daughter on his own.

The pain was too much for him to bear. He could not endure having Rosabel buried or cremated, but there was another option; he could have her embalmed. The embalmed state would, I presume, not last forever, so as one final memorial to Rosabel's beauty, he dressed her in some of her favourite clothes and had an oil painting done of her.

Unfortunately, he wasn't able to pull her dress up over her breasts. Couldn't he have put one of her favourite bras on her body before the artist started work, I wonder? Couldn't the artist have painted a bra or some clothing on afterwards? There *must* be paintings where the subject was wearing something different during the sitting. I think of the things that Louisa Gavreau said, particularly the bit about having your darling wife stuffed, and start laughing to myself. The whole thing doesn't really hold water and I put it out of my mind so I can focus on the job in hand.

There's a Costa directly opposite Mrs Bianchi's place in Portman Street, so I go inside and order a coffee. It's still fairly early, this will be my sixth coffee today and I can feel that I'm already grinding my teeth from the caffeine overload. Still, if any emergencies crop up I'll be on high physical alert. It's moderately warm, so I'm able to sit outside and have a good stare at the house.

The address that Novak gave me just said the street number and 'third floor'. I take a long, leisurely look. These are smart, well-kept brick houses from the mid-1800s with shiny black Edwardian front doors, complete with lion's head brass knockers and ornate cast iron boot scrapers. Nasty looking spiked metal railings with gold tops to deter unwanted visitors and window boxes exploding with colour. If you lived here, you'd need money, no doubt about it. But it isn't quiet. This is a busy road, and just looking to my right I can see and hear three separate sets of road works in progress and each one with a couple of pneumatic drills thundering away.

The ground floor is a company of some sort. There's a gold plaque on the wall, but I can't read what it says. Just after the waitress puts my coffee in front of me, two guys in smart pale grey suits come out of the main entrance, laughing at something. One of them holds a slim attaché case, the other one has pink headphones in. Through the window I can see a young woman working on a computer. There's a photographic print on the wall that looks like a car with its headlamps on in thick fog.

There's a secondary entrance to the right of the main one and I presume this is the access to the other floors. I can see a slim silver oblong with three doorbell buttons and small name plaques. This must mean that there is only one occupant on each floor.

The first floor has shutters inside the windows and they're all closed up. Maybe they're on holiday. Above that, is what looks like another office. There are window boxes and ornate cast iron verandas. The window boxes don't have flowers, but have small pine trees and hardy-looking shrubs. During the few seconds I'm looking, I count five different people wandering around, all in business suits, or, in the case of the solitary female, in a dark grey dress, set off by a string of white pearls.

Third floor is Mrs Bianchi, I presume. Looks like all the others. The light reflecting off the windows indicates double or triple glazing. Well, you'd need it around here. Outside, there are well-maintained window boxes with bright red flowers. I try and run through what I'm going to say when I press her button. I just hope she doesn't have some psycho heavy waiting for me like Novak did.

I look at my watch; it's almost ten-thirty. I finish my coffee and stroll across the road, taking a quick look in each direction for traffic and possible tails. There's nothing, or if there is, they're better than Tote Bag.

I press the button next to the name plaque that reads 'S. Bianchi'. I just hope she still lives there. There's a response almost immediately. A soft, cultured, female voice with no discernible foreign accent. Maybe she's not Italian after all. It may not even be her real name.

'Hello?'

'Is that Mrs Bianchi?'

'Yes it is. How may I help you?'

'My name's Daniel Beckett. I'm a private investigator. I'd like to talk to you about Viola Raleigh, if it's convenient. I'm working for her father. I'm afraid I couldn't get you on the telephone.'

There's silence for a few seconds and I wonder if she's heard me or if this intercom is working properly.

'Come on up.'

There's a loud buzzing and a click. I push the door open and go inside. Everything smells new. The staircase is right in front of me. There's no lift. When I get to the third floor, there's only one door, but it doesn't have a buzzer. It has to be the one. I knock gently and in a few seconds it opens.

I mentioned before that beautiful women easily distracted me and the woman who opens the door to me brings a new intensity to the word 'distraction.' I can feel my heart rate increasing as each second goes by.

I would guess that she's in her late thirties, possibly a little older; it's difficult to tell. She has a large white towel wrapped around her body and the flesh on her arms and shoulders is damp and pink. Her hair is jet black, long and soaking wet. I immediately feel bad that I've got her out of the bath or the shower, which is plainly the case. I swallow so that I can speak.

'I'm sorry, I…'

'What can I do for you, Mr Beckett?'

She's certainly one of the most extraordinarily beautiful women I've ever seen. She's wearing no makeup. She doesn't need to. The slightly olive skin, heart-shaped face, high cheekbones and full sensual lips make me think that she's got Italian blood in there somewhere, but her eyes are something else; startlingly and beautifully Japanese, at a guess, but with an exotic and arresting contrast between the epicanthic folds and the iris colour, which is a striking cornflower blue. Her glance is at once seductive and challenging. Please, *please* don't let her be wearing coloured lenses.

She runs a hand through her wet hair, revealing a damp, unshaved armpit, and looks me up and down. She's maybe five foot nine or ten in her bare feet, so the oriental genes didn't show up in her height, and her figure, from what I can discern, is compact, athletic and curvy. God Almighty. I've forgotten why I'm standing here.

'Er, as I said, I'm working for…'

'Nathan Raleigh. Of course. Come in. I've been expecting you.'

Been expecting me? What can she mean by that? Did Novak give her a call? She used Raleigh's first name, which I hadn't mentioned. This must be the right person; she would only know that through Viola.

'Thank you.' I manage a non-astonished, rather cool and polite smile as I walk into her flat. I can sense the warmth and dampness of her skin and pick up a faint smell of jasmine and rose.

'I have a message for your Mr Raleigh,' she says softly, closing the door behind us.

Before I can turn around to speak to her, my whole world explodes.

There's a searing, astonishing pain which starts in my lower back and spreads up the whole right side of my body. It takes me one second to realise that I've been expertly and savagely punched in the kidney. My eyes are squeezed tightly shut and I concentrate on not falling to my knees in agony. Instantly, in a reflex action I can't control, I twist my right hand behind my back to do what? Stop it happening again? Rub it better? This is a terrible mistake.

Mrs Bianchi grabs my wrist and pushes my arm up

behind my back in a powerful hammerlock. I'm still reeling from the kidney punch as she grabs a handful of my hair, jerks my head back and then uses it to test the structural integrity of a very solid wall. I turn my head at the last second to avoid having my nose broken, but it doesn't make much difference to the overall percussive effect. I'm now in considerable pain and probably slightly concussed.

The idea pops into my head that she's trying to kill me. The how or why of it I can sort out later. For now, I've got to do something to neutralise this attack before it gets any worse. She's still got my arm hoicked up hard behind my back. I have to get out of this lock before she dislocates my shoulder or slams me into the wall again. I spread the fingers of my right hand and push my arm right across my back, narrowing the gap between my bicep and ribs. This enables me to twist my arm out of the lock, and as she's still holding on, do a fast three-sixty turn and throw her half way across the room.

I attempt to go down with her at the same speed and immobilise her in some way, but I'm slightly too slow and she's up on her feet again. We're standing about three feet away from each other and she's taken a defensive stance, her centre of balance low. OK. I know where I stand now. This is karate. Judging from the power of that kidney blow, I really mustn't let her land another one on me.

Her eyes are blank and unemotional and I can see she's taking my whole body in while staring straight ahead. This is something that's being done without any passion. It's clinical and professional, which makes it very dangerous.

She moves in towards me and tries a straight punch

aimed beneath my nose and designed to knock my front teeth out. I block this and try to grab her wrist, but she's too fast and uses a middle finger knuckle strike against my temple. She didn't get it quite right, so I'm still here, if a little dazed, and take two steps back to get out of her range for a second.

'Why are you doing this? What the fuck's wrong with you?'

'She told me. She told me that one day he'd send his people here.'

'What are you talking about?'

My back is killing me. She sidles slowly towards me. I can tell she's going to attempt a kick next. I keep my eyes on her whole body. Her gaze quickly flicks across my chest and then my groin area.

She's so fast I barely see the kick coming, even though I was expecting it. Just before it makes contact with my lower chest, I bat it away and try to grab her ankle, but fail. She fires off three more speedy punches aimed at my face and neck and as I block them I can see a faint look of concern flash across her face.

The towel she has wrapped around her body has become loose and I realise what she's going to do before she does it. She grabs the towel and rips it off her body, twirling it like a lasso. There's a half second delay while my dumb, male brain takes in the lithe, sweating body, the wide hips, the thin strip of pubic hair and the exquisite, ripe breasts. That half-second delay is all it takes and she knows it.

I don't know if you've ever had a heavy, damp towel thrown with considerable force wrap itself around your head, but it's an extremely unpleasant sensation. The painful impact, the slap of the material in your face and eyes, the brief fear of suffocation; it's shocking, painful and disorientating. To have this followed up by two skilled karate kicks to the stomach doesn't improve things at all.

I'm down now, and for the first time I think I'm going to come second in this bout. As I scrabble to get the towel off my face and stand up again I feel a strong grip on my throat and start to feel my consciousness going. My assailant tears the towel off my head and for a second I think she's going to use it to break my neck.

My eyes are stinging and watering and I feel like I've been run over by a bus. I look up through my tears to see Mrs Bianchi sitting astride me, her eyes full of hate and her grip on my throat unrelenting. This is the first time I've had the crap kicked out of me by a naked woman, so at least that's something.

'She said it would happen. She said your boss goes crazy at the thought of anyone else touching his daughter. She said I'd get a visit sooner or later. Well you tell your boss that this is what happens, you piece of shit. The next time, I won't be so gentle. You're lucky you're still alive.'

I've got to find some way out of this before she really *does* kill me. I think her main bone of contention is that I work for Raleigh. Well I do, but I don't think I work for him in quite the way that she thinks. First, I do a quick inventory of my body, find out where the worst pain is and try to block it out. The kidney pain is still at the top of the charts, followed by my chest and then my stomach. This isn't over yet. I try and convince myself that this is just an interlude in our fight and that in the second half, victory will be mine. Optimistic, but it's all I've got at present.

'Listen,' I croak. 'I'm not one of…'

She tightens her grip on my throat and forms her left hand into a fist which she draws back, the knuckle of the middle finger prominent and ready to strike. I don't want another one of those in my face so I shut up.

'What did he tell you to do when you got here? Tell me!'

Objectively, this is very good indeed. Very effective and professional and causing a level of pain that makes me want to give up and go to sleep until it's all over. I'm actually feeling fear, and if I was a genuine Raleigh thug like Purple Tie, for example, I'd have spilt any beans I had to spill by now and be begging for mercy. It's awful, but despite everything, I can't stop myself from looking at her breasts. Well, at least she's giving me a chance to speak. She loosens her grip on my throat slightly.

'I'm a private investigator. I've been working for Raleigh for less than forty-eight hours. He employed me to find his daughter. She's been missing for two years. Someone reported her missing again three weeks ago, so he knows she's still alive. I think that person was you. I just want to ask you some questions. I'm not one of Raleigh's heavies.'

'How did you know about me?'

'I went to see Emile Novak. He gave me your address.'

'Who told you about Novak?'

'I'd rather not say for that person's safety. It wasn't anyone connected with Raleigh.'

OK. I've recovered enough to do something about this. While she's pondering my last answer, I simultaneously grab the hand she's choking me with and push the elbow up and across, throwing her face down onto the floor so hard that she almost bounces back up again. I move with her and lock her arm diagonally across her shoulder, while kneeling down by her side. She lets out a small 'ah' as she hits the carpet. She struggles for a second, then realises that she's close to having her shoulder dislocated and quietens down. The muscles of her back ripple as she wriggles and tries to adjust to a less uncomfortable position. Something in my brain is trying to tell me that this is really sexy. I try to block it out.

'Now listen. You're obviously a senior martial artist. You must realise that everything I've done since your initial attack was defensive. You must also realise that I could dislocate your shoulder right now if I wanted to. I didn't come here to hurt you in any way. Viola obviously gave you some sort of warning about her father and the goons who work for him. I am not one of those goons. I've met them, though, and I know the sort of people you may have been expecting and who Viola may have warned you about. Does any of that make sense to you?'

She tries, unsuccessfully, to get up. I'm sitting side-on to her now on my knees, keeping the shoulder lock on with my right arm. I place a hand on the small of her back, to indicate that she should stay where she is.

'But you are still working for him,' she says, her voice muffled by the carpet.

'Yes. That's true. But I've been trying to find the person who reported Viola as missing. The police knew, but wouldn't share the information. I thought that if I could find that person, then I could find out the name that Viola was working under the night she disappeared. Then I could go to the hotel and try and find out what happened. If that person was you, I just want to ask you some questions. You don't even have to answer them if you don't want to. There'll be nothing I can do if that's the case. I'm going to let you go now, OK? Please don't attack me again. I'm probably going to be peeing blood for a week as it is after that kidney punch.'

My eyes are still stinging and watering from having that bloody towel thrown in my face. A very effective ploy, which I must remember the next time I'm in a fight wearing only a wet towel. I slowly reduce the pressure on her shoulder, waiting for any sudden movements. Despite the damage she's inflicted on me, I really don't like inflicting pain on her. I release her shoulder completely and stand up, walking backwards about five paces in case she decides to have another go. For the first time since coming inside, I take a look at her flat.

I hadn't noticed while she was beating the shit out of me, but everything is predominantly green, black and white. It looks stylish and costly and was almost certainly put together by an interior designer. Walls, ceiling and carpets are white, but two of the walls are covered in green and black bamboo photo prints which look as if the same artist did them. There's a huge grey suede sofa with big matching cushions and two black leather and chrome Bauhaus-style chairs around a big, black wooden coffee table. The table is covered in fashion magazines and books.

On the far side of this room there are two doors; one is leading to a flash-looking kitchen and the other looks like a spare room of some sort. When I came in through the front door, there was a corridor to my left, which presumably must lead to the bedrooms and bathroom. The whole place is enormous and must have cost a fortune.

I watch her as she gets up and pats her hair back into place. There's no sign that she's been in any sort of altercation and she acts as if nothing unusual has happened. She's without any self-consciousness regarding her nudity and walks slowly and with poise across the room, staring at me with mild curiosity.

'Would you like a coffee?'

'Thank you, yes. Black with a dash of milk. No sugar.'

'Come in the kitchen.'

I follow her out of this room and into the kitchen, which is somewhere down the corridor I noticed earlier. She walks like a catwalk model and I have to drag my eyes away from the small muscle movements in her buttocks and the small of her back. I'm still on my guard; I'm not going to let myself get distracted by her body again. Apart from that, I feel slightly dizzy and don't know that I'd be up to another full-on attack.

The enormous kitchen is all chrome with a black, rubber floor. It looks like something out of a superior kitchens catalogue. There's a monochrome photographic print of a dead tree on one of the walls. There are three bar stools. I take my jacket off, sit down on one of them and watch her click on the kettle and prepare the coffee things. As she waits for the kettle to boil, she turns to face me. I really don't know where to look.

'Why does Nathan Raleigh want to find Viola?'

'He said not knowing where she was or what had happened to her was killing him. He wants her to come home. If she's still got a drug problem, then he'll send her to rehab.'

'You said he reported her missing two years ago.'

'Something like that. The police contacted him when she was reported missing a second time. They have to. That was about three weeks ago. Was that you?'

I'm pretty sure that it was. I just want to hear it from her. I wish she'd get dressed. I'm starting to feel the effects of her nakedness.

She pours out two coffees into white tulip-shaped cups with 'Deli-Med' written on the sides in the colours of the Italian flag. She places one in front of me and sits on the other side of the kitchen bar. I can feel that she's thinking about whether it would be prudent to answer my last question. I still can't take my eyes off her breasts.

'I take it that Raleigh laid on the *concerned father* schtick with a trowel.'

'I guess so. He had tears in his eyes. I was moderately convinced.' I look out of the window at the Fifties-style flats across the road. I take a sip of coffee and immediately feel nauseous.

'And what is going to happen if and when you find Viola? Did he tell you that?'

'No. He just said that it would be the end of the job when I found her.'

'Are you ex-police?'

'No. Does that make a difference to anything?' I take a long look at that beautiful face. I'm curious about the racial mix behind it, but I don't think this would be a good time to ask.

'Not necessarily. I don't know how much I should tell you,' she says. 'I'm only concerned with Viola and I don't want to do anything that would put her in harm's way.'

'The police can't act on this at all. You do realise that, do you? If a person like Viola turns up out of the blue, the police will naturally tell the person who reported her missing in the first place, but as she's over eighteen, they can't make her go home or anything. As far as the police are concerned, if she's decided to be a missing person a second time, then that's her business. They're not taking it too seriously. That's why Raleigh hired me.'

'I am afraid that if I help you in your investigation, then I will be complicit in delivering Viola to her father, which is the last thing I want to do.'

'Why? What's the…' I can feel my nausea turning into a strong desire to vomit. Mrs Bianchi gives me a curious look.

'Are you alright?'

'Do you have a bathroom where I can throw up?'

She stands and rushes around to my side of the bar, takes my shoulders in her hands and quickly guides me down the corridor to her bathroom. I turn both taps on and throw up in her sink. 'I'm sorry. I…'

I throw up again. I feel like shit. Mrs Bianchi has her hand on my back. I look up and see the reflection of her nakedness in the sink mirror. She smiles at both my prurience and helplessness.

'This is my fault,' she says. 'Take your clothes off. I'll run you a bath.'

# 12

## CHERRY BLOSSOM

I'm lying in a warm bubble bath in a strange woman's flat. The aches and pains all over my body were on fire when I got in, but now they're calming down a bit and I think I've puked all I can. My back still hurts, though. I take a look at the bottle on the side of the bath. It's Thymes Goldleaf bubble bath with bee pollen, honey and aloe vera. I feel like I'm being spoiled.

I wonder if I passed out for a few seconds, because now Mrs Bianchi is wearing a black raw-cut cotton robe with big blue flower patterns all over it. She sits on the edge of the bidet, leans forwards and rubs the bubbles off my arm, which I'm resting on the side of the bath. Perhaps the last couple of days have been a dream and this is my reality.

'You have attractive musculature, Mr Beckett.'
'Thank you, Mrs Bianchi.'
'My first name is Sakura.'
'Cherry blossom.'
'Oh, very good.'

She hands me a steaming glass with some sort of herbal tea in it.

'For me?'
'It's ginger and red raspberry leaf. It'll settle things down.'

'Thanks. May I continue my interrogation of you? Pardon my nakedness, by the way, Sakura.'

'That's quite alright, Daniel. But I rather felt that it was me that was interrogating you.'

I take a sip of the tea. I feel a slight psychological disadvantage here, but I'll press on anyway.

'Tell me how you first encountered Viola.'

She sighs and puckers her lips. I can't stop looking at her and she knows it. I think this is fairly close to the most insane professional situation I've ever been in. I take another sip of tea.

'I have been involved in various aspects of the sex industry since I was fifteen. I am thirty-seven now. For the last five years, I have been running a discreet and highly priced escort service for bisexual and lesbian women. I was an escort myself and know the business pretty well. I'm still involved in other facets of the industry, but this service is now my main source of income.'

'I didn't know such a thing existed.'

'There aren't many of them, it's true. There are perhaps half a dozen in London. I can't speak for the rest of the country. Many of my clients are happily married women who feel that the time has come to experiment with same-sex relationships. Their lives are so structured that it is difficult to meet other women for one-off, physical trysts. I provide them with genuinely bisexual or lesbian women who are experienced with first-timers and also with clients who are more experienced. I'm sure you've come across the term bi-curious. I help to assuage that curiosity.'

She runs her fingers through her hair and tugs and twists the long strands. I realise that I must have prevented her from drying her hair properly by calling. The tousled look is very fetching, though, but I keep this to myself.

'But they're not all naïve, bi-curious housewives by any means. Many of them are ordinary lesbian or bisexual women who know exactly what they want and just need that type of physical relief when they're in London on business, for example. But all of them have the same basic requirement: that the women they hire must be beautiful, intelligent and be able to be seen with them outside the bedroom. Perhaps they want to spend an evening at the theatre or have a meal in a restaurant. It all depends on the client.

'My girls have to be versatile, sophisticated and should ideally have a working knowledge of a few foreign languages. It's nice if they're university educated and are well spoken. The clients like that. Some of the girls, the bisexual ones and the lesbian ones, had worked as ordinary call girls, doing one-on-one with men and also threesomes with men and women. Working like this was a relief for them. It was not difficult for me to find enough high quality talent. In fact, once I was up and running, I had more offers than I could handle.'

'So Viola was one of your girls.'

'Yes. I don't really have much to do with someone like Emile Novak. He is a distasteful man and I've heard terrible stories about the things he gets up to with his girls, but there's a loose network of people in a similar business and a certain amount of trading goes on from time to time. Novak is old school. His glory days are virtually over now, thankfully.'

'Novak said that he was having trouble with Viola's drug intake and with her lack of enthusiasm for the job.'

'That would be about right. Viola was truly bisexual with a preference for women, like some of the women I just described. I think if she could have started off with just women, she'd have been quite happy with that. Women who hire call girls are not so angry, not so resentful, not so sad, not so desperate, not so ignorant, not so unhygienic, not so violent, not so stupid and not so unpredictable.'

My stomach turns as I think of all the shit she'd had to put up with at the hands of Novak. Presumably Mrs Bianchi knows all about that. 'I'm going to get out now. This bath is starting to get uncomfortably tepid.'

'As you wish.'

I step out of the bath onto a soft, white bath mat. Sakura gently pats me dry with a huge pink towel and hands me another one to put around my waist, which is useful in more ways than one. I feel a little better. She notices an old scar on my left side, five inches under my armpit. Her fingers gently trace the line from back to front. I really wish she wouldn't.

'How on earth did you get that?'

'It's from a skinning knife. It's a butcher's tool.'

'Argument in a butcher's shop?'

'Yeah, it was over the weight of some mince.'

'Ah.'

She watches me get dressed. I can't read the expression in her eyes.

'So you bought Viola from Novak.'

'That's right. I could see through her failings. I knew what she was. On top of that, she was a true beauty and had a firm, voluptuous figure that I knew many of my clients would appreciate. She was one of those women who made the mouth water. I knew that other women would see what I saw when they looked at her.'

I'd like to ask how much Viola cost, but I don't think I will.

'She was beautiful, you're right. I've seen a couple of photographs of her.'

'I brought her to live here, with me. Her looks were not yet ruined and I sought to renovate her. My first task was to get her off heroin. I have been a heroin addict myself, in my time, but I would never have described myself as a junkie. I loved the ecstasy of it and I adored the thrill of the needle, the orgasm of the rush. It fitted my personality and I will never be apologetic for my craving. Viola, however, was a junkie, in my terms at least. She took heroin to forget and obliterate and had a psychological addiction as well as a physical one. I knew it would be difficult to rear her away from it, but I thought it was worth the attempt. I thought I could get her to forget and obliterate through sex.'

'So what did you do? Cold turkey?'

'Basically, yes. But not too suddenly. It took ten days. I gave her diazepam, among other things. Got her drinking a lot of water, isotonic drinks, herbal teas. Does this sound terribly New Age? I hope not. It was total murder some of the time and she attacked me on several occasions. I put up with it all. I used to spend hours holding her in my arms. Gradually, she started building up her strength again. Then, she was ready for her training.'

'Training? In what?'

'She needed to learn how to entertain my clients. How to talk to them, how to be a good companion to them, how to make love to them in such a way that they truly felt they'd had their money's worth. I like them to leave my girls feeling that they have experienced something wonderful, astounding and electrifying.'

'You were like a one-woman finishing school.'

This makes her smile. 'If you like, yes. She became my lover and she became the lover of two of my girls; sometimes separately, sometimes in combination. By the time we'd finished with her she was confident and assertive. The whole process took several months. She was a pearl. She liked to lose herself in the act, which my clients loved.

'I know she had problems and I know this life wasn't the perfect one for her, but at least I'd removed her from Emile Novak and at times she seemed genuinely happy, as happy as any whore can be. We started her with the more inexperienced clients, and then very quickly moved her up. After six months she became the star and we upped her price to the top level.'

'Were you in love with her? Is that a silly question?'

'No, it's not a silly question at all. We were lovers, and sometimes it was very intense indeed. We each took each other to places that neither had been to. I think I was in love with her as much as you could be in love with someone like Viola. Because of what she was doing night after night, day after day, I had to keep a certain emotional distance. One of the other girls, Molly, was infatuated with Viola, but the feeling was not reciprocated. We got on very well, though. She trusted me and yes, I suppose we loved each other as much as it was possible. I've never spoken about this to anyone before. Perhaps it's because you're a stranger.'

She has tears in her eyes. I think she was more attached to Viola than she was letting on. I smile at her. 'Well, I won't tell anyone.'

She brightens. 'I taught her tantric massage, too. I'd been on a two-month course in Beauvais a while ago. I wasn't a qualified instructor or anything, but it's not too difficult to pass the knowledge on if you've had enough practical experience. I've read quite a bit on the subject, too. Viola became very good at it very quickly. She was a fast learner. From the first time that she practised on me, I knew she was a natural. Have you ever had a tantric massage, Daniel?'

'Not so far. Perhaps you could get a job in a spa one day.'

She laughs at the thought. 'Yes. Perhaps I could. How is the interrogation going? Have you got enough out of me yet?'

'Very useful. Just one thing – does Viola still live here? In theory, at least?'

'Oh no. Once she was up and running, so to speak, she was able to rent a place of her own and a very nice place, too. Belsize Park. Would you like to take me to lunch?'

\*

I sit down on one of the Bauhaus chairs and read a magazine called *Femme Actuelle* while Sakura gets ready. My kidney pain is not so bad now, but it's still there. I must remember to take a look at the colour of my urine the next time I take a piss. The last thing I want is to have to go into a hospital and have a load of tests done. My chest is painful where I took those kicks, and at first I thought she might have broken a couple of ribs, but I'm not so sure now. I'll wait a week and see how it feels before I think about having an X-ray. The damage most likely to leave a mark, of course, is the side of my face, after the hammering it took against that wall. I took a look in the bathroom mirror and it looked OK, but I can really do without getting a black eye or sustaining comprehensive facial bruising; it just makes you look conspicuous and sinister, two looks that it's best to avoid in my business.

I wonder to myself whether Sakura would be known as a pimp or a madam. I'm not really sure about the nomenclature used in her profession. I may ask her when we get to know each other a little better, if having already seen each other naked doesn't count. I can feel her presence in the room.

'Shall we go?'

To say she looks amazing would be an understatement. She's wearing a short tight-fitting burgundy velvet dress with wide bodice lacing up both sides from the bottom of the dress to the armpit. This design can obviously not be worn with any underwear. Stockings are out, too, but this hardly matters. She has great legs with a natural tan and is wearing a pair of burgundy velvet ankle strap four-inch heels. Her jet-black hair is swept off her face and held in place by gel. Add to this a slash of bright red lipstick and a touch of blue eye shadow and the effect is stunning.

'I – I don't know what to say. You look amazing. I almost forgive you for beating the crap out of me earlier on.'

She laughs again, placing her hand in front of her mouth. This is a very Japanese gesture and I wonder where she was born.

'There is a pub around the corner that serves meals,' she says. 'Perhaps we could go there.'

I'd seen a sign for a pub while I was sitting outside the Costa, but I hardly think she's dressed for a pub, no matter how classy it may be. It's almost as if she never goes anywhere and isn't aware of normal dress codes.

'A pub? Are you sure?'

'Are you ashamed?'

'What?'

'Are you ashamed to be seen with me?'

I can't tell if she's being serious. 'Of course not. Quite the opposite. I just thought you might want to go somewhere classier.'

'No. The pub will be fine.'

The pub is about five minutes' walk away from her flat. We talk about nothing in particular, though there's a lot I still want to ask her about Viola. I want to know who booked Viola three weeks ago and I still need to discover the name that Viola was booked under so that I can talk to hotel staff about it.

I don't want to push her too hard, though. I can feel she's holding things back and I want the information to flow naturally. If she volunteers any more titbits, they're more likely to be true than anything that might come out as a result of my questioning. I also think she's more delicate than might immediately be apparent.

'How do people book girls from you, Sakura? Tell me how it works.'

I watch her face as we walk along. For some reason, she's looking a little jumpy.

'I have a website. At the moment, there are twenty-four girls on it. The site makes it quite clear that this is for women only. I have had enquiries from men asking if I could supply a bisexual girl for them and their girlfriend, but I always say no. That is not what this is about.

Besides, when men are involved, there is the risk of danger to the girls. And there is the hygiene. Men do not tend to take care of themselves. A few of my girls have worked in conventional prostitution and have had disgusting experiences that they are in no hurry to repeat.'

'So if I was a woman seeking an escort for the evening, how I would I choose which girl I wanted?'

'There are…'

She suddenly grabs hold of my forearm. For a second, I think she's going to attack me again or has seen someone she wants to avoid, but it isn't that. She looks pale and distressed and I can't imagine what the matter is.

'Sorry, I – we'll be in the pub soon. I'll be OK. I hope I'm not hurting your arm.'

'Of course not.' Actually, that's a big lie. Her grip is strong and it's quite painful. If she had shorter fingernails it wouldn't be half so bad.

As soon as we get inside the pub, she lets go of my arm and perks up a bit.

'Sit down,' I say, pointing to a table away from the window. 'I'll get you a drink. What would you like?'

'Thank you – just a glass of white wine. It doesn't matter which type.'

I go to the bar and have a look around while I'm ordering. It's one of those pubs that is attempting to turn itself into a fashionable restaurant. The food is traditional pub fare but with a gourmet twist. It's still not very busy. There's a bunch of loud guys in suits at the far end of the bar and a couple sitting holding hands three tables away from where Sakura is waiting. She's composing herself from whatever the problem was out there. She takes a compact mirror from her handbag and reapplies her lipstick. The guys are just starting to notice her.

I get her wine and another for myself, pick up a couple of menus and sit down across the table from her. She smiles, but it's a fake, nervous smile.

'Here we are. Here's your drink and a menu for when you're ready to order.' I suddenly wonder whether I should be drinking alcohol.

'Thank you, Daniel. I'm sorry about what happened out there.'

'That's OK. To be honest, though, I'm not actually sure what *did* happen.'

'I am agoraphobic. It doesn't happen everywhere, but I start to get panic attacks under certain circumstances. It was the whole thing; the street, the cars going by, the people walking and talking. It's as if the whole thing was just too big and I'm afraid it's going to envelope me and crush me. I get a bad feeling about it and I want to go and hide somewhere quiet. I've been working on controlling it, but it's difficult.'

'Are you OK now?'

'Yes. It seems to be fine in here. That's why I didn't want to go anywhere else. I didn't want to have to walk around for too long.'

'What d'you mean it *seems* to be fine? Do you get it indoors as well?'

'Sometimes, yes, I do. If I'm in a strange or unfamiliar place, or – I don't know – a really *big* place, like a museum, with big high ceilings. It can come on then. But it can also happen in ordinary spaces if I feel stressed for some reason. It can feel as if the room is expanding and I get the same feeling as I did outside just now.'

'Have you seen anyone about it?'

'I saw a cognitive psychotherapist for six months. She showed me how to control it. It's much better than it was before I started seeing her, but it can still take me by surprise. There was a period where I couldn't go out at all. I'm still a little afraid of going anywhere new in case I start panicking.'

'But you feel it's improving?'

'Yes. If I take things slowly. I sometimes take a walk around the block and sometimes go further. It's better at night when there aren't so many people around and it isn't so noisy.'

'Here – have a menu.'

She gives me a shy little smile and takes it. Her colour's coming back, but there's still a small trace of sweat on her upper lip. The demon on my shoulders wants me to kiss that sweat away, but I manage to swat him onto the floor. She seems relieved that she's told me about this and I can feel that she's relaxing a little more. To my surprise, she orders bangers 'n' mash, but the sausages are venison and red wine and the mash is mixed with mustard and red onions. I have the same. A very short guy takes our order.

While we're waiting, she takes a sip of her wine and laughs to herself. 'As you can imagine, I don't go on dates very often.'

'Is this a date?'

'What do you think?'

'Yes, I guess it is.'

'You were asking me about my website before my world started caving in out there.'

'It's alright. You don't have to talk about it if you don't want to.'

'You asked about how you would choose a girl. The site has a page for each one. There are biographical details, which would include the girl's physical characteristics; her age, height, eye and hair colour, vital statistics, skin colour and nationality. There are a few paragraphs about what they are like, what a good companion they are, what their interests are and what foreign languages they speak, if any. There would also be details of their availability. A few of my girls hold down conventional jobs and can only work evenings or weekends.'

'What about photographs?'

'Each girl has a minimum of six photographs. If they want to put more on they can, but the site can't really cope with more than twenty. The guy who did it explained why, but I didn't really understand what he was talking about.

'The photographs are never nude, but just basic glamour shots. I like to show the girls in evening dress, wearing a bikini and wearing lingerie. Those photographs, combined with the physical characteristics, would give you a good idea of what you'll be getting. Sometimes, if the girl wants to be anonymous, her facial features may be obscured, or the photograph cropped so that you cannot see her eyes, for example.'

'So this can be a part time thing for students or whatever.'

'Yes. Six of my current girls are full time university students. Some of them don't care who sees their face on my site, but most of them do. Apart from the basic details of the girl's body, there is usually a sentence or two telling you about their personality and interests. Many of these are made up, as they don't really matter. There is also a section concerning the girl's sexual preferences, what she will or will not do. For example, some girls are good at role-play or domination, others are not, or they may not like it for some reason.'

'I take it that their real name is not displayed.'

The waiter announces his presence with a cough and places our meals in front of us. That was quick. Must be the time of day. 'Here we are,' he says. 'Enjoy!' He has a ring with a green skull on the middle finger of his right hand.

We start eating and the food is quite delicious, if a little too hot. I shall remember this place. Two of the guys at the bar have changed their position so that they can stare at Sakura. I can tell they are talking about her.

'None of the girls have their real names on the site and the client will never know their real name, unless they care to divulge it for some reason or other.'

'What was Viola called?'

'On the site she was just called Natasha. When we needed a surname for an outcall, we used the name Natasha Hart. Oh – and the prices are detailed on the girl's page, too. There's the price for one hour, any additional hours, overnight and dinner date. Sometimes the client may want more. They may want to take the girl with them on holiday, for example; that's a rate that has to be discussed with me.'

'It that common?'

'Not too common, but it can happen. Most common is 'overnight'.'

Three of the guys are now looking at Sakura and laughing. This is incredibly rude, particularly as she's having lunch. I could be her husband, for all they know. I start wondering how long they've been here as they all seem a little pissed. I'm going to change the subject now, to give her a break from all of this.

'Where did you learn karate, Sakura? That was a pretty impressive display.'

She actually blushes when I say this. 'Well, you were pretty hot yourself. Not many people could have faced that. I think I cheated you with the towel. I knew when you saw my body it would give me an advantage of maybe half a second.'

'You were right.'

'I'm a *godan*, but I haven't been to formal classes for a few years now.'

A *godan* is a fifth degree black belt. No wonder I was having problems.

'You'd never know it. I thought I was totally fucked there.'

'But you won, didn't you. You managed to get me off you and onto the floor. I couldn't get out of that arm lock. I couldn't work out what you were doing when you threw me like that.' She pauses to drink some wine. 'I'm sorry I attacked you. I didn't know who you were or what was going to happen. I couldn't take any chances.'

We sit and look at each other for a moment. The guys at the bar are pushing one of their number towards us and loudly whispering, 'Go on!'

'There's a lot of shit going on with Viola, isn't there,' I say. 'Her and her father, I mean. If she was *that* afraid of what her father may do to you, someone he's never even met…'

I don't mention my chat with Louisa Gavreau this morning and I'm not going to. She and her sister's theory about that portrait may not even hold water. It's just a thesis and therefore not worth talking about at the moment.

'She had a lot of demons,' says Sakura. 'Her father was

very possessive of her. He would get very angry if she showed any affection of any sort to anyone other than him. She told me how lonely she was in school. She was afraid to make friends. He had warned her not to. He had quite a fierce temper and a controlling personality, so you can imagine the effect of that on a small child.'

This is very complex and I'm having difficulty making sense of it. 'But her mother was around until she was fourteen…'

'You know about her mother?'

'Yes. Someone mentioned it. Couldn't her mother have done something? You can't relentlessly bully a kid like that without someone saying or doing something, can you? I mean – what the hell was wrong with her father? I can't imagine why he'd be so bloody possessive. It just doesn't make sense.'

We've both finished our meals. The waiter takes the plates away and plonks dessert menus on the table in front of us.

'D'you want a dessert?'

'Let me have a look.'

As she picks up the menu, one of the guys I've been eyeing for the last ten minutes walks boldly up to our table, watched by his giggling friends. He wears a blue suit, has rounded shoulders, a floppy hairstyle and walks with a self-conscious rich kid's lope.

'Excuse me,' he says, more to me than to Sakura. 'But we were just looking at this beautiful lady's dress and, well, we were wondering, er, if she had anything on underneath it!'

He gives me an 'all blokes together' grin, designed to draw me into this terrific wheeze. His hand is now on my shoulder. He's big and sweaty and public school, with the social skills of a protozoan. I catch Sakura's eye briefly. It's almost funny that this jerkoff doesn't realise that he's metaphorically pushed his head into a hornet's nest, but not that funny.

'Fuck off,' I tell him, quietly.

His voice deepens to its true bullying timbre. 'Hey, come on now. No need for that.' He looks back at his mates for support. They're having a good laugh over there. He becomes pally again. 'It's just that we could see flesh all the way down the sides of that rather lovely dress she's wearing and we were wondering if she had any knickers on!'

This brings a huge guffaw from his friends, who are looking at us like we're some sort of entertainment that the pub has booked for its lunchtime customers.

'Or a bra!' he continues, more loudly. He puts on an exaggerated posh voice, though it isn't that much of a push for him to achieve it. 'Doth the lady have on any undergarments, forsooth?'

He's talking about her as if she's not there. I really can't stand that. I look him straight in the eye and hold the sides of my seat, ready to push myself up, when the guy from the couple holding hands walks over. He flashes a police badge and holds the guy's arm above the elbow.

'Would you mind leaving these people alone, please, sir? Go back over to your friends, there's a good chap.'

'I was only having a bit of fun. We just wanted to...'

'I heard what you wanted, sir. Come along now. Just go back to your friends and have a drink. Please don't bother these nice people again.'

He petulantly jerks his arm away from the policeman's grip and slopes back over to his mates, like a child who's just had its favourite toy removed as a punishment for some wrongdoing.

I look up and smile. 'Thank you, officer.'

'I wasn't doing it for your benefit, sir. I was doing it for his.'

'Well thanks anyway.'

He gives me a suspicious look and goes back to holding his girlfriend's hand.

I order toffee apple and pear crumble with cream, and Sakura has the warm chocolate fondant with a scoop of ice cream. When she's finished her first mouthful, she looks up at me.

'Nathan Raleigh had been sexually abusing Viola since she was nine years old.'

I was just about to put a spoonful of toffee apple and pear crumble and cream into my mouth. It never got that far.

# 13

## THE OVERNIGHT OUTCALL

OK.

First of all, I have no proof that what Sakura said is true.

If it isn't true, I just continue with the investigation until I find Viola. When I find her, dead or alive, I inform her father and that's the end of the job. But unless there's some huge, complex conspiracy going on here, I have no reason to doubt Sakura's word about this.

The only weak link regarding this piece of information is Viola. This is something she told Sakura, who had good cause to believe her, but she may have been lying or tampering with the truth in some other way. Who knows, she could even have False Memory Syndrome. She certainly had enough other problems, so why not that one too?

If it is true, I have to decide whether I want to continue this investigation at all. Financially, on the plus side, I've already been given three days' worth of money at double my usual rate. I've done two days already. If Raleigh wants his two thousand back, he can have it, so that's four thousand pounds for two days' work, plus having the crap beaten out of me by Mrs Bianchi as a surprise extra. If I stop now, I won't be seeing the twenty thousand bonus, but if that's the price I have to pay for not working for a leading scumbag, that's fine with me. Fuck him.

But what will actually happen if I stop? What do we have? A high-class call girl who's gone missing and a father who wants her back for God knows what reasons. This is a case that the police aren't interested in. Viola was a missing person, then she wasn't a missing person, then she was a missing person again. If you factor in her occupation, then it's not going to be a high priority for any police force unless someone finds her body somewhere. Plus, if I stop, Raleigh will just get someone to replace me. Worse, he may get Fisher and his goons to take over; a turn of events which I suspect Fisher would be greatly pleased with.

But she may not be dead. She may be out there somewhere, terrified. In one sense, I'm her only hope. But if I rescue her from whatever fate has befallen her, the next stage would be to deliver her to her father, my client, who's been busy destroying her life for the last dozen or so years. By any standards, that would be a despicable thing for me to do.

There are a few other factors floating around which may or may not be connected to what I've just been told.

One of them is Rosabel Raleigh's suicide. This happened roughly ten years ago. I've only got Taylor Conway's word that it happened when Viola was fourteen, but if that's true, then Rosabel may have known what Raleigh had been up to with Viola for close on five years before she decided to end it all. Could her suicide be linked to Viola's abuse? Possible, but even if it is, it doesn't necessarily have any bearing on the case as it stands at the moment and is probably not directly connected to Viola's recent disappearing act.

Then there's Louisa Gavreau's judgement on Rosabel's portrait. That's weird, certainly, but again, I don't know if it's true. The portrait would have been painted when Viola was fourteen. It would have been a presence in her life until she finally left home. Was it meant to be comforting for her in some misguided way or was it meant to be some kind of sick threat? I can't tell.

Would it have been enough on its own to get her on the road to drug addiction and prostitution? Not likely, but you never know. But if what Sakura said is true, it would be a good enough explanation for Viola's drug use, at least, and for her cutting off contact with her father at the first opportunity, and for her telling him about her prostitution, just to piss him off.

Novak said that he found Viola's relative enjoyment of prostitution very unusual. Perhaps she turned to it and *continued* it to purge herself of the memory of her father's abuse in some way, though that could just be psychobabble on my part, and my psychobabble has been unreliable in the past.

Add to all of this the fact that Raleigh may have been lying to me from the off. All that concerned father stuff could have been bullshit of the highest order. *I just want to know what has happened to her and I want her back.* Well, he may have his reasons for wanting her back and off drugs, but he may have a hidden agenda. She's off drugs now, anyway, though he wouldn't know that. It could be that his story about having a clear head for his big arms deal next week may have been a lie, too. Perhaps he's in a hurry for some other reason.

Then there's Tote Bag. I have a strong suspicion that she was set on me by Raleigh or Fisher. I have no proof of this, of course, but it seems the only logical explanation. I can't imagine *why*, though, unless it's just a rich man's way of making sure he's getting his money's worth or he just wants a way of checking on my progress. Whatever, it's still a very singular thing to do and doesn't feel right. Plus it's kind of insulting to my professional integrity and makes me want to break down and cry.

Finally, I mustn't forget what Anjukka told me about Fisher, cruising call girl sites for the purposes of entertaining Raleigh's wealthy clients. That may well be par for the course for arms dealers, but I still have to think of it as suspicious and possibly connected to the whole Viola disappearance situation. But in what way, I can't imagine.

Anjukka. God Almighty, was that only last night? It occurs to me that if Tote Bag was a Raleigh employee of some sort, then he'll know I was on a date with his PA, which I don't much care for.

After we left the pub and walked back to her flat, I told Sakura to hold my hand if she felt wobbly again. That arm-gripping thing not only hurt but also looked a little weird. The roads were busier after we'd had lunch. Three minutes passed before she took my hand in hers. People walking by would have thought we were a couple. I've pushed her quite a lot today, but I still have to ask her about what happened on the night that Viola disappeared. Even if she's not forthcoming, at least I've got a name now: Natasha Hart.

As we take the stairs up to her flat, she continues holding my hand. Despite her kick-ass performance earlier on and her undoubtedly steely mental makeup, she's also quite sweet and gives off a surprising air of vulnerability. As we enter her flat, she turns and kisses me softly on the cheek.

'Thank you for taking me out.'
'My pleasure. Was that our first date?'
'Yes. I rather think it was.'

*

I turn over now and watch her sleeping. She frowns a lot in her sleep, as if she's having a bad dream. At one point, she moans and flings a hand back, hitting herself on the forehead. I pull the sheet off her and slowly kiss her awake, from the neck down to the belly. I lean over and slowly pick my watch up from the floor. It's ten past three. I still want to get to The Bolton Mayfair sometime today, but I still need to talk to her about Viola.

She smiles at me as she wakes up. 'I hope you realise,' she says, 'that in view of your recent injuries, I was gentle with you. It won't happen again.'

'I'll take that as a warning.'

'Yes. You should. Stay there.'

I sit up and watch as she pads out of the bedroom, presumably heading for the kitchen. I have to smile; I certainly wasn't expecting that and I don't think she was, either. I'm trying to remember when things changed between us, as they so obviously did, but can't pinpoint the moment.

When she comes back in, she's carrying a tray with coffee things, plus a plate covered in amaretti cookies, which she puts on the floor next to the bed. I pull her towards me and kiss her. She pulls away after a few seconds and I'm amazed to see that she's actually blushing. Then I think maybe this is an act. Perhaps the whole coquettish, kittenish, vulnerable thing is something she can turn on and off at will. Can you train yourself to blush whenever you feel like it? I remember reading somewhere that the very thought of blushing can make you blush. Oh well; act or not, it's all staggeringly sexy, so I decide to enjoy it for whatever the hell it is.

We sit up and sip coffee like a couple of shy teenagers for a few minutes, then she runs a hand down my arm.

'What are you going to do?'

'What are we talking about?'

'Nathan Raleigh.'

Good. I'm glad it's her that's brought it up and not me. This whole thing is confusing on a lot of levels and it's useful to have someone with a bit of background knowledge to bounce things off. I'll have to keep back some of the stuff I know, though. I'm certainly not going to tell her about Rosabel's portrait, for example. Something like that would only muddy the waters. I suddenly wonder if each of us is using the other through sex to get information or to get something done. Well, if that's the case, it was certainly worth it from my point of view.

'I haven't really given it much thought yet,' I lie. 'I'm not sure whether I should continue, to be honest with you.'

'But then we'll never know what happened to her.'

'That's true. But – if I *find* her…'

'You have to hand her over to Raleigh or you won't get paid?'

I don't tell her about the bonus.

'It isn't that. It's just that my whole line of investigation could be self-defeating. Instead of potentially rescuing Viola from some terrible fate, I could be delivering her into something far worse. But if I tell Raleigh I'm quitting, he'll just get someone else. That someone else may well find Viola and won't have the information that I got from you, so they'll just hand her over to him without a thought.'

'You find yourself in a moral quandary, Daniel.'

'Exactly the words I would have used, Cherry Blossom.'

She punches me in the arm.

'You have to play it by ear,' she says, firmly. 'If I was you, I'd keep going and try and find Viola. You'll come to a point where you have to make a decision about what you're going to do next, whether you report your findings to Raleigh or whether you don't. That point hasn't arrived quite yet. You still haven't discovered what happened to Viola and it's possible you never will. At the moment, you have nothing to lose by continuing and you will also be paid. You may be the one person who can help her. You must do the right thing as you see it.'

'You're right. *If these qualities when adopted and carried out lead to harm and to suffering, then you should abandon them.*'

She turns to look at me, her eyes wide with mock amazement.

'So you are a *Buddhist* now, Daniel?'

'Tell me how Viola was booked that night, step by step.'

'A woman called Mrs Amelia Finch rang me up. She'd seen my website and was making tentative enquiries about booking a girl for an overnight outcall.'

'Did you record the conversation?'

'No. Why would I do that?'

'It doesn't matter. What did she sound like?'

'She was well spoken. Educated accent. Home counties. A tad chary. I couldn't really guess her age. Not that old, but that's all I could discern. Twenties, thirties –

who knows; it's difficult to tell on the telephone sometimes.'

'Did she ask for Viola straight away?'

'No. She just asked some general questions about my service. Basic things, like how she could pay. She said she was happily married, but had been dying to experience sex with another woman for some years. She didn't know that escort services like mine existed.'

'Did she sound genuine?'

'I had no reason to think otherwise. She sounded typical, I would say. It was similar to a lot of the enquiries that I get. She was concerned about how discreet the service was. She didn't want it to be sleazy or dangerous. I assured her that it would be neither of those things. Because she was a first-timer, I told her about the possibility of having a tantric massage.'

'What did she say to that?'

'She was interested. I described what would happen. I told her that the masseuse would be either partially clothed, or, if she wished, totally naked. It would be up to her. I told her that she could stop the massage at any point if she felt uncomfortable with it. She, of course, would be naked during the massage.

'I also suggested that she and Viola – or Natasha as we referred to her – could perhaps meet for a drink or go out for a meal before going back to her hotel room. I tried to give her the impression that she would always be in control of the whole evening, from beginning to end. She seemed very interested in this and wanted more details.'

'Which you gave her.'

'Yes. I told how the massage would proceed from beginning to end. I told her about the exciting intimacy of a tantric massage when given by another woman. I told her which of my girls were qualified to give a massage like this.'

'How many girls was that?'

'There were three choices. It did say on the site, but I didn't want her to have to do a lot of clicking back and forth while she was on the phone. She said she was sitting in front of her computer. I told her that the girls she should choose from were Amber, Anneliese and Natasha.'

'And she chose Natasha.'

'Eventually, yes. She said that she liked Anneliese's looks, but was also quite taken with Natasha. In actual fact, Anneliese is a slightly better tantric masseuse – she's been doing it for longer – but in the end she chose Natasha. She said she liked Natasha's face.'

I watch Sakura carefully as she's relating all of this. She's so lovely. She said that she was an escort herself once, and I find myself wondering how much her services would have been. Very expensive, I would imagine. I snake a hand around her waist and draw her towards me, kissing her neck. She gasps and frowns with concentration and I wonder whether this is a genuine response or not.

'Where are your parents from, Sakura?'

'I was wondering when you'd ask that. Everyone does. My father was Italian. He was from Oristano in Sardinia. He moved to the UK when he was in his twenties. He was a biochemist. My mother was from Nagano in Japan. She was working for a pharmaceutical company in London, which is where they met.'

That would explain the unique combination of features. Talk about exotic.

'Did you feel that Amelia Finch manipulated you into

suggesting Natasha, in a way that you might not have realised at the time?'

'Manipulated? I don't think so. It was me that suggested the tantric massage, for example. No. Wait.' She bites her lower lip and runs a hand through her hair. 'I think she might have mentioned massage in our initial chat. Not tantric massage, but she maybe mentioned something about massage parlours that she'd seen advertised and had been curious to whether the girls there did extras for women as well as men. I said I didn't know. That may have been why I mentioned tantric massage to her.'

'And once you'd mentioned that and she seemed to be interested, it immediately narrowed down her choices from twenty-four to three. And then from three to one – Natasha.'

'Yes. It's possible that could have happened. I don't know. I can't remember every single word that was spoken. No one could.'

'OK. So she wanted to meet Natasha/Viola in a hotel. How does that work?'

'I have very strict rules about that for the protection of my girls. When you are outside the law, you must always be more careful. One of those rules comes from a time when the main clients of call girls were men. The client chooses the hotel. At this end of the market, it will always be a four or five star hotel and it will be in a good area of London. I would expect the client to book a room for themselves, but also to book a room for the girl that they will be seeing.'

'So they have to book two rooms. Isn't that expensive? Don't they object to that?'

'Some do, but if they want one of my girls, it's

something they have to go along with. They can like it or lump it, as they say. It changes slightly if a client is booking two girls. They will book a room for themselves, but they don't have to book separate rooms for the girls. They can share.'

'I don't understand. Why book two rooms if they've booked one of your girls for the night?'

'Safety, pure and simple. The girl will go to the room of the client. They will talk, maybe have a drink. If the girl thinks everything is alright, she will probably spend the night in the client's room. However, if something seems wrong with the client, then they have somewhere to go. The client will have booked the extra room, but they will not have a key for it. It may be that the client is high on drugs or drink. The client may seem unbalanced and possibly dangerous or potentially violent. If this is the case, then the girl is not trapped all night in a hotel room with someone they are unsure about in one way or another. It also saves the girl having to find transport home in the middle of the night. They won't be stranded in a strange area at an inhospitable hour. That has happened to me in the past and it can be very frightening.'

'Do you get many women who are like that? Violent or drunk?'

'Not so far. As I said, it's a hangover from the days when men were the predominant clients of call girls and one I have always thought was a good idea. Some terrible things have been done. Just because you are a prostitute, it does not mean that you can't be savagely beaten or raped.

'You are perceived as a non-person, even today, and you have no rights. Just the word 'whore' is a common and degrading insult against women. Even now, for me, when I hear the word 'whore' or 'hooker' used in jest or as an all-purpose casual insult, it is like a knife being plunged into my heart. It is a reminder of how low down you are, in case you had forgotten.'

God Almighty. I thought I'd got the whole thing in perspective when I was looking at those websites the other day, but the big picture is starting to form in my mind now. The exploitation, the way men perceive women, the way men perceive women that they have paid for and the rights they think that gives them.

I try to steer my thoughts away from it, but I start to wonder why Sakura is a fifth degree black belt in karate and what gave her the focus to get that far, as it can't have been easy. There could be an innocent explanation, of course. Her mother was Japanese. Perhaps she passed her skills onto her daughter like in some film. I won't ask. Not yet. I slide my arm around her waist and let her rest her head on my shoulder. She smells of perfume, sweat and sex.

'OK. So you sorted out the time and date. Amelia Finch booked a room for herself at The Bolton Mayfair and she also booked one for Viola or Natasha. It was an overnight outcall, yes?'

'Yes, it was. There was nothing suspicious about it. Several of my girls had worked at that hotel in the past. It was just another shy, cautious, bi-curious married woman letting her hair down. I insist that all the girls text me soon after they've met the client. If everything seems fine, they'll send me a text saying "Pick up shopping". If everything doesn't seem fine, they'll send me a text saying "We're out of milk". The girls all think this is very silly, as you might imagine.'

'And Viola sent you the shopping text.'

'Yes she did. As soon as I got that, I thought no more about the job. I just hoped that Viola gave the woman a good time and that she wanted to use my company again.'

*My company.* I didn't think about it that way. I wonder how Sakura fills in her tax return. Perhaps she doesn't bother. I lean back and stretch. Sakura runs a hand up my chest and massages my shoulder. I hope she's not starting a tantric. I don't think my body could take it. I'm going to have a three hour-long soak in the bath when I get home tonight.

'How did Amelia Finch pay for this? What normally happens?'

'Well, I spoke to her a week before the date that we'd arranged. An overnight date with Viola was three thousand. I class overnight as fourteen hours. Obviously, we would not be booking her out on that night, and she would probably not work the next day, so we have to have some guarantee that the date will be happening, so we ask for a deposit in cash of, in Viola's case, five hundred pounds.

'The remaining money would be given to Viola within five minutes of her meeting the client. It would normally be in an envelope. Viola would, after some chat and maybe a drink, retire to her room, count the money and send me the text we spoke of. Then she'd go back to the client's room.'

'And it would always be a cash payment.'

'Yes.'

'And how did Amelia Finch get the five hundred to you?'

'She sent it here by courier.'

'Here? Is that – it that safe for you? The police, I mean?'

'There is no evidence whatsoever in this flat of my occupation and I've been doing it for years without any side effects. The police have better things to do than execute stings on madams. Besides, I have contacts with some very senior police officials, some of whom I have known for decades, and two of whom are clients of mine still. They would let me know if the law had any plans for me. It hasn't happened yet, and I've been at it for a long, long time.'

So she *is* called a madam. I'm glad I didn't have to ask.

'I like this. Being in bed with you, talking and cuddling,' she says.

'Really? I'd have thought you were far too decadent and sophisticated for this sort of thing.'

There's that laugh again and the hand going up to the mouth.

'I am not as sophisticated as you might think. Remember, I had bangers and mash for lunch. We could make some popcorn and watch a movie.'

I'd love to ask her how she started in this business. At fifteen, too. But I'm not going to; it's far too clichéd. I'd also like to ask her about her police clients and what she does with them. So now I not only have the name that Viola used at The Bolton Mayfair, I also have the name of the woman who booked her. I have to consider that Amelia Finch isn't her real name. It isn't that difficult to book yourself into a hotel under another identity. I've done it plenty of times.

If she was using a false name, though, I'm wondering how she managed to book two rooms in the hotel. Most hotels will ask for your credit card within minutes, and it'll need to match the one you used if you booked in advance online, so she'll need to have sorted that out, too. They'll also ask for some ID, though many use your credit card as ID. I need to find out what credentials The Bolton Mayfair would ask for.

This is good. I'm one step closer to Viola than I was when I got up this morning and I *have* to find out who Amelia Finch is. If she's a genuine married woman, out for a bit of bi-fun, then she should be easy to trace. If she was someone else, it'll be more difficult, but I'll cross that bridge when I come to it. As Sakura runs a hand down one of my biceps, I think about what to do next. Visiting the hotel is the obvious choice. I need to see who was on duty the night that Amelia and Natasha had their tryst and see if anyone remembers either of them or has any hard information about Amelia. It could be a dead end, but there's still a route I can take while I'm here.

'When did you start to get worried about Viola?'

'Well, when a girl has been on an all-nighter, I don't really expect to hear from her until late the next day. She may need to sleep into the afternoon when she gets home. I would have expected Viola to give me a call sometime that evening, maybe. When she didn't, I didn't really think much of it. I rang her the next day, but she wasn't answering her mobile or her landline. I waited for another twenty-four hours, then took a cab to her flat. I rang her bell, but nobody answered, so I let myself in.

'I've always had a key to her flat, she insisted upon it when she moved in. The place didn't feel as if anyone had been in it for a few days. It was then I started thinking of reporting her missing. I called the police the next day. When I told them she would have been booked under another name and gave them the name of the hotel, they knew what the score was straight away, although the woman I spoke to was too polite to mention anything. She was quite sympathetic, actually, which I didn't expect. She had a lovely, husky voice. I was quite entranced, under the circumstances.'

Olivia. I wonder if I should take her up on that dinner date she mentioned. I'd like to, but I'm not sure it's wise, particularly at the moment. She might become curious about me and start checking me out.

'And that was it. They haven't got back to you,' I say.

'The next time I heard anything about this was today, with you. I told you what Viola said about her father. How he got angry if she got close to anyone else. That was why I reacted as I did when I thought you worked for him.'

'Yeah. That makes a lot more sense in the light of what you've told me.'

'She described what happened to him when he lost his temper. It sounded rather terrifying.' She yawns and stretches, her arms high above her head. I try not to look at the result of this, but it's impossible. 'Viola had some sort of boyfriend a few years back, or maybe he was just a drug buddy. I can't remember his name. Jim? Jake? She said that he was walking back somewhere – I think they'd been out for a meal or something – and these two guys appeared out of nowhere and really badly beat him up. He had to be taken to hospital and have stitches and things. She said that she was sure that those guys were either working for her father or had been employed by him. I wasn't sure whether she was being paranoid or not. Muggings happen all the time, except these two guys didn't steal anything from him, apparently. When she went missing, I was afraid that they'd somehow track me down and attack me. That somehow her father would blame me for whatever had happened to her. When you turned up, I thought it was going to happen to me.'

I wonder if Raleigh had private detectives on this boyfriend or whatever he was. If he had someone following me, someone who he had no need to feel hate, jealousy or aggression towards, then it's quite possible.

For the moment, though, I have to think of friend Amelia as the main suspect in this, though God knows what her motivation may have been.

'Is it possible that Amelia Finch and Viola had such an intense experience that night that they decided to run away together, damn the consequences and cut all ties with everyone they'd ever known?'

She laughs. 'It is a romantic idea, but no.'

'Could Viola have decided that she'd had enough of the lifestyle and make a run for it? Perhaps something happening with that client that repulsed her and made her want to make a clean break, even from you?'

'Unlikely. Viola was too polite. If that was the case, I'd have got a telephone call, at the very least.'

'Has this ever happened to you before, where a girl went out on a job and disappeared immediately after it without getting in touch with you?'

'No.'

'Have you heard of it happening with anyone else?'

'A madam I knew about ten years ago had one of her girls murdered by a client. He cut her face off and left her in the hotel room. That's the closest thing I've ever come across. You read about things, of course…'

'But you've heard of nothing recently. This isn't the latest in a sequence of call girl murders or anything like that.'

'I would have heard.'

She gets up, walks over to her dressing table and sprays some perfume on. When she gets back into bed, she moves in close, assuming her previous position. I wish I could somehow transport this image back to my fifteen-year-old self. He'd have loved it.

'Fine. As we've got no other suspects at the moment, let's assume that Amelia Finch is behind Viola's disappearance. So we've got to ask why. Who would do this? What sort of female would book a high-class call girl for whatever reason and then possibly abduct or kill them? You'd be taking an incredible risk and you'd be leaving a significant paper trail behind.'

'Taking a large amount of cash out of your bank account is a risky thing to do,' she says. 'You'd have to careful about that if you were married, I would think.'

'Not to mention the cost of the hotel, travel, meals etc.'

'And clothing, maybe. Perfume. Lingerie. Sex toys, perhaps. But if people want to keep a secret badly enough, they can usually find a way. The money may not have come out of her own bank account, of course. We're just assuming that it did.'

'She paid you in cash, but I'm not sure that she would have done the same in the hotel. How much would a room in a hotel like that cost?'

'I think about four hundred pounds per night, minus any meals or extras. *And* she would have booked two rooms, don't forget, Daniel.'

'I'm sure the hotel would have taken the cash if she'd offered it, but if she was booking those rooms on the phone, they'd have wanted credit card details. The same goes if you were booking online or arriving there in person.'

'But that's not true, Daniel. About them taking the cash, I mean. Big hotels like The Bolton Mayfair won't take big chunks of cash now. They're afraid of money laundering and getting forged notes.'

'I didn't know. Thanks.'

'As soon as you walked into reception they would ask for your credit card to do a validation on it. The same is true even if you booked online, otherwise they could lose money on people who booked and didn't turn up. If that happens, many hotels will charge a no-show penalty on your card. It would mention this in the small print on their websites and literature. They also need your card details even if you've paid for your whole stay in advance.'

'Why?'

'Because of the extras you didn't think about when you booked. Minibar, using the telephone, all those sort of things. People would have tried to skip without paying for extras in the past and now they've got wise to it. They would have to do a pre-authorisation on your card. They don't want people fucking them over, particularly hotels like The Bolton Mayfair. There are not many people without a credit card of some sort now, and if they exist, they probably wouldn't be staying in a hotel like the Bolton.'

'So it's about ninety-nine per cent certain that Amelia Finch paid for the rooms with a credit card.'

'Yes.'

So you could do a fair amount of this with untraceable cash, but probably not the hotel. I'll have to check this. I want to see the place and, if possible, look at the rooms that our lovebirds stayed in. I'd also like to speak to some relevant staff. I wonder if I can get them to give me Amelia's credit card number. If I can get that, I can get her address, unless there's fakery of a high level going on here.

'Let's assume, for a moment, that it wasn't strictly about Viola. Let's assume it was about you. Is there anyone you know of who might want to set you up in some way? Steal or spirit away one of your best girls? Persuade her to go off with them? Perhaps to work abroad? You said yourself that services like yours were few and far between.'

'Yes, but I also said there were a lot of girls who wanted this type of work. I've had two I've had to reject in the last month. Fashion model types; both delightful and edible, but I'm happy with the number I have now. I'm not greedy and once you start running too many girls, the personal touch goes out of the window. At least that's my philosophy. It isn't shared by others.'

'Who's your biggest business rival in London?'

'That would be Sally Webster. The last time I was in contact with her, she was running about sixty girls, as opposed to my twenty-four.'

'And there's no way she would poach off you?'

'She isn't like that. Plus, we don't – we don't really get on very well. For her to steal from me would be an admission that one of my girls was superior to one of hers, do you see? She would never let me know that a thought like that had entered her head.'

'Any other notable rivals?'

'There's Abigail Gastrell. But her company caters for everyone. Many of her girls are fake bi, and I couldn't say how many are genuine lesbo. Some of these girls will do lesbo, plus lesbo and hetero threesomes, but they're basically hetero themselves. It's all a bit phoney and I don't approve. In a way, though, those girls are *pure* prostitutes, so it's quite admirable, in a way, do you see? None of her girls do tantric, though, and only two of Sally Webster's do it. It may have changed, I wouldn't know.'

'Are Abigail's girls better looking than yours?'

'Are you suggesting that Abigail might steal off me?'

'Not if you don't think so, but remember how Amelia Finch narrowed her choices down from twenty-four to three to one, until she'd booked your most beautiful girl and also one who did tantric. I think it's something worth thinking about.'

'I don't think so. Poaching like that is just not done. I've never, ever heard of it happening. Even Novak was magnanimous enough to see if someone else could do anything with Viola, even if it was for money. Besides, Abigail, apart from the fake lesbo thing, is really top notch. Her girls are always in great demand from wealthy clients and businesses. It's the reason she has so many girls on her books. I told her to stop some years ago, but she just keeps on expanding and expanding. I think she runs over two hundred girls now.'

'Could you do me a favour, Sakura? Could you speak to Sally Webster and Abigail Gastrell? Just a general chat; you don't have to tell them about what's been going on. Just see if you can detect anything in their voices. It may be a waste of time, but we might get something out of it. Even the smallest thing will help. If you feel you can trust either of them, tell them about Viola. You never know, one of them might have heard something through the grapevine, even if it's just gossip.'

She wrinkles her nose in distaste. She obviously

doesn't want to do this, but it's tough. She meets my gaze and nods her head. Good. I start wondering if Novak would be involved, then dismiss it.

First of all, it's doubtful whether he could be bothered to organise something as relatively complicated as Viola's disappearance, and his reasons for getting rid of her would still be uppermost in his mind, no matter how much Sakura had cleaned up her act and profited from her rehabilitation.

Also, if he was involved, he wouldn't have been able to stop himself bragging about it. I still feel angry when I think about him and Jeremy, and can remember every single thing they both said.

'What was the name of the courier that brought you the cash deposit of five hundred pounds?'

'I've no idea. It was just some guy.'

'What sort of courier was he?'

'Motorcycle. He had a helmet, you know? Leathers.'

'Did you get a receipt or anything?'

'No. I just signed something, gave it back to him and he handed me a big card envelope with the money in. Like a FedEx envelope but plain white.'

'Was there a logo or anything on his helmet? Anything on his leathers?'

'I guess so, but I can't remember what it said. Now you mention it, it did look like a uniform. The leathers definitely matched the helmet, in colour, at least. White and bright green. But that's all I can remember. That could have been his personal style, of course.'

'How long between you opening the door to him and shutting it again?'

'I don't know. Maybe ten seconds.'

I get up and allow Sakura to adjust her position,

without me there to lean against.

'Aw. What are you doing?'

'Lie down flat on your back. Put a pillow under your head. Close your eyes.'

'I have a blindfold in the drawer.'

'No. It's OK. No blindfold required just yet.'

'Some lover you turned out to be.'

'You are Satan's daughter.'

# 14

## A LITTLE TRIM OF LACE

I place one hand on her forehead and with the other I gently hold her hand.

'Breathe deeply, slowly and regularly. Inhale so that the air you breathe in travels down to a spot a little below your navel. When you breathe out, release about half the inhalation. We're just going to do a little visualisation exercise.'

'What does that mean?'

'Just shut up and do what I say.'

She keeps her eyes closed and breathes slowly in and out.

'Clear your mind of everything else, and let's go back to that time when the five hundred pound deposit arrived from Amelia Finch. When you took the packet off the courier, what was the first thing you did?'

'I closed the front door, tore the package open and counted the money.'

'By which time, the courier was out of your mind. But your brain must have taken in something about his appearance. You recalled the helmet, his leather and the type of envelope he gave you. We just need a little more. You saw everything. We just need to get it back.'

'Well, the thing I signed was one of those little electric

things. You sign it with a stylus. My signature looked a mess, as if I was drunk.'

'See? That's good. You didn't mention that a moment ago. Then you gave it back to him. He says thanks or something. You're looking at him now. What colour was his crash helmet.'

'Um – green. Green and white.'

'Are you sure?'

'Yes. The green was a bright green. Some sort of pattern. Circles, maybe. The visor was black. It was lifted up. He had blue eyes and a monobrow. Looked friendly. He'd been eating mints, but there was a cigarette smell, too.'

'And the leathers?'

She frowns. 'The same colour. It was like a uniform. The helmet matched the leathers, but the leathers didn't have the circles pattern.'

'Were there any words on the leathers or on the helmet? Anything like a logo?'

'Wait. The pattern wasn't circles. Not really. It was like that plant. On the helmet, anyway. It was…he had a badge on his chest with this plant on it, too. Three leaves. Green. I can see it. I can't think what the word is. It's lucky. It's a lucky plant.'

'A lucky plant? Was it a clover leaf? Three or four heart-shaped leaves?'

'Yes! That's it! Clover!'

She's grinning all over her face, pleased with remembering this.

'Were they called Clover Couriers or something? Do you remember seeing any words at all?'

'I can almost see a scribble across the clover on his chest. But it's not the letter C. At least, I don't think it is.

I can't really see it.'

I try to think what else it can be. Lucky Couriers, maybe? Four Leaf Courier Service? Am I wasting my time on this anyway? No. I might get to speak to someone who actually saw Amelia Finch with their own eyes. It could be the only lead I'll have. Then the answer pops into my head.

'Sakura. Could it have been Shamrock Couriers?'

'Shamrock?' She laughs and nods her head. 'Yes! Yes, that was it! I can see it now. And it was on his helmet as well. Shamrock Courier Services. God.'

'Well done.' I lean forward and kiss her on the mouth. 'Can I use your computer, please?'

London-based, five branches. There's even a photograph of one of their despatch riders (or a model pretending to be one), a glamorous and busty blonde girl leaning against a motorbike, holding her crash helmet under her arm.

'Sakura. Come and look at this.'

She rests both hands on my shoulders and looks at the screen. 'That's it. That's exactly the same uniform.'

'Let's have a look at where their branches are.'

Head office in Chiswick, other branches in Harlesden, Acton, Kilburn and Shepherd's Bush. All West London, none of them local to Sakura.

Their location may be of no use at all, though. I suppose if I was sending a cash payment to someone like Sakura, I might send it from some area of London where I wasn't known if I was uptight about it in some way. Or maybe not. I might not even have to go there in person. Perhaps the courier company would pick up the package from me and take it directly to the recipient. If that was the case, the company would know the address.

Whatever, there's no clue there as to which branch that courier came from. I'll just have to ring all of them.

'So what are you going to do?'

'Well, assuming the money was sent to you by Amelia Finch, that courier either went to wherever she was staying, or she went in personally. I'm betting it was the latter.'

Of course, the branch who delivered the package to Sakura was the very last one I rang. I told them that my name was Bianchi and gave them the date of the delivery. I said that I wanted to confirm which day the courier arrived, as the person who sent it needed the date for their tax return. Total illogical bullshit, of course, but they seemed to buy it and confirmed to me that it was the Chiswick branch I had to visit.

I shower, remind Sakura to have a chat with her fellow madams and take a cab to Chiswick, stopping at a cashpoint on the way to take out some more bribery money. I told the cab driver not to take the Hanger Lane route, but he knew better and we were stuck in shitty traffic for about twenty minutes.

Shamrock Courier Services has its offices on the ground floor of a skyscraper down the Chiswick Roundabout end of Chiswick High Road. I expected to see a lot of motorbikes and vans parked outside, but there's nothing.

Just before I go in, my mobile rings. It's Fisher.

'Mr Beckett? I'm sorry to have to ring you up, but the old man has been fussing about how you're doing. I know you've hardly started, really, but it's hard to convince him that these things take time.'

His tone is too matey and there's a fake undercurrent of collusion, as if we both know only too well that

Raleigh is a bit of a worrier and we both know he's being impatient, the silly old clod. I don't buy it.

'That's quite alright. I'm making steady progress. Nothing of great interest yet, but I think I'm getting there slowly but surely.'

'Excellent. That's what we like to hear. Well, I'll let you get back to work. What are you going to do next? Where will you be going?'

Too many unnecessary questions. What's his game?

'I'm going to see if I can have another chat with that police sergeant.' I lie. 'I think she was being cagey with me but she may have had time to reconsider.'

There's a moment of silence before he replies. 'Oh yes. Good. That's good. I'll let you get on with it. Sorry to interrupt you.'

He didn't believe me, but fuck it. I click off and walk into Shamrock Courier Services.

The guy behind the reception desk is dressed in a smart suit plus a shirt and tie. I didn't expect that, either. His ID badge says his name is Rob Wickham.

'Can I help you, sir?'

I don't think there's any point in lying. I tell him what I am, what I'm doing and what I'm looking for, with a few added fictions thrown in to appeal to his better nature. In fact, I lay the sentiment on with a trowel. I decide against bribing him as I think he'd be insulted. He seems amused, appalled, concerned and entertained by the whole thing and is very serious about finding the correct information. He looks up the date on the computer.

'Package delivered to Portman Street at 14.10. Signed for by Bianchi. Is that the one you're talking about?'

'That's it. If it's not too inconvenient, I'd like to know

the name of your client for this job and whether she came here or you went to her place. I understand that this breaches client confidentiality and we can stop everything right now, if you wish. I'll just tell the mother that I could go no further.'

'Well, if it's helping some poor unfortunate, we can make an exception this once. I think if our client was an innocent party, then they won't mind someone knowing when they came here. After all, we already know the name and address of the person the package was sent to, don't we. How old was the girl who's gone missing, did you say?'

'I didn't, but she was sixteen.'

'Sixteen! Good lord. I'd like to get my hands on some of these people.'

He taps away at his keyboard and frowns frequently. 'Here we are. I wasn't here the day this payment was made, but the client came into the office with the package at 13.15 and paid in cash on the same day that the package was to be delivered.'

Cash. What a surprise.

'Can you tell me the name? It would be very helpful.'

'Name of the client was Lara Holland. Would you excuse me for a moment?'

Well, that was easy enough. He stands up and disappears through a door into a back room. He closes the door behind him. I can smell cigar smoke. Lara Holland. I'm hoping that Lara Holland is Amelia Finch, but that may not be the case. The woman on the phone to Sakura and the woman who booked the hotel rooms and the woman who paid the courier to deliver the deposit may all be different people. If that's the case, this is going to be a nightmare. On the other hand, if I was organising something like this and it was bent in some way, I'd want to limit the number of people involved. It would be easier to trust one person than to trust three. It would all depend on the secrecy required and how much money I was prepared to spend on the whole endeavour.

Rob Wickham returns with a painfully thin black guy who's dressed like he's at the beach and is smoking a slim panatella.

'Sorry about the wait. This is Declan. He was on the desk when Miss Holland made the payment. I've told him what you told me.'

Declan and I shake hands. He holds my gaze. 'I fucking hope you find her, mate. That's too young to go missing, especially in London.'

'Yeah. Me too. Look – I just need you to cast your mind back to this Miss Holland.'

He doesn't hesitate. 'I remember her. Paid with cash. It was thirty quid. Up near Marble Arch. Tony did it.'

'Tony's one of our despatch motorcyclists,' says Rob Wickham, usefully.

'OK. Can you remember what she looked like?'

Declan looks up and to his right. I can see he's visualising her.

'Yeah. I mean you couldn't forget her, really. She was power-dressed, you know? Like she was the director of a successful business. A small business, though. Not too grand. But definitely designer clothing. Expensive. You don't get women who look like that coming in here very much. She was wearing a grey suit. The top was like a bolero jacket. No buttons at the front. The skirt was about three inches above the knee. Black stockings. She had on something dark red under the jacket, but I couldn't quite work it out. It was almost like it was a camisole, you know? Little trim of lace at the top, like she was wearing something a little sexier to offset the suit. Black or grey shoes, I can't remember.'

'Any distinctive accent?'

'No. Southern England. That's all I can say, really. Not particularly London.'

'And she seemed fine, she seemed relaxed, she didn't seem nervous.'

'Maybe in a bit of a hurry, but everyone's in a bit of a hurry. I don't think she was local, though. She had a cab waiting outside with its engine running.'

'That's great. What about her physical appearance.'

'Blonde hair but short. Again, an expensive cut. I've seen a picture of Carey Mulligan with that style, so it can't have been cheap. I couldn't tell if the hair was her real colour or not, but I think it was. Her eyebrows were a light colour, which makes it likely she was a natural blonde. Very, very pretty. Green eyes. She looked like a model.'

'What sort of model are we talking about here? Catwalk model? Page Three model? Glamour model?'

He has a quick think and places a forefinger against his mouth. 'None of those, really. More like your girlfriend's lingerie catalogue model. Pretty and wholesome, but sort of sexy and beautiful at the same time, you know? Bra size could have been a 35DD – I am a bit of an expert – and she was about five foot nine. That height could be wrong, though, as I didn't notice if she was wearing high heels, and if I did I can't remember.'

I smile at him. 'She obviously made quite an impression!'

'Well, like I said, you don't get women who look like that coming in here very much. If women come in here, they're usually secretaries, not boss types. And this one struck me as a boss type, at least from the way she was dressed anyway and her whole demeanour. Having said that, she wasn't that old. Early twenties, I would have guessed.'

'OK. That's great. I won't use up any more of your time. Just one thing. If I do a sketch, like a facial composite, of this woman, can you just tell me if I'm going in the right direction?'

'Sure.'

'Have you got a sheet of paper I could use, please?'

Rob Wickham fetches me an A4 sheet from under the counter. I get out my pen, poise it above the sheet and take a deep breath. Both he and Declan watch my hand, fascinated. I imagine this must be a change from whatever else they'd both be doing at this time of day.

'OK. What shape face did she have? You mentioned Carey Mulligan. She has a heart-shaped face. Would you say that Miss Holland's face was like that?'

'No. This one had a longer face than that and with more prominent, wide cheekbones.'

'Sort of like Charlize Theron? She has what they call a diamond-shaped face. Cheekbones that are wider than the chin and forehead.'

He thinks about this for a moment, as if he's running through films he's seen her in.

'Yeah. Yeah I can see her now. That'd be about right.'

I quickly sketch a diamond-shaped face on the sheet of paper and sketch out a few wisps of blonde hair.

'This starting to look like her?'

'More hair across the forehead. Like a fringe. It was swept back over her ears so you could see her ears. Yeah. That's cool. That's like her without a face.'

'What about her eyes, apart from the fact they were green? What about the eye shape and eyebrows? Keep talking film stars, if that'll help.'

'Big, round eyes. Pretty. Slightly turned up at the side. Angelina Jolie. Eyebrows were pale, but up and down, like a roof shape that a kid might draw.' He makes a roof shape with a finger.

'Got it.'

Both men are watching with fascination now. Declan turns the drawing so it's facing him. 'Hang on.' He goes into the back room and comes out with a green felt pen. He colours the eyes in. 'There. That's her eyes exactly. Eyebrows a little paler, but apart from that – brilliant.'

'OK. Let's do her mouth next. Lipstick?'

'Yeah. Red. Don't know which shade. My girlfriend uses red. This was lighter, but not by much.'

'Mouth shape?'

'Er – well not Angelina Jolie. But not thin, either. Sort of average, I suppose.'

I sketch in a 'typical' female mouth which fits in with and complements all the other features. 'How does that look?'

'A bit fuller than that.'

I alter it.

'Now?'

'Fine.'

'And her nose?'

'Nothing distinctive. Not big, not small.'

'OK. Let's see.' I sketch in an anonymous, but fairly feminine nose that fits the face shape and turn the drawing around to face Declan. 'So how are we doing?'

'That's fucking incredible. That's her. Fuck. You should be an artist, man. Can I make a copy of this?'

'Sure. Could you make me one as well?'

Just before I leave, I stick a hundred on the reception desk. 'This has been really helpful. I don't want any argument. You may have saved someone's life. Go down the pub tonight on me, OK?'

They both grin and looked equally pleased and astonished. I think they enjoyed this. Just as I'm on my way out of the door, Declan calls me back, while waving his photocopy of the rather dishy Lara Holland.

'Can you sign this, please?'

I walk down Chiswick High Road and try and square Lara Holland with Amelia Finch. What did Sakura say Amelia's voice was like? Educated and home counties. That would fit in with Declan's assessment of her voice as sounding southern England, but not London. But there are a lot of people who could be described as speaking in that way; it doesn't mean that Amelia and Lara are the same person, by any means, but something tells me that they are.

I decide to get the tube from Chiswick Park, so I can walk along and have more of a think. If, by a stroke of luck, Amelia and Lara *are* the same person, then I've got something I can show hotel staff at the Bolton, if it comes to that. I smile when I think of Declan wanting a photocopy of that sketch signed. I sense that the hotel isn't going to be as much as a walk in the park as Shamrock Courier Services, though, and I stop at a cashpoint and get out another five hundred.

All in all, this had been quite a good day so far. I've had the disturbing info about the Rosabel Raleigh portrait off Ms Gavreau, Viola's work name at the hotel that night from Sakura and a possible lead to the identity of the person who booked Viola in the first place, even though I don't think she's really called Amelia Finch or Lara Holland.

It's almost five pm now, and I'm wondering whether to go home first or go straight to the hotel. I had considered leaving the hotel until tomorrow morning, but there's slightly more chance I'll be able to talk to staff who were there when Viola arrived than if I visit during the day. That may not be the case, of course. Hotel staff change shifts around a lot, but hopefully the night managers stay the same.

I'm feeling quite tired and still haven't quite recovered from my bout with Sakura. Missing persons is really rather exhausting and time consuming. No wonder the police don't have enough people to cover it. I stop for a moment, and take a look at my face in the window of an estate agent's. Still no evidence of swelling, but I fancy that I've got a black eye coming on the left-hand side. Oh well.

I'm just approaching the tube station when my mobile goes off. My first thought is that it's Sakura, but when I look at the display I can see it's Anjukka.

'Sugar Daddy Dating. How can I help?'

'Oh, Daniel.'

She's sobbing. Before she's said a word, I know exactly what's happened and exactly what it tells me.

'What is it, baby? What's the matter?'

'I've been sacked. I've been bloody sacked.'

'What? What for?'

I think of the lifestyle that her job has allowed her to set up. The clothes, that fabulous flat in Battersea which she obviously loves so much.

'He said I'd breached one of the company protocols.'

'What the hell does that mean? Who said that?'

'Mr Fisher.'

'Fisher was the one who sacked you?'

'He said I was on a month's notice, but I had to leave after a week.'

'After Raleigh's big meeting that he's so concerned about.'

'They're bastards, aren't they. They still want me around to help organise that for them. I should just walk out now.'

'Don't do anything until you see me. Look. Let's meet up for dinner tonight. Selfridge's at eight, OK?'

'I'll need a stiff drink first. I can't believe this. I can't believe this has happened.'

'Don't worry. It'll be OK. Anyway, you said you'd been thinking about leaving for a few months. This might be a good thing for you.'

'I can't wait to see you.'

'I'll be there at eight.'

I click my mobile off and go into the tube station. So that confirms it. Tote Bag was almost certainly hired from Raleigh's office. She didn't have much to report, but she would have given them Anjukka's description and maybe even her address and I guess that would have been enough to infuriate either Raleigh or Fisher or both.

Either there really is a company protocol regarding female staff dating people like me, or they were afraid she might tell me something she shouldn't. Maybe they felt dumb for swallowing her fake engagement story. Maybe they think she really is engaged and were morally outraged and/or humiliated by her showing interest in someone else. Maybe they're just plain jealous. Well fuck 'em. If you work for bastards who think like that, you're better off in another job.

Just as the tube train leaves the station, I realise that I've conceivably got a way of helping her.

# 15

## THE BOLTON MAYFAIR

The Bolton Mayfair is situated in a small, slightly pokey one-way street that must have been quite a fashionable place to live about a hundred years ago. Now, of course, most of the houses belong to various commercial concerns and I don't think many of them are purely residential.

There's a blue plaque on one of the houses letting everyone know that the writer Henry James lived there for a while. I remember reading *The Turn of the Screw* when I was in school and finding it impossibly creepy.

Despite the relative narrowness of the road, The Bolton Mayfair is big, impersonal and classy, and looks like it was built sometime in the last five years. Asking reception staff or management if they can remember the movements of one or two women who stayed here for one night three weeks ago may not be a successful ploy, but I have to try. At the very least, I may be able to confirm that Amelia Finch and Lara Holland are the same person, which means I'll have a rough idea of what Amelia Finch looked like. I can't get over Anjukka getting fired like that.

Once you walk through the big doors at the front and into the spacious reception area, you're in another, air-conditioned world. New-looking black and white marble floors, lots of sparkly white lighting and maybe eight or nine guests hanging around, some checking in, some getting ready to leave and some just loitering. If you were a guest, it would be pretty easy for you to come in or leave without anyone noticing, but hotel staff are pretty sharp-eyed so I might be in luck.

To my right is a spacious waiting area near a fake fireplace with three big black sofas and miscellaneous chairs set around a couple of tables. There's also a stand with magazines and today's newspapers. To my left is a more homely version of the same thing, minus the fireplace, but with cushions on the sofas, a big, flowery print on the wall, real flowers in a vase, more magazines and a low, wide coffee table.

The reception area is dark brown wood with an even larger flowery print on the wall at the back. There are two staff behind it. One of them, a guy in his fifties, is standing up and talking to a blonde woman. There's a girl a few feet away, who's sitting down and typing away at a keyboard. I'll talk to the guy, who looks like the man in charge here. I walk over to the more homely seating area, pick up a magazine and sit down, taking a better look at the place and waiting for the reception guy to be free. He's got an ID badge on, but I can't see what it says from here. I've no idea what I'm going to say to him, but it's better to be straight. Hotel people have seen and heard it all and can usually detect bullshit and spot bullshitters a mile off.

To the right of the reception desk, there's a staircase going down to the lower ground floor. There're no signs there, so it's more than likely for staff use, or maybe there's a spa area or restaurant. Also on my right is a pair of doors which lead into a bar. There are menus on the table, so presumably it's also a restaurant. On my left, there's a staircase and a sign saying 'lifts'. Whichever way you came from, you'd have to walk past reception to get out.

Two hotel porters walk past me and start talking to a family of four who seem agitated and keep pointing at their luggage. Nobody, whether staff member or guest, looks at me twice. A cab driver comes in and starts talking to the girl behind the reception desk. A man in a black business suit runs in, places a big envelope on the reception desk and runs out again. Two girls who are dressed like waitresses walk past and laugh and point at something they can see in the street. All in all, there's a fairly big mix of people here and a lot of activity. If Amelia and Natasha were meeting up here, only their attractiveness would make you look at them.

The blonde woman who was talking to the reception guy turns on her heel and heads towards the main doors. She looks pissed off about something. She bumps into an elderly woman who's coming in and doesn't apologise to her. The guy behind the reception desk raises his eyebrows in amusement and starts to write something down. I think I'll hit on him now. Maybe I'll be a relief from whatever happened with the blonde woman. I've decided that my best tack here would to be totally honest and tell him everything. If he won't play ball, I'll just have to start flashing the cash and see where that gets me.

I approach the desk and catch his eye. I can see his ID badge now. It says 'Mark Kerrigan. Senior Night Reception Coordinator.' Well that sounds like the sort of person I need. At least it's a start.

'Hi. My name's Daniel Beckett. I'm a private investigator working on a missing persons case. I'm sure you're very busy, but I'd be very grateful if I could just have five minutes of your time.'

Of course, it'll be longer than five minutes – at least I hope it will – but five minutes sounds nice and concise. His expression doesn't change, but I can tell he's interested. He has a calm voice with a southern Irish accent.

'Can I ask what it's about?'

'Yes. One of your guests booked a visit from a call girl here about three weeks ago. The call girl has since vanished. I've just got a few questions about the guest and I'd like to know if anyone who was on that night saw anything that may be of help to my investigation.'

That sounded pretty good. The mention of a call girl makes him look rapidly from left to right to see if anyone has overheard any part of this conversation. I give him the date and watch his face carefully. He turns to the girl. 'Ruby, could you take over reception for a few minutes, please? Give Francesca a buzz to come and give you a hand in case it gets busy. I think she's having coffee.'

Ruby stops her typing and takes Mr Kerrigan's place behind the counter. He beckons to me with his forefinger. 'Come with me.'

I follow him through the bar, down a corridor with some shops which are closed and down some stairs until we come to a small office. We go inside, he closes the door, fires the computer up, and indicates that I should sit down.

'Sorry to spirit you away so quickly. Nothing personal. We try not to discuss the peccadilloes of some of our guests in the reception area. The computer will be working in a minute or two and then we can have a look.'

'I quite understand.'

'So what's the score? What's going on?'

'A woman called Amelia Finch booked a call girl from an online service which specialises in supplying bisexual and lesbian escorts. She booked a room in this hotel for herself and she booked another room here for the escort, who was using the name Natasha Hart.'

'Separate rooms? What were they going to do? Phone sex?'

'It's a hangover from the old days, when for the escort's safety, they had somewhere to go if the client seemed dangerous or high or mad or whatever.'

'I've never come across that before. Between you and me, though, we have had lesbian escorts visit this hotel in the past, it's just that they didn't do that thing with the two rooms. OK, let's have a look. What was the date again? Sorry, my memory's starting to fail.'

'Seventeenth of last month.'

He taps something on the keyboard, waits, then taps something else, while squinting at the screen.

'You're in luck. I was on that night. And the name was Amelia Finch, yes? OK. I've got her. Mrs Amelia Finch. She booked the rooms on the fifteenth, two days before they were required. She booked a King Deluxe room including breakfast for herself and she booked a Double Deluxe room for a Miss Natasha Hart, also including breakfast.'

So Amelia Finch expected both Viola and herself to be there the next morning, unless she was being very smart and devious indeed.

'How does breakfast work here if you're a guest?'

'You go down to the breakfast room in the basement and one of the restaurant reception staff will check your name and room number.'

'So you wouldn't really bother booking a breakfast if you had no intention of eating it here.'

He looks at me as if I'm rather dim.

'No, and if you're booking online, which Mrs Finch was, it's not an easy thing to do to book your breakfast by mistake. To do it twice would be even more unlikely. The whole thing isn't set up so you could do that. Also, breakfast adds another fifteen pounds to the bill. You wouldn't book it unless you were going to eat it. There are plenty of places about five minutes' walk from here where you can get a cheaper breakfast and a better one, too, though I didn't say that, of course.'

'Is there any way of checking whether these guests ate breakfast on the morning of the eighteenth? The morning they would have been checking out.'

'Actually yes there is. The breakfast room receptionist would electronically tick you off on the computer when you confirmed your room number.'

'Is that electronic ticking off still on the computer?'

'It should be. I think the computer guys have an info purge every three months.' He looks me straight in the eye. 'You know I shouldn't be telling you any of this…'

He wants to know if he's going to be paid for giving away guests' secrets. I'll let him know that he will be. It'll make him more enthusiastic. I keep the eye contact.

'I know, yeah. I'll be very, very grateful, though.'

'OK. Just so we understand each other.'

He taps away at the keyboard. I look around the office. I'd like an office like this in my flat. It's decorated in exactly the same way as the rest of the hotel; marble floors, classy prints, nice furniture, air conditioning. No windows, though.

'Here we go. There's no record of either Mrs Finch or

Miss Hart visiting the breakfast room on that morning. Ah!'

'What?'

'There's also no record of either of them having checked out. It happens sometimes. We did a pre-authorisation of Mrs Finch's card and took an imprint. She paid in full in advance online and there were no extras, no minibar use or anything else like that. Of course, if there had been any extras we had her card details. That's why we do the pre-authorisation.'

'There was no problem with the credit card that she used to pay for the rooms.'

'None at all.'

'Can you give me the card details?'

He looks shiftily from left to right, even though we're the only ones in the room. 'I can print them off for you, if you like, thanks to the wonders of modern technology.'

'Yes please. So both of these women could have left the hotel at any time the previous night and nobody would have been any the wiser.'

'That's true, yeah. It's an unlikely thing to happen, seeing as the rooms had been paid for in full, not to mention breakfast being paid for, but it's still possible. I was off at ten that night. Someone else would have noticed that neither of them checked out, but that wouldn't have been until around midday or maybe later. As there was no money owed, no one would have made a great fuss about it. I didn't hear anyone mention it. If there was something suspicious, someone would have said something to me, as I was the one on duty when Mrs Finch and Miss Hart checked in.'

He hands me the printout. It's got everything; Amelia Finch's card details, a contact telephone number and an address in SE19, which I think is Crystal Palace or thereabouts. I would be very surprised if any of this was genuine, though the card obviously worked.

'But they both checked in. You're sure of that.'

'Yes, they did. Mrs Finch checked in at 19.15 and Miss Hart checked in at 20.54.'

'I noticed CCTV cameras in reception…'

'Sorry. All that footage is only kept for seven days.'

'Is there any way of knowing whether either of those beds had been slept in?'

'Not on the computer, no. The maids would notice something like that, but it's very unlikely any of them would remember it three weeks on. It happens from time to time, you know? People having affairs booking into separate rooms, that kind of thing. A maid would just see it as a bit of work that didn't need to be done. She wouldn't make a note of it or report it. She'd just see the bed was OK, give the room a clean, move on to the next one and would have forgotten about it by lunchtime.'

'OK. And you were behind the reception desk during the time period that both women checked in?'

'Almost certainly, but I don't recall either of them. That's quite a busy time of night and we have a big turnover of guests here.'

I take out my facial composite of Lara Holland, flatten it with my hands and push it over the desk towards him.

'Does that look like Amelia Finch? I did it quickly, so it's pretty impressionistic, but…'

He takes a long look at it, then places one of his hands over her eyebrows. 'Yeah. Yeah. That's good. I remember her now. Quite striking features. Very pretty girl. But you had to fight to see it, you know?'

'What d'you mean?'

'She had glasses on, for a start, like full-rimmed, you know?' He makes the shape of the frames around his eyes. 'And the hair here is different. Is this meant to be light hair of some sort? Light brown or blonde?'

'I was told blonde.'

'Well Mrs Finch didn't have blonde hair and it wasn't short like this. Her hair was brown and it was definitely shoulder length. It covered her face more than the style you've got here does. It was like a wispy kind of style. But you couldn't mistake those beautiful green eyes. You've got the eyes perfectly. You kind of wanted to reach out and take those glasses off, d'you know what I mean?

'She was quite tall, too. Maybe had heels on. I couldn't really see. Wasn't dressed in anything out of the ordinary. Could have just been smart work clothes. I didn't really take any notice of what she was wearing.'

So Amelia Finch and Lara Holland are the same person. I thought as much, but it's nice to have it confirmed. She was wearing a wig and glasses, but for what reason? Maybe she was just naturally cautious. I take out my mobile and get the photograph of Viola up on the screen; the nice one, the one she had done by a photographer. It only now occurs to me that this was one of a pack of photographs she had done to sell herself on Sakura's site. I'll check with Sakura the next time I see her. I slide the mobile over to Mark Kerrigan.

'Do you recognise this woman?'

He takes a look at Viola's photograph.

'Beautiful.'

'Yes. That's Natasha Hart. Do you remember her booking in? Her appearance may have been different from this.' She has shoulder length blonde hair in the photograph. 'Her hair is almost certainly different from this now. It might be a different colour and it might be a different length and style.'

'Vaguely, yes. Possibly, I mean. I think we had quite a queue at the time, phones going off, all the rest of it. She's the prostitute is she?'

It's a bit of a shock hearing that word so casually used about Viola. 'Yes she is. She didn't return from the job that Mrs Finch booked her for and hasn't been seen or heard from since.'

'I can usually identify them. Call girls, that is. There are a great variety of them. In appearance, you know? Hair is always different, clothes are always different, beauty is different, manner is different and the walk is different. No two the same. But whether they know it or not, there's something about them that enables you to spot them straight away after you've been doing this for a while. It's their manner. It isn't the manner of a guest. I'm always polite to them, though. It's just a job, isn't it.'

'I take it that nobody on the staff would have noticed either of these women leave.'

'No. You don't look at people leaving; you only look at people arriving because you're going to have to do something. People who are going out of the hotel, unless they're checking out, are of no interest to staff unless they're carrying a lot of luggage and want help.' He smiles. 'Or carrying a big pile of towels. Old people you notice, in case they need help. Running, shouting kids you notice. Pissed people you might notice. Sometimes, if you notice people dressed up like they're going out to a restaurant or the theatre or something, you might tell them to have a nice evening if you're not busy. But exiting guests are non-people. Besides, people going out generally have their back to you.'

'So they could have left at any time and no one would have seen them go.'

'That's about it. What do you think happened to her?'

I rock backwards on my chair and stare into the middle distance for about twenty seconds before answering. 'I don't know. But I think Amelia Finch may have some of the answers, so the next thing I have to do is find her and ask her some questions.'

'Well, you've got her address, at least. Just one other thing, and it may be nothing, but I was surprised that she had the title Mrs, you know? She didn't look old enough to be married, but you can never tell, of course.'

'How old would you say she was?'

'Twenty? Certainly no older than, say, twenty-two. It was her complexion.' He taps his cheek. 'Fresh and young. A bit like mine.'

'This has been really useful, Mr Kerrigan. Just one more thing, and I don't know if this is going to be possible. Can I take a look at both rooms?'

'Hmmm. Let me just check.'

While he's checking, I try to get my thoughts straight. If I'm able to check the rooms out, what will I be looking for? I've no idea, really, but something may pop into my head. It could be I'll be looking at the last place that Viola ever stayed in or visited. I don't know. Maybe I'll feel some vibes or something.

'Well, the King Deluxe room that Mrs Finch booked is free at the moment, so we can go and look at that right now. In fact, no one's stayed in that one since your Mrs Finch. The Double Deluxe that was booked for Miss Hart is currently occupied by a couple from Amsterdam. I'll see what I can do. Come on.'

He stands up. I take five hundred out of my wallet and

place it on the table, along with one of my business cards. 'This has already been more valuable than you could imagine. Thank you for your time.'

'My pleasure, Mr Beckett.'

He takes the money and the card, slips them into an inside pocket and off we go.

The King Deluxe room is on the third floor. It's big and airy and although the view isn't up to much, I can't imagine they get many complaints. The first thing you notice is the massive bed, which could easily sleep five. The room has got all the usual stuff, soft sofas, massive television, huge prints, thick pile carpets; it's like every hotel you've ever stayed in, but more so.

The bathroom is full of glass, brown marble, bright strip lighting and chrome, with a power shower, a wide bath, a telephone in the toilet and neat piles of pristine towels everywhere. The whole thing is spotless and smells like no one's ever been in it. Maybe they haven't. Mr Kerrigan follows me in, interested in what I'm doing. He notices a smear on the mirror over the sink, breathes on it and wipes it away with a hand towel. He laughs when he sees I've spotted him doing it 'You'd be amazed at the things that our guests complain about, Mr Beckett. That's probably saved one of our staff an irate telephone call.'

As I walk around, waiting for some revelation to reveal itself, Mr Kerrigan stoops down and runs his hand across a section of carpet to the left of the door, about two feet away from a small writing desk. 'Will you look at that? Scuffs everywhere. Cleaners should have vacuumed it out. Ah well. They probably didn't notice. It's the sort of thing you see when you've had kids in one of the rooms.'

The carpet is pale brown with a complex dark brown pattern all over it. I think it's meant to look like the tendrils of a plant, as there are little flower details every now and then. Mr Kerrigan is rubbing his hand over an area about a foot long, which looks like someone has dug their heel into it and dragged it across hard, with the intention of damaging the carpet. Nothing that a good hammering with a vacuum cleaner wouldn't sort out, but interesting all the same.

Because of the colour and pattern, it would be easy to miss (unless you're Mr Kerrigan), and it's an area of the room you wouldn't walk across much. What's even more curious is that on closer inspection, there are quite a lot of small scuffs and marks. The carpet looks new, and the pile is thick. Mr Kerrigan looks peeved.

'Looks like someone's been having a bloody fight in here. Or playing football.'

But it's probably nothing. I look out of the window. We're on the third floor and I can see it's quite a drop to the outside. Apart from that, I don't think you can fully open the window, which would be usual in a hotel now.

'How would you get out of here if you didn't want to pass through reception?'

'Well, you couldn't. Unless you used the fire escape.'

'Show me.'

We leave the room, turn right into the corridor and then right again at the end into a smaller corridor that's maybe about ten feet long. If you were a guest in any of the nearby rooms, you would never come down here unless it was a mistake, or unless, perhaps, the hotel was ablaze. At the end, there's an escape door with a wide panic bar.

'Can I open this?'

'Yes, but an alarm would go off.'

'What would happen then?'

He points to a CCTV camera about six feet away which points directly at the escape door. 'Security would see a red light flash on the relevant screen and one of their audio monitors would start bleeping. They'd come down to sort whatever it was out. Kids open them sometimes, or just stupid people. Or drunks. Whoever was on duty would look at what that camera was seeing before they decided how quickly to act.'

'So somebody from security would come up here and what then? Would they have to reset the alarm, or does it reset automatically?'

'They'd have to reset it locally – on the door itself – and then they'd confirm the reset in the security office. It's all a bit complicated now. Used to be much easier in the old days. Computers have changed that.'

I squat down and take a look at the alarm pack on the door. It's powered by batteries, presumably.

'So let's say I wanted to disable the alarm on this escape door. I could open the pack here if I had the right key, or just break it off if I had the right instrument, disconnect the battery, then run down to the security office and switch all the flashing lights and buzzers off before anyone noticed.'

'That would be the way to do it, but you'd have to rely on there being nobody in the security office for a start, and of course you'd have to know where it was. Even if there wasn't anyone there, a message stating the time of the disconnect would be logged on the computer system, which you'd then have to hack into and delete.'

'So it would be impossible for me to do that without someone knowing.'

'Basically, yes.'

I look through the reinforced glass of the escape door.

There's a platform outside, which leads to the steps of what looks like an ordinary fire escape ladder. It's new and sturdy looking.

'Can we go and look at the other room, assuming there's no one at home?'

'Certainly. I have to get back on duty soon, though.'

'This is the last thing. You've been very helpful.'

He knocks on the door of the Double Deluxe room that Natasha would have been in. It's on the floor above the other one. There's no reply, so he gets out an electronic key, swipes it and we're inside. He turns to me and grins. 'I hope you've got a good story ready if they come back.'

'I'll tell them we had reports of rats in this room'.

'That should be fine.'

The room is untidy, which isn't surprising, with various items of clothing scattered over the furniture. It's a noticeably smaller room than the one Mrs Finch had, but has all the same amenities. The bed is smaller, but still pretty big by normal standards. I take a look out of the window again. The window is the same type as the King Deluxe; you can't open it and the drop is greater. Apart from that, there's really nothing of interest to see.

On our way out, Mr Kerrigan is smiling to himself. 'You keep looking out of the windows all the time. I can't help but notice. Are you looking to see if someone who was out of their head on booze or drugs could be chucked out the window or out of the fire escape? Or maybe looking for a way someone could dispose of a body? Some way that wouldn't involve dragging it past reception?'

'I don't know. I suppose it's at the back of my mind. It isn't possible, though, is it?'

'Well, now I come to think of it, there is one possibility, though you'd have to know the hotel fairly well to know about it. Come with me.'

We walk down the stairs to Mrs Finch's floor again. We walk past her room and head towards the fire escape, but stop short while Mr Kerrigan pushes open a door I hadn't really noticed.

It's more of a large-ish storage cupboard than a room and it's for the use of the cleaners. There are three of those trolleys that you usually see laden with room supplies; soap, shampoo, coffee, sugar and all the rest of it. All the walls are basically shelves, stacked with supplies and cleaning stuff. There's a window, but it's narrow, perhaps two feet wide. Kerrigan points at it.

'I think we may be entering the realms of fantasy here, but you could shove someone out of this window if you were crazy enough and knew about this room. Of course if you tried to jump from here, the fall would probably kill you as we're on the third floor. The window can't be opened from the outside, and even if it could, you'd have to be Spider Man to scale the wall in the first place. But you can open it from the inside. There's a lock here, see?'

He points to a black handle with a built-in keyhole.

'Wouldn't you have to have a key?'

'Well, yes. But these are pretty easy to open without one. I have mentioned it to security, but they just laughed and said there was no need to be concerned about suicidal cleaning staff. Watch.'

He takes out his wallet and removes a credit card.

'There's a latch bolt at the top and lock bolt directly underneath. But the lock bolt is small, and doesn't quite fit into the strike plate. A lot of this type of lock has this sort of design fault. The hotel probably got them on the cheap, maybe just for these windows. So you can push your credit card like so…'

He pushes his card into the gap between the window and the window frame, and then bends it to the right. I can hear the lock bolt make a loud click as it opens. He then turns the handle downwards and the window opens.

'See? No one bothers about this because you can't break in from the outside. My concern was more to do with cleaning staff stealing stuff and dropping it out of the window to their mates waiting down there with a shitload of bin bags. I can't imagine anyone bothering, though. I mean – who wants tons of miniature soaps and tubs of fake milk? But seriously, it's a safety issue.'

I lean out of the window and look down. I can see what he means. You probably wouldn't survive a drop like that if you jumped, and if you did survive, it would be with broken legs and a variety of serious internal injuries. There's nothing in the alley below, apart from a solitary rubbish bin with the lid broken off and a couple of cardboard boxes.

'Where does that alley come out?'

'The only access is from Stratton Street. You can't get to it from Bolton Street, though I think you must have been able to at one time. The Bolton Street entrance to it is bricked up now. I'm not sure it really belongs to anyone. It isn't hotel property.'

'OK. Thanks for everything. I'll let you get back to work.'

'Ah, that's alright. I enjoyed myself. Any time you want anything else, let me know.'

Before I take the tube back to Covent Garden to freshen up for Anjukka, I stroll up Stratton Street to take a look at that alley from street level. There's a Turkish carpet place on one side and a house on the other. There's nothing stopping you from walking into that alley, it's wide enough to back a car into and there are no signs telling you it's private.

I walk down it towards the bin and boxes I noticed from the window on the third floor. Even though the weather is mild, it's cold enough to make me shiver. This is a place the sun never reaches. I look up at the window of the cleaners' room. The wall is sheer and Kerrigan was right; you'd have to be Spider Man to get up there.

I shrug and head for Green Park tube. Well, at least I know that Lara Holland was really Amelia Finch and that Amelia Finch and Viola were both here at some point. The odd thing is why they left without checking out. I try to put myself in their shoes. Amelia first.

I'm still assuming that Amelia was what she seemed. Booking the courier under a false name may just have been paranoia on her part. She turns up here, checks in and goes to her room, excited about what the evening may bring. It could have been that she was afraid of bumping into someone she knew, which may explain the glasses and wig. If she planned to have dinner with Viola, then it wouldn't have been at the hotel, or she would have booked it online.

Then something happens. Perhaps she gets cold feet. Perhaps she leaves before Viola even gets here. There was a one and a half hour gap between her arrival and Viola's. Maybe that was enough for her to think it through and wonder what the hell she was doing. Maybe the reality of what she was embarking on suddenly hit her now she was actually at the hotel. She panics and leaves the hotel without even bothering to check out, possibly from embarrassment.

Then Viola turns up and checks in. She goes to her room to freshen up. She knocks on Amelia's door, but no one answers because there's no one there. But that doesn't really hold water, because Viola sent Sakura the text saying that everything was OK and she was going ahead with the job.

So an alternative scenario would have to be that Viola knocks on Amelia's door. Amelia answers. They exchange pleasantries and Amelia hands Viola the balance of the fee. Viola goes back to her room to count the money and to text Sakura. She then goes back to Amelia's room to tantric massage her and do whatever else they're going to get up to. I can't speak for Amelia, but I think if it was me and I had hired Viola for the night, I might have ordered something from room service, even if it was a solitary bottle of champagne. It could be that Viola brings her own bottle of champagne, but I don't think that's very likely.

So everything's going to plan, but then something goes wrong. I can't imagine what this could be, but it's so serious that both women flee the hotel, neither bothering to check out. Despite what Mr Kerrigan said, I think both women would have left the hotel via reception, and not through a storage room window that neither of them would know existed and which possessed a drop that could have killed them. And then, to make things even more confusing, why didn't Viola contact Sakura and tell her what had happened?

Then there's another possibility. Amelia Finch hired Viola with the express intention of doing away with her for reason or reasons unknown. But if that was the case, she was taking a hell of a risk and spending a hell of a lot of money. Perhaps she was a psychopath, and none of those things mattered to her. Perhaps she looked at Sakura's site, saw the photographs of Viola and thought to herself, *I would like to kill her.*

So my visit to The Bolton Mayfair threw up more questions, bafflement and dead ends, even if I now know that Lara Holland was Amelia Finch and I've got a passable sketch of what Amelia Finch looks like. Despite all the negatives, though, I feel I'm getting closer to Viola. It sounds stupid, but I feel that she's holding out a hand to me to be rescued or something, and my hand is now a lot closer to hers than it was a couple of days ago. But I'm not sure I want to know what will happen when our hands finally meet.

# 16

## WICKED THOUGHTS

It's only when I get home and get into a hot bath that my body kindly reminds me of the thrashing I received today at the hands of Sakura. I lie there, staring at the ceiling, while trickling in as much hot water as I can stand. I'm trying to have a break from thinking about this case, but as soon as I start anticipating tonight with Anjukka, I start thinking about how she was fitted up by Tote Bag.

If I was Tote Bag, I'd certainly keep that embarrassing episode in Liberty's to myself. It would be too embarrassing and make me look like an unprofessional idiot. In which case, Raleigh, or whoever she reports to, would still think that I was unaware that they had a tail on me, which would be a good thing. I'm surprised, however, that I haven't spotted another one. Maybe they're using someone better.

When I get out, I take a look at myself in the mirror. I look better than I feel. There's bruising around my breastbone from those kicks I received while I was busy with a towel around my head and there's a bit of a black eye starting from those occasions when my skull collided with the wall.

I turn around so that I can see my back in the mirror. There's dark bruising around the area where I received that murderous kidney punch, but at least the pain has gone down now. There's also a big bruise on my shoulder and another whopper on my collarbone. I'm not sure how I obtained those two. I've also got small bruises on the side of both forearms from blocking Sakura's multiple blows. I have to admit it, though, she was really fuckin' good. God help anyone who tried to mug her.

I pick up a London A-Z and look for the address that Amelia Finch gave the hotel with her booking. 59a Acorn Street, London SE19. Sounds like it might be a flat. It's a long shot that it'll be a real address with Amelia Finch actually living there waiting for me with a cup of tea, but if it is, I'll have to go and check it out tomorrow morning. I've never actually been to Crystal Palace, so if nothing else, I'll have got a tiny bit of London tourism out of the way.

Predictably, there isn't an Acorn Street in SE19 or anywhere else, for that matter. Well, I've still got the telephone number. I type it into my mobile, call it and wait. After a little bit of silence, there's an automated message telling me that the number I have dialled has not been found. It's probably a PAYG number which has been discontinued. Mrs Amelia Finch is a very cautious woman indeed. I didn't expect any of her personal details to be true, but I'm still annoyed with this. If she's not the real deal, as presented to Sakura, then what the hell was she? I have to admit I'm totally baffled when it comes to her motivation for all of this.

The other thing is the credit card. Her address and telephone number were fake, but how did she manage the card? The obvious answer is that somewhere there is a real Amelia Finch who is not connected with any of this. She had one of her credit cards stolen and didn't report it missing during the two or so days that fake Amelia required it. That way, it would pass muster with the pre-authorisation check made by The Bolton Mayfair.

But that would be a risky way of going about it. As soon as you had access to the real Amelia Finch's card, you'd have to do the whole thing pretty damn quickly: ring Sakura, book the hotel, book into the hotel, all the time running the risk that the card might be stopped at any time and you'd be found out.

No. It can't have been done that way. Someone, whether it was Amelia or some associate of hers, would have to have high level criminal or banking contacts to get hold of a card with a fake ID which actually worked, which you could actually buy things with and it would be OK. A card that would pass any validation that a hotel cared to put it through.

I'm just making a coffee when my mobile goes off. It's Sakura.

'Hello, Daniel. How are you feeling now? Not too sore, I hope.'

'Are we talking about you beating me up or the sex?'

'Both.'

'Well, treating them as one combined experience, I don't feel too bad, thank you. I look as if I've been involved in a car crash, though.'

'I've been thinking about when we were together,' she purrs. 'I'm thinking about it right now. It makes me feel so good. My body is tingling. I don't know what to do with myself.'

'Sorry – am I being charged for this call?'

She laughs. 'Listen – I spoke to Sally and Abigail after you'd left me this afternoon; left me all alone with only my wicked thoughts for company.'

'Anything interesting?'

'Well, Sally was very reluctant to speak to me and thought I was trying to get something over on her. It took a while to get her to hold a polite conversation. When I told her about Viola she went quiet. She's always feared that something like that would happen to one of her girls one day, and she didn't like to hear it had happened to someone she knew. She felt that somehow the whole thing was getting closer to her.'

'But she hadn't heard of any recent cull of call girls or any unusual gossip?'

'No. But Abigail Gastrell came up with something interesting. I asked her if she'd heard anything on the grapevine and I told her that I was worried about one of my girls, and she said she'd tell all of her girls to be a little more cautious until we found out what had happened to Viola. She was very sympathetic. I've always liked Abigail. We were lovers for a while, but that was years ago.'

'Thank you for that detail. So what was the interesting thing she came up with, Sakura?'

'One of her girls, her name is Eleanor Wallis, rang her up a few weeks ago, and out of the blue told her that she was quitting. It took a while to get Abigail to pin this telephone call down to an exact date, but when she thought about it, she guessed it was either on the eighteenth or nineteenth of last month, because she temporarily removed Eleanor's page from her website on the twentieth – she was able to check the date on her computer. She planned to talk her out of it, but when she spoke to her on the phone, she said that Eleanor sounded frightened, as opposed to bored with the life, or anything like that.'

'And where is Eleanor now?'

'Abigail didn't know. Eleanor hasn't been answering her phone.'

I give my eyeballs a rub with my free hand. Is there a slight, fleeting chance that Eleanor Wallis might be Amelia Finch/Lara Holland? Somehow I doubt it. She might just be Eleanor Wallis. Will this be another dead end? Still, she's from the world of high-class call girls, so there might be some sort of tenuous link.

'Are you still there?' says Sakura, with an impatient edge to her voice.

'Yes. I'm still here. I'm just trying to get my head around this. You don't know what Eleanor looks like, do you, by any chance?'

'No. Would that make a difference?'

'Possibly. If we could get an address for her it could be useful. I'd really like to see her and talk to her, but before that, I'd like to see what she looks like.'

'Abigail isn't keen on giving out proper, identifiable photographs of her girls, if that's what you mean. She said that Eleanor was a university student, which means that even if she was still on Abigail's site, she'd probably have most of her face obscured. That's what they do, girls like that, and she'd have to respect that. Some don't care, of course. Viola didn't care.'

'OK. Can we go and talk to Abigail, in that case? I'd like to ask her some questions. I think I've got a visual identification of Amelia Finch which is fairly good. It's only a sketch, but it worked for a guy at The Bolton Mayfair. If Abigail thinks it looks like Eleanor, then we'll have to find her. If it doesn't look like her, then we can forget about Eleanor being Amelia. It would be good if you could come with me to see Abigail. It'll change the atmosphere if you know her. By the way, the woman who booked the courier to send you the deposit did so under the name of Lara Holland, but that was almost certainly the same person as the Amelia Finch who turned up at the hotel.'

'Interesting. So many names. Of course I'll come with you, Daniel, if you think that would help you in some way. When would you like to see Abigail? Tonight?'

'Tomorrow morning would be better. Ten o' clock, something like that. Where does she live?'

'Ewell.'

'In Surrey? OK. I'll come to your place at nine-thirty. We can get a cab down there. It'll be more like ten-thirty when we arrive. Could you contact her and then send me a text if all that's OK?'

'Of course I will.'

'And you'll be OK, will you? I mean…'

'I'll be fine. In a cab I'll be fine.'

'OK. Tomorrow, then.'

I consider checking Amelia's credit card number with the issuing bank, but can't imagine I'd have any luck there, even if banks were prone to giving out other people's confidential information to complete strangers, which they aren't.

Besides, the person who organised the card would have known there would be a risk of someone trying to track it down, even if it was just the hotel, so any follow-up would be an impasse and a waste of a phone call. Whoever Amelia is or was, she's covered her tracks pretty well. I'd dearly love to know who's helping her with this and why. I don't think it's something you could do on your own.

There are so many pieces of half-baked information here that it's giving me a headache. Part of me is trying to struggle with what Amelia's motivation might be, but then I start thinking *motivation for what?*

Motivation for visiting a courier company and using another name? Motivation for booking a couple of hotel rooms then leaving without checking out? Motivation for arriving at the hotel in disguise?

And, of course, the fact that both she and Viola didn't check out of the hotel might have been pure coincidence. The fact that Viola disappeared might have been nothing at all to do with Amelia Finch. I must ask Sakura whether this lack of checking out of hotels is a common thing in her world.

I get dressed and prepare to leave for my date with Anjukka, then remember I have to make one more call.

I put my jacket on, make sure I've got all the other crap I need and head down to Exeter Street, which already has more than its fair share of lost tourists and bewildered theatregoers.

Just as I'm strolling past the wine bar at the end of the road, I notice a guy walking past me in the other direction and give him a half-second peripheral glance. He's aged between fifty-five and sixty-five, short grey hair, big nose, long sideburns, medium height, sports jacket, white shirt, dark green tie with thin red stripes, grey trousers, black leather shoes, fit looking, carrying the *Daily Telegraph* and walking with purpose.

He's walked past The Lyceum Theatre so he's not going in there. He's walking on the side of the road with no entrances to anywhere, no shops to look at and no hotel entrances of any kind. He doesn't look lost, doesn't look like he's a theatregoer and doesn't look like a tourist. What he *does* look like is someone who's totally out of place in Covent Garden.

I turn left into Wellington Street and after about a minute, have to cross over the road at Tavistock Street. I don't turn my head to my left, but I can see him down the far end, across the road from the back of Covent Garden Market. He must have turned right at the end of Exeter Street and doubled back. Smart. I get out my mobile, press a button and keep walking down Wellington Street, but not too fast.

'Hi. I don't know if you remember me, but we met the other night.'

I can hear Natalie's dirty laughter on the other end. 'How could I forget? I've been thinking about you.'

'Really?'

'Well what do *you* think? You've ruined me for other men.'

I stop and look in Penhaligon's window, using the screen of my mobile as a reflective surface. Grey Hair has caught up and is about one hundred yards behind me. He's dumped the newspaper. I continue on my way and take a left into Russell Street. There's a café bar about ten yards away. I go in, order a double espresso, take my jacket off and sit at the front, looking out at the street.

'Well the reason I was calling you…' I say.

'Ye-es?'

'…was to see if you fancied having lunch with me tomorrow.'

'At your place? I could get a cab over if you want.'

He walks past the café and looks in briefly. He tried to make it look like a casual glance, but it wasn't good enough.

'No, not at my place. I'm a little busy tomorrow, but I can get a cab over to where you work. Is there anywhere we can go for lunch near you? Expense is no object.'

I'll be charging it to Raleigh, is what I mean. The waitress puts my espresso in front of me. My new shadow is going to be pissed at this. He's going to have to hang around and look innocuous while I finish my coffee and whatever else I decide to do to put him on edge so he'll make mistakes. I'm damned if I'm going out with Anjukka with another fucking tail on me.

'Hmm. Well there is a lovely oyster bar not too far away,' she says. 'Do you like oysters? I hear they're an aphrodisiac. Something to do with amino acids, apparently. I could take the afternoon off to see if that's true, if you like.'

'I'm not sure I'd be able to handle you on aphrodisiacs.'

She gives me the name of the oyster bar and we arrange to meet at twelve-thirty. She'll book it, as it's nearly always busy. I say that's fine. I finish my espresso, get up and put my jacket on and leave the café.

I'm wondering where this guy came from. I'm sure I'd have noticed something if he's been following me all day. I have to assume that he's Tote Bag's replacement, or maybe the replacement of her replacement. I try to think about where I've been and where I could have picked him up.

After I left Anjukka's place this morning, I got a cab to see Ms Gavreau in Old Bond Street and after that walked up to see Sakura, who royally beat the shit out of me. I took Sakura to lunch in that pub and then back to her place. After that I took a cab to Chiswick to speak to the courier company, and then got the tube up to Green Park to talk to Mr Kerrigan at The Bolton Mayfair, then another cab to Exeter Street. Raleigh doesn't know where I live, so if he was behind it, as I suspect, then my big-nosed friend must have tailed me back to my flat without my noticing.

Of course, there's always the possibility that he wasn't working alone. After the failure of Tote Bag, someone may have thought a two-person team might have been the thing to do. I had a feeling that someone was tagging along just before I visited Louisa Gavreau.

I try to remember who I noticed as I was walking along Old Bond Street; fat guy on his mobile, girl with great legs, old woman with walking stick, middle aged guy in cream suit. Was that him? Did he have a change of clothes with him? Had he been on my tail since I left Anjukka's this morning? Quite possibly, if Tote Bag had reported back to Raleigh and he'd identified Anjukka as the woman I was with.

Depending on the timeline, Raleigh or Fisher may have given Grey Hair Anjukka's address. If that's the case, they've succeeded in pissing me off; I don't like being followed and I don't like people knowing where I live. I decide I've had enough. I'm not going to spend another evening steering Anjukka across roads and into shops and I'm not going to keep checking reflections to see who's behind me.

I can see him walking away from me into the market. He stops, bends down to tie a non-existent shoelace and bears right towards the shopping colonnade opposite the main entrance. I'm about ten yards behind him as he pauses and starts innocently eyeing shop windows.

It isn't that crowded here for early evening. There's an old couple looking in another shop window about ten feet away from my man. Two groups of five tourists are heading towards the same area. Two girls come out of the front door of the shop he's pretending to look into. Each big shop window along here has a recess next to it with either a door or a door-sized window.

I have to act quickly. I jog up to him and brightly say, 'excuse me.' Before he realises what's going on, I grab his upper arm and steer him towards one of the doors. He looks surprised and is about to say something, but it never comes out. With only a gap of about nine inches between my fist and his solar plexus, I punch him just the once, with as much *ki* as I can manage. He inhales loudly with the pain and slumps against the door, his face pale. I know that will incapacitate him for the few minutes I need to leave the area and get a cab. I feel bad about it as I know what that must have felt like, but if he doesn't want events like that in his life he should work in insurance.

I get out of my cab at the side of Selfridge's, walk into the store and head for the perfume department. I'm a little early and intend to buy Anjukka a gift of some sort. After all, it's indirectly my fault that she's been fired.

I ask the glammed-up assistant for something not too flowery and she suggests a bottle of Mitsouko by Guerlain. Spicy, earthy and woody, she tells me.

She sprays some on her wrist and holds it out to me. Perfect. I get it gift-wrapped and head for the main entrance. I recognise her from behind immediately; it'd be hard not to. She's wearing a black pencil skirt, red top with short puff sleeves, black stockings with seams and red patent leather high heels. That retro look again but it really suits her. People walk by and look at her as if she's something to do with the shop. She kisses me, I hand her the perfume and we stroll along Oxford Street once more.

'Is this a sympathy date because I've lost my job?'

'Absolutely. That perfume is a sympathy gift, too. All this sympathy makes me feel good. I feel on top of the world. It's nothing to do with you.'

'Raleigh is such a dick. I don't know what I'm going to do.'

'Don't worry about it. Really.'

'So how's your day been?'

'Interesting.' I've got so many things I could tell her, but something is stopping me. It isn't professional reticence; I just don't think it would be a good idea. I don't want her exploding at Raleigh because she's found out that he or Fisher had me tailed last night and inadvertently got an insight into her personal life. That would give them too much information, about her and about me. There is one thing I can tell her, though. 'I went to see this woman this morning. Her name's Louisa Gavreau. She lives in Old Bond Street.'

'Does she know anything about Raleigh's daughter?'

'No. But she knows a lot about portrait painting.'

She stops walking and stares straight at me. 'You *didn't.*'

'No pressure on your part. But she said she could do it in two five-hour sittings. She even works evenings and weekends, but that's to accommodate people who work, which wouldn't really apply to you, would it.'

She punches me on the arm, then puts both arms around my neck and kisses me. It's a kiss that makes passers-by turn their heads away in embarrassment and that's the best kind of kiss there is. 'Thank you,' she says, finally. 'That's given me something else to think about and something to look forward to. We can discuss some poses later on tonight. I have a few ideas.'

'I'll give her a ring and get some dates, if you like. You

can always cancel if they're no good. You could go and have a look at her studio if you wanted to. She seemed very nice and I saw some of her work. It was excellent. I can't wait to see the results. I'll hang it in my bedroom and you can come and see it whenever you're in the mood. How's Raleigh doing with his big meeting next week?'

We continue walking, with me trying to stop myself looking for tails in shop windows. There's a fishy-looking guy right across the road, but then he meets and kisses a girl who obviously goes for fishy-looking guys.

'Hm,' she says, not really wanting to discuss work. 'There's a very funny atmosphere around the place at the moment, not that that's anything new. Mr Raleigh and Mr Fisher had a bit of a shouting match this morning. I couldn't hear what it was about. I'm sure it's all connected with the Oman thing. I could be wrong, though.'

'What sort of a shouting match? Who was in charge of the shouting?'

'Oh, Mr Raleigh, definitely. Mr Fisher was just mumbling in reply. It was as if he'd done something wrong and Raleigh was giving him a bollocking about it. Then Fisher came into reception and fired me, as if it was all my fault, whatever it was.'

'Forget about him. They're a pair of twats.'

They're certainly getting edgy about something. Is it my progress, I wonder? I can't imagine it went well for Fisher when Tote Bag called her report in, which makes me wonder why they're having me followed in the first place.

If Fisher was using an investigations company of some sort, they'd have been on the phone to him as soon as

Tote Bag's cover was blown. They would have grovelled to him, apologised profusely and got someone else on the job straight away.

Fisher, shall we say, would have identified Anjukka from Tote Bag's description (and who knows – she may have taken photographs) and then someone would have made Grey Hair an emergency replacement. Grey Hair would have been supplied with Anjukka's address and he or Fisher would have assumed I would be spending the night there, which is quite flattering, in a way. At that point, of course, they didn't know where I lived, but they do now.

So what does this tell me? Well, not much, other than the fact that Raleigh and/or Fisher are/is easily rubbed the wrong way and make panicky decisions under pressure, often with a big dose of self-interest thrown in for good measure. And that, despite his macho appearance and manner, Fisher is basically Raleigh's man-bitch and is maybe a little frightened of him or just afraid of losing his job and its associated authority. He's also, I suspect, not very big on women in general. But fuck it. I've come a long way in three days and when all this is over, I'll never have to have any contact with them ever again.

As we think about where to go for a pre-prandial drink, a tall, stunning-looking woman with tied-back strawberry blonde hair is walking towards us at quite a pace. She's wearing a fabulous, cobalt blue lace wrap dress with skyscraper heels and to say she's making heads turn would be an understatement. She gives me a smug, knowing smile as we make brief eye contact and I know without any doubt that she's Grey Hair's replacement, or perhaps his co-worker.

Well, by now I don't really give a damn, at least not this evening. It's the investigation into his own daughter's disappearance that Raleigh's sabotaging here by pissing me off, and in one way or another he'll pay the price for it.

After walking for a while, we find a bar in Margaret Street and Anjukka talks animatedly about possible poses for her portrait purely to wind me up, while I try to think of excuses for later on tonight when she asks me where all my bruising came from.

# 17

## RETRO GIRL

'My darling Sakura, it has been much too long, you foxy, bewitching slut you!'

If Anjukka had an older sister in the world of 1950s retro styling it would surely be Abigail Gastrell. As soon as Sakura and I are admitted into her large, Edwardian semi-detached house in Ewell, I feel somewhat disorientated, as if I've unexpectedly stepped back in time into an idealised version of what things weren't really like, but *could* have been like in a British/American hybrid of sixty years ago. If your interior designer was crazy.

It's perfect, from the palette-shaped coffee table, through the mint green, turquoise and pink furniture to the print of The Chinese Girl by Tretchikoff on the wall. The blue/black Eiffel Tower linoleum on the floor and the cherry red and white polka dot curtains are the icing on the cake. There are similarities with Louisa Gavreau's place and I'm sure they could exchange ideas, but Louisa's décor has more *depth*, I suppose, and is more art-based than this. This is tastelessness and camp raised to the level of art.

Abigail herself fits in perfectly. With ruby-red lipstick and ultramarine eye shadow trowelled on, she's wearing a canary yellow dress which is covered in garish, cartoony flowers of white, orange and turquoise. There's almost certainly a bullet bra underneath and her figure brings a new meaning to the word hourglass. She must have an absolutely tiny waist and the dress accentuates this with the help of a black patent leather belt. Big bottom, too, which always helps.

She also has the most amazing red hair, which is tied back in a long ponytail. It's like a combination of Hot Housewife and Rockabilly. It sounds outlandish and bizarre, but the final effect is dazzlingly sexy. I wonder if she dresses like this all of the time and decide that she probably does.

As soon as we're inside, she grabs Sakura and pulls her into a huge, sustained hug, and I stand around feeling like a spare prick at a wedding as she grabs Sakura's ass, digging her red lacquered fingernails in deep, as if she's trying to draw blood.

As I watch them smooch like teenagers at a village hall disco, I wonder if this 1950s image was the one that Abigail used when she was an escort herself, which I presume she was, and I wonder about the age range of the sort of men who would have gone for it. Sixty-something Bettie Page fans, probably.

Her image is so amazing that it's difficult for me to guess how old she must be. At least thirty, without a doubt, and maybe as old as mid-fifties; but whatever it is she wears it well.

After what seems like an age, she turns to look at me, with a piercing, appraising stare that makes me feel extremely self-conscious and young.

'And this must be Daniel.'

I shake her hand. 'Hi. I'm pleased to meet you. I hope you don't mind us barging in on you like this.' Did I just say that?

'Not at all. Not at all. You are helping Sakura, so you are my guest and my friend. Even though Viola was not one of my girls, I feel a physical pain whenever I hear about someone in our line of business who may be in jeopardy. And you know about my Eleanor, of course. Let's go into the kitchen and we can talk.'

Did she say *in jeopardy*?

The kitchen is done out as a 1950s American diner. A massive sunburst design clock takes up one whole wall and most of the other surfaces are covered in retro adverts for Coca Cola, Route 66 root beer and other Americana. It's fantastic, and would be a great venue for a party. She even has an enormous pink Smeg refrigerator. As Sakura and I sit down, she fires up an enormous royal blue espresso machine and turns to look at me once again.

'Do you know Sakura through, er…'

She taps her cheekbone to indicate my black eye, which was worse when I woke up this morning; it's now brown with green around the edges. Sakura quickly answers her. 'No. We are not connected in that way.'

'Oh. OK.'

I look at both of them and wonder what they're talking about. Then it dawns on me. The three of us laugh briefly in our different ways and for different reasons. Sakura catches my eye and winks. Shortly, Abigail sits down opposite me and we sip our coffees for a few moments.

'So Sakura tells me that you think Eleanor's recent unusual behaviour may be linked to that of Viola's disappearance.'

'I wouldn't say that. Not exactly. But it's possible. There could be a tenuous link. To be honest, I haven't got anything else at the moment. Let me show you something.'

I take my drawing of Lara Holland/Amelia Finch out of my pocket and hand it to Abigail. She takes a long look at it and smiles. 'When did you meet her to do this? I don't understand.'

So Eleanor Wallis is Lara Holland is Amelia Finch. Now we're getting somewhere.

'I didn't meet her. Sakura told me that a woman called Mrs Amelia Finch booked Viola for a night in The Bolton Mayfair.' She nods. She's heard most of this from Sakura, but I keep going anyway. 'She paid Sakura a deposit in cash which was delivered by a motorcycle courier. I visited the courier company and one of the guys there gave me a description of the woman who paid them for that job. That drawing is from the description I was given.

'They told me her name was Lara Holland. When I showed that drawing to a manager at the hotel, he identified her as Amelia Finch, except Amelia Finch wore glasses and what we assumed was a wig when she visited the hotel.'

'This is Eleanor Wallis,' says Abigail, finally. 'There can be no doubt about it. This is an excellent likeness. It's almost photographic. Could you – could you draw me like this? I'd love to have one of these of me. In a thick red plastic frame. Don't know about the felt pen eyes, though.'

I have to laugh. 'Sure. Whenever I've got time I'll come down here with my pencil and sketch pad.'

'Or I could come to your place.'

'It's always a possibility.'

'Let's make it soon, eh?'

Sakura bursts out laughing. 'Oh, *stop* it Abigail!' She turns to me and laughs. 'She'll fuck anything, Daniel. Don't get too flattered.'

'Thanks. I won't.'

Abigail giggles. 'I'm sorry, darlings. I can't help myself. So let me get this straight. One of my girls, who was primarily heterosexual the last time I checked, hires a bisexual call girl from one of my rivals, my darling Sakura here.'

'That's right. She hired her for the whole night.'

'But to protect her identity, for whatever mad reason, she called herself Mrs Amelia Finch. I like the 'Mrs', by the way, don't you? Such a nice touch. It's funny how that title can add a touch of respectability to a person, isn't it, Sakura.'

'It certainly is, Abigail,' says Sakura, smiling. Abigail reaches across the table and holds Sakura's hand. These two should get a room. I can see Abigail looking from Sakura to me and then back again.

'You don't think, Sakura, do you, that perhaps the three of us…'

'Not at the moment, darling,' says Sakura, grinning.

'So, Daniel,' says Abigail. 'Why do you think she used another name when paying for this motorcycle courier?'

'I have no idea why she should have done that. There was no real need for two deceptions. One would have been fine. But, it did delay my investigation very slightly, so perhaps that was the intention, to muddy the waters a little. I went to the courier company in case they'd sent a bike to her home to pick up the money. If that was the case, I'd have had her address, but she went there in person, so no address, at least not a genuine one, but I got a physical description which tied her to Amelia Finch at the hotel.'

'I'll tell you now, Daniel, I cannot *imagine* why she would have done this. Let me tell you a little about Eleanor Wallis. She's almost twenty-one and she's studying for a bachelor's degree in Diplomacy and International Relations at London Metropolitan University. Her college work always comes first, but she's available most evenings and virtually every weekend.

'She's very good when it comes to entertaining businessmen who want someone to take to dinner and who want everyone to be jealous of them when they see her. She's intelligent, articulate and can talk about a wide variety of subjects. You would never guess that she was a call girl, which is something that makes her price so high, apart from her looks and body, of course. Your drawing is good, but it doesn't do full credit to her. If you saw her in person, you'd see why she's so popular. She's exquisitely beautiful and has a strong sexual presence. I'll show you some photographs later, if you like. She's one of the best at GFE that I have.'

'What's GFE?'

Abigail laughs. 'Girlfriend experience, darling. No rush; kissing and French kissing, cuddling, going out for a meal, or maybe to the theatre. Whatever. Guys want a pretend girlfriend for the night, or maybe even for the week. They want a *nice girl*. Sometimes they take them on holiday with them. Maybe it's something they've never had in their real life. Maybe they've never walked down a street with a beautiful girl on their arm. Maybe they've never had other guys being jealous of them, thinking *what has he got that I haven't?*

'You're a good-looking man, Daniel, but even you must have had difficulties at certain stages of your life with girls. Maybe a girl you wanted to go out with wanted to go out with someone else. Perhaps you didn't have enough money to take a girl out on a date in the way some girls like it. Maybe some girls just didn't like you or you were making the wrong choices for various reasons. Now try and imagine what it must have been like for some of the ugly fat fucks that *we* get!'

She laughs raucously at her own joke and Sakura and I cruelly join in. I like her. You can quite easily imagine going to the pub with her and it being a real laugh. She's rubbing my leg with her foot under the table.

'Thank you, Abigail. I feel a lot better about my past failures now.'

'You're welcome, Daniel. The more successful and rich and powerful the men are, the more ugly, gross and boring they are. It's one of the rules of life, Daniel, my love. We're the happiness safety net for guys like that. Actually, that's quite good. I might use that on the site. The Happiness Safety Net. Hm.'

'OK, Abigail. So Eleanor was very good at her work, and there's no obvious reason why she would have booked Viola for a tantric massage and lesbian experience.'

'No. If she'd wanted a lesbian experience, she could have taken her pick from a number of my girls for nothing. Christ, I'd have had her myself.'

I take a sip from my coffee, but it's cold. Abigail notices. 'Let me get you another. Sakura?'

She turns to talk to us as she makes more coffee. I'm trying to focus, but I keep wondering what she'd look like naked and what her breasts are like without the pointy bra. 'You see, Daniel darling, all I knew about this was that she rang me up and said she'd decided to quit. I couldn't bloody believe it, to be honest. She was making a fortune and she was saving it.

'She planned to take a couple of years off when she'd done her degree and travel around the world. It was so unlike her. She loved the money, too. That's why she worked so hard. For some girls, the money becomes an addiction. We never talked about it, but I think Eleanor was like that. She serviced more clients than any other girl who's on my books. She also liked the buzz of wondering what the client was going to be like when she was on her way to a job.'

'What makes it so odd, Abigail,' says Sakura, 'is that both Eleanor and Viola left that hotel without checking out. Eleanor had paid in advance, there were no extras, so the hotel wasn't that bothered, but it's still strange. She'd even booked breakfast for both of them.'

'How did she pay for the hotel?' asks Abigail.

'A credit card under the name of Amelia Finch,' I say. 'The hotel pre-authorised it and it seemed to pass muster. I can't imagine where she'd have got it from, though I don't think it matters that much. It was just a prop in the whole scam, if scam it was.'

'And she rang you, Sakura,' says Abigail. 'She must have given you the whole spiel about wanting to try it with another woman and you didn't notice anything suspicious? My darling, are you getting old?'

Sakura gives her a quick, insincere smile. 'No, I didn't notice anything suspicious. I guessed her age at somewhere in her twenties or thirties. She said all the usual things. She was very convincing. But then we are the ultimate actors, aren't we, my dear.'

'If this was her first time doing this sort of thing, I'm not sure she'd have been so convincing,' I say to Abigail.

'Do you think it's possible she'd been coached? I don't mean in the way she spoke, more in what to say, how to make it sound real? There was a certain slyness involved in the way she manipulated Sakura to suggest Viola to her.'

'It's possible,' says Abigail, nodding her head and ponytail. 'But then she knows the score about services like Sakura's. We all do. And Eleanor has done bi sessions in the past. She's done hetero threesomes and les threesomes. She may well have picked up *bi-curious housewife* chat from a client and was bright enough to recreate it.'

'OK. OK. So she can do this and she did it, but the bottom line is what happened that night in the hotel that caused Viola to vanish into thin air and make Eleanor retire and sound frightened? Tell me about her phone call. How frightened did she sound?'

'Well, it's not as if her teeth were chattering or anything, my love, but I could tell she was lying to me and wanted the conversation to end as soon as possible. She was trying to disguise the fear in her voice, but she couldn't. She sounded really rattled, Daniel, which is so unlike her. She's very placid usually, very calm. She actually clicked off while I was still speaking.'

'And she's not answering her mobile.'

'No. It's dead.'

I take out a piece of paper I have in my pocket and slide it over to her. 'Is that her number?'

'No. I've never seen that number before.'

'That's the number that was on her hotel booking details. That one doesn't work, either.'

Abigail frowns. 'I'm getting worried about her now.'

'Could you try her mobile number again? Right now?'

Abigail fishes her mobile out from a kitchen drawer and presses the number. She frowns and hands it to me. Nothing.

'Has she got another mobile? One she uses for family and friends?'

'She may well have; lots of the girls have mobiles they use exclusively for their work with me, but if she has, I don't know what the number is. Some girls use the same mobile, but slide in a different SIM card for when they're working. They usually keep this in their purse. Do you want to see her page on my site? I've taken her off public view since she called me, but it's still on there in the way that these things are.'

'Sure.' I'm half wondering if her computer will be a gigantic 1950s model with huge tape drives, but I doubt you could get one of those in the house. The three of us go into the living room, grab some chairs and sit around her desk. I'm disappointed to find that it's just an ordinary PC, but at least it has a photograph of Monroe in a bikini on the side of the CPU.

She types something in the search field and Eleanor's page pops up on the screen. I say Eleanor, but her professional name is Celia. Celia Valentine. There are ten photographs of her, two of each type; evening dress, sexy lingerie, bikini, see-through baby doll and arty, tantalising, subtle nude. These are professionally done and remind me of the photograph of Viola that Raleigh gave to me. I can feel my heart rate increasing as I look at them and it feels a bit weird that I'm sitting here ogling with two sexy women, but they're ogling too, so that makes it OK, I guess.

'Her body is heavenly,' says Sakura, touching the screen with the tips of her fingers.

'She has no inhibitions at all,' whispers Abigail to Sakura. 'You two should meet. You should meet her too, Daniel. When all of this is over, perhaps the four of us could have dinner.'

'I don't think I'd survive it.'

I'm quite pleased to see how close my sketch of her was to the real thing, but the real thing is far more beautiful, as Abigail mentioned. The blonde hair that Declan described seems to be her natural colour and style and she has a 'girl next door' smile and demeanour that combines with her voluptuousness to stunning effect. Like Abigail said, you could take her out to some posh restaurant and no one would ever know what she was. An evening with someone who looked like this would be the GFE of the punter's dreams.

*"Intelligent, elegant, beautiful and sophisticated, I will be a passionate, inventive and friendly companion. I'm fantastic company for the theatre or dinner and am able to hold lively conversations about most topics. Apart from my native English, I am also fluent in Italian and French, and am currently studying Arabic and German. I am a natural blonde and I have a slim, athletic figure (though a little on the busty side!) and love all sorts of sports, especially riding, tennis and golf. I'm extremely easy to get along with and if you're looking for a high quality, very discreet GFE who won't rush things, then you need look no further."*

Studying for a bachelor's degree while simultaneously learning two new languages? I'll bet Eleanor was top of the class all the way through school.

Underneath Celia's blurb is a box detailing her physical characteristics and sexuality, plus a load of acronyms like COB, COF and BBBJ that mean nothing to me, though I can make a good guess at the last one.

Beneath that is another box that details how much her

various services cost. There's also a thing you can click on to see her reviews. There are a lot of them. This is just like Amazon. I know that most of this stuff here is bullshit, but I still can't quite square it with the Amelia Finch storyline.

'What sort of guys booked her, Abigail?'

'All sorts, really. Businessmen, politicians, rich guys generally. Foreign guys liked her. That classic English rose thing, you know? She was a very popular choice when it came to going on holiday, whenever she could fit it in with her studies. She's been to more foreign countries than I have!'

'So – sorry if I'm being naïve here – so these girls kind of work for themselves and are paying you a percentage for being on your site and the reputation that that gives them.'

'Something like that. But I'm more than an Amazon trader. They need training and advice. Someone like Eleanor; they don't know all the tricks intuitively, you know? They think they do, but they don't. Some things they need to be taught. Also, they need a shoulder to cry on sometimes and they also need medical checks and all the rest of it. I do more for them than you could imagine. They could do it without me, but it can be a lonely, depressing, dangerous place when you're on your own.'

'And this telephone number down here to book her. Is that your number or…'

'That's me, yes. That's my number.' For a second she makes meaningful eye contact with me and rubs my leg with her foot a bit more forcefully. 'The girls would never put their own telephone numbers on the site. That would be asking for trouble in more ways than one.'

'Well, you know her work rate – did she need to do

any moonlighting?'

'Financially, no. Unless someone offered her some fabulous amount of money for half an hour's work, of course. I think she'd do it, but then most of us would.'

I look at Sakura. She meets my gaze. She's thinking the same thing as I am.

'Do you think there's the possibility that somebody could have paid her a great deal of money to maybe set Viola Raleigh up in some way?' I say. 'To ring up Sakura and pretend to be Mrs Amelia Finch, housewife, who was seeking to expand her sexual horizons? And to then supply Eleanor with a shitload of cash and a false credit card to cover all the expenses? And tell her what to do and when and how to do it? And the end result of it all was one frightened Eleanor and a disappeared Viola?'

'I don't understand,' says Abigail, frowning. 'Why would someone do that?'

'I don't know. But the only alternative to that is that Eleanor had decided to treat herself to a tantric massage with a top call girl on her own time, and thought that the way to do it would be to use two fake identities, one of which came complete with its own credit card, address and telephone number.' I let this hang in the air for a moment before continuing. 'I checked the address on her hotel booking, by the way. It doesn't exist. And after she'd finished, she decided to leave the hotel – which she'd booked into in disguise – without checking out. And within forty-eight hours she'd quit being a call girl.'

'Well, when you put it like that, lover…'

'Do you have an address for her? I've got to see her. She's almost certainly the only person who knows what happened to Viola. If she's in trouble, and I think she may be, I can help her.'

Abigail is plainly reluctant to give me the address. I can't imagine what the reason must be. Does Eleanor still live with her parents or something? Is she the daughter of a famous politician? I can tell that Abigail is vacillating. I have to push her on this.

'Listen, Abigail. I'm sure you've got a million reasons for not giving out the addresses of the girls who work for you and I can probably work out a lot of them for myself. But there's plainly something creepy going on here and I've got to find out what it is. One girl missing and another gone into hiding; you must realise that something isn't right. This could come back to you in some way. It could come back to your other girls.'

'I don't mean to be rude, Daniel, but would you mind if I had a brief confidential confab with Sakura for a moment?'

'Not at all. You two stay here. I'll go and look at your fabulous living room.'

I get up and leave the kitchen, closing the door behind me. I sit down in an extremely comfortable, fluffy pink armchair, clasp my hands together above my head and stretch, getting a sharp twinge in my lower back as I do so. I was peeing a little blood last night and this morning. I'll give it two more days to go away before I visit the hospital.

I'm a little disappointed to see that Abigail has a modern television in here, but I think getting a black and white model with a nine inch screen and two channels would be pushing it even for her. I can hear her and Sakura talking in hushed voices in the kitchen. I can only hope that Sakura is persuading her to give us Eleanor's address. When you look at it from Abigail's point of view, it's quite logical that she'd be reticent about giving anything like that to me. Apart from the fact that she doesn't really know me, the whole story we've been feeding her sounds strange, confusing and unlikely.

I don't really know what's going on myself anymore and I'm trying not to think about it too deeply. I just think that a face to face with Eleanor would clear a lot of things up. This is the closest I've been to Viola and I'd really like to bring this job to some sort of conclusion now. I'm also sick of being followed by people.

While I'm waiting, I call a local minicab firm and order a car to take us back to London. I don't know what Sakura's plans are, but I'm obliged to make that lunch date with Natalie. I must remember to type all these expenses into my computer so that I can present them to Raleigh when this is all over.

The kitchen door opens and Sakura and Abigail come in, Sakura holding a piece of paper in her hand.

'Sakura said I could trust you and I'm trusting you with this,' says Abigail, nodding at the piece of paper. 'Please don't do anything that would frighten her or harm her in any way. Tell her she can come and stay with me if she wants to.'

'I just want to talk to her. I just need some facts, that's all. If she can't help, we'll leave her alone, I promise. There's just one more thing. You said she serviced a lot of clients. Do you have their names on some sort of database? I don't know if I'll even need this, but I'd like to see a list going back, say, six months, if that's at all possible.'

'Now you are asking too much, Daniel,' says Sakura. 'Besides, with all the subterfuge that has been going on, do you think you might be seeing a list with many genuine names on it?'

'OK. I'm sorry. It'd probably be a waste of time, anyway. It's been lovely to meet you, Abigail.'

'And you too, Daniel,' she says, kissing me on the lips. 'Please let me know what's happening. You've got me worried now. And don't forget about sketching me one day.'

She passes a small piece of paper into my hand. I slide it onto my trouser pocket.

'I won't. And thanks for the address and all of the other information. It's been really useful. I mean it.'

After Abigail and Sakura have given each other a goodbye grope, I hand Abigail one of my business cards. You never know. I can hear a car outside and it's the one I ordered. Before we can get out of the house, he toots his horn impatiently.

'They're so rude around here,' says Abigail.

As the car heads towards London, I run over the street details I managed to notice after we'd left Abigail's house. There was a silver Skoda Fabia parked almost directly across the road that wasn't there when we arrived. There was a guy sitting in the driver's seat studiously reading a newspaper. He wasn't stupid enough to be reading it upside down, but he was stupid enough to have such an expression of studied casualness on his face that it had to be phony.

Just before our car pulled off, a bright yellow Ford Ecosport, driven by a woman with strawberry blonde hair, overtook it. Her hair wasn't tied back and I didn't see her face during my one-second glance, but I'll bet anything it was Wrap Dress from last night in Oxford Street.

So now they're mobile and there are two of them.

# 18

## CHAMPAGNE AND OYSTERS

By the time the minicab drops us both off in the West End, I've lost sight of our two tails and haven't noticed either of them for about ten or fifteen minutes. I did consider offering the driver a couple of hundred pounds to pull over and let me do the driving, but I decided it wasn't worth it, and I doubt whether he'd have played ball, surly bastard that he was.

Both Sakura and I sat in the back of the minicab, and after a few minutes, the driver realised that we weren't in the mood for conversation. I put my arm around her and turned to face her, talking about nothing in particular, so that it only needed a slight turn of my head to look out of the back window to see if either Yellow Car or Silver Car were following us. Sakura was a bit pale and shaky, but said she'd be fine as long as she didn't look out of the window too much.

For about fifteen minutes, it seemed as if we were clean, but once we were on the A3, I could see Yellow Car about half a mile behind in the slow lane. Our driver was changing lanes to overtake as the mood took him, and was travelling between fifty-five and sixty-five. Yellow Car remained in the slow lane but persistently matched our speed, changing lanes whenever necessary.

Five minutes later, Yellow Car had dropped out of

sight, but then I spotted Silver Car overtaking us in the fast lane. He was quite a way ahead of us before he slowed down and kept just ahead of us in the middle lane. Shortly after this, Yellow Car appeared again, but once more was keeping her distance.

These two were pretty good, randomly disappearing and reappearing with no apparent logic to their movements, but one of them always had us in sight, and I guess they were communicating. If Raleigh and/or Fisher were responsible for these two, as I supposed they were, then I think they must have changed companies. There is no way that Tote Bag and Grey Hair were in the same league as Yellow Car and Silver Car. The fact that at least one of them had tailed our cab all the way down to Abigail's is proof of that. This is slick, professional surveillance that makes the other two look like amateurs.

Just as we were approaching Wimbledon Common, they both seemed to have disappeared, Yellow Car only fleetingly appearing again as we crossed over the Thames into Fulham. The next and last time I spotted Silver Car was when he was way behind us on The King's Road and had got caught behind a slow-moving lorry.

I arrange to meet Sakura after my lunch date, get the minicab to drop me outside Marble Arch tube station and give Sakura a handful of cash to pay him with. I don't tell her about our two friends.

Before the cab driver whisks Sakura away, I get her to open her window.

'Will you come with me to Eleanor's place? If she's there, I don't think she's going to open the door to me if I'm on my own. In fact, it's probably better if I hide around the corner until she opens the door to you. It's sneaky, but we have to see her.'

'Of course I will. I'll tell her who I am and that I'm a friend of Abigail's. Don't worry. We'll work something out.'

'Listen, Sakura. Could you do me a favour? Don't answer the door to anyone and don't buzz anyone up. Not until this is finished. I have to talk to someone regarding this case. I'll probably be an hour or so. When I've finished, I'll get a cab to your flat. When I'm outside, I'll call you.'

'Whatever you say, Daniel.'

I don't tell her who my lunch date is with, but it wasn't a complete lie about it being connected to the case, just a partial one. As I run down the stairs to get the tube, a young guy in a bright yellow jacket overtakes me and bumps into my shoulder. 'Sorry, mate,' he says, patting me on the back. 'Late for a date! Take care.'

Well at least he apologised.

\*

'You're late!'

'Only ten minutes.'

Natalie is sitting at the bar looking sexy and pretending to fume while inspecting the menu. I'm not sure exactly why you'd have a menu in an oyster bar, but they do. She passes me a copy and it's obvious that they do lots of other stuff and about fifteen different varieties of oyster. I order two half pints of Guinness as I'm flicking through it. I don't want to rush things, but I can't wait to meet up with Sakura and see what Eleanor Wallis has to say, if she'll speak to us, that is.

This place is called Gilray's Oyster Bar and it's situated in Carey Street, around the corner from The British

Library of Political and Economic Science. I wonder if Eleanor ever goes there. From outside it looks like something out of Dickens, but the interior, at least, smells and looks new and the restaurant section at the back is bright and modern.

Even though we're sitting at the bar, a waiter comes over and asks us if we'd like to order now as they're a little busy. Natalie, who's evidently been here before, orders a dozen Gillardeau oysters with a glass of champagne and I go for half a dozen tempura oysters with wasabi, also with champagne. I don't think I could eat a dozen oysters right now. I can always pinch some off her plate if I get hungry.

Natalie sits up on her stool and crosses her legs, an action which gets a none-too-subtle gasp of appreciation from a couple of old guys standing near us as they get a clear view of the tops of her hold-up black stockings.

'So what have you been doing since we last met, Daniel? Bare knuckle boxing or something?' She grins and squints at my black eye. I haven't looked at myself in a mirror since I got up this morning, but I'm sure it looks worse. They always do before they get better.

'No. I was beaten up by a beautiful half Japanese/half Italian dominatrix.'

She laughs. 'I knew it.' She takes a sip of her Guinness. 'I've been thinking about the other night quite a lot. I'd like to do that again. Soon. I'm serious. I'm still tingling from it. When are you free next? Tonight? This afternoon?'

'I'll have to consult my diary. But as you say, it'll have to be soon. Let me know when the tingling starts to wear off.'

She runs a hand through her red hair. 'I will.'

'So how's work?'

She rolls her eyes heavenwards and sighs. 'Bloody exhausting.' There's that Australian accent coming out again. 'I run a department with four people in it and there should be eight.'

'What was it you said you did again?'

I know what she said she did, but I want to guide the conversation towards Anjukka. I think of Anjukka and that damn body of hers and for a second feel dizzy.

'I'm a senior paralegal in a big law company. I've been working flat out for the last three months, preparing trial bundles, taking witness statements and all the rest of it. We've got a lot of big, complicated cases on at the moment and it's getting me really stressed out, yeah?' She moves closer to me, places a hand on my thigh and whispers. 'That's why I need…well, you know what I need, honey.'

A waiter walks briskly by to intercept a couple in the doorway. I imagine that places like this are pretty well booked solid at lunchtimes, considering the location and the amount of workers nearby.

'It sounds like a really taxing job,' I say. 'It's quite a coincidence, actually…'

She moves closer. 'What is?' I can smell her perfume mixed with her sweat and the alcohol she's been drinking. I'm starting to get intoxicated with it. I have to keep reminding myself that this is the middle of the day and I'm on a case. It's difficult.

The couple at the doorway are quietly altercating with the waiter. His tone of voice is polite but firm. He's having none of it.

'Well, I was talking to a friend of mine the other day…'

'A female friend?'

'Well, yes. She was. Female, I mean.' What the fuck am I talking about? I hear the waiter say, 'two days.' Is that really how far you have to book in advance for this place? That's not too bad, actually. Natalie leans forwards a little more until her face is about nine inches away from mine.

'And what did she say? This female friend of yours.' I can't help myself. My hand is on her leg now and it looks like we're going to be kissing in a moment. I'm wondering if this sort of thing is acceptable in an oyster bar at lunchtime.

'Miss Codlin? Your table is ready.' A young waitress who we follow to our table rescues me. As I get up, I glance at the doorway where the couple who can't get a table are finally giving up and going to sit at the far end of the bar instead. The woman has her hair tied underneath a rather psychedelic crimson bandana, but there's no mistaking Wrap Dress.

Now this is taking the piss. It's almost laughable. Perhaps the whole point is to unsettle me, but why? If I was Raleigh, and was hiring me, the last thing I'd do would be to bother with all of this crap. It might genuinely put me off my stride and the end result would not be as expected, viz. the discovering of what happened to Viola. It might annoy me so much, that I'd resign from the case, which is what I've been close to doing the whole way along. I can only assume that Raleigh is not as bright as he seems, and is a little naïve when it comes to hiring private investigators.

Two glasses of champagne are placed in front us. Natalie, already missing the physical contact, twines both of her legs around one of mine. This is very off-putting and I'm having difficulty remembering what I was talking about. Oh yes.

'Well this friend of mine is a paralegal. Works for some big company, gets a very good salary, but she's moved away from the legal work and wants to get back into it.'

'How much notice does she need to give?'

'Well, between you and me, I reckon she would walk out this afternoon, if something else came up. She's getting a lot of unwanted male attention where she works. She fucking hates it, to be honest.'

Natalie rummages in her handbag, pulls out a business card and hands it to me. 'Tell her to give me a ring. Once all the paperwork's sorted I could take her on next week and screw her old job.'

Our oysters arrive. Wrap Dress and her friend (or should that be colleague?) are sitting at the bar. 'That's great, Natalie. She'll be delighted.'

'I hate guys who fuck you around in work. As far as I'm concerned, it's the absolute worst thing that you can do. All these little men exercising their wanky power over girls who wouldn't look twice at them in real life. It's pathetic.'

She sprays lemon juice over her oysters and swallows two of them in quick succession. The wasabi paste on mine is extremely hot and my eyes start to water.

'You've been here before, I assume.' She nods her head. 'Is there another exit apart from the one over there?'

'You planning on running away from a girl who's gulping down aphrodisiacs?' She's taken her shoes off under the table and is rubbing one of her feet against my leg.

I decide to tell her the truth. Fuck it. 'I'm a private

investigator, Natalie. I'm working on a case at the moment, and a side effect of that case is that I've got these people following me everywhere.'

'You're fucking with me, yeah?'

'No. Don't look over at them straight away, but there's a couple at the far end of the bar by the front door. The woman's got a red bandana on. They've been trailing me all morning.'

She runs a hand through her hair and shakes it from side to side, quickly taking in Miss Wrap Dress and her pal. 'Got 'em. Jesus Christ, Daniel, is this true? Fuck. You being you and you doing that – so fucking exciting. I need to go to a hotel with you right fucking now.'

'So is there another way out? Don't worry – I won't be leaving until we've finished lunch.'

'See over there by the sign pointing to the toilets?'

'Yes.'

'There's an exit there. It comes out at the back of this place, but you're right by the rear entrance of the pub next door. You can go through the pub and come out the front and skip down Star Yard. Then there's a little road straight ahead of you that comes out on Chancery Lane.'

'Great. Thanks.'

'So do I get a reward for telling you that?'

'Another glass of champagne?'

'Not quite the reward I was hoping for, but that'll do for the moment.'

By the time we've finished lunch, I'm thinking about what to do. It's difficult, because all of Natalie's conversation leans towards sex and it's a bit distracting. Still enjoyable, though. Part of me can't be bothered to shake these two dummies off, but another part feels I'm obliged to, just for the practice, if nothing else. Initially, I thought they'd been told to wait until a table was free, but now I just think they're hanging around the bar waiting for me to leave.

'They certainly can't take their eyes off you, can they,' says Natalie, grinning broadly. 'You want to give them the slip now?'

'It might be an idea.'

'You owe me big time for this, Daniel. I'm helping your friend out with a job, I've given you a getaway route and now *this*!'

'Now *what*?'

'Call me and make it soon. My brain is frying.'

She wipes her mouth with a serviette, gets up and strides straight over to Wrap Dress, stops and stares at her, and then slaps her across the face. Hard. 'You fucking bitch! You leave him alone or I'll fucking kill you, you cow!'

I don't wait to see or hear what happens next, much as I'd like to. I get up, walk over to the toilets and follow Natalie's escape route until I'm on Chancery Lane and can hail a cab. Nice lunch, though; my eyes are still watering from it. I put a hand in my pocket and pull out the piece of paper that Abigail Gastrell handed me this morning. It just has one word written on it: 'Call.'

# 19

## COFFEE AND CIGARETTES

Eleanor Wallis lives in a white, wisteria-covered detached house in Stockwell Park Crescent, about five minutes' walk from Stockwell tube station. It's a tidy looking place and appears to have been recently decorated. It's got a basement and I can see that the front part has been converted into a kitchen.

It's a quiet, very leafy road and would be a nice place to live. I wonder if she rents this or shares it with anyone else. If she's saving her money, I doubt that she owns it, though I'm sure she could afford it, from what Abigail was saying about her work rate. Parking is by permit only and there's a brand new red Alfa Romeo MiTo outside, which could well be Eleanor's.

Sakura is wearing sunglasses when she gets out of the cab and I wonder if that helps her condition, but I don't ask. We stand outside the house for a few minutes, just looking.

It's a flat-roofed house. There are three upstairs windows and the blinds are down on each one of them. Two downstairs windows, either side of the front door have curtains which are both drawn, one of them only partially. Everything is still.

There's a gate at the side of the front garden, which leads to a small garage, which has both doors closed.

There's no obvious way to get to the back of the house, other than climbing over the garage roof. I listen for any type of noise that might indicate there's someone inside, but there's nothing; all I can hear is the tweeting of the birds and the sound of distant traffic.

I decide that we've stood around looking suspicious for long enough and indicate for Sakura to follow me up the eight concrete steps to the front door. I stand to the side, out of sight, as Sakura presses the doorbell just once, for about two seconds. It sounds like the bell is at the back of the house.

There are two glass panels on the front door. I didn't know this before we came here, but just in case, asked Sakura to wear something ordinary so as not to alarm anyone who might be inside looking out. Ordinary, for Sakura, is a dark blue silk Stella McCartney V-neck dress complete with five-inch heel strappy sandals. Her legs look great and with her hair slicked back and full, fabulous makeup, she looks like a model. It's hard to believe they're the same legs that almost crushed my ribcage the other day.

After thirty seconds of silence, she gives the doorbell another press. Still nothing. Then I hear a dull bump from inside the house. It's so faint, that for a moment I wonder if I imagined it, but about thirty seconds later, there's another one. There's definitely someone or something inside.

Sakura rings the bell for a third time, then turns to me quickly and nods sharply. Soon after, I can hear someone walking inside. She opens her clutch bag and produces what looks like a very small box of chocolates. I give her a questioning frown and she smiles and shakes her head at me. She's looking into the hallway and speaks to someone that I can't see.

'Darling? Are you alright, darling? Abigail was worried you were ill. I'm Sakura. I'm a friend of Abigail's. We've know each other for twelve years. I live near you. She asked me to bring you some chocolates. She asked me to ask you if you needed anything. Any shopping or something.'

Well, if I was Eleanor, I certainly wouldn't answer the door now. Someone I don't know trying to gain access to my house through proffering sweets would be pretty damn suspicious, not to mention terminally creepy. Sakura holds the box against the glass.

'They're Vosges, Eleanor. Caramel marshmallow by Vosges. Abigail said that you loved them. But it's OK. I can take them away and bring them back another time. Or I can leave them on the step. Actually, no. Someone might take them if I leave them on the step. I'll go. I hope you feel better soon.'

I can hear the lock on the door slowly opening and the second I hear the latch click I hit the side of the door hard with the ball of my hand. This has two results, the door opens wide and Eleanor Wallis is knocked against the wall, and her arm is pinned against it by the door.

Her eyes are wide open with shock and with her free hand she lashes out and scratches the side of my face. It hurts like fuck; I can't imagine what the damage will be to my matinée idol looks. She goes for a follow-up, but Sakura is too fast and catches her wrist, locking her arm at the elbow and pushing her into the centre of the hallway, where she staggers from side to side for a few feet. I close the door behind us and wait for the next assault, while Sakura attempts some speedy damage limitation.

'Eleanor. Listen. We're not here to hurt you,' she says in a half-whisper. 'We're here to help you.'

Eleanor is not in the listening mood and runs towards the back of the house. I can't imagine where she's going. She turns left into some room or other and I follow. Whatever she's going to do, I can't have her escaping now and she looks desperate enough to try anything.

As I get to the door that she's disappeared into, a solid-looking crystal vase comes flying towards my head. I block it without thought, sending it flying across the room, but worry that it's broken my wrist. As it smashes on the floor, she runs to the fireplace and returns with a fire poker with a nasty hook on the end. She's fairly determined to kill me with this and takes a frenzied run at me, slashing wildly from left to right.

*"Intelligent, elegant, beautiful and sophisticated, I will be a passionate, inventive and friendly companion."*

I manage to get away from the doorframe and into the room, to give myself more space. As the poker cuts through the air again and again, I look around the room to see if I can spot anything I can use against it, like a chair. No chair; at least nothing I can lift up. Insanely, I find myself thinking how pretty she is, despite her face currently being a fierce mask of anger. She's also been drinking; I can smell her vodka breath from here.

Sakura follows me into the room and I feel a little safer, though I'm suddenly reminded of her violent reaction to me when I first turned up at her place and wonder if there's a link here. Women who feel so threatened by certain men that their immediate instinct is to try and kill *any* male visitors. I have to qualify that; their immediate instinct is to try and kill *me*.

'Darling, I'm sorry.' Sakura's voice is calm and soft.

'I'm sorry we had to do that, but you wouldn't have let us in and we *had* to get in here and talk to you and help you. We had to. This guy here is OK, but if you keep swinging at him with the poker, he might have to do something that will hurt you to make it stop.'

Eleanor holds on tightly to the poker. There's no way on earth that she's going to let go of it. Her knuckles are white, her breathing is ragged and she's as white as a sheet. She's also swaying slightly; she's more pissed than I thought she was. It's only now that I notice there are loads of empty vodka miniatures on virtually every surface in this room. Who the hell buys that many miniatures? Then it clicks; this must be one of the perks of her job. These are all refugees from various hotel minibars; stuff she's nicked while the client is showering. It's not only vodka, it's scotch, gin, brandy, schnapps and even Campari and Malibu.

'Look,' says Sakura, reaching into her bag again and fetching out the chocolates. 'They're real. We were only talking to Abigail this morning. She told me about these chocolates. She told me about the other ones that you liked. The coconut and curry one; she told me about that, too. We're friends, darling. You can call Abigail now if you don't believe me.'

Eleanor is still hyper and wild. Something has clearly tipped her over the edge and she's looking rather crazy. The fear and booze is making her shake. She's dangerous like this, and could get a lucky strike with that poker that could inadvertently kill one of us. What were the sports mentioned in her bio on Abigail's computer? Riding, tennis and golf, I seem to remember. The golf, if that was true, would give her a good, powerful swing with that poker. She looks fit, too, but she also looks fucked. She's wearing a wrinkled white linen shirt with various liquid stains down the front and a pair of beige cargo crops, which look like she's spilled an entire meal down them in the recent past, or puked down them.

'Get out of my fucking house,' she hisses at both of us. 'Get out of my fucking house or I'll kill both of you. Do you understand? Get out now!'

'Darling…' Sakura starts to say something, but is cut short by Eleanor rushing at her at full speed. She takes a wide swing with the poker, which would have come down hard on Sakura's collarbone, and probably fractured it, but Sakura quickly sidesteps it and gives Eleanor a hard knife hand strike on the base of her neck. That's the end of the attack, as Eleanor drops to the floor like a puppet that's had its strings all cut.

Sakura and I both take deep breaths at the same time and look at each other.

'That was good,' I say. 'Accurate.'

'Thank you. Let me see your hand. I saw you deflect that vase. Very fast. I was impressed.' She takes my right hand in both of hers and lightly runs her fingers down the side of it. 'It's starting to bruise already.'

'Stop touching me in a sensual manner.'

This makes her laugh. 'Let's get her undressed and get her in a bath. She needs to sober up.'

I pick the unconscious Eleanor up in both arms and follow Sakura upstairs. We're both assuming there'll be some sort of bathroom up there. When we find it, Sakura turns both taps on and I take Eleanor into what must be her bedroom. There are empty miniatures in here, as well. We undress her and I carry her into the bathroom and gently lower her into the bath.

'Her hair looks like it could do with a wash. I think it

would be best if you do it. Pour some bubble bath in there, as well.' I hand Sakura a bottle of orange and vanilla aromatherapy bubble bath and she pours a couple of capfuls under the flow of tap water. Eleanor moans as she starts to regain consciousness and she begins to rub the side of her neck, which must be hurting like a bastard. I don't think it would be a good idea for her to open her eyes, discover she's naked in a bath and find some guy she doesn't know looking at her. 'Can I leave this to you, Sakura? We don't want to freak her out completely.'

'Of course, Daniel. Perhaps you could go and make some coffee. I think she'll need some.'

The first thing I do is to go in the small toilet downstairs and look at my face in the mirror. There are three big scram marks from the cheekbone to the jaw on the same side of my face as the black eye. They're moderately deep and blood trickles from them. I soak some toilet paper in warm water and dab at my face until the excess blood has gone, then attach a couple of toilet roll sheets to the marks. Just like when you cut yourself shaving, but rather more serious and terrible-looking.

I stick a kettle on in the basement kitchen and eventually find the coffee things and some mugs. I keep thinking, *I'm getting there, I'm getting there. I'm getting there.* In three days, too, though I'm not at the finishing post quite yet. I try to remember how long I told Raleigh this would take. I think I told him less than a week. Well, that was accurate enough, I suppose. I'm still rather irked about all the people he has following me, though, and still can't work out a sensible motive for it.

While the kettle's boiling, I run upstairs to the ground floor and go into the room where we had the fight with Eleanor, find the poker and slide it underneath a sofa. I'm not having her touching that again. As I head back down to the kitchen, I can hear Sakura talking in a low voice upstairs. I hope she's able to get this girl into the right mood to talk to me. And a girl is all she is; Abigail said she was almost twenty-one. *Almost.* God Almighty.

I find a tray, put all the coffee stuff on it, plus the box of caramel marshmallows, and take it all into a small sitting room at the back of the house. There's a small but very well kept back garden, with a greenhouse, a couple of benches and a large concrete Buddha. I wonder if any of Eleanor's neighbours have any suspicions about her second occupation. It's doubtful. Erratically timed comings and goings are part and parcel of student life, so they're probably not bothered.

This is a nice, sunny room. I imagine Eleanor coming back here after a night's work and sitting here reading, sipping a glass of white wine. I wonder if she's got a boyfriend. She's a university student, so it would be unlikely that she didn't get offers. Perhaps she doesn't mix with the other students at all. Perhaps that's the price you pay. Perhaps she's regarded as reticent or snobby. I remove the toilet paper from my face and stick it in my pocket.

When she comes in the room, she's calmed down considerably and is not brandishing any weapons. She's still cautious, though, and frowns suspiciously as she looks at me. I have no idea what Sakura was talking to her about up there, but it seems to have done the trick.

She's wearing a plum-coloured towelling robe with a big hood, her face is pink from the bath and her hair is still wet. She seems smaller than when she was in attack mode and is actually rather petite. I would guess that she's about five foot three or so; definitely shorter than Sakura.

Her complexion is healthy-looking, fresh and glowing, and without makeup she looks about seventeen. She's much, much prettier than her photographs and despite myself and all that I know, part of my brain is screaming, *what the fuck are you doing working as a prostitute?*

She looks like the sort of wholesome, dream girlfriend you imagined yourself going out with (if you were very, very lucky) when you were in school. And that's just it, isn't it. Abigail said she was one of the best at the girlfriend experience and now I can see why.

I smile at her and pour out the coffee. She takes one of the chocolates and pops it in her mouth, giving me a petulant little frown at the same time. She has to be brought down into some sort of peaceful reality again after the shock of our forced entrance and the adrenaline rush of her frenzied attack and its neutralisation. Sakura helps with this. She has a very calming presence and sits on the edge of her seat, completely still. I can feel that Eleanor is still fearful and agitated, but she's got to trust us both if I'm going to get anything out of her.

None of us speak for a couple of minutes, then Sakura looks at the box of chocolates. 'Can I try one?'

'Of course,' says Eleanor. She looks at me and smiles slightly. 'You can have one as well, if you like.'

'Thanks.'

'You're welcome.' She's unsure of what's going to happen or what we're going to say, and glances nervously around the room.

'Is this your house or do you rent it?' I say. Well, that's a crap beginning, but it's better than nothing. She looks slightly puzzled that I should ask such a thing. She finishes eating her chocolate, drinks some coffee and lights a cigarette, tipping the ash into an enormous ashtray with a picture of the Arc de Triomphe at the bottom. I wonder if it's a souvenir from some holiday or other. Maybe it was a gift.

'I rent. But they let me do what I like with it.' Her voice is soft and slightly croaky. There's also a very slight slurring to her speech, which is not too surprising considering the amount of miniature empties around the place. As she leans forwards to tip some more ash onto the Arc de Triomphe, I have to force myself to redirect my gaze from her full breasts to the floor. 'All the furniture is mine and I redecorated the whole thing last year. Decorating is my hobby. Do you like it?'

'It's great, it's great. The whole place is really light and airy.' I nod towards a black and white photographic print; a woman in a headscarf cooing at a small bird in a cage. 'And Silvana Mangano above the fireplace.'

This comment perks her up a little. 'You recognise her! Oh wow, I love her and I love her films. I thought she was so beautiful and sexy.'

Silvana photographs, fridge magnets and the rest were still very popular in Italy, but she's not so well known over here. 'I've never seen that photograph before,' I say, smiling at her.

'Neither had I! I just had to have it as soon as I saw it.'

We talk about her prints, furniture and decorating for a few minutes longer. It's almost as if our violent welcome had never happened. What I'm in awe of is how she has the time to study for a degree, be a call girl, learn new languages *and* decorate a house. She must have incredible drive and energy. Then something reminds her of who we are and why we might be here and she looks downcast again. She pushes the tips of her fingers into her eyeballs as if she's trying to clear a headache.

'I think I'm in deep shit. Do you know anything? Have you heard anything from anyone? Am I in deep shit? I don't know anything. Tell them I don't know anything and I don't remember anything. Am I in deep shit? Everything was going so fucking well. Tell me.'

'I'll be honest with you, Eleanor – I don't know,' I say, keeping my voice as soft as I can. 'We're here because you were in The Bolton Mayfair three weeks ago with a client called Natasha Hart. Natasha Hart disappeared that night and hasn't been seen since. We're just looking for her, that's all. If you can't help us, you can't help us.'

She looks downwards and starts nibbling at one of her fingernails. 'I don't know anything about…anyone called that. Sakura told me that this Natasha was one of her girls and that she was worried about her. That's all I know.'

She's afraid and she's lying. I can't force her to cough up the info, but I can try and be gently persistent. 'Why did you tell Abigail that you were stopping working as a call girl, Eleanor? What happened that made you make that decision?'

'I – I didn't like it anymore. What's it got to do with you anyway? I can stop if I want, can't I?'

I take a deep breath. 'I don't know what's the matter, Eleanor. I think you're frightened and I don't know why. But I know that you booked Natasha Hart for an overnight outcall. You spoke to Sakura here. You said your name was Mrs Amelia Finch. You wanted a tantric massage. You were very convincing. You sent the deposit to Sakura here using a motorcycle courier and you gave the balance to Natasha Hart in the hotel. When you went to the courier place in Chiswick, you used the name Lara Holland. The guy there gave me a description of you and I made this drawing.'

I show the rumpled facial composite to her. She looks nonplussed.

'When I showed this drawing to the hotel night manager, he recognised you, except he said that you were wearing glasses and had shoulder length brown hair. He told me that you paid for your room and for Natasha Hart's room, including a breakfast for each of you the next morning, but that you both left without checking out. He pre-authorised the credit card that you used to make the booking. Please, Eleanor, we're not the police. We're not criminals or heavies. I'm a private investigator. Sakura here hired me to find Natasha. You were the last person to see her. That's why we need your help.'

It's not the whole truth, but the whole truth can be just a little too complicated sometimes. Luckily, Sakura doesn't react to this small deception.

Sakura leans forwards and places her hand over Eleanor's. 'Who did you think we were when we came in here and you attacked us, Eleanor? I can understand why you attacked us and we were in the wrong to come inside your home like that.'

But Eleanor isn't listening now. She has her head in her hands and she's crying. 'I'm so fucked up. I have so fucked up. I was so fucking stupid.'

'Tell us. What is it, Eleanor?' says Sakura softly. 'What happened at the hotel?'

She shakes her head. I light a cigarette and hand it to her. She takes a deep drag and shakes her head again. 'Please can you just go? I don't know what I'm going to do but I don't want you here. I don't want anyone here.'

'Listen, Eleanor,' I say. 'Whatever is it, and whoever you're afraid of, I can help you. I don't know who we're dealing with here, but I assume it's men, and the sort of men who put the frighteners on women, and reduce them to the sort of state you're in, are always weak pieces of shit.'

She looks up at me and laughs briefly through the tears.

'I don't work for you and I don't intend to, but I guarantee that nothing will happen to you while I'm alive. But you have to help me with this. I have to know what happened in that hotel.'

I let her cry it all out and finish the cigarette. I look at Sakura and she tips her head to the side slightly, to indicate that we might be in with a chance for a logical chat now. I'm starting to find this stressful and exhausting. The scratches on the side of my face are stinging and throbbing to remind me that they're still there. I think Natalie will like these scratches, actually. I must take Natalie out somewhere soon and I've got to give Anjukka a ring to get her to ring Natalie.

'We can take it easy, Eleanor,' I say, as calmly as I can. 'We don't have to talk about that night at the hotel. We can just chat about what led up to it. Did somebody approach you about doing this? Is that what happened?'

When I was at Abigail's, I put forward the idea that someone had coached Eleanor with the phone call to Sakura and all the rest. Now I've met her, I don't think she'd have needed coaching in much, but I'm sure she didn't think all of this up by herself.

I keep getting an image of a shadowy figure looking over Eleanor's shoulder, telling her what to do and making threats if she didn't obey. Eleanor isn't sobbing anymore, but tears are still running down her face.

There are a few minutes when all three of us are completely silent and still. I'm not going to say another thing. She has to carry this forward herself now. She lights another cigarette and blows the smoke up at the ceiling. 'I can't give you an exact date. Abigail would be able to do that if it was really necessary. She keeps all the details of our outcalls on her computer.

'I went on an outcall with a guy called Bill Coleman. He booked me through the site. It was just another job. Nothing unusual about it. It must have been three or four months ago.' She examines one of the fingernails she's been worrying. 'Normally, I wouldn't have remembered the guy's name or the hotel, but I remembered this one.'

Bill Coleman. Yet another name. 'Where did you meet him, Eleanor?'

'He suggested The Bolton Mayfair. He said they had very nice rooms and he liked staying there whenever he was in town. He said he'd stayed there at least half a dozen times and that the food was very good.'

'What was he? A businessman from outside London?'

'I supposed he was. I didn't know anything about him. Usually it's when you meet up that they start talking about their jobs.' She looks straight at Sakura. 'As you'll know, it's the most popular topic of conversation with most men.'

Sakura smiles and laughs, covering her mouth with her hand. 'And, of course, their wives.'

'Oh yes,' says Eleanor, smiling for the first time. 'They always like to talk about their wives. I know some of their wives better than they do. The wives of my regulars, anyway.'

Eleanor and Sakura exchange a little small talk about the foibles of male clients, but this is good; it's relaxing her and showing her that she and Sakura have some shared experiences. It'll help her trust us. I suspect that there's something deep inside her that she doesn't want to talk about and you have to let these things float to the surface naturally, if at all possible.

'Had you ever been to The Bolton Mayfair before, Eleanor?' I say.

'No, it was my first time. It's very nice inside and Mr Coleman had booked a King Deluxe room, which was fantastic.'

'I've seen those rooms. They're huge, aren't they.'

The smile vanishes from her face. It's as if thinking about the hotel room had drained the energy from her body. I can feel her anxiety and it's giving me a bit of a chill in my stomach. She starts to look her age once more.

'You won't go to the police, will you? I don't know why I'm saying that. I haven't done anything wrong, not really. I was just in the wrong place at the wrong time, that's all. But you won't go to the police, will you?'

'About what, darling?' says Sakura, sympathetically.

'About all of this. About what I'm going to tell you. I used to think I was pretty tough, you know, mentally. I'm quite clever. I can analyse things and work them all out. But it's been burning a hole in me. I thought it would get better after the first week, then I thought it would get better after the second week, but it didn't work like that at all; it's actually getting worse. I really don't know what to do about it. I didn't see anything in the papers, so I don't know what's going on.' She leans forwards, confidentially. 'I've been drinking a lot. I thought that would kill off everything and then I could go back to things as they were before. But it's not just me feeling guilty. It's the fact that I just know they'll be looking for me. It's why I'm afraid to go out and I don't answer my phone. I think that everyone's going to be after me. I did go to the local shops yesterday, though.'

I smile and nod. I don't know what on earth she's talking about, but at least loads of stuff is coming out now. It's just up to me to make some sense of it all.

She pours us all another coffee and offers the chocolates around. 'I've been fucking up my college work, too. Not seriously and I thought I'd have been able to catch up by now with a clear head, you know? I can keep a lid on it all, usually. But I can't concentrate and – I never thought I'd hear myself saying this – I feel depressed, you know? It's three big essays and some smaller stuff. It was about theorising security and war. I know what to do and I understand it all, but I just can't bring myself to get down to it. And I've been missing lectures. I wrote to them saying I was ill but I can't keep saying that indefinitely. I can usually keep a lid on it all.' She wipes the tears from her eyes but they keep on coming.

'Don't worry,' says Sakura, reaching forwards to hold Eleanor's hand. 'I'm sure you'll be able to catch up, once this is all over.'

Once what is all over? I don't think I'm really sure anymore. I've got to get Eleanor back to talking about her timeline. 'Eleanor, you were saying that normally you don't remember your clients' names or the name of the hotel, but you did this time. Why was that?'

'Because he didn't want sex. This lovely big hotel room with this huge bed, but he didn't want sex. And the cost, too. The cost of me, I mean. All of that money and he didn't want sex. Sometimes my clients will just want to talk, but not usually on the first visit.'

'How long did he book you for, darling? An hour?' says Sakura.

'That's the funny thing. It was overnight. He said he was doing it to show good faith.'

'So you made good money for doing nothing, darling?'

'Well, yes. And he gave me a tip of fifteen hundred on top of the fee. But I didn't stay there once he'd talked about the deal. I got back here about a quarter to eleven that night.' She suddenly leans forwards and grabs my wrist. 'Could you stay here with me tonight? I could make a bed up, but I'd feel safer if you were in my bedroom with me.'

I take her hand in mine but remain professionally noncommittal. I have to say that I'm quite impressed with my restraint in this matter and am now pretty close to sainthood. 'You said you didn't stay at the hotel once he'd talked about the deal. What was the deal?'

And then Eleanor Wallis/Amelia Finch/Lara Holland/Celia Valentine tells us about the deal and everything starts to slowly capsize.

# 20

## THE DEAL

Since I started this case, there has been something at the back of my mind which I've been ignoring, mainly because it's weak, conventional thinking, which I don't ordinarily do. When Eleanor starts talking, a part of me is pleased that my instinct has been proved right, but another part wishes it wasn't.

'He said he'd pay me for the night and he was pleased to do it,' says Eleanor. 'He said he thought I was beautiful, but that I wasn't to take offence.'

'Offence at what?' says Sakura.

'That he didn't want to have me. He said that under normal circumstances, he'd love to spend the night with me, but these were not normal circumstances. This was something special. This was something that could get me a lot of money if I played my cards right.'

'OK,' I say. 'What did he say then?'

She lights another cigarette. She's getting through them quickly, managing to finish each one with about six deep drags. She keeps rubbing her eyes, touching her face and pursing her lips. 'He started talking about this guy. He said that this guy was a friend of the family. I don't know why, but I didn't believe this, I just kept nodding my head in an understanding way. I'm used to doing that.'

She glances at Sakura. 'You know what I mean? When you're listening to stuff that you're not really interested in, but it's part of what you have to do to keep them happy?'

'Yes, Eleanor. I understand,' says Sakura, nodding her head and smiling.

'Anyway, as I said, I didn't believe what he was saying, not the details, anyway, but the general theme seemed convincing to me. He said that this friend of the family was an old guy whom he'd known for many years. This guy had helped him when he'd been down and all that sort of crap. I kept looking sincere, thinking I'd be getting out soon, but I'd still be paid for a whole night.

'As he was talking, I started thinking about what I'd do when I got home, you know? I was thinking that I might send out for a pizza and watch a film or something. He kept on talking about this guy, as if he was trying to convince me that this guy was Father Christmas and David Attenborough rolled into one. So *nice*, this guy was, so *kind* and *understanding*. Well, believe you me, I was starting to think I wanted this guy to adopt me, you know?'

I have to laugh at this. For the first time, Eleanor makes eye contact with me and smiles, as if we're having a normal conversation. Idiotically, I start to ponder asking her out for dinner when this job is over. 'So – what was he doing? Was he building up to getting you to do something for this male Mother Theresa?'

She giggles and starts chewing at her thumbnail. 'He told me a story about this guy and all the hardships he'd had to endure. He was a widower. He'd had a beautiful wife once and she had died and it had broken his heart. The one thing that had kept him sane was his daughter. She was beautiful and sweet and all the rest of it. She was the light of his life. You can imagine it, can't you; all the clichés came pouring out. I feel like I'm relating some bloody fairy story. She was just like a princess. I hated her immediately. Shall I make some more coffee?'

'I'll do it.' Sakura gets up and goes into the kitchen. Eleanor watches with slight concern as she leaves the room. I can't blame her; Sakura has a soothing and reassuring presence. But I've got to keep Eleanor in full flow, even though I can predict what's coming next.

'So was there a problem with the daughter? Had something happened to her?'

'Well, I wouldn't use the word *problem*, exactly, but she was very affected by her mother's death and went off the rails, as they say. She had a drink problem, then boyfriend problems, then a drug problem and – shock of shocks – had eventually drifted into the oldest profession. I mean – can you believe it? That poor girl!'

'Well I'm appalled, Eleanor. I think I may throw up. Do you have a bucket?'

'Oh, don't worry about that. This carpet's old.'

We both laugh as Sakura returns with some more coffee. She makes eye contact with me and nods slightly. Eleanor takes two or three rapid sips of her coffee and licks her lips.

'Anyway, he said that her father was desperate to get in touch with her again, but didn't know how to go about it. He hadn't seen her for years, apparently. Then he found out she was working as a call girl for one of those agencies that caters for bisexual and lesbian women.'

'How long ago was this?' I ask. 'How long ago did he find this out?'

'I can't remember. I don't think he gave me an exact date, but I think it was probably in the last three or four months. That's the impression I got, anyway. Could be wrong.'

'How on earth did he discover which agency his daughter was working for?'

'I don't know. Mr Coleman didn't share that piece of information with me.' She scratches her head. 'I didn't like him, this Mr Coleman. He was very pleasant on the surface, but there was something nasty about him. Something deep down. I can't really put it into words. It was as if he was secretly looking down on you, secretly sneering at you. It was as if he hated your guts beyond belief but someone was paying him to be nice to you. He was trying hard, you know? But he just couldn't prevent the poison from dripping out.'

I leave a gap of about thirty seconds before I speak again. I stand up to stretch my legs and look out of the window at the garden.

'What did Mr, er, Coleman look like, Eleanor? Could you give me a rough description?'

'Very big, like he played rugby or something, you know? Very tall, too. I mean, *you're* tall aren't you, but he was definitely taller than you.'

'Six foot four? Six foot five? Something like that?'

'Yes. Yes, I would think that was about right. Um, looked like he spent a lot of time in the gym, but *too much* time in the gym, you know? Where the shoulders and all the rest start to look freakily big, like you *know* he works out and it's a bit of a turnoff, yeah? Guys don't realise how revolting that look is to most women.'

'Hair?'

'Shaved head, but you could see he was trying to disguise male pattern baldness.'

'Age?'

'Fifty-ish, perhaps. The baldness made it difficult to be more accurate than that.'

'Accent?'

'South of England somewhere. That's the best I can do.'

It's Fisher. So what the hell was he playing at? Was he really working on behalf of Raleigh? Was he working alone to impress his boss with the most wonderful present of all? Does Raleigh know about any of this? Does Raleigh share his most intimate secrets with Fisher? Some of the facts were familiar, but it sounds as if they were twisted around to create a more effective sob story for Eleanor.

I've been wondering about Fisher since I spoke about him with Anjukka, and had a mild suspicion that he might be screwing over Raleigh in some way or other. It may be more complicated than that, however. I'll have to keep pressing.

'So what did Mr Coleman suggest to you, Eleanor?'

She frowns and looks at the floor. Her speech is faster now, as if she can't wait to get it all out. 'He said he'd come up with this plan. A plan that would make this lovely old guy happy again. He said that this man had come to terms with his daughter being a call girl, but they'd had a row about something unconnected with that, and the daughter wouldn't get in touch with him anymore.

'His plan was that someone would hire his daughter for the night. It would have to be a woman, because of the type of agency she now worked for. I know about these agencies. They sometimes get male callers, but they don't ever send girls out to them.' She looks at Sakura to get confirmation of this.

'It's true,' says Sakura. 'Some men contact me from time to time. They think they can get two les or bi girls out to do a show for them or something and eventually they'll join in!' She laughs at the audacity of such men. 'There are plenty of places you can get that from, but it's not the sort of service that I'm offering. Sometimes I'll send two girls out, but only if it's for a woman.'

'So I think the idea,' says Eleanor, 'was that this was a sure-fire way of getting this man's daughter in a place where they'd definitely know where she was going to be and at what time. Mr Coleman said that it was important that father and daughter should be reunited on neutral ground, so to speak.'

I sit down again, take a large gulp of coffee and a deep breath. 'OK. So Bill Coleman knew about agencies like yours, Sakura, and he knew which one of them that Viola worked for.'

'Who's Viola?' says Eleanor, looking confused, as well she might be.

'Viola is Natasha's real name, darling,' says Sakura patiently. 'You know what it's like.'

'Of course,' says Eleanor, smiling. Then something wipes the smile off her face and she starts to sob again. 'I'm sorry. I'm not usually weepy like this. I think it might be delayed shock. This has all been very traumatic for me, even though I've tried to rationalise it as much as I can. I'm scared as well. I try to put how much I'm scared to the back of my mind, but it keeps on creeping up on me.

'I've been drinking quite a bit. Did I tell you that already? And sometimes I watch some television or a film and if I get wrapped up in the story I forget about everything for a while. Dramas are the best, especially if they have a complicated plot. Then suddenly, something will trigger the memory again.'

I'm a little bit lost here, I have to admit. It's plain that we haven't had the whole story yet and that the whole story is troubling her in some way. What can she have delayed shock from? What has traumatised her that she's been trying to drink her way to oblivion for three weeks? If Fisher is behind it, I'd be only too happy to give him a little trauma of his own.

Eleanor composes herself and lights another cigarette. 'So that was it, really. Oh, and the money. I was a bit dubious at first and I think he picked up on it. He said if I did this job for him and did it well, he'd give me ten thousand pounds. Five thousand now and the other five when it was finished. That seemed like a pretty good couple of days' work to me.'

'You're kidding. Ten thousand. Just for ringing up Sakura and pretending to be a client of one of her girls.'

'Well, it wasn't just that, was it? I had to go to Chiswick and…let me go back a bit. He gave me a piece of paper with the name of the website. He suggested a sort of personality for me; a married woman who wanted to experiment with her lesbian side. He seemed to know a lot about it, like he'd been reading up on it.

'He told me the name of the girl I had to book – Natasha Hart. He told me that it would sound more convincing if I pretended that I hadn't been with a woman before and I was to keep pressing until tantric massage was suggested. That would limit it to three girls.

'He showed me the website in the hotel room and we looked at all the services offered and then we looked at the profiles of the three girls who did the tantric and then we focussed on Natasha. I memorised all of her details and specialities, so that if one thing failed and Sakura tried to fob me off with someone else, I'd have some other reason for choosing Natasha to fall back on, understand?'

'Yeah,' I say.

'Something I could come up with quickly, even though I'd have the website in front of me when I called her up, see? I didn't want the person on the other end of the line to hear typing.'

'And then you limited your choice to Anneliese or Natasha,' says Sakura. She's smiling, but she's not at all impressed with herself for being fooled so easily by a twenty-year-old girl. It's understandable, though. Eleanor is very well spoken, posh even, and her voice is quite low, with very little girlishness in it.

'That's correct. I tried to make it seem as if I wasn't decided, and that's what Mr Coleman told me to do, but after pretending to think a bit, I told her I wanted Natasha as I preferred her looks.' She suddenly looks up at Sakura. 'I'm sorry. This is really weird that I'm talking about what I did with you and you're actually here in front of me and we've already spoken on the telephone and I lied to you about all of this. I'm sorry. I didn't mean any harm by it.'

'That's quite alright,' says Sakura. But I can tell she's perturbed by the whole thing and just wants Eleanor to get on with it so that she can find out what happened to Viola.

Eleanor twists her hair around one of her fingers. 'We ran through it in the hotel room, there and then. I pretended that Mr Coleman was the person I'd be speaking to and I explained about myself and I explained why I wanted to try it with another woman. It was easy. I've been with bi-curious women and I've spoken to them and I can remember what they said. I can remember their nervousness. Mr Coleman looked really pleased and impressed. We had quite a laugh about it. I thought that this was going to be the easiest money I'd ever made.'

This is clever, I have to admit. It's what I would have done if I was manipulating someone like Eleanor; taking her through it step by step, as if it was just a harmless prank with sentimental overtones. Everything being organised for her; being told what to say and how to say it. Fisher, and possibly Raleigh, must have spent lot of time preparing this before procuring Eleanor to be their agent. And Eleanor would have been exactly the right girl to pull it off.

'Where did the name Amelia Finch come from, Eleanor? Did you make that up yourself?'

'Oh no. She had to be called Amelia Finch because that was the name on the credit card he gave me. He said that it actually belonged to someone called Amelia Finch and that it would work and I was not to worry about it. The only reason I had the card was for the hotel booking. He said that there was no other way around it. Everything else could be done with cash, but not the hotel. Not that hotel, anyway.'

'How much cash did he give you?'

'Apart from my five thousand, he gave me three thousand five hundred in a separate envelope. An overnight outcall with Natasha or whatever you called her was three thousand. The extra five hundred was for assorted expenses. It was very generous of him, though perhaps he didn't realise quite *how* generous. I had four hundred and fifty left over.'

'What were the expenses?'

'Getting to Chiswick and hiring the courier to deliver the five hundred deposit to Sakura here.'

'Why Chiswick? Why that courier?'

'No reason. Mr Coleman said he'd picked the courier company at random. As long as it wasn't in the West End, it was OK. He seemed to be a bit concerned that Sakura or whoever might try to find where the money came from for the deposit. He thought that if it wasn't a courier in the West End it would be too much of a pain to visit it and check it out. He said that Chiswick seemed far enough away but not too much of an inconvenience for me. I got a cab there and back.

'The deposit delivery had to be done by courier as he didn't want anyone involved to see me before the meet with Natasha. If that happened, they'd know I was young and not the person I was pretending to be on the telephone. He didn't want to do it himself, as he didn't want to be connected with any part of this in case Natasha got suspicious and it would spoil everything for his nice old friend.'

'Was he afraid that Natasha would recognise him? Did she know him?'

'I don't know. That never came up. I mean, she'd hardly be hanging around the courier's office. He just wanted the whole thing to be handled by me, from beginning to end. It was just to do with that, I think. Just security. No link between me and him and his nice old friend. He didn't want the fuss of doing the courier, was the way I read it. I'm babbling, aren't I.'

'You're doing very well, Eleanor. Why did you wear a wig and glasses when you went to the hotel? Was that Mr Coleman's idea, too?'

'Yes it was. He said it as an afterthought, I think. I don't think there was any real reason to do it; nothing sinister or anything. He put it forward as a bit of fun.

Something to give the whole endeavour a little excitement and subterfuge.'

So if Raleigh wasn't directly involved with this plan, then it was certainly being done for his benefit. Fisher was wasting a lot of energy and time with the Chiswick courier thing and the disguise at the hotel; both had no point other than to excite Eleanor, if indeed she needed excitement as an incentive. Perhaps Fisher thought she did.

In fact, the whole act that Eleanor had to put on during the initial phone call was a bit of a waste of space, too. As long as the client was paying the money and understood the protocol, I doubt whether Sakura would have turned down whoever was on the other end of the phone.

But manipulating her into suggesting the tantric massage which led directly to Natasha/Viola was smart, but not that smart. She could have just asked for Natasha up front and Sakura would have been none the wiser. She could have just said she saw Natasha's photograph and fancied her.

Perhaps Fisher just got some sort of kick out of all that chicanery and felt muddying waters would be a good thing under the circumstances; just his inept way of playing it safe, perhaps. Or perhaps he'd anticipated that Sakura might take more notice of any booking that involved Viola, so a little artifice might be useful.

'So that was it. He told you what to do, ran through the scenario, gave you the credit card, the expenses money and the first half of your fee…'

'And he gave me a PAYG mobile, too. I was to make the call to Sakura on that then dump it after the meet. Until then, I had to hang onto it in case either Sakura or

Natasha tried to contact me about anything, just for continuity's sake. Once everything was over, I was to dump the phone, take the SIM card out and dump it separately.'

'You wouldn't have told Abigail about all of this,' says Sakura.

'No. This was nothing to do with my work for her. This was private and it was a lot of money. Oh yes – and I had to book two rooms, one for me and one for her. I'd heard of that, but had never done it myself.'

'Sakura,' I say. 'How would Mr Coleman have come across Viola in the first place? Would it have been purely by chance? Raleigh, if he can be believed in the light of all of this, hadn't been in touch with her for two years, in which case, he wouldn't know about your involvement with Viola or your site. He wouldn't know that you existed or that Viola was one of your girls.'

'I don't know, Daniel. I'm really at a loss. There's only one explanation, really.'

'What would that be?'

'If Mr Coleman looks at lots of high-end call girl sites. London-based ones, I mean.'

'He does. Raleigh's PA caught him at it. I think he hires call girls as part of his job. Raleigh has a lot of important, rich clients who like to be entertained with girls, as you might expect.'

'Well, my site has links to twenty-two other sites. Three of them are like mine, the rest are more like Abigail's. But they're all high-end. He might have just come across mine and taken a look out of curiosity.

'If he knew what Viola looked like, he may have recognised her from her photographs. Everything else was fake, basically, but Viola never had her features fuzzed out or her photographs cropped in any way. It's usually students who have that done; sometimes glamour models do it, as well.'

'That's right,' says Eleanor. 'Mine weren't cropped or fuzzed out because I thought my face would sell me and so did Abigail. She thought I had lovely eyes and a sexy mouth.' She giggles. 'Plus the fact that I don't give a tuppenny damn who sees me.' She runs a hand through her hair several times to dry it off. I wish she wouldn't do that.

'OK, Eleanor. So you've got all the stuff he gave you; what was the next step? Would you be seeing him again?'

'No. Well, there were no plans to at that stage, anyway. He seemed happy enough with my understanding of the whole thing. He kept going over details again and again, but there was no need to really. I got it all the first time. To be honest, I don't think he was as clever as he made out. The way he spoke, you know?'

'So you left the hotel with your money, your phone and your Amelia Finch credit card.'

'That's right. I thought it was a really good deal, you know? On top of that, it seemed as if I'd be helping someone. The only thing that unsettled me slightly was Mr Coleman himself, like I said before.'

'Why?'

'Well, apart from the other stuff, there was a threatening tone in everything he said. He tried to disguise it and was cheery and chummy, grinning and smiling all the time, but it was as if he'd learnt it on a YouTube tutorial or something.

'I've come across a lot of very unpleasant people since I've been doing this, and I could feel he was one of those. It was the way he kept eye contact with me while he was telling me what I had to do. It was as if – this is hard to put into words – it was as if he was giving me orders and if I didn't carry them out to his liking, say I skipped with the money and didn't book Natasha for example, then I had better look out, you know?

'There was like a simmering threat of violence beneath everything he said. It was as if he was angry all of the time and was just managing to keep a lid on it.'

'Yeah, I know what you mean.'

'But it was a bit insulting, too. I mean – for that amount of money, there was *no way* I would have not continued with the whole thing and gave no impression that that might be the case. I still had another five thousand coming, for a start. I already had plans forming in my mind about what I was going to do with all that money, you know? I was going to save half of it and blow the rest on clothes and perfume!' She laughs again. I keep forgetting what a tough operator she must be.

'OK. Can we go on to the night that you met Natasha in the hotel?'

And now she goes pale again. She licks her lips and swallows a lot and I can tell she's going to throw up. I pull her to a standing position, put an arm around her shoulder and quickly get her into the small toilet, where she vomits into the sink. I turn the tap on and splash water around, poking the solid bits down the plughole with my finger. There aren't many solid bits. I keep on holding her shoulder tightly. Sakura is right behind me and fills a small glass up with tap water, holding it near Eleanor's face for when she's ready to drink.

'Splash some water over your face and then drink some of this, darling,' says Sakura, gently. 'You're OK. You're going to be OK.'

Eleanor spits into the sink. 'But I'm not OK and I'm not going to be OK,' she says, before throwing up again. I think about the fear that Raleigh and Fisher have instilled in Sakura and in this girl, then what they did to Anjukka, and then what Raleigh did to Viola and the knock-on effect that caused Rosabel to kill herself.

All that money and all that power, and at the end of it they're just a pair of toxic wankers. I already have an immeasurable amount of loathing for them, and have a feeling that it's going to get worse. And I'm starting to experience that familiar revulsion that I have for myself; for helping people like this and for working for people like this. I stroke Eleanor's hair and stare at my reflection in the mirror above the sink.

# 21

## *FERME TES YEUX*

It takes Eleanor about ten minutes to recover. Sakura makes some more coffee and the three of us sit around finishing Eleanor's posh chocolates before continuing.

'I'm sorry about your face,' says Eleanor, as if noticing the scratches for the first time.

'Oh, think nothing of it. It's an occupational hazard.'

'He's used to being attacked by women. He gets tetchy if he misses a day,' says Sakura, smiling at me and patting the back of my hand.

'It wasn't me that gave you that black eye, too, was it?' says Eleanor.

'No. That was her. Don't ask. If you feel ready, Eleanor, can we talk about the next time you went to The Bolton Mayfair?'

'Yes. That was about three weeks ago. It was strange. It was one of the few times I'd been to a hotel in London when I wasn't working. When I went in, I felt everyone was staring at me and that they all knew I was a call girl, when actually I was the customer of one, so to speak. I was innocent!'

She lights a cigarette, places it on the edge of the ashtray, then holds her coffee cup in both hands. 'I felt a bit silly wearing the wig and the glasses, to tell you the truth. I mean, they looked good; I'm not saying they looked silly or anything. I spent about an hour getting the wig right before I went out that night. I don't think anyone really noticed me, but you always think that they do when something is making you self-conscious and I felt self-conscious going into a hotel to meet this Natasha. I was also feeling a little trepidation about all the cash I had in my bag. The whole thing was a little unsettling for me.'

I remember what Mr Kerrigan said about Amelia Finch's beautiful green eyes, how they made you want to reach out and take her glasses off. I look at Eleanor and he was right. For a dizzy second, I forget what it is I'm doing here and allow myself to get lost in them. She notices, smiles quickly and looks at the floor. Great; now she thinks I'm just like all the others.

'What time did you arrive at the hotel?'

'I can't remember exactly. I think Mr Coleman told me to get there before eight. I think I may have been a little early, possibly before half past seven.'

'The hotel said seven-fifteen.'

'Was that it? Yes. That sounds about right. I checked into my room and then I went to the bar and had a couple of glasses of white wine. I read a book. That was weird, too. I was in the hotel for a perfectly innocent reason. Correction: a relatively innocent reason. But as I was sitting in the bar, I could feel people looking at me and I got the feeling that they knew, you know? That they knew what I was. Not what I was doing there on that particular evening, but what I was. It's not as if I was dressed conspicuously. I was wearing a plain black skirt and a black sleeveless top and some subtle silver jewellery.

'Though to be fair, I often wonder if hotel staff suspect what's going on so much when it's a woman hiring another woman for sex. In a lot of hotels, when it's a man hiring you, you can tell they know the score, especially if you're a regular visitor. But then there are so many hotels in London. Even with the number of outcalls I've done since I started, I've rarely visited any hotel more than three or four times. Just a thought. Anyway, I realised I didn't like it. I knew how a normal woman must feel when she's mistaken for a call girl. I felt quite indignant!'

'I think they were just staring at you because you were beautiful, darling,' says Sakura. 'You have a very striking figure. Voluptuous and athletic. You would stand out in any hotel anywhere.'

'Some guy came up to me and asked if I wanted a drink. It's so annoying when that happens. Just because a woman is on her own in a hotel bar men think she's a prostitute!'

This gets a laugh from all of us. I can see why Eleanor does good GFE. She's smart and funny. I like her.

'OK,' I say, still laughing. 'So what happened next?'

'Well, after I'd been in the bar long enough, I went back up to my room to get ready for Natasha. I wasn't sure how far we were going to go while waiting for her father. I mean, I wouldn't mind *trying* a tantric massage, just to see what it was like, but I didn't want to be naked and sweating and in the middle of a screaming whole-body orgasm when the old man came in, you know?'

This puts an image in my mind which I have to eradicate immediately for the sake of my sanity.

'Mr Coleman said that it wouldn't be long after Natasha arrived that there would be a knock at the door.

I was to say that it was champagne that I'd ordered from room service. I'd open the door and then this wonderful father/daughter reunion would occur. I'd smile at everyone, make my excuses and leave. Then I'd go online and spend my ten thousand pounds!'

She laughs again, goes to light another cigarette and realises her packet is empty. She excuses herself and gets up to get some more in another part of the house. Sakura places her hand on mine.

'I am starting to get nervous now, Daniel. Her moods are so up and down that I can't imagine what we're going to hear from her next.'

'It'll be OK. I think she's quite strong, really. I think she has a lot of things going on in her head because of this. Most of her anxiety is because she doesn't know what's going on or who anyone is or what their motives are or were. This is taking a long time, but I think the soft approach is working with her. She's being dying to talk to someone about all of this, even if it's going to be painful for her.'

'Well, at least she's not wielding a poker anymore, Daniel.'

'Yes. I miss that.'

Eleanor returns with a fresh packet of cigarettes, takes one out and lights it. The smell of the smoke is quite unusual and not at all unpleasant. I take a look at the packet. They're called Cigaronne. I've never heard of them.

'So there I am, waiting in my swanky hotel room for Natasha to arrive. I'd decided to create a persona for her visit so she didn't get suspicious. It was rather like acting a role. I'd be a little shy, a little naïve, I'd laugh nervously, but I wouldn't lay it on too thickly. I had to remember that I was trying to fool someone who was in the same profession that I was, so I'd have to be very good. I just hoped that I didn't have to keep it up for half an hour or something.'

'So then Natasha arrived,' says Sakura, softly. This must be a curious experience for her. Not only is she getting a first-hand account of how one of her girls works from the client's point of view, but she's also hearing about what might be the last moments in the life of a former lover. Someone she rescued from heroin addiction. Someone she taught, probably in the most intimate way possible, the various tricks of the trade for being a call girl who only serviced female clients.

'Well, yes,' says Eleanor. 'She must have arrived shortly before nine o' clock. She'd already booked herself into her room and she called me on the hotel room telephone from there. Said who she was and would it be alright if she came to my room. I said yes. She was on a different floor.

'She knocked on the door and I got up and answered it. I was quite taken aback when I saw her. I mean, she was incredibly beautiful, but it wasn't that, particularly. It was the way she looked, the way she was dressed. She had 'professional woman at a conference' down to a T. She even had a briefcase. Quite clever, I thought. Of course she would have had a bag with all her bits and bobs and clothing with her. She'd have dumped that in her room. We kind of air-kissed just after she came in. I thought that was nice.'

'So what did she say, Eleanor? Did you chat much?' I'm starting to get butterflies in my stomach. I can almost see Viola entering the hotel room. I can see both women staring at each other, sizing each other up. Viola wondering how this client will respond to her touch, and Eleanor wondering when Natasha's dad will turn up so she can go home; wondering how convincing her pretence will be and how long she can keep it up for.

'The moment she came in,' says Eleanor, 'I think she thought something was not right. She looked at me and I noticed a tiny little frown flash across her eyebrows. Barely noticeable, but I saw it straight away. I think it was my age. I think she was expecting somebody older.'

'That's probably right,' says Sakura. 'Most of my clients are at least mid-thirties. Eleanor here was able to pass herself off as older on the telephone, but in person it would not be so easy for her.' She looks at Eleanor and smiles. 'You are too fresh-faced and innocent, my darling, too virginal and unsullied.'

'That's my cross I have to bear,' replies Eleanor, amused by Sakura's humour. 'Natasha immediately put me – or should I say Mrs Amelia Finch – at ease. She was charming and lovely. I made us some hotel room coffee and she talked me through what would be happening with the tantric massage.

'I'll tell you what it reminded me of. It reminded me of the Avon Ladies that used to come to the house when I was in school, but more posh and definitely sexier. It was as if she was talking to me about some new line of face cream, as opposed to a multi-orgasmic G-spot massage. I must admit, part of me wanted to just lie down and let her do it to me. She asked if I would like her to be naked while giving the massage or just partially naked. I didn't know what to say immediately, because I knew we weren't going to get that far.'

'But you said something.'

'Yes. I said I'd like her to be naked. Then she asked

me if I had any preference for the sort of oil she would use on me during the massage. I said I didn't know, so she suggested using sweet almond oil scented with rose and neroli. That sounded nice so I agreed. I was starting to feel a little bad that she was going to all this trouble for nothing.'

Eleanor has tears streaming down her face again, but she isn't sobbing. Well at least that's something. Sakura leans forwards and holds both of Eleanor's hands in hers.

'That is when you gave Natasha the money, yes?'

'Yes. I handed her the envelope and she kissed me on the cheek and said she was just going to pop down to her room to get everything ready and she'd be back in a few minutes. She suggested that I take a shower and get into a robe. Well I hadn't planned on that. Of course, Mr Coleman hadn't planned on it either, neither of us had, so we hadn't discussed it.

'I couldn't think what to do. It would spoil Mrs Amelia Finch's image if Natasha came back to the room and I was still dressed and sipping hotel room coffee. I didn't know what to do. The real Mrs Amelia Finch would have just got undressed and had a shower like Natasha said. She'd be under a hot spray of water and she'd be getting excited and maybe even aroused at the thought of what was to come. And here was I wondering what the hell to do next.'

'So what did you do, darling?' asks Sakura.

'This is going to sound crazy, but when I heard her knock on the door again, I took my top off so that I was just in my bra and skirt. I let her in and she looked surprised. I told her that I was more than a little shy; I was incredibly uptight about this and about sex in general. That's why I hadn't got undressed yet. I was having a teensy-weensy panic attack. Then I had a brainwave; something that would make that sound like a plausible story.

'I told her that I'd ordered a bottle of champagne from room service. She said that that sounded like a good idea. She said she liked champagne. She had a big bag with her now and she said that she was going to go into the bathroom to get changed. She was very nice. She said that there was no need to rush, that we had all night. She said that she would make it good for me, that I could relax, and that I would never forget it and I would never forget her. As she went into the bathroom, I breathed a huge sigh of relief.'

God Almighty; I'm going to have an anxiety attack listening to this. Eleanor lights another cigarette. The tears are still streaming down her face. She sips at her coffee, though it must be cold by now.

'About five minutes later, Natasha came out of the bathroom. She was dressed in a lovely silk kimono robe. She looked so gorgeous. The robe was, I don't know, I guess you'd call it ivory. The colour, I mean. It wasn't see-through, but you could see through it, d'you know what I mean? It looked like it had been painted on, particularly around her breasts. I liked it. The fabric fell beautifully. It occurred to me to ask her where she got it from, but I didn't in the end. It was tied with a sash belt, but seemed designed to fall open when she leaned forward. It's as if it was caressing her body as she walked along.'

Eleanor leans forwards and looks Sakura in the eye. 'She seemed so nice. She wasn't that much older than me. I know the way she spoke to me was an act, I do that act myself, but apart from all of that I could imagine us being friends, being in the same business and everything. I could see beneath the act, is what I mean to say. There was a nice person underneath that act.

'She went into the bedroom and set up this little burner device which she used to heat up the oil for the massage. After a few minutes, this lovely smell filled the bedroom and the rest of the room. She put a thing like a big, thick pale green towel onto the bed. The bed was big, but this hung over the sides. She put a white sheet on top of the towel. She kept bending over while she did all these things and the robe kept falling open. I know this was part of the whole thing, you know? It was to titillate the client. She pushed the bed a few times to see how firm it was. I was wondering when the hell this guy, her father, was going to turn up.

'I could see what she was doing. The whole atmosphere in the bedroom was getting intoxicating. The rose and the neroli from the warmed-up oil, the perfume she was wearing. I didn't know what it was, but it was very musky.'

'It's called *Ferme tes Yeaux*,' says Sakura.

'So there I was, still wearing a bra and my skirt. I took my shoes off and left them outside the bedroom. I was wearing these four-inch heels and my feet were starting to ache, so it was quite a relief to get them off. They were Pleaser Fabulicious ones and you know what they're like.'

I smile at her. 'I never wear anything else.'

She laughs. 'God. How tall would *you* be in *those*?'

'So Natasha was preparing the massage things in the bedroom.'

'Yes. Then there was a knock on the door. A quiet knock. Not like room service would do, d'you know what I mean? This was a secretive knock. For a crazy moment I was thinking that it must be the champagne, then I remembered that was just a story. I remember being quite relieved. I was thinking that all of this would be over soon and I could go home.'

She looks in her coffee cup to see what's left, then unsteadily places it back on the saucer. She lights another Cigaronne and looks at the lit end.

'It's going to be hard for me to describe to you what happened next. It all took place really fast. There are bits of it that I can't remember very clearly. I've been dreaming about it, to tell you the truth. I've been dreaming about that whole evening. Some mornings I wake up and feel relieved because it was all a dream, then I realise it wasn't and get this terrible sinking feeling. I keep getting bits of what happened mixed up and in the wrong order.'

She bites one of her fingernails. Her nails are so perfectly manicured that I want to reach out and stop her, but don't. She keeps swallowing, as if she's got a bad taste in her mouth that she's trying to get rid of.

'Don't worry about the order of things or being precise, Eleanor. Just tell me what happened as naturally as you can. Backtrack if you have to. I won't mind.'

She inhales some cigarette smoke and then presses the balls of her hands into her eyes. She breathes in and out rapidly, as if she's starting to hyperventilate, but then she stops.

'I opened the door and there was Mr Coleman and this old guy. This had to be the father. He smiled at me. He seemed very nice. A bit like your favourite granddad. But his eyes were dead. He was staring right through me. You know how some people do that? It was as if I wasn't there for him; as if I didn't exist.'

I ask her to give me a quick description of the father.

She does. There could be no doubt that it was Raleigh, or his identical twin.

'Mr Coleman smiled at me, as if we were old friends. He put a finger up to his lips for me to keep quiet. It was as if we were in on some lovely surprise for someone or other. A birthday surprise, maybe. The father guy came into the room and looked around as if he'd never been in a hotel room before. He smelled of old-fashioned aftershave or cologne or whatever. Mr Coleman followed him and quietly closed the door behind him, but not quietly enough, because Natasha heard it and asked if that was the champagne. Mr Coleman nodded to me and I said yes, it was the champagne.

'Then Natasha came out of the bedroom. I noticed that her robe had fallen open and you could see her breasts. I remember thinking how similar our body types were. I saw her take in the two men for a fraction of a second, as if they might be hotel staff who'd come into the room with the champagne, then her eyes widened. She opened her mouth to say something, but nothing came out. From the expression on her face, I knew immediately that something wasn't right. I'm talking in clichés, aren't I?'

'It's OK, Eleanor.'

She looks down at the floor, an expression of concentration on her face.

'Her father smiled at her and said something I didn't catch. He held his arms out, as if he expected her to run into them and give him a big hug. She turned and gave me a terrible look, as if I'd betrayed her or something. I'll always remember that look. It was hideous. Then she just went berserk and launched herself at him, punching him again and again in the face and the chest. He had his arms up to protect himself like this.' She crosses her hands in front of her face. 'Then Natasha started shouting and swearing at him. She looked crazy. Then Mr Coleman got behind her and grabbed the back of her neck so she couldn't move. Her father slapped her across the face and pulled the robe off her so she was naked. I started to feel ill. I didn't know what was happening or what I should do.

'He started shouting at her about how she was his property and how nobody ever, ever left him; ridiculous stuff like that. The he started to grab her body and it was like he'd totally lost control of himself. He was trying to kiss her and fondle her. She was struggling and kicking out at him, she even spat at him, but she couldn't really do anything because Mr Coleman was stopping her from moving. He'd let go of her neck and he was holding both of her arms.

'She wriggled and swore, trying to get free. It was terrifying and disturbing. I'd been rooted to the spot until then, but I started to think that I wanted to get out of there as fast as possible and sod the rest of the money, you know? This was getting violent, nasty and incomprehensible. I'd been in situations a little like this before and I was frightened. He kept on saying that it was his right to do this. He kept on calling her his property all of the time. I'm sorry if this isn't entirely accurate, but it was all a bit of a blur. She kept on kicking and spitting and swearing and you could see he was getting annoyed with her.

'Mr Coleman put his arms around her in a tight bear hug from behind. He was smirking. I looked around for my stuff. I could see my top, but it was over a chair about eight feet away. I felt stupid being in my bra when all this was going on, whatever it was. My shoes were near the bedroom where I'd taken them off and my bag was on a coffee table.

'Then the old guy said to Mr Coleman to get me out and for him to go with me. He said that he had everything under control and would deal with everything now. Mr Coleman grinned and nodded his head at the old guy. He – the old guy – grabbed Natasha and was trying to drag her into the bedroom. I was surprised he was so strong, because Natasha looked pretty fit. I grabbed my top and put it on, and then I grabbed my bag. I was so relieved that I was being allowed to get out.

'I asked Mr Coleman for the rest of my money, but he just laughed. I asked him again and he slapped me and told me to shut my fucking mouth or things would get nasty for me. You know that expression 'seeing stars'? I finally understood what they meant by that. He slapped my face so hard that I could taste blood in my mouth. He really didn't have to hit me that hard, you know? I think he enjoyed it. He was grinning like the cat that got the cream. I was shocked because I thought we were working together on this.

'I was wondering if anyone else in the hotel could hear all this noise. Perhaps someone would call hotel security and someone would come up to see what on earth was going on, but they didn't.' She taps some cigarette ash onto the Arc de Triomphe again. 'This sounds like it was going on for ages, doesn't it. But it wasn't going on for ages. It was all like a couple of minutes, tops.'

I turn to look at Sakura. Her eyes are starting to fill with tears.

'So the old guy was slapping and punching Natasha and dragging her into the bedroom. She was putting up a hell of a fight. The whole thing was unreal. It's like it wasn't really happening and I was watching a film or something, you know? But part of me knew what was going on here. Part of me knew that it was some weird sexual thing that the old guy had for her and that he wanted everyone out so he could get on with it. I wondered if he was really her father. I think he was shocked that she was putting up that much of a fight. I don't think he had expected that.

'I was just going to get my shoes, when without warning Natasha landed a really good right hook on the old man's jaw. He was, like, stunned for a moment, and in that moment she kicked him in the balls. I mean, she was bare-footed, but it still did the job, you know? It was freaky watching this because she was naked.

'He groaned and his face went grey. At first, he looked like he was going to cry, then he looked angry; really angry. It was scary. He was bent in two for a few seconds, then he straightened up. His eyes were bulging out of his head. He balled his hand into a fist and punched Natasha hard in the face. Despite his age it was a really hard punch. I'm sure it would have knocked me out.

'Then I'm not sure what happened. It looked as if she was leaning backwards and for a second she righted herself and was standing up straight again, then she lost her footing and she fell backwards and sideways. There was a little writing desk; wooden, quite solid. She hit the back of her head on it really hard and then she was on the floor. That was when everything went quiet and still, apart from the old guy's panting.

'Her head was at a really grotesque angle. Her mouth was hanging open and her eyes were open, too. I knew that she was dead straight away. It's just one of those things, isn't it, when you just know like that. It was really strange; one second she was being really feisty and fighting back and the next second…'

Sakura has gone quite pale. She has her hand over her mouth and is trying to hold back several huge sobs. Eleanor looks at her in alarm and tears start to fill her eyes again.

'I'm sorry. I'm sorry to have to tell you this. I should have done something, but I couldn't. I don't remember everything that happened after that. The old guy looked at Natasha and then looked at Mr Coleman. He bent down and started kissing her face and stroking her hair. He started running his hands all over her body, as if he was testing each square inch for signs of life. He was smiling and doing this fake laugh, as if everything was alright and she was messing around, pretending to be dead. He was *pawing* her and smacking his lips. It was creepy beyond belief.

'I started to feel faint. I was thinking that he'd just killed his daughter and now he was acting like this. It didn't seem normal. He kept saying that she was alright. That she'd just bumped her head. That she was still alive. That everything would be the same. That she'd still be his little girl and things would go on as they always had. Just loads and loads of stuff like that. I remember thinking that he was deranged. That was the word that came to mind. Deranged. Mr Coleman just stood there like he didn't know what to do, like he was waiting for instructions.

'The old guy looked up and looked straight at me, as if he was seeing me for the first time. Then he looked at Mr Coleman and said he should make sure I didn't leave here. He had to think. I could feel my insides turning to jelly. Mr Coleman pointed at me and ordered me to sit down, so I sat down on a dining chair. Mr Coleman went into the bedroom to look around.

'He kept watching me, to make sure I wasn't going anywhere. I put on a bit of an act. I sat totally still and stared in front of me, as if I was frozen with fear. He picked up Natasha's bag and put it on the bed. He started stuffing her things into the bag. I just knew that if I didn't get out of that room right then I'd never get out. When you do this sort of thing you get tuned in to danger pretty quickly and I knew that I was in danger, and that every second that went by I would be in more danger.

'I don't know what made me do this, but I noticed that Mr Coleman was having a problem zipping Natasha's bag up. He was swearing under his breath. I picked up my shoes and made a run for the door, hoping that they hadn't locked it from the inside. But when the old guy realised what I was doing, he stood up and blocked my way.

'He grabbed my upper arm really tightly. Again, I was surprised how strong he was. I still had my shoes in my hand. I dropped one onto the floor and used the other one to smack him in the head with it as hard as I could manage. I knew about using heels as a weapon. I knew they could be dangerous. I wanted to fucking kill him. I wanted that heel to go through his skull into his brain. He screamed and immediately released my arm. I got out of there as fast as I fucking could. I could hear him calling Mr Coleman, but he was calling him James, not Bill.'

I remember the strange scar above Raleigh's eyebrow. So *that's* how he got it.

'I ran down the corridor. I remember being amazed that it was empty, but then, as I said, the whole business only took a couple of minutes and there probably wasn't as much noise as perhaps I thought there was. I went down the service stairs and ended up near some bar on the ground floor. I don't think anyone noticed that I didn't have any shoes on, or if they did, they didn't care. I still looked pretty smartly dressed.

'There were two nerdy guys looking at me. I went straight up to one of them and asked him in my sexiest voice if he would mind coming out to the front of the hotel with me so that I could get a cab. I told him there was an ex-boyfriend lurking around that I didn't want to bump into. He was very gallant and so was his friend, who insisted on accompanying us. It was stupid, but they believed it and it was the best I could come up with at the time.

'As we were leaving, I saw Mr Coleman. He was out of breath. I think he was going to try and stop me, but when he saw the two guys, he stayed where he was, glowering at me. I think if it had been one guy he might have tried something, but two of them put him off. He watched me leave the hotel and I turned back to look at him and he gave me a look, a smirk, that said he was going to find me, you know? That he was going to kill me, that's the impression I got. He didn't have to say anything. Just that look was enough. Needless to say, I didn't bother to ask him for the rest of my money.'

She laughs for the first time in what seems like ages. I think she's relieved to have got all of this off her chest.

'So I got a cab back here and I haven't really been out since. I was frightened. I didn't think it was safe to go anywhere or to do anything. I only realised this morning that I'd forgotten to dump the mobile and the SIM card that Mr Coleman gave me. I knew there was no way on earth that Abigail would give Mr Coleman my home address, but then I didn't think he was going to ask her for it.'

'Why not, darling?' Sakura has recovered somewhat and is dabbing her eyes with a handkerchief.

'Well think about it. If Mr Coleman went barging into Abigail's house – even if he could find out where it was – and said to her that he wanted my address, then she'd want to know why. But, of course, he couldn't possibly tell her, could he? So then she'd have no reason to give it to him.'

That sounds fairly logical, if a little bit foggy. Then it dawns on me. It's so blindingly obvious that I feel like kicking myself. Raleigh had wrong-footed me right from the start. Both he and Fisher had always known that Viola was dead. My assignment wasn't to find Viola, it was to find Eleanor, the only witness to Viola's death, and like an idiot I'd led them straight to her.

The night at the Bolton after Viola had died, Raleigh and Fisher had to act fast. They'd made an attempt to keep Eleanor in the room with them, but it had failed and she'd escaped. That didn't matter, though. They could deal with her later.

They probably assessed that there was a chance of her going straight to the police, but the likelihood was that she wouldn't. They would be hoping that she would just take the money and run.

She would be frightened by what she had witnessed. She would be frightened of Fisher and what he might do to her. She would be frightened of going to the police in case she got into trouble. She was a prostitute; her instinct would have been to lie low and hope it all went away.

Their main priority was to cover up Viola's death and

remove her body from the hotel without anybody noticing.

The period immediately following Viola's death would have been a stressful time for Raleigh, and for Fisher, too. Neither could be a hundred per cent sure how Eleanor had acted after she'd left the hotel. If she *had* gone to the authorities, then they could expect a knock on the door at any time.

Fisher had used a false name and Raleigh had never been identified at all, but if Eleanor spilled the beans, it wouldn't be long before the police discovered that Bill Coleman was really James Fisher and that would lead them directly to Nathan Raleigh.

The Amelia Finch credit card would be a good place for the police to start, not to mention the PAYG mobile, which Eleanor didn't get rid of. There could even be fingerprints on it if they were lucky, not to mention the fingerprints all over the hotel room. And if they acted quickly, they'd have the hotel's CCTV footage of both Fisher and Raleigh from that night.

They could also visit Abigail Gastrell, who would have a record of Fisher's initial hiring of Eleanor for that evening when they set everything up. Fisher would have paid for Eleanor by credit card and he'd have paid for his room at the Bolton in the same way. But they didn't have to worry; Eleanor had no intention of going to the police.

Then something happened that would have caused Raleigh and Fisher to breathe a collective sigh of relief: Sakura reported Viola as a missing person. When Olivia Bream telephoned Raleigh, he must have thought the game was up. But it was a courtesy call, to let him know that his daughter had been reported missing yet again. There was no mention of Eleanor Wallis and no mention of Viola's death.

So far, so good. But they weren't in the clear yet. Eleanor was still out there with all that information in her head. She had to be tracked down and eliminated.

This was not a job that Fisher could take on. His hands would be tied. If he attempted to locate Eleanor through Abigail Gastrell, he'd be implicating himself and Raleigh if the circumstances surrounding Viola's death ever came to light.

Abigail could refuse to give him any info regarding Eleanor. She could call Eleanor to warn her and Eleanor might decide to go to the police. Abigail could go to the police herself. Anything could happen.

Then they hatched a plan. Raleigh could use Viola's renewed missing status as an excuse to hire someone to find her. His story would sound completely plausible and the police could even confirm it. No one need know that it was really Eleanor he was looking for, and, of course, no one would know that Viola was dead. With a bit of luck, they could have Eleanor in their clutches as a side effect of the futile search for Viola. Then, three weeks later, I walk in through the door.

It would explain all the surveillance and Fisher's matey phone call checking on my progress. I have no idea if Sakura and I were followed here, but I think it's pretty likely. I get a sick feeling in the pit of my stomach and feel angry at being taken for such an idiot. As the enormity of the whole situation starts to dawn on me, I hear a car door being slammed shut outside, and then another.

# 22

## BLUE TIE, ORANGE SHIRT

'Eleanor. Is there a lock on your bathroom door?'

'Yes there is. Why?'

'Sakura. Take Eleanor upstairs and lock both of yourselves in the bathroom. I think we've got visitors.'

'Do you want me to stay with you, Daniel?' says Sakura. 'I mean, I can help if…'

'Thanks but no. Just wait in there until I come and get both of you. Don't make any noise. Sakura – if anyone tries to come inside and it's not me, let them have it. Be merciless.'

Both women look uneasy as they leave the room and head upstairs, particularly Eleanor, who's gone as white as a sheet. I run up the stairs after them and go into Eleanor's bedroom, which has a view of the street and, more importantly, has lace curtains so I can look out of the window without being seen.

There's a silver BMW 5 Series parked across the road and two big guys in suits have just got out and have already started heading across the road. One of them is Blue Tie from Raleigh's office. The other one I don't recognise, but he's cut from the same ex-military cloth. Blue Tie is hiding something underneath his suit jacket.

I try to work out what they're going to do. Presumably, they're not going to offer Eleanor a few thousand pounds, a luxury cruise and a fur coat to go away and forget everything. They may not even know what happened in the hotel. They're probably just under instructions to lift Eleanor and take her to Raleigh and Fisher, who will then dispose of her.

Their thinking probably goes like this: Eleanor (or Celia as they must still know her) is a prostitute, someone that no one will miss if she is made to vanish. She just doesn't matter and she barely exists as a human being. She wasn't even staying at the hotel under her real name or her professional name. It was a bit of moonlighting that even her madam didn't know about.

What happened to Viola cannot be allowed to leak out. Raleigh would be in deep shit just for what he did in the hotel and if all the details came out in court, everything he's ever worked for would be in ruins. I doubt whether he'd have a very good time in prison, either, all things considered. Neither Raleigh nor Fisher could have foreseen what happened in the hotel, so Eleanor was an unexpected hassle that had to be sorted out as soon as possible.

Then, of course, there's his big Oman deal next week that he so wanted to have a clear head for. Was that a lie? The whole thing? No, it can't be. Anjukka knew about it. But could they have made it up and told her about it to make it seem so convincing? Perhaps I'm seeing too much conspiracy here. Perhaps all my speculation is bullshit. Perhaps there'll be a happy ending to all of this, but I won't order the champagne and caviar just yet.

I try the toilet door to make sure it's locked properly. It's OK. You could kick it open, but hopefully it won't come to that. As far as I'm concerned, those two heavies will not be coming up here. Not if I can help it.

As I go down the stairs to face them, I realise that Sakura and I will also have to be dealt with by Raleigh. Quite apart from the Eleanor situation, Raleigh and Fisher will have to assume that we know the whole story and will have to be silenced.

Would Raleigh resort to murdering everyone who could harm him with the information about Viola? I have no idea. But I can think about all of that later. I'm having enough trouble keeping the horror of the whole thing out of my head as it is.

By the time I get downstairs, I can see two besuited shapes right outside the front door. If I was in their position, I'd want to get in here as quickly and as inconspicuously as possible, deal with the three of us and leave, though I can't see how they'd get us out into the car without someone noticing. This is not a particularly busy road at this time of day, but if you were driving past and saw three people being manhandled into a big BMW by a couple of gorillas like that, you might consider calling the authorities.

Of course, they can circumvent all of that by killing us right here. That's what I would do, and sort out the problem of the bodies another time.

I don't want them to have to smash the door down; I want them in here, with me. I wonder what I'm going to say when I let them in, and try to think of a witty one-liner that'll slay them.

I walk up to the front door and open it. Blue Tie sees me and smirks. He's going to have his revenge for those bouncer remarks I made the other day, I can see it in his eyes.

'Hi, girls,' I say, brightly. 'She's in the back room.'

They walk in as if I'm not there. Then Blue Tie grabs

the front of my shirt and slams me into the wall. He's very strong indeed. If I wore false teeth, they'd be on the floor by now. Little white stars dance about in front of my eyes. I feel nauseous and faint. He turns to his pal, who I must call Orange Shirt.

'Keep this fucker here. Close the door.'

Orange Shirt doesn't speak, but he certainly obeys. I take a good look at him for the first time. He's bald (aren't they all?), grim-faced, and has a grey moustache. Quite old for this game, I think, but he looks wiry and muscular underneath the suit. Something tells me you don't give a guy like this any chances. If you don't get him effectively the first time, he'll kill you. He closes the door quietly, turns, and punches me hard in the stomach. I groan and bend double with the pain. I'm not acting; that was a bastard of a punch. I'm aware that I'm not as fit as I might be after my bout with Sakura and I have to keep taking that into account.

I catch sight of Blue Tie, who's now about five feet away. He's moving slowly and with deliberation. There are three possibilities that the term 'back room' could cover and he's cautiously looking from left to right. I'm glad he's thick; it'll give me the time I need to deal with him. For a second, I think he's carrying some sort of truncheon, then I realise it's a telescopic stun baton. So that's what he was hiding under his jacket. I'm familiar with these things. They carry about eight hundred thousand volts and it's best not to touch the business end.

I start to straighten up and Orange Shirt is about to give me a second helping, but I turn to the side and ram my shoulder into his solar plexus with as much *ki* as I can manage. He looks shocked and staggers back. Before he can make his next decision I bring a hammer fist down hard on his collarbone, breaking it. His shoulder sags on that side and his face goes grey to match his moustache.

I head-butt him to give him something to think about, hit him hard on the same spot again and push down with my thumb. I can hear the broken halves of his clavicle grind against each other. I'm aware that one of those halves could rupture his subclavian artery and he could die, but there's no time for sentimentality.

Just as Blue Tie is turning around to see what just happened, I'm running towards him down the corridor as fast as I can. He's about twelve feet away and I have to judge this perfectly or I'm screwed. In the brief moment that he still has most of his back to me, I give him a flying kick just beneath his shoulder blades. This knocks him forwards onto the floor, but he's still holding the stun baton.

As I'm now on the floor as well, I spring up onto my feet before he can do anything else, but he must be tougher than I anticipated, as he gets up with an unexpected nimbleness, turning towards me and brandishing the baton. He looks pissed, but I've made him lose his temper, which is a good thing.

He's such an idiot. He's got all that voltage and all he needs to do is to prod me with it, but instead he's slashing away as if he's holding a broadsword. Despite this poor technique, I can still do without that thing touching me and taking it off him will be a risky endeavour.

I crouch low and take in his entire body, watching for any slight twitch that might indicate what he's going to do next. He's giving himself away with his gaze, though knowing where he's going to strike doesn't necessarily mean I can avoid it.

He's grinning as he makes the baton whistle through the air, assured of victory. I'm half hoping that he's so stupid that he couldn't work out how to turn it on, but I can see a little green light and hear a humming noise which tells me otherwise.

'Is this how you deal with people wearing flip-flops?'

For this I get a fast couple of swipes that just miss my head.

'You're fucking dead.'

Another swipe, another miss. Can't place his accent. Not Israeli as I'd first thought.

'You're wasting time. Your fiancé needs an ambulance.'

His eyes flicker with the tiniest bit of concern over to where Orange Shirt is lying on the floor. I can hear him moaning softly, so the end hasn't come quite yet.

'You'd better go and sort him out or the wedding's off.'

'I'm going to sort *you* out, you fucker.'

'Are all your comebacks that snappy?'

'Fuck you.'

He's very angry now and his slashing technique gets more frantic and naturally sloppier. He telegraphs all his movements like an amateur, so I'm able to dodge them all, which makes him even angrier. But I can't keep this up indefinitely and I don't know what other guests may soon be arriving. Orange Shirt moans a little more. Blue Tie uselessly attempts to cut my head off with the baton but this time I catch his wrist and twist it the wrong way while turning my body in the opposite direction.

Despite his weight, the pain gets him off his feet, flicks him through the air and throws him into the wall. He grunts and drops the baton, which I kick out of the way.

A throw like that would have finished most people, but this chump is strong. When he tries to get up I kick him hard in the side of the head, and then do it again with greater force. The second kick splits his cheek open and draws blood. I bend down to check him, jamming my thumb into his fresh wound to discourage any valiant resistance.

He's incapacitated but breathing hard, so he's not out cold. I grab his collar, pull him up to a good position (for me) and punch him several times in the face. Then I pick up the baton, work out how to operate it and give him a ten-second burst in the chest. He jiggles about just like they do in cartoons. I slap him on the face a few times, but there's no response. Blood pours from the side of his mouth.

I try to remember which side of their vehicle these two fuckers were getting out of. Orange Shirt was on the pavement side, I think, so he must have been the driver. I go over to him and check all of his pockets until I find the car keys. I take the keys, his wallet and his mobile, slip them in my pocket, run upstairs and tap on the toilet door.

'It's me. You can unlock the door. You two have got to get out of here.'

Sakura pops her head out and looks from left to right to see whether I'm lying or not, and I can't blame her. Anything could have been going on out here.

'Eleanor. Can you gather up an overnight bag's worth of stuff? Take any valuables, credit cards etc. Hopefully you can come back here tomorrow. Go and get dressed and grab whatever you need. Quick as you can.'

She nods her head and disappears into her bedroom. She looks ill again. I take Sakura's hand and drag her down the stairs after me. 'Have you got anywhere you can go? You can't go back to your place and Abigail's is out of the question, too.'

She thinks for a second and nods her head. 'Yes. Yes, I know where I can go.'

'You'd better take Eleanor with you. Is that OK?'

Sakura stops when she sees the two groaning heaps on the floor. 'What happened to them?'

'They should count themselves lucky that it wasn't *you* they had to deal with.'

Eleanor runs down the stairs and passes us by as she looks for things to stuff in her holdall. She also stops when she sees Blue Tie and Orange Shirt. 'God. Who are they? What have you done to them?'

'These guys were coming here for you. You've got to remember, Eleanor, you were the only witness to what happened to Natasha. I think they were sent here to take you away somewhere. What was going to happen to you then, I have no idea, but I suspect they were going to make you disappear.

'The night at the hotel was three weeks ago. If you'd gone to the police, Coleman and his friend would have known about it by now. They were pretty sure you were just going to hide out and hope it would all go away, and they were right. They hired me to find Natasha, but really they hired me to find you.'

'You keep talking about 'they'.'

'The guy you knew as Coleman was actually called Fisher. He works for a guy called Raleigh. Raleigh was the guy in the hotel who killed Natasha.'

'Whose name is really Viola,' she says, almost laughing at the complexity of it all.

'Yes. Viola was his daughter, that part was true. He

started abusing her when she was nine and I think he felt he was owed some more quality abuse time with her. When he discovered the sort of agency she was doing escort work for, he decided to set her up, but he needed a female to hire her. That was you. Is that red Alfa Romeo outside yours?'

'Yes it is.'

'Tell me when you're ready to go. Sakura will give you directions. I don't know where you'll be going and it's better that you don't tell me. I know you're pissed, but you'll have to drive.'

Sakura prods Blue Tie with her foot. 'What about these two?'

'They'll have to stay here. This one will come around in about ten minutes. The other one is in a more serious state. He's got about twenty minutes left if he's lucky. Either this one will call an ambulance for the sick one, or he'll spirit him away somewhere. I don't know how he's going to do it, because I'm taking their car.'

Eleanor races upstairs to get some more stuff from the bathroom. Sakura looks a little pale and panicky. She holds onto my forearm, just like she did on that first day as we walked down Portman Street. 'I don't feel so good, Daniel.'

'You'll be OK. You've got to be. Here's what's going to happen.' I search Blue Tie and take his mobile, his wallet and a bunch of keys. I put them in my pocket. 'When Eleanor is ready, we'll go to the front door. I'll go out and check the street to make sure there are no more surprise visitors or any sort of backup team out there. Once it's clear, you and Eleanor get in Eleanor's car and go wherever you're going to go. Choose a convoluted route if you can manage it. I shouldn't think you'll be tailed but don't take any chances.'

'How did those men know we were here?'

'I don't know. We were tailed by two cars on our way back into London from Abigail's, but the last time I saw either of the cars was in the King's Road.'

'While we were in the taxi? You didn't say anything.'

'I know. Don't worry about it. I saw the driver of one of the cars when I was having lunch, but I managed to give her and her friend the slip.'

I think about Natalie and smile. I hope she's OK. There's something wrong with the sequence of events here, but I can't put my finger on what it is.

I try to think what I did before I came here. I got on the tube at Marble Arch and took the Central Line, getting off at Holborn and walking down to the oyster bar in Carey Street to meet Natalie for lunch.

I've been a lot more switched on since Tote Bag and Grey Hair, and wasn't aware of being followed when I approached Carey Street. However, Wrap Dress and her colleague turned up at the oyster bar. How did Wrap Dress manage that?

The last time I saw her in her yellow car was just before the minicab approached Fulham. If she'd driven straight to Carey Street, she could have easily got there before me, but I hadn't told anyone where I was going. The only two people who knew about the oyster bar were me and Natalie. I couldn't be a hundred per cent sure, but I don't think that Wrap Dress's companion was the guy who was driving Silver Car, so whoever he was, he'd come from somewhere else.

So she gets to the oyster bar a little after me and isn't too fussed that I'd clocked her. Natalie does her jealous girlfriend act and I slip out the back way, get a cab to

# Kiss Me When I'm Dead

Sakura's place and we head down here. I didn't notice us being tailed, and I was keeping an eye out for it.

I close my eyes and try to visualise Eleanor's street just after the minicab dropped us off. No cars passing by. A woman with a pram on the other side of the road talking to an older woman. They were arguing about something. Sustained car horns in the next street. People shouting. Two very attractive young black women leaving a house about ten doors down on Eleanor's side of the road. One of them was pulling a bright red cabin suitcase that was the same shade of red as Eleanor's Alfa Romeo.

We'd been here around forty-five minutes before Blue Tie and Orange Shirt turned up. Unless my instincts are deteriorating badly, they didn't tail us here and could have had no intelligence regarding our whereabouts. Ah well, fuck it.

I take a look into the street from one of the front rooms. I can hear Eleanor thumping around upstairs. There's a postman delivering letters to the house opposite and he looks genuine. A man with a long beard walks past the house. He's late thirties, wearing a combat jacket, an Avril Lavigne t-shirt and he's talking to himself. Apart from that, it's clear.

'OK, ladies. Can you come to the front door, please? Have you locked up the back of the house, Eleanor?'

Eleanor has a think about this. 'It wasn't unlocked in the first place.' She dumps her bag on the floor. It's huge and stuffed with clothes.

'Where are you going, Daniel?' asks Sakura.

'Raleigh has this place in Holland Park which he uses as an office/home hybrid of some sort. I think that's where he'll be. If he's not there and if Fisher isn't there, I'll wait for them. I don't know what I'm going to do or say, but I have to find out what's going on here. Until I do, neither you nor Eleanor are safe.'

'I know the Holland Park place. Viola told me about it. She went there sometimes. You are in danger, too, aren't you.'

'From Raleigh? It's possible. But don't worry. It'll be OK. I promise. Eleanor – are you OK to drive? You're not seeing double or anything?'

'Of course!' She smiles brightly as if nothing irregular is happening.

'OK. It's just that you still sound slightly pissed. Don't take any risks, don't drive quickly and don't do anything that will attract the attention of the police. I don't know where you're going, but when Sakura tells you you're close, find a public car park to put your car in. Somewhere five or ten minutes' walk away would be good. Whatever you do, don't park outside wherever it is you're going. OK?'

Sakura kisses me on the side of the mouth. 'Take care.' I watch as she and Eleanor get into the Alfa Romeo and wait until I see it speed off. I just hope Eleanor doesn't do anything crazy like drive through a shop front.

I do a quick, final check on Blue Tie and Orange Shirt. Orange Shirt is mumbling and perspiring, Blue Tie is snoring. Eleanor doesn't appear to have a landline and I've got both of their mobiles. Good luck with that one, boys.

I think about what Sakura said before she left.

*Take care.*

Something about that phrase. I've heard that somewhere else today. Marble Arch tube. The guy in the bright yellow jacket. He bumps into me, apologises, then pats me on the back. 'Late for a date! Take care.'

I don't fucking believe this. I take my jacket off, run my hand down the back, and there it is; a small, transparent disk about five millimetres across, decorated with barely discernible printed circuitry. Now I wonder where *that* came from. I peel it off carefully and stick it on the heel of Blue Tie's left shoe.

This, of course, would explain Miss Wrap Dress turning up at the oyster bar and my two supine friends here. If I'd been thinking straight, I'd have given the arrival of my oyster bar friends a little more attention, but there's nothing I can do about that now.

It was a very slick attempt and it almost succeeded, were it not for Blue Tie and Orange Shirt underestimating what would happen to them as soon as they set foot in Eleanor's house.

I get inside their BMW, turn it over and drive off.

## 23

### THE COOL ROOM

As I head over Vauxhall Bridge, I make an attempt to rationalise what the fuck's been going on. I get it down to five sentences.

1. Raleigh is a rich, twisted bastard who's been abusing his own daughter.

2. This abuse puts her on a trajectory to becoming a junkie and a prostitute.

3. Raleigh somehow views her as being his property and decides that if anyone's going to be having sex with her it's him.

4. Somehow he eventually gets lucky, finds out how to hire her for the night and uses Eleanor as camouflage.

5. Things turn bad, he accidentally kills his daughter and to tidy things up hires me to track down Eleanor, the only witness to the whole thing.

Except he tells me that the job is to find a daughter that he already knows is dead. Well, I don't feel *that* duped or stupid; I have to take each job on face value and if your job appears to be helping someone, you don't automatically assume that they'll be lying to you to hinder the investigation.

I pull over and stop the car for a moment, keeping the engine running. I try to look at things from Raleigh's point of view. What happened in the hotel was unfortunate, but it wasn't intentional. It was the result of unforeseen circumstances, if Eleanor's account can be relied upon. He could have called the police, explained exactly what happened and Fisher would have backed him up. If the police investigated properly, they could even have tracked down another witness, Eleanor Wallis, who would have given the same account as everybody else who was in the room.

So Raleigh would almost certainly been charged with manslaughter. It would have gone to court and the case would have been reported in the newspapers. This is a man who most people would not have heard of, but journalists would do some digging and it would all come out. His enormous wealth, his connections to other countries and to various UK politicians and institutions would have been revealed. It would be a big news story and the sleaze factor would bring it to the attention of the tabloids and television.

And if they dug a little further, the truth about his wife's suicide would come out. In the light of what I know now, her suicide would almost certainly be linked to Raleigh's behaviour with Viola. And after Louisa Gavreau's comments about Rosabel Raleigh's portrait, there would, I imagine, be a lot more newsworthy stuff to come.

If Fisher had been the only witness to what happened in the hotel, they could probably have concocted some variation of the truth between them. They could have spun the same yarn that Raleigh fed me; that of the doting father trying to save his daughter from a life of sin and get her into rehab. The altercation that killed Viola would have to remain the same, but at least the reason that Raleigh was there in the first place could be altered to Raleigh's advantage.

But with Eleanor as a witness, things would be different. If Eleanor was tracked down and put on the stand, her account would put a different, seedier slant on the whole thing. With her evidence out in the open, questioning of Raleigh and Fisher would be more aggressive and the whole truth would come out sooner or later. It's conceivable that the police investigation might even lead them to Sakura, and she would be able to confirm the implications of any statement made by Eleanor.

So Raleigh would be disgraced, ridiculed and ruined. His business would collapse and he'd be in prison. He'd possibly even die there. Fisher's collusion in the whole thing may get him a prison sentence, too. I'm not really sure how that would work. Maybe I should ask Natalie or Olivia one day.

But all of the scandal, all of the ridicule, all of the disgrace, all of the humiliation; it could all be avoided, as could the prison sentence and the ruination of Raleigh's business interests and reputation. Things could go on just as before as long as Raleigh and Fisher kept their heads and thought of some smart way to locate Eleanor.

All Raleigh and Fisher had to do was to spirit Viola's body away, find Eleanor and shut her up. They'd never be able to pay her off. Even putting the frighteners on her would be unreliable. One day, she might come back to haunt them in one way or another. She could move abroad and blackmail them from somewhere safe. They'd have discussed this. This woman was a prostitute. She sold her body for money. Anything could happen.

No. The only thing to do with Eleanor would be to kill

her. If I was in a job like Fisher's and was constantly thinking of effective ways to protect my boss and get him to pat me on the head for being a good boy, then that would be the first thing that would pop into my skull.

I guessed Fisher was ex-military. Perhaps he'd been a mercenary. Perhaps his mind-set was to kill first and ask questions later. And someone like Eleanor, who he'd regard as barely human and a piece of meat, well, why the hell not? Once you've killed a few dozen people, one more doesn't make much difference to you. You know the score. You know how it all works. You know how to file away the guilt into a part of your brain that you never visit. You know the risks, you know how to manipulate and bribe, and you know how cover-ups work.

Raleigh's wealth would doubtless enable him and Fisher to execute and smokescreen something like that, and the way they would regard someone like Eleanor would make getting rid of her easy for them on all levels. Who knows – they may have done something like it before. Raleigh would be taking a huge risk with this, but he's probably of an age where he would see the risk as worth it. If it turned out to be a gamble that didn't pay off, so what? He'll be dead pretty soon anyway.

And now to me and Sakura. Are *we* safe? I don't think Blue Tie and Orange Shirt knew that Sakura was in the house, so even if they manage to report back to Raleigh, it would still only be me who would be walking around with Eleanor's knowledge in my head, as far as he would know.

I indicate, move out and continue driving along the Chelsea Embankment, wondering what exactly I'm going to do if Raleigh is there in Holland Park. A display of righteousness indignation perhaps? 'How *dare* you hire me to track down your daughter when you know damn well that she's dead? Who do you think you're dealing with?'

Plus, of course, the amount of money he was offering me to find his daughter, dead or alive. That was obviously bullshit and was just a spur to get me to Eleanor a little faster. I wonder if I could take legal action against him for deceiving me. Probably not.

But it's more serious than that. I'm going to have to assume that I'm in danger as soon as I walk into Raleigh's office. If he's there, he may be surprised to see me on my own, assuming that I was going to be dragged in semi-conscious by Blue Tie and Orange Shirt.

I could, of course, just walk away from all of this now. But then I'd be another loose end, just like Eleanor was. I've been looking over my shoulder enough for the last few years without having yet another reason to do so. I also have to keep reminding myself that they know where I live. That doesn't matter so much, but I'd still prefer it wasn't the case.

And, despite myself, I'd prefer not to leave Eleanor and Sakura at the mercy of a major tosser like Raleigh.

I park a few streets away from Raleigh's house and leave the car unlocked on a double yellow line because that's what I'm like. Before I get out, I take a look at the contents of Blue Tie and Orange Suit's wallets. I can't remember which wallet belongs to which person, but the contents are similar; a fair amount of cash, credit cards and in one case a membership card to something called Club Mirabeau. Both wallets, however, contain an identical slate-grey key card. I have no idea what doors these may open, but I slip them both in my pocket along with the cash.

I get out and begin the walk to Raleigh's house with

still no clear idea of what I'm going to do or say. I have to admit that I feel rather numb. It seems like this whole thing has been going on for weeks rather than just a few days. I decide that once I've got myself checked out in a hospital, I'm going to go on holiday somewhere hot. It's going to be tough to decide who to take with me, if anyone.

I walk past Raleigh's house on the other side of the road at first. It's a wide road with big trees and lots of parked cars, so I shouldn't be too conspicuous. There doesn't seem to be any unusual activity outside the house, but that indicates nothing. As I pass it, I take a quick, hard look at the front door. It's difficult to see any detail, but apart from an old-fashioned door handle, the only locking device seems to be a black oblong on the left-hand side.

After I've walked down the road for about two hundred yards, I cross over and head back to the house. I actually don't know what I'm doing and wonder if I'm subconsciously putting off confronting Raleigh for some reason. I decided that's bullshit, and when I'm outside the house I run up the steps as if I'm a normal visitor.

To my right is the buzzer that I first pressed only three days ago. On the other side is the black oblong that I noticed from the street. If I'd known I was going to be making a visit, I'd have asked Anjukka who was going to be here today. On impulse, I take one of the key cards from my pocket and wave it across the front of the black oblong. The door immediately clicks open.

Once I'm inside, I close the door behind me, stand still and listen. I can hear the low hiss of the air conditioning, but nothing else. I walk down a corridor until I come to Anjukka's office. It's empty and her computer is turned off. Well, this wouldn't be too unusual. She said that most of the company's day-to-day work was done at their HQ in the City. Then I notice her big brown leather holdall by the side of her desk. Why is that there? Would she have brought that in and left it here if she wasn't working? Is there anyone here at all, I wonder?

I walk across her office and push open the door that leads to the area where Fisher's goons tried to search me. The first thing I notice is that the high-pitched whine of the faulty security camera has gone and there's no sign of any of the little red lights. Well, perhaps that's not so strange. If there's no one here today, then there's no need for anyone to be spying on them. Still, I was surprised that no alarm went off when I came in here, key card or no.

I decide to take a look around Raleigh's office. Surprisingly, the door is unlocked. The first thing I see is Rosabel's portrait. She's staring straight at me, as if she's threatening to tell Raleigh that I'm in here without his permission. Somehow, though, I think she'd be pleased. Even as I turn away to look at the rest of the office, I can feel her eyes boring into my back. It's odd; the last time I was here I thought I was looking at a portrait of a living woman.

I'm curious to find out what would happen if I tried to remove the Monet from the wall. I'm sure that would set off a silent alarm that's linked to the local police station. Perhaps I've already unwittingly set off an alarm just by coming in here. Perhaps the police are already on their way. I pat Lincoln the dog on the head as I walk past him.

I take a look at one of the enormous Natuzzi sofas and it's tempting to just lie down on one of them and go to sleep. I really must try to go to bed early tonight.

There are two doors leading out of this office apart from the one I came in through. One of them is the one that Raleigh appeared from the other day, surprising me as I was looking at Rosabel's portrait. I open it and find myself staring into an empty corridor. There's a smell of new carpets. I can see a kitchen at the end of the corridor and head towards it, pushing open the two doors to my right as I proceed.

The first door leads into a bedroom that doesn't look like it's used very much. There's a double bed, a big freestanding wardrobe, a couple of chairs and an en suite bathroom. The second door opens to reveal a small sitting room. There's a sofa, three big armchairs, a coffee table and a huge flat screen TV.

The kitchen is big but doesn't have much stuff in it. There's a wide window which looks out onto a large-ish garden. The garden has been concreted over and most of the plant life is in terracotta pots of varying sizes. That's not to say it isn't attractive. There are lush bamboos growing here, plus a good variety of ornamental trees.

The kitchen and the two rooms are possibly used by Raleigh as a little pied-à-terre when he's staying here overnight. I leave the kitchen and walk back into the hall, again standing still for a few seconds to see if I can pick up signs of anyone else being in the house. Once again, everything's totally silent. I'm a little uneasy about this. There's no reason on earth why this house shouldn't be empty in the middle of a weekday, and Anjukka said it wasn't the main office, but the place just seems too big to be deserted at this time of the afternoon. And getting in here was just too damn easy.

I go back into the office and try the second door, while Rosabel looks on indifferently. Although it looks like the one I've just gone through, this one is locked. Luckily, it's a basic two-lever mortise lock and it takes me five seconds to pick it with a useful tool I have attached to my key ring. I don't really know why I'm bothering to do this, but I feel compelled.

Unlike the previous door, this one opens into almost total darkness. I carefully pat my hand against the wall to my right, trying to find a light switch. I don't really want to explore whatever's here if there's a chance I'm going to fall over something. After that fails, I pat the wall to my left. I'm just starting to wonder if Raleigh has a torch somewhere in his office, when my hand finally finds a small switch, a little lower down than you'd normally place one, almost at hip height.

When I turn it on, I'm greeted by yet another corridor. This one is carpeted much like the first one and from what I can see, leads directly to the back garden. There's fussy red flock wallpaper on the walls and lots of expensively framed prints of countryside scenes on each side. A little over the top for a corridor, but then it's Raleigh's corridor, to do with as he wishes.

The lighting is muted here, and as I walk along, I can hear the door to the office closing behind me with a loud click.

There's a door at the end with a Venetian blind covered in a cherry blossom pattern. It's very pretty. This door leads out to the garden. It's an unusual layout, but maybe Raleigh likes to take a stroll around his shrubs in between power meetings.

I walk towards the cherry blossom door to see if I can get out to the garden. I know that it's probably locked, and I don't really know why I'm doing it, but I somehow think it's worth a try.

I turn the handle, but there's no give at all. I pull one of the slats down and look out into the garden. Same view as from the kitchen. I turn around to head back to the office, but as I approach the door, I can see that there's no obvious lock or handle to the office on this side. There obviously was a handle there at one point, but it's been removed. Now why on earth would you do that? What a stupid thing to do, and how stupid of me not to check. This means I'm trapped in this corridor. The only thing to do is to break out of the cherry blossom door into the garden.

Then I notice a straight line travelling down the wall on my right about five feet away from the back door. For a moment I wonder if I'm hallucinating, then I spy another one about three feet away. Is this a door? The light in here is pretty dim, but it was the flock wallpaper that prevented me from seeing this when I passed it the first time and the prints take your eye away from it. I wonder what would happen if I gave this area a hard push?

To do that, I'd have to take two of the prints down, so I do. I lean them up against the wall on the opposite side of the corridor. I place my hand flat against the wall and push. Nothing happens and it feels pretty solid. But about a foot beneath my hand, I can see that the wallpaper is slightly worn, as if someone has been attempting the same thing as me, but slightly lower down. Normally, this would be covered by one of the prints and would not be noticeable.

I place my hand on the worn area and give it a tentative shove, wondering why I'm actually doing this. There's a little bit of give so I push harder and the door that isn't a door swings open.

I'm immediately hit in the face by a blast of cool air and my first thought is that this is some sort of wine cellar, but on the ground floor. I take a tentative step inside and a light flickers on without me doing anything. I assume I must have stepped onto some sort of pressure pad.

It isn't a wine cellar. It's just a very chilly room with nothing in it apart from a wooden sideboard and a single leather sofa. A bizarre print hangs on the wall, featuring a floating naked woman holding an hourglass in one hand and a plumed helmet in the other. There's a drinks tray on top of the sideboard with a few bottles of spirits and some glasses. What kind of a room is this? Does Raleigh pop in here for a scotch and soda when he's feeling stressed? And why is it so cold?

There's yet another door to my left. What's behind *this* one, I wonder? This is getting to be like a Grimm's Fairy Tale. Well, I've gone too far with this now and I can't say I'm not curious about this place. I'd come here to find what the hell was going on with this guy and now I've ended up snooping around his house like a burglar.

This new door isn't disguised in any way and it doesn't appear to have a lock, just an ordinary handle like you might find in a normal house. I grab the handle, push it down, open the door and step inside. This time the blast of air that hits my face isn't chilly but most definitely frigid. No automatic light switch-ons, but the interior is already lit up by half a dozen halogen lamps built into the ceiling. They're all low wattage, so things are quite dim, apart from two brighter ones in the centre of the room which are aimed downwards at an angle of about forty-five degrees.

The two of them sit side by side on a pair of slate grey

hi-tech wheelchairs like you might find in a hospital. These are not the type you can push yourself along with; these are transport chairs that someone else would push, and there are multi-directional castors on each of the four legs.

I have a mental exercise that I sometimes use to cope with fear, especially if I think it's going to get in the way of clear thinking. I try to imagine the fear as a sheet of paper which I then crumple up into a tight ball and throw into some deserted corner of my brain; out of sight and out of mind. It usually works, but not this time.

I can feel a chill running up my spine which makes the hairs on the back of my neck stand on end. I can feel the chill spread to the sides of my face and I'm aware of my heart racing and my palms sweating.

They're both naked. Rosabel is certainly the scarier of the two; her facial features are pinched, her lips are pulled back in a grimace, her hair is straw-like and her breasts are shrivelled and seem to be too high up on her chest, certainly higher than in her portrait. You can see the shape of her skeleton underneath her skin, which I think you'd have to describe as parchment-like.

Her body looks like it's been treated with some sort of thick makeup, perhaps to partially disguise the scars on her abdomen. I presume these are the result of the embalming process. She certainly bears little resemblance to the beautiful woman in the portrait, but that was painted over ten years ago. Perhaps the fact that I still recognise her at all means that the embalmer, whoever it was, made quite a good job of it.

She sits in the same pose as the portrait, head turned slightly to the right, hands on her lap. I start wondering how difficult it would be to dress and undress someone in this condition. I start wondering about how they did it for the portrait. Is that the reason her breasts were exposed? Was there some difficulty with getting the dress onto her body? Was she too stiff? Was it all too awkward? But that's ridiculous. Any decent artist would have been able to paint the clothes on afterwards, but that makes the pose even more creepy and disturbing.

I take a deep breath and walk into the main part of the room. There's no mistaking Viola. She still looks like the girl in the photograph, and without all the knowledge I have in my head, could almost pass muster as a living human. Her hair is still thick and shoulder-length, her eyes, which are possibly glass, stare straight ahead, all the intelligence and flirtatiousness expunged; no longer humorous, no longer tragic.

Her body is still voluptuous, but the muscle tone is different, and as you get closer to her it's obvious that this is a corpse, albeit one in an unusual posture and condition. She sits in the same pose as her mother, hands on lap and back straight, but I can see there's something wrong with her left side. The shoulder is slightly hunched at a peculiar angle and the arm looks somewhat twisted, causing the back of her left wrist, as opposed to the palm of her hand, to rest on her thigh. The curve of her waist is abnormal, as if a few ribs have been removed. Something has happened to her. She's been damaged.

I touch her cheek with the back of my hand and then pull it away quickly when the softness I expected isn't there. There's a moderately strong chemical smell in here, similar to the one I noticed on my first visit to Raleigh's office. At the time, it reminded me of carbolic soap, and I'm sure it's a phenol of some sort, but mixed up with several other smells that I can't identify.

In the far corner of the room there's piece of equipment that looks vaguely scientific. It's like a long, narrow, silver tub about four feet high and it's on three castor wheels for easy movement. There are two rubber tubes coming out of it and a couple of metal ladles hanging off the side. God knows.

To my left, there's a silver trolley, but there's nothing on it. Next to that is a cream-coloured, freestanding medical cabinet with three drawers. I pull one of them out and it's full of scalpels, syringes, scissors and several instruments I can't identify.

As a contrast to the creepy scientific-looking stuff, there are a couple of old-fashioned wardrobes made from some dark wood. One of them is slightly open and I can see two or three dresses hanging up. So what's that all about? Does Raleigh treat his former wife and daughter as a couple of luxury, life-sized Barbie dolls?

For the sake of my own mental stability, I tear my eyes away from the pair of them and take a look inside the wardrobes. I look in the one that's already open. There are all sorts of gowns and dresses in here; some of them look and smell new, other not so new. From the look of them, I would guess that they are/were Viola's, though nothing is certain in the world of the insane.

At the bottom of the wardrobe are a variety of shoes, ranging from espadrilles to seven-inch heels to plain black court shoes. There's even a little Tupperware box with half a dozen bottles of perfume inside. I push the clothes away from the right-hand side and can see a couple of racks screwed into the wood. One of them has three belts hanging from it and the other one has a couple of pairs of stockings. Nothing, really, that you wouldn't find in a living girl's wardrobe.

The second wardrobe isn't open, but a quick tug at the handle rectifies that. Again, this is filled with clothing, but there are also coats in here, including a silver fox fur coat. I run my hand down its length. It's real fur. There's a faint smell of a flowery perfume that is probably coming off the clothes.

The clothes in here are more luxurious and expensive-looking and I guess this is Rosabel's stuff. I pull out a drawer at the base of the wardrobe. This is full of lingerie, as well as a couple of unopened boxes of perfume. One of them is in a pink box with Victoria's Secret: Bombshell on the side and another says Absolutely Irrésistible: Givenchy. At the base of the wardrobe are a load of shoes, mostly in disarray. There is also a pair of what I think would be described as 'mules' with high heels and pink fluffy stuff at the front.

I close the doors and look around the room once more, only now noticing that the walls are solely decorated with photographs of Rosabel and Viola. I take a deep breath as I stroll around. Without realising it, I'd been producing a lot of adrenalin. There's only one shot of them both together, sitting on a bench in front of a big hedge. There's no mistaking Viola, but she's quite young in this; maybe nine or ten. Rosabel is smiling, but her eyes are expressionless.

I guess that this room must be the ultimate shrine to both of them, but it doesn't just have the clothes and the photographs, it has the women themselves. I try to put myself into the mental state where you might do something like this, but I can't.

I walk back to where Rosabel and Viola are sitting and take another look. Could either of them ever, *ever* imagine that it would come to this? I'm trying to get my brain to work out the implications of what I've found in here, but all it can manage is a kind of debilitating sadness. I don't even know who the sadness is for. Rosabel? Viola? Raleigh, even?

I can't tear my eyes away from them; it's like looking at some obscene, erotic art instalment and I'm mesmerised by it. I'm wondering whether the best thing to do would be to hand this entire, nauseating, odious matter over to the police.

And then my head explodes.

# 24

## A MOUTHFUL OF BLOOD

The first thing anyone does when regaining consciousness is to take a deep breath. This happens even when you've been asleep. It's the shallow breathing that does it; your body wants a little more oxygen and it's telling your brain what to do to get it.

But I don't know what's happened to me yet, and I don't want to let whoever may be watching me realise that I've come round. I keep my breathing shallow.

I do a quick tour of my body, in no particular order of importance. My back is the first thing I notice. Quite apart from the residual agony from Sakura's expertise, there's a hot pain radiating from an area about six inches below my shoulder blades and it feels like the muscles there are cramping up.

I remember staring at Rosabel and Viola, then experiencing a colossal jolt of pain that snapped my head back so hard that I thought my neck had been broken. After that, nothing; I have to assume that someone jabbed me with an ultra-powerful stun weapon of some sort.

Despite that, I think I've only been out for about five or ten minutes. From the cold, I think I must still be in the same room as Viola and Rosabel, or maybe the one just outside. I'm sitting in a chair with my head slumped forwards. It's very bright. If I am in the same room, either someone has been hitting the dimmer switch or I'm sitting next to Rosabel and Viola in their special spot-lit spot.

Both of my shoulders ache and that's because my hands are tied behind my back. I give my wrists a miniscule twitch, but there's no give at all. I can feel the tight binding of a plastic wrist tie. There are a number of ways of getting out of these, but most don't work if your hands are behind your back, so I'll put that problem on ice for the moment.

I don't have to move my feet to know that my ankles are tied to the legs of the chair by the same method. The feeling in my hands and feet is starting to get fuzzy and they're both probably starting to get discoloured by now. I think it can safely be said that I'm not in a good place at the moment.

I allow my consciousness to expand into the room. In thirty seconds I can tell that there are two people in here apart from myself. Whoever they are, they're not talking – to each other or to me. I listen out for breathing, inhale gently for scents; anything to give me an idea of who or what I might be dealing with. To my right, I can hear soft but erratic breathing and I can smell perfume. I run the scent through my mind to see if it's at all familiar.

It's Mitsouko by Guerlain, the perfume I bought for Anjukka. Is she sitting there, silently watching me? Is she in on this in some way? I can feel the other presence in front of me and to my left. No perfume, but a mix of male sweat and deodorant. Whoever it is, I can hear them shift slightly in their seat and hear a gentle creaking of wood. I can feel the focus of both of them on me. I suppose I've got no real reason to continue this pretence, but I do it anyway. Just to give myself some time to think.

I should have known better, of course. It was just a little too easy for me to get in here and snoop around the place. I felt something wasn't right when I noticed that the security cameras were switched off, but didn't think it was significant enough to exercise any caution.

I can hear Raleigh's voice now. It's distant and muffled, as if he's talking on the telephone in another room. He and Fisher must have been in the house all along, listening and watching; seeing what I would do; and what better moment to get the drop on me than while I was in a predictable state of shock upon discovering Rosabel and Viola.

I try to imagine what must have happened when Eleanor's narrative ended. Raleigh and Fisher were left with a corpse on their hands. Eleanor had run away, but that could be dealt with later. They had to somehow get Viola's body out of the hotel room and back here without anyone in the hotel noticing.

It couldn't have been easy. I try and put myself in their position and ponder what I would have done under the same circumstances. If it was me, I'd have left her there; too much risk and hassle with security cameras, staff and other guests. But Raleigh wasn't me. This was his daughter and he had other plans for her. Was he thinking about embalming her as soon as he realised he'd killed her? Would that have been the first thought that entered his head?

I have no knowledge of the legal ramifications concerning embalming in the UK at all, but I'm sure a death certificate would be involved somewhere along the line; probably a doctor, too. But in Viola's case, if no one knew she was dead in the first place, and she was registered as missing, you could probably bypass all those inconveniences if you were careful enough and clever enough.

In fact, the name Viola Raleigh only appeared on the radar when Sakura reported her as a missing person three days after her death, and the police attitude to that was predictable. This was a woman who'd already been reported missing once and she was obviously working as a prostitute, so the possibility of her being dead would not have been seriously considered.

Could the same thing be true of Rosabel? Could she also have died without anyone knowing about it? When I first met Raleigh, he spoke about her as if she was alive. When I was talking to Anjukka about Rosabel's portrait, she said that she'd never met Raleigh's wife, as if she fully expected to one day.

Is Raleigh such a control freak that no one is allowed to leave his personal orbit without his permission? Not even if they die? I'm almost looking forward to hearing his excuses for all of this. I'm sure he's rationalised it all to the nth degree and would be delighted to bludgeon you over the head with his reasoning.

But things can't have been airtight; not with a loose cannon like Viola around. Taylor Conway knew that Rosabel was dead. Someone told him. A friend of Viola's called Antonia. She said that Rosabel had shot herself. Was it some big family secret that Rosabel had died? Was no one meant to know? Did Viola let the cat out of the bag to Antonia one night when she was totally hammered on something?

I try and imagine a scenario where Raleigh comes home and finds Rosabel lying on the floor dead with a gun in her hand. Could someone as rich and powerful as

Raleigh cover something like that up? Of course he could. Fisher may not have been around to help him then, but there were probably other Fishers who would do anything for their amiable, powerful, obscenely wealthy boss.

I mull all of this around in my head for a few moments. Is Raleigh mad? No. He's just an unusual variety of perverted tyrant who's always been allowed to do as he wished because of his money. I'm sure he has a million ways of justifying it all to himself and to others. I'm sure he thinks that us normal folk are just too stupid and unworldly to understand the mysterious ways of the exceedingly powerful.

At least I hope that's the case. Any alternative is much too unsettling to contemplate.

'So is our private *dick* back in the land of the living?'

It's Raleigh. His voice comes as a shock. I can hear him walking towards me and then he's standing behind me and has placed his hands on my shoulders. I can feel my skin beginning to crawl.

'He should be,' replies Fisher. 'I didn't give him the full treatment. Maybe he's faking.'

Fisher grabs a handful of my hair, jerks my head up and slaps me hard across the face. Twice. More like an open-handed punch, really. I quell the anger I'm feeling, open my eyes and give him a resigned look. He looks pleased that he's seen through my façade. He slapped me on the side of my face where Eleanor scratched me and it feels like it's on fire.

'He's with us now, Mr Raleigh,' he says with a smirk. 'You don't look very well, Mr Beckett. A bit under the weather, are we?'

I don't reply. I look over to my left and see Anjukka. She's about six feet away, tied to a chair in much the same way I am, and has been positioned so she's facing me. She looks pale and frightened. There's a wide strip of silver gaffer tape across her mouth and there are tears streaming from her eyes.

She's wearing a glamorous dress with a mottled pattern of dark red and black, but the front has been ripped down and her bra cut through and pulled to the sides to reveal her breasts. The fact that her arms are tied behind her back makes them jut out in a way that impudently attacks the senses.

As I look at her, I'm reminded of Rosabel's portrait and wonder whether this is a coincidence or not; one of Raleigh's *things*. It hardly matters. In one way or another, both Raleigh and Fisher are going to pay dearly for this.

'We thought we'd invite your girlfriend to the proceedings, Mr Beckett. Or should I say *one* of your girlfriends,' says Fisher, with a sneer in his voice. 'You're a very busy man, aren't you.'

Despite his cockiness, he looks angry and I can tell he hates me just on principle. That's fine with me. I take pride in being hated by people like Fisher.

For a couple of seconds, I'm not sure precisely where I am, then I realise that I'm facing the door that I came in through before encountering Raleigh's cadaverous harem. I look up and get dazzled by the halogen lights that had previously illuminated Rosabel and Viola, who have been wheeled over to the left-hand side of the door, presumably out of harm's way. Rosabel is looking straight ahead, but Viola's wheelchair is angled a little to her left, so that she seems to be looking straight at me. It would be true to say that I've never been in a position quite like this before. The next time it happens I'll be ready for it.

Raleigh places a fake Regency chair about three feet

away from me, sits down and smiles. It's as if I've come for a job interview, not that I'd know what that was like. He nods towards Anjukka.

'Not my idea, Daniel. The dishabille, I mean. Fisher here's always had his eye on her so I allowed him this little treat. I must say, though, she has magnificent breasts. I always thought that would be the case. It's interesting, isn't it? Usually, a woman's breasts are never quite the shape you thought they would be when you were imagining them naked, but in the lovely Anjukka's case they are exactly as I imagined, and believe me, I have been imagining them a lot. What about you, Fisher?'

Fisher nods his head, pleased to be asked his opinion by his boss, whom he so clearly loves and respects. 'Yes, sir. I think they're pretty close to how I imagined them. Perhaps a bit bigger.' He looks straight at Anjukka, licks his lips and blows a kiss at her.

'What about you, Beckett? Were they as you imagined?' says Raleigh.

'What happened to Viola, Nathan?' I say, ignoring him. 'She looks a bit damaged on one side. You really must take better care of your embalmed women.'

'Ah, yes. Most deplorable. I take it you know what happened in the hotel by now. As you can imagine, we had a little problem when it came to removing Viola from her room. Luckily…'

'The cleaner's supply room. You dropped her out of the window.'

'How did you know that?' He looks a little angry. Perhaps he thought he'd been clever and no one would work it out.

'I tried to think what I would have done under the same circumstances if I was you. I've got a dead girl on my hands, I can't leave her in the hotel room, I can't call the police, I can't get her past reception, so I have to think of another way of getting her out of the hotel without anyone noticing. I see a lot of security cameras by the fire exits, so those would be out of the question.

'Then I try that little door and go in that little room. Who discovered it? You? Fisher? It's a store room with nobody in it and no cameras. It's got a window that opens. It's a bit of a drop, but beggars can't be choosers. There's an alleyway beneath the window. I could back a car up into it and shove her in the boot after I'd pushed her out. There's a chance I'd be discovered, but if I'm very quick I might just get away with it. I take it the phrase *respect for the dead* doesn't mean that much to you. You prick.'

Raleigh nods at Fisher, who, with all his strength, punches me on the side of the face. I can taste blood in my mouth after that one and feel dizzy. I poke one of my molars with my tongue. It feels slightly loose and there's a tiny blast of pain, so I don't do it again. Just for the sake of it, I try to stretch my wrists apart against the plastic tie, but there's still no give. And there was I hoping that it might have magically slackened so that I could make a spectacular and heroic escape.

Something makes me look at the silver trolley I'd noticed earlier. There's a long, thick plastic thing about nine inches long with a green flashing light on it. Looks like the same model as the one that Blue Tie was waving around. I wonder if they have plans to use it as a torture device.

Well, this is all extremely interesting. I don't think these circumstances can be explained away by viewing Raleigh as an avaricious control freak with several unpleasant personality disorders. I'm beginning to think he has to be just plain mad. And I'm tied to a chair in his Chamber of Insanity.

I make eye contact with Anjukka for a couple of seconds. I attempt to transmit to her the idea that *everything will be alright, nothing will happen to you and I will get us out of this*. I don't know if it worked, as she still looks terrified, but I thought it was worth a try. Quite apart from her alarming situation, there's the added trauma of the cadavers. She'll probably need therapy for six months just to stop the bad dreams.

'I have to say, Beckett,' says Raleigh, with a sincere, avuncular tone that I find both reassuring and creepy, 'that you've done a pretty good job under the circumstances. We didn't give you much; just the name of that idiot Conway and the police bitch, and we knew you'd get nowhere there. We couldn't give you *that* much or you'd have got suspicious.

'Of course we knew where Mrs Bianchi was located, obviously, but we had to keep that to ourselves. We knew you'd find her eventually. We had faith in you. We needed an outsider to track the girl down. Someone good; someone who we were certain would lead us to her. But I was concerned that you may not want to share your discoveries with us when you found out the truth. That's why I've been using a security company to track you the whole time. You probably thought I was being stupid.

'Their operatives were very impressed with you, particularly as you had no reason to suppose you were being tailed. Not at first, in any case.' He laughs mirthlessly. 'They described you as a slippery customer. Attaching that little device to you was a last resort. They were confused by your movements and had no idea what you'd do next.

'My company developed that bug, if it's of any interest to you. It's able to pinpoint an individual within a radius of ten feet. I was very impressed with it. I'm sorry you destroyed it. It was a prototype.'

'You can deduct the cost from my fee.'

'After you visited Miss Gastrell, we thought you might lead us straight to Celia Valentine. The security operatives were surprised when instead, you just went to keep a bloody *lunch date* with a woman who seemed to be unconnected to the whole affair. Too old to be Celia, apparently, and with an Australian accent, they said.'

'What – do you think I don't eat all day or have a social life?' For a moment, I don't remember who Celia is, then I remember that Celia Valentine is Eleanor's work name. Working in the sex industry must be exhausting; I don't think I'd have the memory skills for it.

'When you finally arrived at the house in Stockwell, we knew that it had to be Celia Valentine's. By that time there could be no doubt about it as far as we were concerned. She was one of Gastrell's girls. It was the next logical step after you'd seen Gastrell, your lunch break notwithstanding. We had a feeling you'd take either Bianchi or Gastrell with you and we were right. Bianchi is a real beauty, I am told.'

'Not your type. She's still breathing.'

'We expected that Miss Valentine would be extremely paranoid, and with good reason. She was never going to open the door to a solitary unknown male like you. We retired the security team and my men took over. Once that bug was placed on you, your goose was cooked, so to speak.

'That's lovely, Nathan, but won't this security

company be a loose end for you? Aren't you going to have to get them all down here and drown them in the bath or something?'

'They had no idea what the job really was. Their only contact was with Mr Fisher here, who has been invaluable throughout the whole proceedings. He told them that you were his son-in-law and that he suspected you of philandering. Your behaviour over the last few days made that seem very convincing indeed. I must admit, Mr Beckett, I'm quite in awe of your womanising skills. You succeeded expeditiously with young Anjukka here where so many before you had failed. I hope her fiancé will not be too upset.'

He thinks he knows everything, but he doesn't. I'd like to ask a couple of questions about all of this, but I'm in so much pain and discomfort at present that I can't think straight. Apart from that, this thing has become so complex that I wouldn't know where to start. There's only one thing that has been puzzling me since I found out about Raleigh and Fisher visiting the hotel.

'How did you manage to track down Viola in the first place? The chances of you finding her on the internet must have been millions to one. She may have even worked for someone who didn't have a website.'

'Well,' says Raleigh, beaming. 'It was pure luck. Well, that's not strictly true. It was very fortunate, all the same. As I'm sure you can imagine, I deal with people who like to be entertained on a grand scale. Mr Fisher deals with that side of things.'

'Grand scale meaning prostitutes like your daughter. You obviously deal with the world's crème-de-la-crème, Nathan. Well done. I'm insanely jealous of you.'

Raleigh nods at Fisher who punches me in the face

again. It's on the same side as last time, which is a little annoying. That tooth is looser now. I'll have to visit the dentist if I survive all of this. I spit the blood out of my mouth and it goes all over Fisher's trouser leg. He looks pissed, but doesn't do anything. I take it he has to have Raleigh's permission to hit me.

'I should be careful how you speak to me, Mr Beckett. You are in no position to be so conceited.'

'Of course, sir. Sorry, sir.'

He glares at me and nods his head in an *enjoy yourself while you can* manner. I'm glad I'm annoying him. It's all I've got at the moment, so I'm savouring it.

'Mr Fisher was arranging the entertainment for my current business dealings with Oman. While he was busy with his research, he came across a link to Mrs Bianchi's site. Her speciality was not what we were looking for, but Mr Fisher was curious and investigated further.'

'You mean he wanted to look at sexy photographs of lesbian prostitutes. Is he allowed to do that during office hours? Should you not be docking him some pay?'

He ignores this. I can't blame him; it wasn't that funny. I'll do better next time.

'How is the business with Oman doing, by the way? They're not going to be very pleased with all this, are they? I've heard they're none too keen on dealing with mentally ill cockroaches who abuse, kill and then embalm their own daughters.'

He ignores this, too. My days as a salon wit are plainly over.

'Mr Fisher had never met Viola,' continues Raleigh, 'but he had seen photographs of her. Despite the fact that she was displayed under the name of Natasha, he immediately knew it was her. He came and told me. I have to tell you, Mr Beckett, I was quite shocked when I discovered what type of site it was. I had no idea that such things existed. And to think of my Viola offering her services in that manner; it was shocking to me. I suppose I should have expected it. I should have expected anything. She was out of control.'

'Out of *your* control, you mean.'

I can feel some blood drip out of my mouth as I speak. I hope my appearance isn't alarming Anjukka too much. It's ridiculous, but I don't like her seeing me like this. Part of me is afraid she might not be interested anymore.

'Yes, Mr Beckett. Out of *my* control. It may seem strange to someone like you, but I loved my wife and I loved my daughter. When Rosabel took her own life, it almost killed me. I couldn't bear to be without her.'

'So you embalmed her. Great.'

'Not me, Mr Beckett. It took a lot of work, but I was able to find a gentleman from Austria that was able to perform the task and keep his mouth shut. But I assisted him. In fact, he let me do most of the work under his strict supervision. He was very pleased with me, particularly the care with which I embalmed Rosabel's arteries. He even made a joke about me going to work for him in Vienna, if I ever needed another job.'

'Well, it's never too late to acquire new skills.'

'My darling Rosabel shot herself in the head with one of my guns. Luckily it was a small calibre bullet. It entered her head through the temple and came out of the top of her skull. Minimal exit wound, so my gentleman was able to repair the damage with very little effort.'

Raleigh walks over to Viola, strokes her hair and places his hands on her shoulders. I feel a chill run through me.

I wonder if he takes her for a stroll down the road in that wheelchair when the weather's nice.

'But Viola – Viola was all my own work,' he continues. 'I took my time, Mr Beckett. It was done with love. A father's love. I'm sure that Mr Drasche would have been proud of me. Admittedly, there was some damage that I was not skilled enough to repair, but I don't think it's too bad. I think if her face had been damaged, I might have requested his presence once more, but I think things turned out very well. She is as beautiful in death as she was in life. She is perfect. Have you ever embalmed anyone, Mr Beckett?'

'You know, Nathan, someone was asking me that just the other day.'

Another nod, another punch. Same side again. Ouch. I'm wondering whether I can claim my dental expenses from Raleigh. Probably not.

'I don't think you're taking me seriously, Mr Beckett. Embalming is not a science, as far as I am concerned. It is an art. Viola was stiff when we got her back here. I had to massage her body to break the rigor mortis.'

'I'll bet anything you enjoyed that, you old perv, you.'

Another nod. This time, Fisher savagely punches me in the stomach. I compartmentalise the pain and act as if it was nothing, but I've thrown up slightly into my mouth and can taste the tempura oysters and wasabi. This makes me think of Natalie. I hope those security folk didn't discover who she was or where she lived. I swallow the vomit. Raleigh is gearing himself up for more self-deluding bullshit.

'You're very funny, aren't you, Mr Beckett. And you really have no idea. You look at Rosabel and Viola there and you think this is some sort of freak show. Some mad old man with an unusual, offbeat hobby. Someone who needs psychiatric treatment.'

'That would be about right. Especially the last bit.'

'But it's to do with love, Mr Beckett, love and loss. I couldn't bear the thought of life without Rosabel. She was a troubled woman and she took her own life, it's true, but she is still mine, and she will always be mine. No one I love leaves me, Mr Beckett. I'm not going to watch them being lowered into the ground or turned to ash. They're still mine. They're still my possessions, as they were in life, to do with as I wish.'

I take a quick look at Fisher. He's beginning to get tears in his eyes from this insane crap. Oh fuck.

'The same goes for Viola. I could have given her a life of quality, adulation and luxury. I would have done absolutely anything for her. I was prepared to get her off drugs. I was prepared to overlook the way she sold her body. Can you imagine the pain I was in from all that she got up to in her life? All the men that had had her? All the women? When she should have been safely in my arms?'

'Well this is all very interesting, Nathan, but I'm kind of tuning out now. I have some other patients to see. Perhaps you could book another session with my secretary. I think we've made good progress today.'

Fisher gets another nod and I get another punch. At least this one was on the other side of my face, though it was still pretty hard. I'm starting to get a bit of a headache now and my scratches from Eleanor are on fire again. Raleigh drags himself away from Viola's chair and walks towards me. He seems pretty calm. I don't think I like that. He takes hold of his chair again and sits down close to me. He's smiling.

'Listen, Nathan,' I say. 'Obviously this is heading for

some sort of climax, so if you can cut out all the self-aggrandising deviant bullshit and get on with it, I'd be extremely grateful as I'm getting bored now. By the way, I take it your wife shot herself because she knew what you'd been up to with Viola since she was a little kid. Would that be an accurate assessment? I mean, let's face it, they're both dead because of you, aren't they. Because you're a major freak asshole.'

He really doesn't like this one bit. His face is going red and he's clenching his fists. He walks over to me, and for a moment, I think he's going to hit me himself, but Fisher gets another nod and I get another punch. This one is so hard that my chair and I get knocked to the floor. The back of the chair crushes the side of my bicep as I land and it hurts like a bastard. I wonder if I'm still going to get paid for this. I decide to find out, even though I'm on the floor and on my side.

'Oh, and Nathan – I found Viola for you. There she is, over there on that chair next to her mum. I was wondering if I could buy the portrait of Rosabel with the twenty thousand you owe me.'

Fisher drags me and the chair up to a sitting position again. I'm waiting for yet another punch, but it doesn't come. Raleigh is trying to compose himself, but he's still red-faced and shaking. I don't know why I'm doing this, really. Part of me thinks that I could get Fisher to hit me so hard that it'll break the chair, but then I'd still have the problem of the wrist ties, but that wouldn't be insurmountable.

'I'm sure you've worked out, Mr Beckett, that we need some information from you. That is why you are here – that is why we *allowed* you to be here – and that is why Miss York is over there, tied to that chair.'

'Celia Valentine,' says Fisher, speaking rather than punching for a change.

'I'm sure you've surmised that that is why we hired you, Mr Beckett,' says Raleigh. 'Celia was the only witness; the only one who knew what had happened in the hotel. Initially, we had fears about her contacting the police, but as I had hoped, she was too scared. Besides, who would believe the word of a common prostitute?'

'She was hardly common at those prices, Nathan.'

'When she ran away that night, we couldn't do much about it. That was why we hired you, of course, as I have already said. And I have to say you did it very well. Things were going very smoothly right up until the last moment. We almost had her and we almost had the other whore, too, for good measure.'

They know Sakura was there. One of the goons must have been in touch and they must have heard me tell her that I was on my way over here. That's why I'm in this situation now. Damn. How careless of me. Well, at least they still don't know Eleanor's real name, which is something. If I never get out of here she still might have a chance of escaping these lunatics.

'And what were you going to do to Celia, Nathan? What was going to happen to her?'

'That's none of your business,' barks Fisher. 'You just tell us where the whore is and nothing will happen to young Anjukka there.'

'Really? I don't believe you. I don't believe either of you. You've really fucked this up. Too many people know what happened. It's a mess, isn't it, Nathan. You and your bitch here don't know what the fuck you're doing, do you.'

Fisher's face goes into meltdown at the mention of the

b-word. His nostrils flare as he looks at Raleigh and silently beseeches him for permission to wallop me for it. Raleigh gives him the nod and I brace myself as well as I can. There's an element of fear that comes from total helplessness, but you just have to store it in one of the spare rooms in your brain and not let it get to you. I just keep telling myself that something will happen and the situation I currently find myself in will stop. After all, it can't literally go on forever.

It comes from above and lands on my cheekbone with such force that it rocks my head downwards and could easily have broken my neck. For a moment the chair tips backwards and I get ready to land on my back, but then it veers to the left on one of the back legs and I land on my side again, the impact knocking the air out of my lungs with a grunt. I hear Anjukka scream and then sob as well as she can with that gaffer tape across her mouth. I start thinking about her mouth and I think about kissing it. I don't look at her, though. That would make me too angry and I'm angry enough as it is.

Fisher picks me and the chair up again, but he does it roughly for my maximum discomfort, and I can feel my brain shudder in my head as I'm plonked back into position. The plastic wrist tie is still in place and as tight as ever.

I try as well as I can to act as if that didn't just happen. It's difficult.

'What are you going to do to Anjukka if I don't tell you where Celia is? Are you going to kill her? That is, of course, assuming that I know where Celia is, which I don't. That was your last chance back at her house. Your two Neanderthals had a chance to grab her, but they fucked it up.

'You're not thinking straight, Nathan. You think you can get me to tell you where Celia is and in return you'll let me and Anjukka go? With all that we now have in our heads? You *have* to kill us. Because if we walk out of here, we're going straight to the police. I realise you haven't had much time to formulate some brilliant plan, but you really are a pair of dimwits, aren't you. And I would stop getting your monkey to hit me so much. If he kills me accidentally, you're both screwed. But you're screwed anyway. There's no way out of this for either of you.'

I may have just signed our death warrants.

Fisher leans forwards and puts his face right next to mine. His breath is terrible. 'Who the fuck are you, Beckett? Do you want to know why we hired you?'

'Well, I assume it was because Mr Raleigh there wanted tips on how to pick up women who were still alive.'

'Your recommendation from Italy seemed kosher enough. Then we checked to see if you held an SIA licence. Everyone in your line of work has to have them now. Private investigators, bodyguards, even bloody security van drivers have to have them. But you don't have one. Why is that, Mr Beckett?'

'The forms were too difficult to fill in.'

'Was it the criminality checks? Was it the documentation that was needed? It isn't difficult to get one as long as you've got all the info they need. So why would you avoid getting one? In your fucking line of business, with all the money you must make and all the jobs you must get. Why would you risk blowing it? I'll tell you why. You're bent, Beckett. I don't know in what way. I don't know where you come from, but as soon as I tried checking you out in any depth, I came to a dead end every fucking time. It's like I'm standing here talking to you but you don't really exist. Now what sort of person would that be?'

'A mysterious and enigmatic person.'

'Yeah, right. I sent two of my best boys to pick up the whore. One of them is in intensive care. He may not live. He used to be a major in the Welsh Guards. He's one of the toughest men I've ever worked with. And my other boy. He's a veteran of the 601$^{st}$ Special Forces Group.'

'Really? What the hell's that?'

'Czechoslovakian army. When he rang me, I asked him how he was. He said he felt like he'd been run over by a truck. He bit half his tongue off when you used the stun baton on him. He said you knew what you were doing.'

'I'm flattered. Was he difficult to understand on the phone?'

Raleigh drags his chair closer to me and sits down again. Perhaps he's getting fatigued. 'Hi, Nathan,' I say, in as friendly a way as I can manage. 'How're things?'

'You must have realised that once you found out what was really going on, we couldn't have you walking around telling everyone or going to the police,' says Raleigh. 'We suspected that you were expendable and we were right. You were just the sort of person we needed. No one will miss you, will they? You're some sort of non-person. We'll make it quick for you if you tell us where the whore is.'

'Oh, well now you've really hurt my feelings, Nathan. I really looked up to you. But does the same apply to Anjukka? Is she a non-person, too? Do you think you can get away with making her disappear and nobody will notice? Oh, Nathan. They're going to take Rosabel and Viola away from you. I don't think they're going to let them share your prison cell. They're quite strict about things like that.'

As I'm saying this, the enormity of it hits me. I'm just trying to bullshit him and make him rattled, but I'm worried about Anjukka. She's fucked, basically. I think about Natalie and the chance Anjukka may have had for a new job at her company. All gone. Is it all my fault?

My mind is racing to find a way out of all of this, but the bottom line is I'm tied to this fucking chair and I can't escape from it. I try to think of something to say that will turn Raleigh against Fisher, but nothing comes. I just decide to keep digging a big hole for myself.

'What's the body count going to be like at the end of this, Nathan? Me, Anjukka, Celia Valentine, Mrs Bianchi? Where's it going to stop? You won't get any real peace of mind until you've got hold of Abigail Gastrell and killed her too. That'll be five murders. Not to mention the manslaughter of Viola under pretty awful circumstances. When the police get hold of you – and they fucking will – they're going to be throwing away the key. Same goes for your poodle here. You'll be a mass murderer, Nathan. Good work.'

Raleigh seems to drift away for a moment. He looks over his shoulder at Viola, stares adoringly at her, and then turns back to me.

'You don't know what you're talking about, Beckett. You have no idea of what can be done if I want it to be done.'

'You want this all to disappear. You think you can get hold of Celia Valentine and kill her so your pathetic rich man's life can go on as if nothing has happened and your latest big billion dollar deal can go through next week without a hitch. It's not going to happen. When is the weak link in all of this going to appear? Who's it going to be?'

I turn to Fisher, who is clenching and unclenching his fists. It's been a few minutes since he's hit me and he must be getting withdrawal symptoms. 'I tell you, Fisher. If I was this scumbag here,' I nod at Raleigh so he understands who I'm talking about, 'I'd be thinking about getting rid of *you*. Think about it. You could bring the whole thing crashing down. You know too much. You could blackmail your boss. You could make a fortune from this. He's been thinking about getting rid of you for a while. You were head of security here when that kidnapping attempt happened. He's always looked down on you because of that. He thinks you're a fool.'

Raleigh and Fisher start laughing. Well, it was worth a try.

'Shut this idiot up, Fisher. I need to think.'

Fisher doesn't need asking twice. He punches me in the stomach once more and then gives me a terrific backhander under the chin. I think I actually lost consciousness for a couple of seconds there. Well, at least they haven't killed me yet. They still must think that I can lead them to Eleanor. I also think that all that I've said has bought me some time, or not, as the case may be.

I hear the noise before they do. It's like a muffled click. It sounds vaguely familiar, as far as muffled clicks go, but I can't quite place it. Raleigh picks up on it before Fisher does.

'Did you hear something then, James?'

I raise my head to watch what Fisher does or says. He tilts his head to one side, listening. 'Nothing, Mr Raleigh. Just house noises.'

Raleigh purses his lips together and exhales impatiently

through his nostrils. 'Go and have a look, will you? I heard something then. Sounded like a door closing. It was definitely on this floor.'

Fisher gives him an obedient nod and leaves the room. Normally, I'd try and say something smart to irritate Raleigh, but I'm feeling too fucked. I watch as Raleigh gets up and approaches his embalmed family again. I think again about all of the clothes in those wardrobes, not to mention the lingerie and perfume. Does Raleigh dress Rosabel and Viola up? I really can't imagine what he gets up to with them. Well, I can, but I'd prefer not to think about it.

He starts to tidy up Viola's hair, then frowns and produces a comb from his pocket. The look on his face as he combs her hair is priceless. It's a combination of lust, subservience and simple-mindedness. I suppose Rosabel's hair would fall out if he tried combing it after all this time.

I catch Anjukka's eye and smile at her as well as I can. God knows what my face must look like. I mouth 'It's OK' at her and get a faint nod of the head in return. I don't know if it is OK, though. It probably isn't, but I couldn't think of anything else to do.

Raleigh walks back over to me, places his hands on his hips and stares meaningfully at Anjukka. 'Mr Fisher could do some very bad things to this young lady if you don't give us what we want, Beckett. Very bad things that you would have to witness.'

'I've been invited to this crazy party next Halloween, Nathan. I was wondering if I could take your girls with me.'

I can see Fisher coming through the door. Something's wrong. His face is grim and pale. Then I see why. There's a gun pointed at the back of his head and Sakura is holding it.

# 25

## CHOKE-OUT

It's a Bersa Thunder 380 pistol with a silencer attached. It's made in Argentina, fires 9mm rounds, and is used by the police and by civilians. My information may be out of date, but I didn't know you could get silencers for these. Silencer or no, if Sakura pulls the trigger that close to Fisher's head, his face will be all over the wall on the other side of the room.

Her arm is outstretched, which is good. There's a danger he could spin around and take the gun off her, but as she's standing at arm's length behind him like that, he could make a fatal mistake. Having said that, I've no doubt that his entire focus is on getting the gun in *his* hand and not hers.

Raleigh looks astonished, as if he can't quite believe what he's seeing. I have to remind myself that he's never met Sakura and will have no idea who she is. As she and Fisher enter the room, she turns briefly and gives me a wink. I manage a brief, involuntary laugh at her panache.

'That's one of my guns,' says Raleigh. 'Where did you get that from?'

'Shut up,' she replies, waving the gun briefly in his direction. Well that's a good start, anyway. Any minute now she's going to see Rosabel and Viola and I don't want her to get freaked out. Fisher is trembling with rage and Raleigh has gone as white as a sheet.

'Sakura. Listen. Keep the gun aimed at his head. If he turns to face you or says anything smart, shoot him. Then shoot the other guy. You can guess who these two are. They've got Viola and her mother in here; they're both dead and they're both embalmed. They're behind you next to the door. Don't turn around and look at them, at least not yet. Keep your mind on Mr Fisher here. Don't let anything distract you.'

She nods. She looks a little sick and I can see she's perspiring. I just hope she's not going to have one of her attacks. I get the feeling that she doesn't quite know what she should do next, so I'm going to have to step in, despite the fact that I'm helpless and semi-delirious.

'Now listen carefully, you two pricks. You have to imagine that that gun is in my hand. I'm sure it doesn't require a great stretch of the imagination to guess what I would do if either of you made a move I didn't like. If I tell this lady to shoot you, she'll shoot you. Do you understand?'

Both men nod their heads, which to be truthful, I didn't expect.

'Get over to the wall and get down on your knees facing me, hands behind your head. Now.'

They walk over to the wall on my left-hand side and do what they're told. So far so good. Raleigh keeps looking at Fisher, willing him to do something heroic and marvellous. Fisher doesn't meet his boss's gaze, keeping his eyes on Sakura and the gun, occasionally glancing at me with hate-filled eyes. He's trying to look relaxed and cool, but he's like a coiled spring. This is going to have to be sorted out fast.

Sakura licks the sweat off her upper lip. There's an almost imperceptible trembling in the arm that's pointing the gun and I'm sure Fisher has noticed.

'Good. Now listen, Sakura. In a moment, you're going to have to do something for me, but you're going to have to keep your eye on those two with the same level of focus you've got now.'

She nods her head again. The gun is still pointed at Fisher, who I can see she rightly perceives as the greatest threat.

'These two are in a desperate situation and they're waiting for a break in your concentration so they can grab the gun and overpower you. That must not happen. I want you to come over to my right-hand side and get my key ring out of my right trouser pocket.'

She walks backwards towards me, gun still raised and aimed at Fisher's head. I can feel my heart thumping in my chest. When she's close enough for me to smell that musky perfume, she slowly slides a hand into my pocket.

'No funny business, Sakura.'

'As if I would.'

She dangles the key ring from one of her fingers.

'See those two grey metal strips? One of them has a serrated edge. You're going to use that serrated edge to saw through the plastic tie that's around my wrists. You'll only need to saw through it once and it'll fall off. It's going to be tricky, but you mustn't look at the wrist tie when you're sawing through it. Don't worry if you accidentally cut me. Keep looking at our two friends there. Keep aiming the gun at them. Once more, if they move, shoot them; and keep shooting.'

These words are not particularly for Sakura. They're for the benefit of Raleigh and Fisher. I have to keep reinforcing the idea that they're in imminent danger of meeting whichever supernatural being they worship.

Sakura finds the right metal strip and holds it between two fingers.

'You're going to have to squat down while you do this. Try not to lose your balance. If it's easier for you, you can rest the butt of the gun against my thigh to keep it stable if you have to fire. Now try and saw through the plastic. Just keep your aim steady.'

She squats down beside me and keeps the gun pointing in the right direction, never taking her eyes off her targets for a second. She's very good. Apart from looking a little green around the gills, she seems totally in control and is actually quite scary, her cold expression contrasting with the beauty of that unique face. If I was Fisher right now, I'd definitely think twice before trying anything. She turns her head a little to the right and gets a good view of Viola and Rosabel.

'Oh God, Daniel.'

'I know. I know. Keep it out of your mind for now. Concentrate on this.'

I can feel the metal strip against the inside of one of my wrists as she fiddles around trying to find the right position and angle. There is a quicker way of getting this type of tie off by lifting the locking bar with a credit card or something, but you need two hands for that, so it has to be this method.

I look over at Anjukka and give her what I hope is a reassuring glance, while putting as much pressure as I can on the plastic tie with my wrists. The position that Sakura has to be in is giving her problems with the sawing action that's required. She wobbles a couple of times and I'm afraid she'll lose her balance and drop the gun, but after a minute I can feel the plastic snap apart and my hands are free.

'OK. That's good. Now you can stand up again. Keep your attention on those two. Don't fall asleep.'

'I knew I shouldn't have taken all those Valium.'

She smiles at me, but she's not looking at all well. Not surprising, really. She's had a traumatic, exhausting day, has just seen the embalmed corpse of a former lover and it's barely the evening. She stands up and places the key ring on my leg.

As I try to rub some feeling back into my wrists, fingers and hands, I can see Fisher staring at her with total contempt. He turns towards Raleigh.

'This bitch is the pimp. He called her Sakura. That's the name on the site. Sakura Bianchi. She's the one who's been pimping your daughter to fucking lesbians. It's a fucking disgrace. It's fucking disgusting.'

Raleigh's face goes dark red, but he doesn't say anything. Fisher shouts at Sakura.

'You better put that gun down, girly. You're in enough shit as it is. You don't know what you're getting yourself into here.'

Sakura ignores him. I don't.

'Tell him to shut up, Raleigh, or I'll get her to shoot your girls over there.'

'You wouldn't dare,' says Raleigh angrily.

'Oh, wouldn't I?'

I'd expected to see some cuts on my wrists, but there are only deep red and purple marks. I still can't articulate my fingers properly. I'm just about capable of taking the serrated tool on my key ring and starting on the ties around my ankles.

Once those are out of the way, I attempt standing up

for the first time in God knows how long. I feel woozy and faint as I straighten up, but I know that will pass. Most of the pain I'm feeling is in my abdomen and face, plus some residuals in my back, but it's fading with every second that passes, or it better be. I can't wait to see my face in a mirror.

I take the gun off Sakura and quickly look it over. The safety was on, which went unnoticed by Fisher. I click it off. I check the magazine and it's fully loaded. It isn't in very good condition and hasn't been oiled for a while. I've never liked guns that aren't maintained properly. They can be a menace. I can see Fisher watching me with curiosity.

For the first time I wonder where Sakura got this gun from. Raleigh said it was his, but I can't imagine that she got hold of it here. If he has guns on the premises, they'd all be locked up. I wonder where she took Eleanor. Wherever it was, is that where she got the gun from? And where is Eleanor now? I just hope she's safe somewhere.

I look around hoping that there'll be some more wrist ties like the ones they used on me, but I can't see anything. I'm sure there are some somewhere in the house, but I'm not going to waste any time looking.

'So what are you going to do now, Beckett?' sneers Fisher. 'Are you going to execute us? I don't think you've got the balls.' He turns to Raleigh. 'I don't think he's got the balls, do you, sir?'

'For God's sake stop it, Fisher,' Raleigh mumbles. 'You heard what he said.'

'Yeah, I heard what he said. That's probably all he's got the balls for; shooting dead women.'

'Fisher!'

The next thing I have to do is untie Anjukka. I'm still a

bit too flipped out to have a clear plan yet, but the first thing I think I have to do is get Anjukka and Sakura out of here. What I'm then going to do with Raleigh and Fisher I have no idea.

I hand the gun back to Sakura. 'As before. Any sudden movements, kill them both. Aim for the centre of the chest.'

'You honestly think she'll kill us, Beckett?' Fisher's hands are slipping away from the back of his head and are no longer making contact with any part of it.

'As you were, Fisher. Hands on the back of your head.'

'You people don't know anything about killing. It's people like me who have to dirty their hands with killing, to protect scum like you.'

I crouch down in front of Anjukka and rest both hands on her thighs. 'I'm going to take that tape off your mouth, but I'm going to have to take it off in one quick sweep, otherwise it'll be murder. OK?'

She silently agrees. I try to take one of the corners in between my fingers. It takes a few attempts as there's little feeling in them still. 'I'm going to count to three.' I rip the tape off on two.

'You bastard.'

'Had to be done. Are you OK?'

'I think so.'

She looks terrible, but then I guess I'm no oil painting at the moment, either. I get behind her and am about to saw through her wrist and ankle ties, when I realise that I can lift the locking bars and use the ties on Raleigh and Fisher. I should have thought of that before I cut through the ones on my ankles, but I was in a hurry.

I take a credit card out of my wallet and start work. This would be considerably easier if I had more feeling in

## Kiss Me When I'm Dead

my fingers, and it's like trying to play the piano wearing thick gardening gloves.

'Daniel.'

I look over to Sakura. She doesn't look at all well. Because of the state I'm in, this isn't going as fast as it should be.

'Hold on, babe.'

Eventually, I manage to flip open the locking bar on the plastic tie that's around Anjukka's wrists. I put the tie on the floor for later use. Fisher is still working on Sakura. I start fumbling with the ties around Anjukka's ankles. The feeling in my fingers has improved, but it's still taking me a frustrating amount of time to do this.

'Hey! You!' bellows Fisher. 'You Japanese whore or whatever fucking nationality you're meant to be. You stupid bitch. All of this is your fucking fault. Your fucking girlfriend over there. Your whore. Have you had a good look at her yet? Go on – take a look at how sexy she is now.'

This seems to be having more of an effect of Raleigh than it does on Sakura, though I know it must be difficult for her not to look at Viola. It was looking at her that got me a blast from that stun gun.

'There's no need for that, Fisher,' Raleigh says. 'And don't refer to Viola as a whore. Remember your place.'

But Fisher can't help himself.

'If she's not a whore, what is she? I want her pimp to take a good fucking look at her. See how she's ended up. I bet the two of them were at it, as well. Is that how it was, Mrs Bianchi? Are you a fucking lesbian whore as well?'

I know what he's doing and he's getting on my nerves now. Maybe he's not trying to goad her. Maybe he's in serious denial about who it was that set Viola up in that hotel in the first place.

Anjukka rubs both of her wrists in turn, then takes her ruined bra off and throws it on the floor, doing up the front of her ripped dress as well as she can. My hands are shaking and it's difficult to get the edge of the credit card into the lock. The ties they've used on her ankles are slightly different from the one they used on her wrist.

'Go on, Mrs Bianchi. Take a good fucking look at your best girl!'

I've freed one of Anjukka's ankles and start on the last tie. I have to admit it; these things are really good. Much better than rope. I look up at Sakura. The hand that she's holding the gun in is shaking badly. Fisher is aware. She has tears in her eyes and she's white and sweating profusely.

'Oh, boo-hoo,' gloats Fisher like a five-year-old playground bully. 'Are we sad, Mrs Bianchi? Is that a couple of thousand a week down the pan? Because that's all she meant to you, wasn't it. She was like a prize cow that you milked for money.'

'Fisher!' Raleigh is getting red-faced with anger. He doesn't understand what Fisher is trying to do. But I do.

'Sakura. Ignore him. I'll be there in a couple of seconds.'

But I don't have a couple of seconds. In the same moment that I pop the last of Anjukka's ankle ties, I see Sakura's attention wander for a micro-second as she wipes the sweat out of her eyes, then I see Fisher make a swift move and see something shiny flash through the air.

Sakura drops to the floor, clutching the knife that's in her shoulder. Fisher is fast and he has the gun in his hand a second later. For an awful moment, I think he's going to shoot her, but he aims the gun at me.

'Hands behind your head, fucker.'

I do what he says. I have no choice. Sakura is moaning softly. The knife looks like it's in two inches deep. Good throw. It looks like it's missed the artery, but I can't be positive. I just hope she doesn't try to pull it out.

This is my fault. I'd taken a cursory glance at Fisher and decided he was weapon-free, but I was thinking about guns, not throwing knives. I should have done the whole thing the other way around. I should have disabled Raleigh and Fisher and then freed Anjukka, but my thinking was muddled. Fuck it. I don't know what I'm doing. I stand up slowly and put my hands behind my head. I feel pretty nauseous and weak.

Fisher is looking pleased with himself. He steps over Sakura and gives the knife a vicious kick as he passes by, whether to drive it in deeper or just to cause more pain I can't tell, but it's something that I won't forget, even if he does, and I won't forget the deep moan of pain that escapes from her mouth.

I walk backwards so that I'm standing directly in front of Rosabel and Viola. Fisher thinks I'm trying to retreat and allows himself a little sneer; the cowardly private eye afraid of the big army man with the gun. He helps Raleigh up to his feet. Raleigh looks a little rattled by all that has happened, but Fisher is still looking to him for instruction. Despite his air of macho authority, he's still like a little child, and has to have someone to tell him what to do.

'I thought I could trust you, Fisher,' says Raleigh, angrily.

'You can, sir. All those things I said about Viola, they were...'

'You called her a whore.'

'Well, sir, with all due respect, that's what she was. But I was trying to…'

'What are we going to do about all of this, Fisher? This is a damn bloody mess, isn't it. If your men had done their jobs properly at that bloody tart's house, none of this would be happening.'

'That's because of *this* idiot.' He waves the gun in my face.

'Well *you* were the one who thought he'd be a good bet, I seem to recall.'

'Could you not talk about me as if I'm not here?' I say. 'It's extremely rude.'

Fisher aims the gun at my abdomen. 'If you don't want a slow, messy, painful death you'll shut the fuck up right now. In fact, I don't really care whether you shut the fuck up or not. I think I'll just kill you for the pleasure it'll give me. You're going to have to die anyway, it may as well be now.'

Raleigh looks worried. 'Not until he's told us where Valentine is, and for God's sake don't wave the gun in that direction. You might hit Viola or Rosabel.'

'I'm sorry, sir, but I'm starting to get impatient with this. I'm just doing my job. I have to keep this bastard under control. The fact that he's standing in front of your wife and daughter is neither here nor there. Besides, a bullet from a gun like this isn't going to do that much damage. They are already dead, sir, if you don't mind my bringing it up.'

'Well if you're not going to do anything about it, then I suppose I'll have to. Keep the gun on him.'

Raleigh walks towards me. For a second, I can't imagine what he's going to do, then I assume he's going to wheel Rosabel and Viola out of the way.

'Sir. I wouldn't go near him if I were you.'

'Oh, good God, Fisher. Look at him! He's in no state to do anything. You've been beating him senseless for the last half an hour. He looks like he's been in a serious road traffic accident. Keep him where he is, by all means and keep the gun on him. I'm just going to get the girls out of harm's way. Then we can make a decision about what we're going to do about him and these others.'

'Sir, the best option now is to finish him off. Let me shoot him. I'll take care of everything. I can make it like he was never here. Same for the bitch. Both of the bitches.'

Raleigh ignores him.

'Then we can get back on track and find this bloody Valentine girl. Torture it out of him if necessary. And if you think the whore knows anything about it, torture her as well, if she's still alive.'

I can see Sakura move, but Fisher is blocking my view of what she's doing. She's lying on her side and she's been so quiet for the last few minutes that I'm worried that she might have died.

Raleigh is about two feet away from me, and flashes me a look of seething contempt that I personally find really upsetting. Then something strange happens to his face. It's as if a small, red explosion has erupted from his left eye. I'm sprayed with a sizeable amount of blood and tissue, and so are Viola and Rosabel. It seems as if he's staring at me with his other eye while his jaw drops down and his mouth hangs open stupidly.

Then he drops to his knees. Then he falls forwards so his face is in Viola's lap. Fisher's eyes are wide with horror. His face is white. He's grimacing in pain. It looks like he's turning the gun so that he can look at it side-on. There's something wrong with his leg. In the distance, I can hear a woman scream.

I don't have any idea what's happened, but something makes me lunge forward and ram my shoulder into Fisher's chest before he turns the gun in the right direction again. He goes down hard and yelps in pain. The gun goes flying across the room. I don't understand why he's hurting so much and I don't particularly care.

I try to pin him to the floor and it's almost successful before he roars with rage and pain and head-butts me. This almost knocks me off his chest, but not quite. I feel my eyes roll up into my head for a second, then I grab his larynx in a grip that's intended to remove it from his neck and just go crazy, punching him as hard as I can in the face, again and again, breaking his nose, his front teeth and his jaw.

But he's a strong, tough bastard. He spits blood into my face and catches me on the side of the head with a hammer punch that almost knocks me off his torso and onto the floor. He tries it again, but I block it and bring an elbow down hard into the centre of his throat, which stalls his progress for a couple of seconds so that I can whack him hard on his broken jaw.

He's struggling like mad, but I get a sense that he's not firing on all cylinders. Then I see why and my heart sinks. It's the knife that he threw at Sakura. It's sticking out of the back of his leg. She must have pulled it out of her shoulder and dug it in when he and Raleigh were bickering a moment ago.

I grab the flat handle of the knife and screw it around in his leg until he screams in agony. The pain must be excruciating, and that's what I want. I want him to pass out from it so I can sort out everything else that's going on in this madhouse. After about thirty seconds of this incessant torture, he flops backwards and is almost senseless. For good measure, I apply pressure to both his carotid arteries until I get a choke-out and leave him on the floor, unconscious, kicking him in the balls for good measure when I've got up. He's fucked now, so I can leave him alone for a while without worrying about him too much.

I take a quick look to where Sakura is lying and there's blood everywhere. It's pouring out of the wound in her shoulder and soaking her clothing. The knife must have severed an artery. I reckon she's got about ten minutes and then she's dead.

She's still breathing, but it's ragged and shallow. This has got be done fast. I rip her blouse away from her shoulder so I can get a good look at the knife wound. It's just less than an inch wide. No good.

Anjukka is standing against the wall, hyperventilating. I grab her arm and drag her across the room to where Sakura is lying.

'Are you OK, babe? You're going to have to help me now or she's going to die. Understand?'

She nods her head. 'What can I do?'

'Wait there and hold her hand. I'll be back in a second.'

I pull open the drawers in the medical cabinet I noticed earlier, unwrap a fresh scalpel blade and slide it onto a metal handle. I grab a big pair of scissors and head back to where Anjukka is sitting, stroking Sakura's forehead.

'Your dress is fucked anyway. Do you mind if I cut some material off it? I'll buy you a new one next week.'

She rolls her eyes and lets me cut a few strips off it with the scissors. This is not the most hygienic way of doing things, but it's all I have at the moment. I use the scalpel to cut into the knife wound, increasing its width to around four inches. Predictably, Sakura screams and jerks violently while I'm doing this, but not too badly as she's so weak. The pain must be pretty awful. I just wish she'd faint.

'Can you hold her down? Lean with your knees pressing down on her if you can. She mustn't move now.'

Anjukka turns her head quickly away when she sees what I'm doing. I press the material from her dress into a ball and push it into the wound. Sakura screams again and thrashes her head from side to side. Hopefully this will stop the bleeding until we can get proper medical help.

'What are you doing?'

'It's OK. The knife severed an artery.' I place my mouth close to Anjukka's ear and whisper. 'When she took it out to stab Fisher she started bleeding to death. I think I may have stopped it, but I can't be sure yet. You have to take over here now. You have to press down here as hard as you can.'

'OK. As long as I don't have to look at what I'm doing.'

The dress material is already getting soaked with blood. Sakura has calmed down a little and is mumbling to herself. Anjukka manages to push the material from her dress into the wound, while looking the other way. I can't say I blame her.

I count to ten and then test for a pulse in Sakura's wrist on the side of her shoulder wound. Nothing there. Good. That means we've blocked the artery.

'That's fantastic, Anjukka. Keep that pressure on.

Don't let her move. Keep kneeling on her chest to keep her immobile. I'm going to call an ambulance.'

Fisher is still out and I don't think he'll be coming round for some time. I run into Raleigh's office and call an ambulance from his landline. I tell them that I've got a woman with a serious knife wound who's bleeding to death and that they need to get here yesterday.

When that's sorted, I make a visit to Raleigh's little kitchen and wash the blood off my hands and off my face. I take a tea towel from the draining board and sling it over my shoulder. When I return to the office, I empty the contents of Anjukka's holdall onto the floor, then start work on Raleigh's safe.

It's a combination lock which is a real pain. I try to calm myself down so that all my attention is on the safe. I've only got one option here and that's lock manipulation, which involves using the lock against itself to get it open. Just like in the movies, this involves careful listening, working out the number of wheels and discovering the contact points.

After three or four minutes of listening to frustratingly quiet drive pin clicks, I have all the possible combinations in my head. The third one I try works and the door swings open. I can't imagine how stressful this would be if you did it for a living.

There's a little foreign currency in here, but not that much, and most of it is GBP. I make a quick assessment of what's in each bundle of notes and remove about seventy thousand, placing the money in neat piles at the bottom of the holdall. That should cover my fee and medical bills with a big bonus for each of my reluctant associates.

I move the remaining money around so everything

looks right, close the door, give the combination dial a good hard spin and wipe my prints off with the tea towel. I don't think anyone will notice what's gone missing. Raleigh isn't interested in anything anymore and Fisher probably had no idea exactly how much was in there in the first place. Besides, he's going to be too busy with hospital, court and prison to worry about anything else.

As I refill Anjukka's bag with as many of its original contents as will fit, I get my mobile out of my pocket and call DS Bream. She'd better be on duty. I was hoping that I wouldn't have to involve the police, but once an ambulance crew see what's in that room, they're unlikely to keep it to themselves.

I can hear Sakura moaning from the other room. Well, at least she's still alive. I go to see how she is and it doesn't look good. Her breathing is shallower than when I left and her complexion is almost translucent. I crouch down across from Anjukka and take Sakura's hand in mine.

'You're going to be alright. Just hang in there.'

She attempts a smile. 'Stop talking in clichés,' she whispers.

I can hear sirens in the distance.

# 26

## A MAN OF MANY SUSPICIOUS TALENTS

'What the fuck happened here?'

From her demeanour, I can tell immediately that Olivia Bream is basically on my side and doesn't perceive me as the chief perpetrator of any crimes. Well, not much, anyway. This is good. I'd like to gently remove myself from the whole thing and disappear into the night, but I can't really see that happening and certainly don't want to have to go to court. I'm going to have to handle this very delicately.

I sit opposite her on one of the Natuzzi sofas, in exactly the same place as when I sat here opposite Raleigh and Fisher a couple of hundred years ago. Anjukka is with us, but she sits on an upright chair near Raleigh's desk with a blanket over her shoulders, draped there by a kind ambulance person. She's staring blankly into space, but is otherwise doing fairly well, all things considered. I try to stop my eyes from glancing at her holdall, and hope she doesn't go rummaging around in it looking for something.

'It's an interesting scenario, isn't it?' I say. 'I can imagine this cropping up in some police training programme in years to come. It'd be an advanced course, obviously.'

DS Bream smiles at me. 'Have you looked at yourself

in a mirror? You look like absolute shit.'

'Thank you. You, on the other hand, look very lovely.'

She laughs then blushes. 'When you called me, I thought you were going to ask me out to dinner. I didn't expect to be facing hell on earth in Holland Park.'

It's nice hearing that husky voice again. I'd forgotten about how desirable she was, but it's all coming back now. 'It had crossed my mind, but then I remembered you saying that you were overdue for promotion and wanted something big and spectacular.' It hurts to speak, I notice.

'Well, you certainly got me that. I had to call in quite a few favours to be put in charge of this, but I managed to convince my boss that all of this was an extension of Viola Raleigh's missing persons case.'

'Some extension.'

'Quite. Who was the other woman? The dead one, I mean. The other dead one.'

'That was Rosabel Raleigh. She was Viola's mother. She committed suicide about ten years ago or thereabouts. She shot herself. Somehow it was never reported and no one noticed she'd gone. She obviously didn't make much of a mark on the world. I think Raleigh was pretty adept at covering things up and getting people to help him. He even managed to get a portrait of her painted after she'd died. That's her over there.'

Olivia looks up at Rosabel who stares back coldly. 'Yes. Yes, I can see it. What a strange thing to do.'

'You're telling me.' I remember my promise to Anjukka and remind myself to sort out a sitting with Louisa Gavreau.

'Why did she shoot herself? Do you know?'

'I can't be sure, but I think it may have been because

her husband was carrying on with her daughter.'

'Jesus Christ.'

I explain about how I'd been duped by Raleigh. How the job of tracking down Viola Raleigh was really the job of tracking down Eleanor Wallis with a view to silencing her forever about Viola's death in the hotel.

I tell her how I'd visited Miss Wallis in her home with Mrs Bianchi and discovered what was going on. How we got her to a place of safety and then how I came here to confront Raleigh about his duplicity. I don't mention the presence of Fisher's boys and the likely fate of one of them.

'So they tortured you and tried to find out where you'd hidden her.'

'Correct. They also threatened sexual violence against Miss York here if I didn't tell them where Miss Wallis was hidden.'

Olivia looks over at Anjukka for confirmation of this. Anjukka nods. I'm glad it's a woman dealing with this. I look at Anjukka's holdall. I can't help myself.

'So how did the gun come into it?'

'That was brought here by Mrs Bianchi. She was the woman who reported Viola missing a few weeks back. You know – the woman you wouldn't tell me about. My suspicion is that she took Miss Wallis to Viola Raleigh's flat, for which she had a key. I think that's where the gun came from. It was one of Raleigh's. He recognised it. I think Viola must have pinched it. I think if she hadn't turned up with it, myself and Miss York there would both be dead now.'

'So Mr Raleigh was shot with his own gun.'

'I don't think it was looked after very well. I don't think Viola bothered. That might have been the reason it went off. If that isn't poetic justice I don't know what is.'

'Do you have the address for Viola Raleigh's flat? I'll have to talk to Miss Wallis.'

'No. Only Mrs Bianchi knows that.'

She sighs. I know there's a problem here and it's Sakura being in possession of an illegal firearm and using it to threaten people, even if those people had me and Anjukka tied to chairs and were beating the crap out of me with a view to locating Eleanor Wallis and probably killing her. I'm mentally willing Olivia to overlook this. She's going to have to overlook quite a bit.

'So anyway, I told Mrs Bianchi how to control the room while she untied me. I then took the gun, which incidentally still had the safety on. It was while I was freeing Miss York there that I temporarily handed the gun back to Mrs Bianchi.

'Mrs Bianchi isn't well. She not only has some weird form of agoraphobia which also manifests itself in unfamiliar places, she also had to be in the same room as her friend Viola Raleigh.'

Olivia smiles wryly. 'Friend?'

'Well, you know. She knew that Viola was dead, but she didn't know about the embalming. Anyway, she was getting sick, Fisher goaded her and for a moment she lost her concentration. Fisher threw the knife at her, hit her in the shoulder and he managed to get hold of the gun. It was while Fisher was threatening me with the gun that Mrs Bianchi pulled the knife out of her shoulder and shoved it in Fisher's leg.

'Something happened then and I'm not sure what. In retrospect, I think I heard Fisher scream. Either the pain caused Fisher to pull the trigger, or the gun went off on its own. As I said, it wasn't in very good nick, so the latter is a strong possibility. Whatever, Fisher shot his boss through the head. The end.'

'Why is Fisher in there lying on the floor looking like he's picked a fight with The Terminator?'

'I had no choice. I think he was stunned for a second when he realised what he'd done. He's a big guy, ex-soldier, and I was fucked by that time. I had to give him everything I had to incapacitate him. He kept fighting back.'

'How inconsiderate of him.'

'I was already injured and it was getting worse. I know he looks bad, but it was all necessary. Anything less and I wouldn't be talking to you now and Miss York wouldn't be sitting over there. You may not have even known about any of this. We'd have all vanished off the face of the earth and no one would have been any the wiser.'

She rubs her eyes and allows herself a tired laugh. 'God Almighty, I don't know how I'm going to write this up. What a shambles. I saw Mrs Bianchi as they were taking her into the ambulance. She's lost a lot of blood. You'll have to prepare yourself for the worst with her, I'm afraid. The paramedic said she'd already be dead if someone hadn't cut her open, sorted out that knife wound and stopped the arterial bleeding. He was very impressed with that. Was that you?'

'I'm too modest to answer that.'

'A man of many suspicious talents.'

'She's not stupid. I think she knew what would happen when she pulled the knife out. She did it to stop me being shot.'

We look at each other for a moment. I can't tell what she's thinking. I have to press home my advantage.

'When I asked you the other night why you'd joined

the police, you said it was because you wanted to do the right thing, and to stop people doing the wrong thing.'

She clasps her hands behind her neck, stretches, stands up and slips her leather jacket over her shoulders as if it's cold in here. 'Both of you need to get yourselves sorted out.' She looks at Anjukka. 'Have you got somewhere you can stay? I don't think you should be on your own tonight. Have you got relatives in London?'

Anjukka shakes her head. 'My parents live in Melrose.'

'She can stay with me. I've got a spare bedroom. She'll feel safe.'

'You both need to get yourselves checked out by a doctor. Particularly you, Mr Beckett. You look like death warmed up. Do it as soon as you can. I'll type up a couple of statements for you both tomorrow when I've had a chance to churn all of this around in my mind. You can come in when you feel able. You can read both statements and if you feel happy with them as they are, you can sign them.'

I look at my watch. I can't believe it's only seven-forty. It was less than ten hours ago I was in a cab heading for Ewell to see Abigail Gastrell.

'OK. Thanks, Olivia. What's going to happen to the women?'

'The ones in there, you mean? They'll be buried, I suppose. We'll have to contact next of kin, if there is anyone. Someone will have to take care of the funeral expenses. There'll be quite a lot of paperwork to sort out on those two, particularly the mother. Like you said, why did no one notice she'd gone?'

'I'll pay for the funeral expenses for the two of them. Let me know when you've finished with the bodies.' I didn't know either of them, but what the hell. The irony is that I'll be paying with Raleigh's money. I just hope I don't have to pay for Sakura's as well. I don't know who'll be paying for Raleigh's funeral. A fuckin' pauper's burial would be too good for him. Maybe someone could dump his body in a skip somewhere. 'What would have happened if Raleigh had turned himself in after Viola had died?'

'He'd have been charged with involuntary manslaughter. Maximum sentence would have been life. And of course there was preventing a lawful burial for both the mother and the daughter and God knows what else. We can only guess at what might have happened. It would depend on the court and how good his lawyers were and how good the prosecution was. He'd be ruined when it all came out, that's for sure. In a way, I wish he was still alive. I'm sure that all of this is the tip of the iceberg. I'd love to have got him in court.'

Two of the ambulance crew walk past with Fisher on a stretcher. He's not looking good, but should consider himself lucky that he's still alive.

'I should put a police guard on him if I were you,' I say. 'He's in a lot of shit and I wouldn't put it past him to try and get away once he's recovered.'

'Once he's recovered? In that case, we'll put a guard on him in about a month.'

Olivia says goodbye to both of us and arranges for a car to take us both back to my place. In chivalrous fashion, I insist upon carrying Anjukka's holdall for her.

On the way back, I run through the loose ends in my mind. Blue Tie and Orange shirt are a problem, but only if Orange Shirt dies. If that doesn't happen, I'd expect both of them to make themselves scarce until they can find employment elsewhere. I don't think that Orange

Shirt is the type to go howling to the police accusing me of GBH. He's far too much of a man for that.

I have no idea where the police will start as far as charging Fisher is concerned. There's his involvement in setting Viola up in the first place, his presence in the hotel room when she died and his collusion in hiding her body. I'm sure they can get him on something just for that lot, though I'm not sure what. I'm also pretty sure he knew about Rosabel, even though he wasn't around when it happened, so that's conspiracy to conceal yet another death and probably perverting the course of justice, too. He shot and killed Raleigh, of course, which will be involuntary manslaughter.

Then there's what he did to Anjukka, which must include abduction, sexual assault and the threat of death, not to mention GBH or attempted murder against Sakura, which could turn into a murder charge proper if she dies.

And then there's me. Assault with a stun weapon, grievous bodily harm, threat of death, torture, attempted murder…

Oh fuck it. I'll just leave it to the police. I'm sure if they dig around a little in his past, they'll find lots of other stuff, too. I'm just concerned that when it goes to court I'll have to testify against him for what he did to me and I'd prefer not to be that conspicuous. I guess I'll just have to brazen it out. Of course, he may want to press charges against *me*, for hammering him like that, but I somehow doubt he'll bother.

\*

When we get back to Exeter Street, I let Anjukka have

the first soak in the bath, and I graciously allow her to use the last of my Radox Herbal Bath Muscle Therapy. I throw her ruined clothing in the bin, swallow the dihydrocodeine the paramedic gave me and start to make some coffee. I had considered going down to some of the still-open shops and getting her a new dress, plus some other things, but we can always do that tomorrow.

Besides, I don't want to give the shop assistants a fright. I don't feel that bad, but as DS Bream so kindly mentioned, I look like death warmed up and the left side of my face is swollen thanks to Fisher's efforts. I'll get myself fully checked out with a doctor as soon as the opportunity presents itself.

I unzip Anjukka's holdall, take the money out and hide it in one of the kitchen cupboards behind a load of tinned food that I've never bothered to eat. I can't remember how far I'd got with the coffee. Not far. I'd loaded up the Siemens with beans but hadn't switched the damn thing on. I place some cups and saucers on the kitchen surface and go into my bedroom to lie on the bed for a few seconds, just to rest my eyes.

I don't wake up until the next morning.

# 27

## LOOSE ENDS

'She's still very weak,' says the bearded doctor who looks too young to have grown a beard. 'She lost a lot of blood and her heart stopped twice. She was in theatre for two hours. We had to give her three transfusions. I'm sorry, but I can only allow you five minutes with her. She needs to sleep.'

Sakura was taken to St Mary's Hospital in Paddington. She had to be resuscitated in the ambulance. This guy clearly thinks she is very lucky indeed to be alive. I'm only allowed to see her because Olivia gave the hospital a call and told them I was the closest thing she had to a relative and that I had saved her life and that she'd be pleased to see me. She obviously wasn't taking the state of my face into account. When I finally had the nerve to inspect myself this morning I looked like I'd gone ten rounds with a heavyweight boxer who was being assisted by Bruce Lee.

'Will she be OK? I mean…'

'There's no lasting damage. Very tricky op on an artery in the shoulder. Bit of awkward internal stitching, but she'll be as good as new in a few months. She'd been attacked by some maniac, according to the police. Normally, we wouldn't allow visitors for a few days, but someone from the police rang and said we should make an exception with you.'

'So everything's fixed now.'

'Yes. She'll have to have her upper arm and shoulder in a cast for a couple of months, just to stop unnecessary movement and to encourage efficient healing. Remember. Five minutes. It's for her benefit.'

He looks quizzically at my face. I can tell he'd like to know the story behind it but it would take far too long and he'd probably think I was making it all up.

She's in a clean, white recovery room on her own. I've brought her some Muscadet grapes, a big bunch of sunflowers, a copy of *Vogue* and a dark red lipstick called Private Party. The nurse who's in the room when I arrive looks at me as if I'm insane. She takes the flowers from me and goes off somewhere.

Sakura is propped up in the bed as if she's been reading, but her eyes are closed. She's attached to a drip and a heart monitor. She's wearing a blue and white hospital robe and there's a shitload of bandaging over her shoulder, along with traces of dried blood, felt pen marks and what I assume are iodine stains.

I sit down next to her to her and look at her face; still beautiful and sexy despite everything. I place a hand over the one of hers that isn't wired up to everything. After about a minute her eyes flicker open and she turns her head so she can see who it is, smiling when she sees it's me.

'When can I see the baby?' I say, as sincerely as I can manage.

'You are not to make me laugh, Daniel.'

'I've brought you some lipstick.'

'Thank you. I'm going out tonight. I was afraid I'd have to borrow some off one of the nurses.'

'How do you feel?'

'Drugged. It's not unpleasant. I've always been fond of diamorphine.'

'Have you been told what happened?'

'No. No one's spoken to me apart from medical staff.'

'Do you remember stabbing Fisher in the leg?'

'Just about.'

'I don't know what happened, whether it was the gun or whatever, but he shot Raleigh. Raleigh's dead. Fisher's probably here somewhere, but don't worry, he's in no condition to do anything and won't be for a long, long time.'

She nods her head. 'Good. I'm glad Raleigh's dead. I wish I'd done it.'

'Well, you did in a way, if that's any consolation.'

Tears start to fill her eyes. 'Seeing Viola like that. So shocking. It didn't really register at the time because of everything else. Her whole life, ruined because of him, and even after she was dead he couldn't leave it be. He was a monster.' She sniffs and smiles at me. 'My heart stopped a few times, the doctor told me. I told him that couldn't be. I don't have one.'

'You'll be back to normal in a few months. A few weeks of physio and you'll be able to beat me up again.'

She smiles and holds my hand tightly, but tears start to form in her eyes.

'I knew Viola was unhappy, but I did what I could for her. I knew I could never cure her of whatever was eating away at her. I felt so sorry for her. Whenever I used to think of what she went through when she was with Novak, it upset me greatly. He and his friends, they treated her as if she was an animal; less than an animal.'

God Almighty, I'd almost forgotten about Novak and

Jeremy. It seems ages ago, rather than at the beginning of the week. At the time, I remember being repulsed by his glee in what he'd done to Viola, as if she hadn't had enough by that time.

When I think about what he told me about Jeremy and his mates from the snooker club, my mouth goes dry and I feel a ball of loathing in the centre of my chest. If anyone was less than an animal it was Novak and his boy. I keep thinking about Viola crying and praying on her mattress each night during Novak's training. I keep thinking about her having to lick the toilet clean while Novak filmed her debasement at the hands of Jeremy and his mates.

*She was like a pig at a trough.*
*She was like a filthy fucking pig.*
*She had been totally and utterly debauched.*
*All the fun of the fair.*

'Have you seen a doctor yet, Daniel?'

'Sorry? Er, no. Not yet. I need a complete check-up, but I think I'm going to see my dentist first. I've got a shaky tooth courtesy of Fisher.' I tap the side of my face. Ouch. 'It feels like it's cracked. Hurts to touch it.'

'Your face is very swollen on one side.'

The nurse returns with the sunflowers in a huge vase. She gives me an order to shut up and get out using only her eyebrows.

'I'm going to have to go, Sakura. I'll come and see you tomorrow. Try and get some sleep.'

'Bring some eye shadow. It's difficult to flirt with the doctors and nurses without makeup. Dior 5 Couleurs Iridescent will be fine. You can get it in John Lewis. I'll pay you back.'

'You don't have to. It'll be my pleasure. After all, you

saved my life.'

'And you saved mine. They told me what you did.'

'Then we're square.'

'Yes. We're square.'

I shouldn't be telling you this, but there were tears in my eyes when I left that room.

\*

By the time I'm walking towards Coptic Street it's past eleven and there are a lot of people about. It's pretty boisterous and most of the noise comes from the pissed crowds leaving the pubs after chucking out time. There's also the comings and goings from the Pizza Express and a nice-looking Greek restaurant that has a smartly-suited, smiling guy out the front reluctantly turning people away.

On the other side of the road from me, there's a man of about forty throwing up in the gutter while a much younger girl in a red leather jacket rubs his back and talks encouragingly to him. There are lots of groups of girls, usually four or five strong, wandering around in the sort of gear that tells me there must be a club around here somewhere. I can hear a distant bass thump about five hundred yards away, so maybe that's the place they're looking for.

Four guys in their twenties pass by me and one of them notices my face. 'Walk into something, did you, mate?' he says. His friends laugh, but I don't think they knew what he was referring to. Further up the road, a solitary man is singing in Welsh.

The snack bars either side of Firmheath Enterprises plc are both closed, although one of them is still dimly lit from the inside with what looks like Christmas tree lights.

I stand at the door fiddling with my keys. People walk past me but nobody really pays me any attention.

It takes me about thirty seconds to get the door open, go inside and close it quietly behind me. As I tap the five numbers into the keypad and open the reinforced steel door, I can already smell the chlorine from the pool. I keep thinking about DS Olivia Bream and her reasons for joining the police force.

*Doing the right thing. And stopping people doing the wrong thing.*

Ten minutes later, I'm walking down Shaftesbury Avenue towards Covent Garden. My mobile rings. It's Jodie, the blonde birthday girl from the bar in Tavistock Street. We arrange to meet for a drink next week. Hopefully, most of my cuts, bruises and swellings will have disappeared by then and my appearance won't alarm her too much.

## THE END

# Books by Dominic Piper

Kiss Me When I'm Dead

Death is the New Black

Femme Fatale

Bitter Almonds & Jasmine

Printed in Great Britain
by Amazon

41896384R00253